HOUSEBROKEN

HOUSEBROKEN

Three Novellas

Yael Hedaya

Translated by Dalya Bilu

Picador USA
A METROPOLITAN BOOK
Henry Holt and Company
New York

www.picadorusa.com

Picador® is a U.S. registered trademark and is used by Henry Holt and Company under license from Pan Books Limited.

For information on Picador USA Reading Group Guides, as well as ordering, please contact the Trade Marketing department at St. Martin's Press.
Phone: 1-800-221-7945 extension 763
Fax: 212-677-7456
E-mail: trademarketing@stmartins.com

Library of Congress Cataloging-in-Publication Data

Hedaya, Yael.
    [Short stories. English. Selections]
    Housebroken : three novellas / Yael Hedaya ; translated by Dalya Bilu.
        p. cm.
    Contents: Housebroken—The happiness game—Matti.
    ISBN 0-312-42090-0
    1. Hedaya, Yael—Translations into English. 2. Love stories, Hebrew—Translations into English. I. Bilu, Dalya. II. Title.

PJ5055.23.E33 A23 2001
892.4'36—dc21   00-046908

Originally published in Israel under the title *Shlosha Sipurei Ahava* by Am Oved, Tel Aviv

First Picador USA Edition: July 2002

10 9 8 7 6 5 4 3 2 1

For my father

Contents

HOUSEBROKEN

He was a shy dog, so the neighbors were surprised when one morning he got up from his mat, leaped on the old woman climbing the steps with her shopping bag, and ripped off her ear. He was a retiring dog, a shadow of a dog, with the build of a hyena and the gentleness of a bird. He always walked on tiptoe, his tail folded between his legs; he had short, thick brown fur, drooping ears, and long, fragile legs which might have possessed an aristocratic grace but for the fact that they trembled all the time.

He was one and a half years old, but he seemed older. The curve of his spine, the slump of his tail, the hanging pelvis with the ribs sticking out like wings gave him a deflated look, but it was mainly the way he walked—half sitting, shrinking, apologetic, as if evading imaginary kicks. The old lady was fond of him, and sometimes she would stop on her way home from the market, choose something from her basket, a chicken neck, a slice of cheese or salami, a sesame cracker, and throw it onto his mat before resuming her slow climb to the top floor. Only when the dog heard her door close and the key turn twice in the lock did he get up, sniff the offering, pick it up gingerly with his teeth, let it drop, circle it a few times, pick it up, reconsider, and then, looking from side to side, snap it up and swallow.

The neighbors had always ignored him. They were used to the sight of the dog dozing on the mat, lying outside one of the apartments, the one with a sign on the door bearing two names written in round letters—a woman's and a man's—and a childish drawing of a dog.

Now the old lady's groceries were strewn across the second-floor landing—chicken, potatoes, onions, apples, a grapefruit, a melon which had rolled into a corner, green bananas, sliced smoked turkey wrapped in white paper, a bar of dark chocolate, a head of garlic, and a bunch of parsley, lying in a little pool of blood.

That morning the old lady had planned to give the dog some smoked turkey, but before she had time to bend down and rummage in her baskets, the dog pounced and knocked her to the floor. She let out a shriek of surprise. The dog was surprised as well. He retreated and circled the old lady a few times, taking care not to step on her. She tried to get up but fell back again. The dog came closer, wagged his tail, and looked deep into her eyes. She turned onto her side, gripped the railing with both hands, and tried to pull herself up. He began to lick her face, and the old lady, who was heavy and short of breath, gave up and rolled over on her back again, let her hands fall to her sides, and sighed, and then the dog seized hold of her left ear with his teeth, and with one pull tore it off.

The old lady pressed her hand to the wound, which was spurting streams of blood, and screamed. The neighbors came out to the floor landings. A man wearing rubber flip-flops approached and removed her hand from the place where her ear had been. "He bit off her ear!" one of the neighbors shouted from her doorway, pointing with her cigarette toward the dog, who was hugging the wall and trembling, his tail between his legs and the ear dangling from his mouth. A few of the neighbors panicked, slammed their doors, and locked them. The man in the rubber flip-flops said they should get rid of the dog before he bit off the other ear, too.

But the dog sat back on his hind legs, looked at the old lady, whose screams had given way to rhythmic, desolate sobs, and then at the neighbors clustering around; he stood up, dropped the ear on the floor, and tottered back to his mat, where he waited quietly until the ambulance came and the men from the city pound. He saw how they put the old lady on a stretcher, how a hand in a plastic glove picked up the ear and dropped it into a bag. He listened to the neighbors giving the victim's particulars and watched two paramedics carrying the stretcher down the stairs.

The city dogcatchers said they would have to put the dog to sleep, but first he had to be quarantined to make sure he wasn't rabid. One of them asked the neighbors to step back, while the other went down to the street and returned holding a long iron pole with a loop at the end of it.

"No!" yelled the older dogcatcher. "Get the stun gun. You can't catch him with that. He's dangerous."

"Yes I can," said the younger one quietly. "Just get these people out of the way."

"Back into your houses!" ordered the older man, clapping his hands. "Everyone inside!" The neighbors remaining on the landing went back to their apartments obediently, but they kept their doors ajar to watch the dog being trapped. The dog lay on his mat in a ball, both pleased and embarrassed by the attention, his eyes closed, his nose touching the tip of his tail, and one of his ears pricked up.

"Look at him," said the older dogcatcher. "He's trying to pull a fast one, the bastard. Get the gun."

"Let me do it," said the young one. "He doesn't look dangerous to me."

"You're so wrong," said the older one. "I know his sort. He's bluffing. Just look at him. He's cunning. Look at his ear moving. He's only pretending to be asleep."

"He's always like that," whispered a neighbor dressed in a dirty pink bathrobe, peeping out from behind her door. "That's how he sleeps."

"Lady, get back inside. Please!" The older man gave her a push, then wiped the sweat from his forehead with his hand.

The two men stood and looked at the dog. His eyes were closed, his ear twitched a little, and his ribs rose and fell with his slow breathing. He looked too peaceful to attack anyone. The young man approached him, holding the pole in both his hands like a spear, trying not to make any sudden movements, but suddenly the dog opened his eyes and the catcher, who took a step backward, saw that he was wagging his tail.

"He's wagging his tail," he said, without taking his eyes off the dog.

"Don't trust him!" the other man whispered. "He's bluffing!"

"Are you wagging your tail?" said the young one. "Are you a friendly dog?" And the dog stood up, then sat down on his hind legs, and lowered his eyes shyly.

"What's going on?" hissed the older man. "What's he up to now?"

"Shhhhhh . . . ," the young one whispered. "He's not doing anything. Shhhhh . . . good dog!" And he aimed the loop at the dog's head.

"Watch out," said the older man. "I'm telling you, watch out!"

The young catcher leaned forward and went down on one knee. He tightened his hands around the pole, and moved it right and left until the loop hovered over the dog's head. The dog lifted his head and looked up at it. Then he looked at the catcher kneeling next to him, holding the pole and biting his lower lip in concentration. He turned his eyes to the loop again, which looked like both a snare and a halo.

"Quick!" whispered the older man, who was sweating heavily.

The young one lowered the loop until it touched the dog's nose; the dog sat still, looking upward, and didn't move even as the loop slowly encircled his head. The catcher jerked the pole back and the loop tightened around the dog's neck. The dog then stood up, dropped his tail between his legs, sidled along the wall, and led the catcher to the stairs. He descended slowly step by step, the metal disks on his collar rattling, and when he reached the entrance the older man was already standing there, holding the door open. He pressed his back against the door and watched his young colleague leading the dog to the yellow van. The dog stood until the young catcher opened the back doors of the van, then jumped in and bowed his head for the loop to be removed. He stepped into one of the empty metal cages, which the man shut slowly behind him, even though it was unnecessary. It was clear to the young catcher, and to the older one, who sat down in the driver's seat and wiped the sweat from his forehead, and to the neighbors, who crowded into the street to watch the final stage of the capture, that the dog wanted to go.

2

The man sat on the floor in the bathroom. He watched his friend bathing his baby daughter. He looked at him intently, following every movement, admiring the way in which he supported the baby's back with one hand and held her little head above the water with the other, sailing her body to and fro and making noises like a ship: the hoots and coos and gurgles of a doting father.

The man looked at his friend and said to himself that he must remember these details. That bathing a baby was exactly the kind of thing nobody ever explained to you—you just had to know. He wanted to be sure that when he had a baby of his own he would be able to give her a perfect bath, exactly like this one. He didn't want to make any mistakes.

He rested his arm on the ledge of the bath and dipped his fingers into the water, feeling the temperature, the warm soapiness,

the little waves made by the baby's kicks. He picked up the bottle
of baby soap and began to read the label. He wanted to know what
it was that turned ordinary soap into baby soap. His friend looked
at him and smiled, and the man felt suddenly embarrassed, as if
he had been caught reading something forbidden—something pure
intended for babies and fathers only, which in his bachelor hands
turned into pornography.

He stood up, wiped his hands on his jeans, and handed the
father the baby's white terry-cloth bathrobe, which had a little hood
like a monk's habit. He knew the ritual by heart. The father took
the baby out of the bath and wrapped her in the robe. He hugged
her to his chest and pressed his lips to her head and combed her
downy yellow hair with his fingers. Then he carried her to the
nursery with the man following like a faithful retainer, holding
the tiny hand poking out of the robe between his two fingers. The
father laid his daughter down on the chest of drawers, asked the
man to keep an eye on her, and left the room. The man remained
alone with the baby, flanking the chest of drawers, tense and ready
to save her if she fell, but the baby lay quietly on her back, trying
to catch the edge of the terry-cloth sleeve in her mouth. The father
came back with a bag of disposable diapers and put it down on the
floor. The man asked whether he could help and the father smiled
and rubbed his nose on the baby's belly and asked her what she
thought, whether they needed any help, and the baby laughed and
kicked her legs in the air. The man picked up a round flat jar of
ointment and again found himself reading the label. Then he put
the jar down and picked up the box of talcum powder, which had
pictures of elephants and giraffes on it, and sniffed the talc. He
put it down and picked up a bunch of colored plastic keys and
shook them in front of the baby, who turned her eyes toward them
for a minute. The man was pleased, thinking to himself that he
was quite a success at this, but then the baby turned her eyes back
to her father's face as he bent over her and fastened the diaper
around her waist, and she smiled. She put out her hand to touch
his face and the father kissed her fingers. The man put the keys

down on the chest of drawers, next to the talc and the ointment, left the room, stepped on a rubber dog which let out a sharp squeak and startled him, went out onto the balcony, and lit a cigarette.

3

The woman stood in her kitchen cooking spaghetti. She put a handful of spaghetti into the pot and looked at the fan of pasta half immersed in the water and half leaning on the side of the pot. She knew exactly how long it would take for the fan to collapse. It would begin with a small, barely perceptible movement of a few spaghetti sticks, which would slide into the water and drag the others down after them. In two minutes they would all sink into the pot, sliding downward with a tired, submissive movement, but there would always be two or three particularly stubborn ones that would have to be pushed in with a fork.

She took a can of tomato paste out of the cupboard and opened it. Then she unhooked the colander from where it was hanging above the stove, stood it in the sink, and waited. She took the package of spaghetti out of the cupboard and read the cooking instructions, even though she already knew them by heart: eleven minutes. A strange number, she thought. Odd, not even.

She lifted the pot off the stove and emptied its contents into the colander. Then she put it back on the flame, poured in some oil, shook the spaghetti in the colander, and returned it to the pot. She added tomato paste, salt, pepper, and paprika, and stirred it all with a fork. The contact of the spaghetti, oil, and tomato paste with the bottom of the pot produced spitting, hissing noises, and a smell of aluminum and starch spread through the kitchen, mixed with the sweet scent of cheap spices. The woman took the pot off the stove and placed it on a wooden board on the table. Then she sat down, spread the kitchen towel over her knees, and began to eat. This was her lunch. It was a kind of punishment.

4

The man and the woman sat in the car and talked. It was a warm evening at the beginning of October and the windows were open. They smoked cigarettes and flicked the ashes out on the sidewalk. The dog lay under a bush and peered through tired, half-closed eyes at the cigarettes' glowing tips, which looked like two fireflies inviting him to come and play in the darkness. But he didn't trust the fireflies. They were one more illusion of false hope that he had to treat with caution. This was the eighth day of his wanderings, and he was hungry and thirsty and tired. He was five weeks old and for the first time he began to feel the stirrings of what would ripen a year later into real despair.

His mother was a mongrel who had strayed from the fields to the city and littered under the concrete pillars of a quiet residential building. For a month she had suckled him and his three brothers. Early in the morning, before daybreak, she would emerge from hiding to scour the garbage cans lined up on the sidewalk. One of her front legs was broken. On the night she had strayed into town from the fields, wary of the people but oblivious to the cars, a taxi had hit her. The taxi had carried on driving while the dog went on running. For several hours she ran through the streets, past shops and cafés and restaurants, her injured leg folded inward, her heavy belly almost dragging on the asphalt, until she reached the little street and slipped under the building with the pillars, lay down on a sheet of cardboard, and gave birth to four puppies.

Whenever she returned from her scavenging expeditions to the garbage cans—where she swallowed the pickings quickly, almost without chewing—she'd lay down on the cardboard and her injured leg would twist, resulting in a cry of pain which eventually drew the attention of the neighbors.

An old man came down the stairs, holding a broomstick in his hand. At first the dogs saw only his feet, shod in rubber flip-flops, but then his knees, thighs, the bottoms of his short trousers, and his face suddenly came into view, and the bitch sprang up, bared her teeth, and growled at him. The man let out a curse and withdrew; he did not return that day. The next morning the mother rose slowly to her feet and licked each of her pups, a slow, sad lick, lingering longest on the head of the firstborn as if trying to convey a message to him with her tongue. Then she limped off in the direction of the garbage cans, walked past them, and never came back.

At noon the old man returned, accompanied by two other men. One carried a long pole with a loop at the end and the other scattered scraps of red meat over the lawn. The puppy's younger brothers ran outside, wagging their tails and whimpering, tripping over their feet in excitement and gratitude, but he preferred to withdraw deep between the pillars of the building and hide behind a pile of broken bricks that smelled of dust and spiders. The dogcatchers waited for the mother to emerge, in the meantime picking up the puppies. They exchanged a few words with the disappointed old man, who swore to them repeatedly that yesterday a crazy dog had tried to attack him right under the pillars.

The dogcatchers and the old man stood on the lawn and waited but the mother did not come back. One of the catchers collected the scraps of meat and picked up the pole, while the other clasped the three puppies to his chest. The old man felt that the bitch had betrayed him. For the sake of the residents' safety he tried to persuade the men to wait a little longer; in a whisper, so that the puppies wouldn't hear, he pointed out that "families with children" lived in the building. The catchers agreed to stay and the man went upstairs to return with a tray laden with glasses of juice and cookies. The catchers ate and drank at their leisure, and afterward they thanked the old man and left, taking their traps and the puppies with them.

Darkness fell, but the puppy didn't dare come out from behind the pile of bricks, so he stayed there all night. In the morning he lay down on the sheet of cardboard, which was soaked with urine and memories, and at noon his hunger drove him outside, to the dazzling light and the lawn which still smelled of raw meat. He crawled over the lawn, sniffing and whimpering quietly to himself, and he forgot his terror of the man with the flip-flops and the other men who had caught his brothers. A column of ants led him to a wet cookie. He snapped the booty up between his teeth and ran with it to the cardboard. After devouring the cookie, he laid his head on his front paws and fell asleep. When night fell he woke up to a new hunger, worse and more painful than the one before. He went back to the lawn and looked for the friendly ants, but he couldn't find them. He began to bark with shrill little barks, and a window opened above him, a man's head poked out, and a smell of frying meat flooded the air. It was the first time the dog had barked and he realized immediately that he had made a mistake and escaped into the street.

For a week he roamed the neighborhood, sleeping under bushes and parked cars. Now and then small children noticed him and tried to drag their parents over, but the parents usually tightened their grip on their child's hand and pulled them away. Once the dog passed a restaurant and someone threw him a chicken leg. He ate the leg and remained sitting on the sidewalk, under the generous table, but a gigantic woman came out of the restaurant and kicked him. During the course of the week he grew accustomed to all kinds of kicks: the hard kicks of café owners and shop salesmen when he sought shade and attention, the not-quite-so-hard kicks of people rejecting his attempts at friendship, and the weak kicks from feet he stumbled over in the busy streets, which were so halfhearted and incidental that they sometimes seemed to him like caresses.

Now the car door opened and a woman emerged. She leaned through the open window, and the man inside kissed her. Then she turned around, stood with her back to the car, and took her keys out of her handbag. The dog heard sounds of laughter and whispering, and opened one eye. The woman was leaning into the car again, her one leg resting against the door and the other raised in the air, and the man was kissing her and trying to pull her back in. Then she straightened up, the driver's door opened, and the man got out, slammed the door, and came around to the sidewalk.

He slouched against the passenger door. The woman stood facing him, playing with the bunch of keys, which clattered every time she threw it into the air and caught it in the palm of her hand. The man leaned toward her and whispered something in her ear. The woman took a step backward, shook her head, and went on bouncing the keys in her hand. The puppy opened his other eye and pricked up one of his ears.

The man said: "But why not?" And the woman kept quiet and smiled and went on rattling her keys. The puppy crawled out from under the bush and wagged his tail.

At first they didn't notice him. They embraced and kissed, and the bunch of keys was caught between them and the puppy heard only sucking noises and whispers and again: "Why not? Just for coffee." And again the keys rattled, and the puppy ran up to the man and woman, his tail between his legs, his head bowed and tilted to one side.

The woman saw him, bent down, and put the bunch of keys on the sidewalk. The man said: "Look, what a poor little puppy."

"He's so thin," said the woman and scratched the back of his neck with her fingers.

"He's friendly," said the man.

"Poor little thing," said the woman.

"Look how happy he is," said the man, and sat down on his heels. With one hand he stroked the puppy's belly and with the other he stroked the nape of the woman's neck. Then they kissed again, but they went on scratching and tickling the belly of the puppy, who immediately succumbed to their fondlings.

"What are we going to do with him?" said the woman and put her hand on the man's shoulder.

"Let's go up to your place," said the man.

"But what about him?" she said, and looked at the puppy now lying on his belly, his head resting on his paws and his tail thumping the sidewalk.

"It doesn't look as if he belongs to anyone. You want a dog?"

"I don't know. Do you?"

"I can't," he said. "I'm hardly ever home."

"Actually I'd like to have a dog, but I don't know if I need that kind of commitment right now," said the woman.

"I certainly don't," said the man and put his hand on the woman's thigh. She sat back on the sidewalk and said: "That's enough."

"So are we going up to your place?" asked the man.

"Yes," said the woman and stood up. "But just for coffee."

"And what about him?" the man said and looked at the dog.

"We'll give him something to eat, and when you leave you can take him out again," said the woman.

"Okay," he said, and kissed her again, this time gently, on her cheek. "After coffee I'll take him out."

But the man and the dog stayed over.

5

Each of them slept in his own place—the dog on a little rug at the foot of the bed, and the man in the bed next to the woman. The man and the woman didn't go to sleep right away. First of all they took care of the dog. They took out almost the entire contents of the fridge and put them on a plastic plate which the woman removed from beneath one of the potted plants on the balcony. The dog's meal included a full container of cottage cheese, a few slices of hard cheese, some smoked turkey, and mocha-flavored yogurt. The man and the woman were in a generous mood. The woman put the plate down on the marble counter and asked the man if he thought it was enough. The man hugged her from behind and pressed his lips to her neck.

The dog sat on the floor next to the fridge. He understood instinctively that this would be the source of his happiness tonight, and maybe not only tonight but forever, and the man pushed him aside with his foot, opened the door, peeped inside, and took out three eggs. He broke them onto the plate with one hand and threw the shells into the garbage can. The woman picked up the plate, turned toward the man, and they kissed again. The dog jumped into the air.

Finally, the woman remembered him and she laughed and said: "Poor little thing, I'm starving you." She freed herself from the embrace, bent down, and put the plate on the floor. The dog devoured the food. The man leaned the woman against the fridge and lifted the hem of her dress. The dog ate, whimpering as he did. His whole body trembled with excitement. He ate quickly without tasting, but when he progressed from the rim of the plate to the middle and discovered that there still was more food he slowed down and closed his eyes, abandoning himself to the mixed tastes of the eggs and cheese and turkey and mocha. He polished the meal off and then licked the plate clean. Then he turned it over, pushed it along the floor with his paw, stuck his nose under the edge, and then turned it over to lick the bottom again. When he discovered that the plate had nothing more to offer, he suddenly felt both satisfied and anxious and ran into the bedroom.

The man and the woman were rolling around on the bed naked. The dog found their clothes strewn like signposts from the kitchen to the hallway to the bedroom, which was dark and sounded of grunts. Now that the dog was full he wanted to play and began to run around the bed. He heard the man and the woman laughing and whispering, and when he saw the man's naked foot poking out of the sheet he stood on his hind legs and sniffed the warm, rough heel. The man kicked him. The dog fell on his back and rolled on the floor. He stood up and wagged his tail. He knew that this time it was a good kick.

With his stomach full, he was subject to a strange mixture of happiness and restlessness. The happiness he remembered dimly, distinct from all other memories, as a square of cardboard; the restlessness was still fresh and painful and detailed: leaves, scorching asphalt, thirst, thousands of kicking feet, and one chicken leg which was either part of the happiness or the restlessness, the dog didn't know which. He circled the bed, again stood up on his hind legs, and laid his head on the mattress. He tested the man's side and then went around to the woman's side, but neither wanted to play.

He ran to the kitchen, sniffed his plate, and licked it again; then he flipped it and kicked it and dragged it over the floor until he grew bored and returned to the bedroom. On the way he collected a sock which smelled like the rough, warm heel. He shook it between his teeth and growled, but the sock, the man, and the woman didn't cooperate. He sat next to the door and looked at the bed rocking in the dark. He missed the man and the woman.

He barked one of his experimental barks—he wasn't quite accustomed to the sound and he wasn't yet sure of its meaning—and when there was no response he ran to the living room, the sock dangling from his mouth, and crawled under the sofa. He was almost asleep when he heard water running in the bathroom. He hurried there, full of hope, and saw the woman stooped over in the bath, her back to him. She turned and smiled, aimed the shower head, and sprayed him with water. He sneezed and drew back, and when the woman came out of the bathroom he ran to the living room, beckoning her with his head to follow him. He crawled under the sofa and waited, but the woman didn't come.

The house was quiet now. The dog went into the kitchen, where the fluorescent light was on, and looked from a distance at his plate, which was lying upside down next to the balcony door. He couldn't remember what had been in it that had driven him so frantic with joy. He sniffed at it again, and went back to the bedroom. The man was lying on his stomach and the woman was lying on her side. The man's arm was wrapped around the woman's waist, and the woman's leg was lying at an angle across the man's legs. The puppy curled up on the little rug at the foot of the bed,

closed his eyes, and let out a long breath that contained both bit-
terness and resignation. He pricked up one ear to remain on guard,
to defend the man and the woman against all possible enemies,
and then sank into a long, sound sleep.

6

In the morning the man woke up and went to the bathroom. He
peed and yawned and for a moment was alarmed to feel a wet
tongue and sharp teeth rubbing against his ankle. Then he remembered the puppy and the events of the night before and smiled,
flushed the toilet, and bent down to stroke the dog's head. He
went into the kitchen, picked his shirt up from the floor, collected
his belt and shoes from the hallway, and returned to the bedroom,
where he found his jeans waiting for him on the floor in a kneeling
position with his underpants inside them. He gathered his clothes
together and put them down on the bed, on his side, and began
to get dressed quietly, trying not to wake the woman. But the dog
barked—this time it sounded almost like a real bark—and the
woman woke up.

The man apologized, but the dog was beside himself with joy.
Now they were both awake, which doubled his chances of getting
love. He dashed around the bed barking, and then he ran into the
bathroom and peed on the floor. He went back to the bedroom,
feeling a little guilty without knowing why. The man was sitting on
the edge of the bed and looking around the room for his sock. The
woman crawled over the bed on her elbows and knees, put her
arms around his neck, and said: "Are you leaving already?"

"I'm late for work," said the man, "and I can't find my sock."

"Should I help you look?" asked the woman and rubbed the tip
of her nose on his ear.

"No," said the man. He looked at the dog and asked: "Well?
Should I take him with me and let him go somewhere?"

The woman nodded.

"Will you come over this evening?" she asked.

The man picked the puppy up in one hand and waved him in front of her and asked her if she wanted to say good-bye to him.

"No," said the woman.

"Not even a kiss?" asked the man.

"No. I don't want to get attached. So are you coming over this evening?"

The man sat back down on the edge of the bed, clasped the puppy to his chest, and said: "Actually he's rather cute, don't you think?"

The woman didn't answer. She saw the man murmuring sweet talk to the dog and the dog wriggling in his arms, and suddenly she felt demeaned, because this was exactly the way he had talked to her in the night, and exactly the way she had wriggled in his arms. She hoped the man would fight for the dog, take pity on him, find a corner for him in his life, but she knew he was going to get rid of him without thinking twice.

She said: "So will you come over tonight?" and put her hand on his thigh. The man threw the puppy into the air, caught him, threw him up and caught him again.

"Be careful!" she said. "Did you hear me?"

The man sat the dog in his lap, felt one of his paws with his fingers, and said: "Do you think he'll be big?"

She lay down on her stomach next to the man, stretched out her hand, and touched the dog's wet nose with her fingertips.

"I can't find my sock," said the man.

"I'll give you a pair," said the woman and she wanted to get up and go to the closet, but the man put his hand on her shoulder to stop her.

"Are you sure?" asked the woman.

"Sure," said the man.

"So will we keep in touch?" asked the woman.

The man stood up and said: "We'll see. I don't know."

He pushed his bare foot into the shoe and tied the laces.

"Should I let myself out?" he asked, but the woman pulled the sheet over her head and didn't answer. "I'll let myself out," said the man, and he left the room, carrying the delighted puppy under his arm. From the door he called: "Good-bye!" The woman jumped out of bed and ran after him, clutching the sheet, her hair wild, her face swollen, and her eyes glittering with tears.

"Leave him here!" she said.

"What?"

"Leave him here," she said.

"Are you sure?" asked the man.

"Yes," said the woman, "I'm sure. I want him."

The man shrugged his shoulders, handed the dog over, and kissed the woman on her cheek. He gave the dog a little pat too and went away.

7

The dog knew that yesterday he had been a stray and today he was a pet. There was a price to pay, though, and he was happy to pay it. All day long the woman chased after him and swept him up in her arms and pressed him to her breast and buried her face in his neck and wet his coat with her tears. When he whimpered in protest she would put him down on the floor, mutter something, throwing herself onto the living-room sofa to leaf through the newspaper, stare at the TV, or dial phone numbers, and the dog would gain a few precious minutes of freedom, which he used to explore.

Once, when the woman was talking on the phone, he managed to climb onto the bed. He stepped carefully, treading on the sheets and pillows, which with every step let loose a cloud of familiar smells: the smell of the woman and the smell of the man, and when he poked his nose into the gap between the two pillows and made a thorough study of the scent line down the length of the bed, he caught a sharp and unfamiliar odor—the smell of them both. He returned to the living room feeling excited, and again the woman swept him up in her arms and hugged him and smothered him. He squirmed and whined, so she put him down on the floor and dropped back onto the sofa. He sat on the carpet and looked up. He liked the woman, but he was afraid of her.

Toward evening, she calmed down. She spoke on the phone some more while the dog lay at her feet with his eyes closed, nibbling the tip of one of her rubber flip-flops.

"The bastard!" the woman shouted into the phone and resumed her crying, and the dog was afraid that it was going to start all over again, the hugging and the kissing and the sobbing and the choking. He raised his head to look at her but all he saw was agitated knees and fingers holding a burning cigarette.

"Are you listening?" said the woman. "I acted like a total idiot! An idiot! I don't know what came over me. We kissed a little and he came upstairs and that's it. It happened. It just happened.

"Yes, it was nice. It was more than nice. It was wonderful.

"In the morning.

"I tried! I've been trying for hours, but you weren't home. Where were you?

"I don't know. About ten o'clock, right after he left. He was going to leave without even saying good-bye. You get it? You see what kind of a person he is?

"Because I heard him getting dressed. He thought I wouldn't wake up.

"Maybe. But even if he'd left a note, that wouldn't make it okay.

"I woke up.

"Nothing. We didn't even have coffee. He said he had to go to work.

"I don't remember. He told me yesterday. Something to do with film production.

"I don't know. He told me, but I don't remember.

"That's it. And I asked if he wanted to keep in touch.

"Yes, I did.

"I know.

"You're right. It was a mistake. And just to prove it he said he didn't know.

"But I haven't got the strength for these games anymore. I haven't got the strength.

"Yes. He said: 'We'll see. I don't know.'

"That's what he said: 'We'll see.'

"Yes. I'm sure.

"I don't know what it means. Probably no."

The woman burst into tears again; the dog stopped nibbling the flip-flop and began licking her ankle, and the woman bent down and picked him up, but this time she didn't choke him; she sat him carefully on her lap and began feeling the fur on his neck and said: "I forgot to tell you, I have a dog.

"Just a dog.

"A stray.

"I don't know. Ugly. A puppy.

"Maybe two months. Small.

"We found him last night. When he brought me home, it was under my building.

"But I couldn't just leave him outside. He was starving. That's why he came up with me in the first place, to feed the dog. That was the excuse. He said he'd take him away afterward.

"No. I wouldn't let him. I don't know why. I felt sorry for the poor little thing. Do you think he'll call to ask about the dog?

"I don't know. I can't throw him out now. Maybe I'll wait a day or two. Let's see what happens. Let's see if he gets in touch. You want a dog?"

When she hung up the woman dried her tears and went to the bathroom. The dog heard her shouting and then she came back into the living room. She shook a finger at him. He dropped the rubber flip-flop and lowered his eyes. He knew he had done something bad, but he didn't know what. The woman burst out crying again, but it wasn't the same crying as in the morning and the afternoon, it was different, flat and deflated.

"Sonofabitch!" she shouted. "What do I need this for?"

She went into the kitchen, got a stick and a rag, and went back to the bathroom. He followed and watched her mopping up the puddle on the floor and crying. She turned her head—just as she had done at night when she caught him looking at her—and for a minute he filled with joy, but then the woman threw the wet rag at him. He was alarmed and ran to hide under the sofa. The woman ran after him. She kicked the sofa and hurt her toe. Now she cried in a different way, which alarmed him more than all the other kinds he had heard before. She hopped around the room, holding her foot in her hand and crying, but all of a sudden she stopped. He saw her kneeling and stretching her hand toward him, so close it was almost touching him, and pulling out the sock, which was now full of holes and fuzzy dust. He didn't protest or try to take the sock back. Something in him wanted to make friends with the woman and something in him wanted to go back to the street, but he made no move, because he knew she was dangerous now—she was quiet, not kicking or crying, just walking around the room with the white sock crushed in her hand, whispering: "It's all because of you."

8

In the evening the man arrived carrying a big plastic bag in his arms. The woman let him in and resumed her place on the sofa, opposite the TV, without saying a word. The dog was glad to see him, and the man was glad that someone was pleased to see him. Neither of them could see that the woman was glad as well.

The man stood in the doorway and said: "I bought some stuff for the dog."

The woman said nothing, just turned up the sound on the television.

He came into the room and began spreading his purchases out on the table: a brown leather leash, a collar, a deep plastic bowl, a big bag of dog biscuits bearing a picture of a plump, furry yellow puppy—not at all like the wild ingrate who had wrought havoc in her house—and a rubber bone which the dog snatched from the man's hand and carried off to the bedroom. The woman looked at him and thought: He's taking over the house.

The man sat down next to her on the sofa and put his hand on her thigh. She remembered that she'd done the same thing in the morning, when she'd wanted something from him—it was apparently a universal gesture of distress. She moved away and went on staring at the screen. She thought: What gives him the right to come here? The man asked her what she was watching and she didn't answer. He asked her if it was any good and she still didn't answer. He asked her what was up and she stayed silent. He asked her whether she was angry and she shrugged her shoulders. Then she took a cigarette from the pack on the table, lying under the leash and the collar and the big plastic bowl.

"I bought things for your dog," said the man, also staring at the screen. The woman blew smoke out of her mouth and said: "He's not my dog."

The man was glad she was talking to him. He leaned forward and took a cigarette from her pack, lit it, and flipped the match into the ashtray with a macho kind of movement. She thought: What gives him the right to take one of my cigarettes? The man began to tell her about his day at work, tapping the cigarette on the edge of the ashtray and describing the movie director he was working with—an egotist but a genius, and the woman thought: He's an ass kisser.

Again he put his hand on her thigh, and the woman ground her cigarette out. She picked up the collar and said: "What gives you the right to come here?"

The dog was running back and forth between the bedroom and the living room with the bone in his mouth, beside himself with joy. The woman felt sorry for him because it was so easy to make him happy and even easier to take his happiness away. She felt a sudden urge to make him miserable, but she controlled herself. The man kept quiet. He knew he had done something wrong, but didn't know what it was.

"What makes you think you can just come here without letting me know?" asked the woman, opening and closing the collar buckle.

"I thought you wanted me to come," said the man.

"Who said?" she asked.

"That's what I understood from you."

"And what if I wasn't home?"

"But I knew you would be."

"How?"

"I thought you're free."

"And if I'm not?"

"But you are."

"But what if I wasn't?"

"Then maybe I'd come back later."

"And what about the things for the dog?"

"I'd have left them outside the door. Or brought them back later, or tomorrow. I don't know. I didn't think about it. What difference does it make anyway?"

"So did you come for me or the dog?" asked the woman.

"What did I do?" asked the man. "Why are you angry?" When he saw the dog running up and down the hallway with the bone in his mouth, he whistled and the dog dropped the bone and jumped into his lap.

"I don't want him on the sofa," said the woman. "Put him down."

"Why not?" said the man and scratched the dog's belly. "He's not hairy."

"He might have ticks," said the woman. "And anyway, he has to have some limits. If he doesn't learn them now, there'll be no stopping him. He has to be trained."

"So it sounds like you've decided to keep him," said the man.

"I haven't decided anything. He's a difficult dog."

"So are you going to tell me what I've done?" asked the man. "Was I wrong to bring stuff for the dog? Is that what made you angry?"

"Why *did* you bring all that stuff?" asked the woman. "What do you care? This morning you wanted to throw him out."

"Me?" shouted the man. "*I* wanted to throw him out?"

"Yes. You wanted to leave him in a field somewhere. Or in the street, where he'd get run over or caught by the city dogcatchers. If I hadn't kept him here he might be dead by now. Such a little dog. He'd have died! I don't understand why you didn't bother to call before you came."

"Because I don't have your number."

"You don't have my number?"

"No. You called me. Remember?"

"Yes," said the woman and put out her cigarette. He was right. She'd called him. She was the one who'd made the mistake of calling him in the first place.

"You smoke a lot," said the man. "You smoke twice as much as me."

"That's because I'm nervous," said the woman. "I'm twice as nervous as you."

"Why?" asked the man and tried to embrace her, but the woman stood up, took the ashtray and the cigarettes and matches, and went to the kitchen. The dog, who remembered the kitchen as a happy place, ran after her.

"I'll tell you why," she shouted to the man from the kitchen as the dog sat down next to the fridge. "Because you behaved like an animal. I asked if you wanted to keep in touch and you couldn't bring yourself to say yes."

"What did I say?" asked the man, standing in the kitchen doorway looking at her. "I don't remember."

"You said, 'We'll see. I don't know,'" said the woman in a mocking tone.

"But I didn't say no."

"So you *do* remember."

"I don't remember saying that I didn't want to go on seeing you. That's what I remember."

"So why did you have to say 'We'll see. I don't know,' if you knew that you did want to?"

The man bent down to pat the dog and said that he didn't understand what she was talking about. The truth was, he thought, that he didn't know whether he'd wanted to see her. He'd just come. "Has he eaten today?" he said, pointing to the dog's plate lying upside down next to the porch door.

"No," said the woman. "I forgot to feed him."

"So should I give him some of the biscuits? Should I put them in the new bowl?" asked the man.

"Do what you like," said the woman and she emptied the ashtray into the garbage can and watched the cigarette stubs sinking into the remains of the spaghetti she had eaten for lunch yesterday. Then she washed the ashtray thoroughly and put it on the drying rack. "You can do whatever you like," she said. "He's your dog just as much as mine."

The dog received a bowlful of special biscuits for puppies. Then the man and the woman got ready to go out to a restaurant. The man said: "I'm sorry if there was a misunderstanding. I'm sorry if I hurt your feelings. I didn't mean to." And when the woman looked at him suspiciously, he stroked her cheek and said: "I really don't remember what I said this morning," and the woman said: "Never mind. I don't know why I jumped on you. I had a bad day. The dog was really annoying. I don't know what I'm going to do."

"You'll have to train him," said the man.

"If I decide to keep him."

The man said: "You'd better make up your mind."

The woman said: "I know nothing about training a dog."

And the man said: "I'll show you."

Then they argued about what restaurant to go to. The man said: "It's my treat," and the woman said: "But you paid yesterday, today it's my treat." He embraced her and said: "You're a sucker—that was just coffee. You didn't even have any cake. Why didn't you have anything?"

"Because I was too nervous," said the woman.

"You didn't miss anything," he said. "The cake was disgusting."

The woman said: "Yes, I could see you were suffering."

The man said: "But it looked good in the window."

The woman said: "Yes, it did."

She went into the bedroom to get dressed and asked the man to take the dog for a walk. "He's been in the house all day," she said, "and he peed on the bathroom floor." But she said it without anger; she even sounded pleased. The man put the collar around the dog's neck, but the collar was too big, and he asked the woman if she had something with a sharp point he could use to make a hole. The woman, who was in a better mood now, shouted from the bedroom: "Next to the stove, in the top drawer on the left, there's a pair of scissors." The man found the scissors, took the collar off the dog's neck, placed it on the kitchen table, pierced it with the point of the scissors, turned it around, picked up the collar, and, looking at it, said: "Come here. Let's try it on."

The dog had begun to understand the man's language. He came up to him, dropping the toy bone, which had started to lose its appeal.

"Perfect," the man said to the dog and he attached the leash to the collar. "We're off," he said to the woman. "Wear something sexy."

The woman stood in her panties in front of the long mirror on the closet door. She noticed a red scratch on her stomach and didn't know if it was from the man or the dog, but she preferred to think it was from the man. The black dress she had worn yesterday was lying on the floor. She thought of the puppy and picked it up in alarm. She spread the dress out on the bed and turned the reading lamp toward it to examine it closely, but the dog seemed to have spared it. In any case, she couldn't wear the same thing tonight. She surveyed the closet, searching for something sexy, but she couldn't find anything—she had used up her one sexy dress. Then she considered whether the man was being serious when he said: "Wear something sexy."

9

The man and the dog went down to the street. The collar felt tight around the dog's neck, but he was so happy to be going for a walk that he kept running on ahead. The man was suddenly seized by anxiety. All day he'd wondered whether to see the woman this evening or wait a few days to make the rules clear or not see her at all and be cold on the phone if she called. He didn't know where he stood on the issue. He had been on so many blind dates in the past year he was afraid his improved dating skills had impaired his ability to discriminate.

The date with the woman had been arranged by a friend who he'd first met on a blind date. They had gone out for two months, he had sometimes slept at her place, and they had talked long into the night. He told her everything he knew about himself. She told him about her past, her ex-boyfriends, the hopelessness of the present, her hunger for a relationship, and he nodded in silent agreement. He broke up with her, but he asked if they could stay friends. She was important to him, he said, and he didn't want to lose her. And she said: I don't want to lose you either.

Afterward she started arranging blind dates for him with her friends and the friends of her friends, not sure what she enjoyed more: seeing him reject them or them reject him. She always had to hear the story from both parties, and she always pretended to take his side, because she wanted him to go on dating her girl-friends, breaking up with them, and telling her all about it on her balcony at night. But most of all she wanted him to sleep over, worn out by talking.

This time he'd decided to be passive. He'd said to his matchmaking friend: I'm not calling anyone. If they want to call me, fine.
I won't say no. She said: I gave your number to the friend of a
friend. I saw her on the street once and she looks okay.

He felt so passive he didn't even ask what she looked like and
how old she was and what she did. The woman called that afternoon. She had a pleasant voice. He didn't notice any signs of ner-
vousness. She told him she was a translator, working from home,
it didn't bring in a lot of money but she managed to make ends
meet; she was thirty, and this was the first time she'd taken the
initiative and called someone for a blind date. He asked her
whether she was generally shy and she said yes, but if she'd been
really shy, she said, she wouldn't have answered his question. The
man thought: She sounds clever. The woman asked if it bothered
him that she'd called. He said no, on the contrary, and they arranged to meet that evening in a café much favored for blind dates,
because it was noisy and there was no possibility of privacy. When
he got dressed for the date, hesitating between comfortable old
jeans and a new pair that he hadn't worn before and were a little
tight, he remembered that he'd forgotten to ask how he would
recognize her.

He came fifteen minutes late, having deliberately ignored a few
good parking spots so as not to arrive on time. He wanted to punish
the woman for taking the initiative and calling him. By the time
he decided to park he couldn't find a spot and had to leave his car
in an expensive parking lot. Nevertheless, as he walked to the café
he felt pleased with himself.

The woman was waiting at a table for two, which was placed
between two larger tables, where four couples were sitting. His
date looked lost at her table. Usually he was the one waiting for
the stranger he'd called, who'd arrive late on purpose, apologizing
and checking him out before she sat down on the other side of the
table he had chosen after much hesitation. When he saw the
woman hemmed in by the two large tables, smoking and darting

nervous glances at the door, he saw himself in a new and touching light. He felt a rush of affection for the woman waiting at the table. He hoped she was his date.

He went up to her and introduced himself and they shook hands. Her hand was small and cold. She asked if the noise and the crowds bothered him, if he wanted to go somewhere else. He said it was up to her. She said: I don't know. What do you think? And he said they should stay where they were, he didn't have the energy to look for another parking spot.

She was short and thin with shoulder-length straight black hair. She had beautiful eyes and lips and a charming, almost imperceptible little scar under her chin. He asked her right away how she'd gotten it, which seemed a good way to break the ice. She smiled and said: I fell off a swing when I was a little girl. She asked whether he had any scars and he said that he had a big, ugly one on his knee, from a piece of broken glass when he once fell off a seesaw. She said: It's either swings or seesaws.

He thought of a little girl with black hair on a swing. He liked the idea. She didn't look really grown-up even now—her slight build, her smile, and the little scar made her seem childlike, someone he wanted to save from falling off a swing, and also to go to bed with.

In the morning, after he'd left, his conscience bothered him. He shouldn't have said that he didn't know if he'd come back. He should have at least given her a yes or a no. It was the maybe that drove them crazy, he knew, but still he never managed to stop himself. And she was actually okay, this woman. They'd had an enjoyable evening. Most of the time she listened. She seemed interested and asked questions, good questions—the kind that showed real curiosity—and he answered willingly. He remembered that he'd hardly asked her about herself and he felt a little guilty. He'd been inconsiderate. On the other hand, she'd said that she was shy. Really shy people were grateful when someone else talked. This increased his desire for her. In the afternoon he decided not to see her again because she'd broken one of his rules: she'd asked

if he wanted to keep in touch. She's dependent, he said to himself.
Or else she doesn't know how to play the game. On the other hand,
she might be playing a different game, one he wasn't familiar with.
The possibility would never have occurred to him two or three
years ago, even a year ago, when he was more sure of himself and
less lonely.

He had never had a relationship that lasted more than two or
three months, and they had always revolved around negotiations
about when they would see each other again. The negotiations
were tedious and predictable, and he always won, because he was
the one who said when they were over.

He was thirty-three and he was tired of his own rules, games,
and negotiations. They were fine in themselves, as rules, games,
and negotiations—this is what his matchmaking friend, who admired everything he did, always said—but most of his friends were
already married and living by different rules and having different
negotiations, which seemed a lot more important than his, and they
were playing with their children.

The man was so lost in thought that he didn't notice the distress
of the little puppy, who began coughing and choking but who went
on running ahead, refusing to let the tightness of his collar spoil
the joy of his freedom. The man stopped and bent down and
opened the buckle of the collar. Since there was no hole in a more
suitable place, he decided to let the dog loose and see if he would
run away. The dog stayed with him. Although there had been one
terrible moment of uncertainty that afternoon, when the woman
had chased him and tried to kick him, he had already forgotten it.
He had a short memory and he wanted a home.

10

When they returned from their walk, they found the woman sitting on the living-room sofa. She was wearing faded jeans and a black tank top whose straps fell off her shoulders. Neither the man nor the woman wanted to go out to eat but they didn't want to disappoint each other, so they said nothing. The man wanted to sit on the sofa next to her, watch television, and order a pizza; the woman also wanted to stay at home and see how things developed. She was tired.

She had gone out with two men in the past year before she met the man. She had met the young lawyer at a party. They danced and then he took her to see his apartment on the tenth floor of a frightening marble tower uptown. She admired his furniture, even though it repelled her. It was like the building and a bit like the lawyer, who was very tall and pale. All evening he kept urging her to look out the window, even though the view was of a big freeway intersection and a few distant factory chimneys. Afterward they went to bed.

In the morning the young lawyer said he wanted to cook dinner for her. Tell me what you like, he said, and I'll make it. She almost said that she liked everything, but the thought of another evening in the apartment with the roads and the ugly furniture depressed her. She told him she was busy. A few days later he called and invited her to dinner at an expensive restaurant. She said she wasn't interested in seeing him again, and when she hung up she imagined the young lawyer walking around his big apartment with the cordless phone and looking out at the asphalt and the chimneys. She wondered if he was wearing the white terrycloth bathrobe with his name embroidered on it in gold letters, the bathrobe she had seen hanging on a chrome hook in his bathroom. She felt sorry for him.

She remembered how they had sat on the white leather sofa in his living room, sipping white wine and staring out into the darkness. She remembered how he had stood up to pour her wine, and when he sat back down next to her the leather had squeaked. He put his glass on the low table—four metal legs topped with a sheet of milky glass—and said: We can have sex if you like.

They went into the bedroom and took off their clothes in silence. They each put their clothes on one of the identical chairs standing on either side of the bed like sentinels. To her it seemed more like a tedious ritual before going to sleep than the prelude to a one-night stand. She lay on her back on the bed and let him run his thin fingers over her belly and seek her lips in the dark. When he kissed her she said to herself that his tongue was like a lizard's, quick and automatic and greedy. The young lawyer turned onto his side, opened the drawer of the nightstand, which had apparently been made to match the coffee table in the living room, and took out a pack of condoms. With the same practiced skill as when he had poured her wine, he drew one out of its wrapper and fitted it onto his penis. She knew she had made a mistake but consoled herself with the thought that it was a good thing he was taking the proper precautions, even though the whole thing already seemed to her as ugly and industrial as the view from the window.

Two weeks later she went on her first blind date. The divorced painter had arranged to meet her at a bar downtown. He was fifteen years older than she was. He was short and stout and he had a gray beard and thin gray hair tied up in what looked like a pigtail. Her first blind date's teeth were stained with nicotine.

The divorced painter showed no interest in her at all. He talked about himself, his painting, his genius, his poverty, and his three teenage daughters who made his life miserable. He bad-mouthed his ex-wife too, and it seemed that he was still in love with her. The woman sat opposite him and drank her beer in silence. The divorced painter said it was important to him to make it clear that he wasn't looking for a relationship. He emptied his glass of brandy, leaned over the table to touch her cheek, and said: "I'm looking for a fuck."

The woman said: "At least you're honest."

The divorced painter said: "When I'm horny, I'm honest."

She asked: "How long has it been since you fucked anyone?" And she thought that he was very different from the young lawyer, who was slick and milky and opaque, like his coffee table and his nightstand. She thought that fate had presented her with two extremes; once she knew both, maybe she would finally be able to identify what lay between them, the happy middle, the compromise that everybody talked about all the time.

The divorced painter said: "I haven't had a fuck in six months. And you?"

"I fucked someone two weeks ago," said the woman.

The divorced painter brought his face close to hers. His breath smelled bad. A blend of cigarettes and cheap brandy and something else. He beckoned the waitress and ordered another brandy for himself without asking the woman what she wanted. He crumpled his empty pack of cigarettes, took one of hers, lit it, and said: "You want to fuck me?"

Suddenly it seemed to the woman that she longed for the young lawyer, but she knew it was too late to invent such longings. She said to the divorced painter: "Yes, I'll fuck you if you like."

And afterward it turned into an act of charity. The divorced painter didn't have a car, because he was poor and because he didn't believe in cars. She knew this was a lie he told himself, and that the lie was part of the bad smell coming from his mouth—a smell that would soon become a part of her. She thought of the divorced painter's ex-wife, who had thrown him out of the house. She imagined the divorced painter wasn't only a terrible husband, but a terrible painter as well. They took a cab to her home and she paid. The driver, a young, attractive man—someone who looked like a student, someone who only a few years earlier could still have been her boyfriend—looked at her in the rearview mirror as if he felt sorry for her. For a moment there was something thrilling about being a victim.

They went up to her apartment and the divorced painter spread himself out on the sofa and opened his fly. She didn't turn on the light. She knelt down next to the sofa and began to fondle him. The divorced painter asked: "Do you have anything to drink?" And the woman said: "There's some wine in the fridge. Should I get it?"

He said yes, bring whatever there is. She went to the kitchen and opened the fridge and took out the bottle of white wine she had received as a gift and was saving for a special occasion. Punishment should be celebrated too, she said to herself. She pulled out the cork and poured a full glass for the divorced painter. She drank tap water and heard him calling from the living room in a voice hoarse from cigarettes. She returned to the dark room where he had already stripped naked. His clothes were on the floor and he was on his back, his hands clasped behind his head, waiting.

She said to herself: I'll remember this. If I remember it, I won't do anything like it ever again. If I never do anything like this again, maybe my life will be better. She placed the glass on the table and the divorced painter took it, drank, and belched. It occurred to her that she had been deceiving herself all evening: the young lawyer and the divorced painter were not two extremes, but two ends of the same extremity. She stood for a moment without moving and thought: Maybe I'm not looking for a relationship either. Then she bent down over the divorced painter and gave him a blow job.

The divorced painter groaned and writhed like a lizard but nothing happened. He didn't have an erection and he didn't bother explaining or apologizing. She stopped and took a sip of his wine. The divorced painter got up and roamed naked around the dark room, looked out of the window, and said: All you can see from here is apartment buildings. You should see the view from my studio. An authentic, alienated, industrial landscape. You don't see landscapes like that anymore. And she said: Yes.

The divorced painter got dressed, swallowed the rest of the wine in one gulp, and asked if he could take a few cigarettes to last him until he got home. She said: "Take the whole pack." When he was gone she got undressed and took a shower and put on her favorite big white T-shirt, brushed her teeth, and went to bed. She felt nothing. Even the longed-for disgust, like the relief of vomiting after nausea, failed to come.

11

The man saw the woman sitting on the sofa in her faded jeans and black tank top, and thought of the little girl who had fallen off the swing. He wanted to hug her. He sat down on the sofa and they both began looking for ticks in the dog's coat. Their fingers dug and twisted and met, and there was a moment of peace and reconciliation in the air, at least from the point of view of the dog, who had fallen asleep in their laps.

They couldn't find any ticks and after a while they disappeared into the bedroom. When they emerged it was already very late. We never went out to eat, said the man, and he sat down on the sofa next to the dog and turned on the television. Get off, said the woman and pushed the dog off the sofa. She sat down next to the man, stroked his thigh, and said: "Should I make something?" The man nodded. He was hungry.

The woman went into the bedroom and came out wearing panties and the man's purple T-shirt. The man asked if he could help with anything and she said: "Sit. I'll call you when it's ready." The dog ran into the kitchen after her.

She took a big onion, tomatoes, black olives, and a little jar of anchovies out of the fridge. She chopped the onion, peeled a few cloves of garlic, put a pan on the stove, and heated up some olive oil. Then she opened the freezer and took out a little bag of basil she had frozen a couple of months ago, maybe more, she couldn't remember how much time had passed since she last went to the market. She would go there to pick out the freshest fruit and vegetables and herbs and exchange secret smiles with the vendors, as if they too were invited to the big meals she cooked for her friends, the dinner guests who always came in couples.

Sometimes the couples would phone and ask if they could bring a friend, a guest from abroad, someone who had dropped in to visit, someone they had conjured up for her out of thin air, and she would lay an extra place at the table, a plate and glass and fork and knife and spoon for her prospective date. By the time the first course was over, she knew that nothing would come of it. Whether she served stuffed prunes, fried eggplant sprinkled with pine nuts, tomatoes baked with herbs, roasted peppers, or summer food— figs filled with goat cheese, a salad of green beans with garlic— she knew that nothing would come of it.

The woman stood at the sink and held the bag of frozen basil under a stream of warm water. She heard the television in the living room—an old musical on the movie channel—and saw the bag change color under the water, become transparent, the green leaves appear, the layer of ice melt and wash into the sink, and she felt that she too was thawing, awakening the cook, who had grown tired, had rebelled, and had sunk into a long sleep.

"What should we call him?" asked the woman after they had finished eating and emptied the leftover spaghetti into the dog's new bowl.

"I don't know," said the man. "First you have to be sure that you want to keep him. There's no point in giving him a name and then throwing him out."

"But at least we can think of names," said the woman and cleared the dishes off the table. "So we'll have one when we do decide."

12

The joy of cooking took hold of the woman like a violent recurring outbreak of a malignant disease. In the morning she woke early, got out of bed, closed the bedroom door quietly behind her, and took the dog with her to the kitchen, so he wouldn't disturb the man. A soft light entered through the balcony door. The dog moved around the room, sniffing at the cracks between cupboards, the gap under the fridge, the wooden legs of the chairs on which the man and the woman had sat the night before. She looked at him and suddenly felt full of love. She had always wanted a dog. She had always thought: When I have a home of my own I'll have a dog. But now it occurred to her that things could happen the other way around. She took the remains of the salami and cheese out of the fridge and put them in the dog's bowl. She poured water out of his aluminum pan and replaced it with milk. Then she put the kettle on to boil for coffee and leaned against the marble counter to watch the dog, eagerly eating and drinking, unaware of his new role. She thought: I have to fill the fridge. I have to do a big shop today. The dog finished his food and began to drag his bowl across the floor. The woman took the bowl and put it on the counter so the noise wouldn't wake the man. She sat at the table and drank her coffee. The dog sat on his haunches and looked up at the counter. The man, the woman, and the bowl were now his whole world.

Suddenly the woman was seized by anxiety. She remembered yesterday morning. She reminded herself that she was sitting in the kitchen, enjoying the quiet, the soft light, the dog, and her shopping list, because of the man asleep on his stomach in the next room.

Maybe he had other plans. Maybe when he woke up he would get dressed quickly and say that he was late for work; maybe this time he would agree to drink coffee out of politeness while all the time he'd be planning his escape. He would sit in the kitchen and play with the dog and drink his coffee and smoke one of her cigarettes, but she would know he wasn't really thinking about the coffee or the dog but about what he would say, if she dared to ask (even in her calmest voice, although he would see through the calm, and the tone of indifference acquired over years of experience). So, will I see you tonight?

When she was younger, she had promised herself never to play games. During her twenties she had kept this promise. She had a few short affairs which she herself broke off, always with an honesty and directness that astonished her partners, and always with a certain degree of cruelty. I won't play games, she would explain to the girlfriends who rebuked her. Later she met the young lawyer and the divorced painter. They were a game, but its purpose was to lose as much as possible. She was good at this. It frightened her to be so good at something so bad.

After the young lawyer and the divorced painter the woman began an investigation of relationships. She asked her friends—the ones who seemed happily married—how it had started: how they'd met the men, what they'd done, what they'd said, what they'd worn, what they'd felt—as if she were asking for a recipe and overlooking the fact that cooks always left out a secret ingredient.

The woman shut the dog in the bathroom and tiptoed into the bedroom. The man was now sleeping with the sheet drawn up to his chin and one foot sticking out. She opened the closet door, took out a T-shirt, and picked up her jeans and bra from the floor. She carried the clothes to the living room where she got dressed. On the sofa she found her black tank top rolled into a ball. She remembered how the man had taken it off last night, how he had asked her to raise her arms and pulled the top over her head as if he were undressing a baby. As she sat on the sofa and dressed herself, she thought that there had been a big difference between the first night and the second. There had been something paternal in the way he had pulled the top over her head and patted her rumpled hair into place. She remembered the night she had spent in the young lawyer's tower, the half-night on this sofa with the divorced painter. She hadn't touched the young lawyer, the divorced painter hadn't touched her, and even before she had gone to bed with them she had known she didn't want to see them again. It wasn't the same with the man.

She went into the bathroom, where the puppy greeted her with joyful barks, brushed her teeth, and washed her face. Then she closed the door behind her and heard the puppy scratching it. In the kitchen, she took a pen and paper and wrote the man a note. She liked writing notes. It gave her a feeling of control. She wrote: "Good morning! It's quarter past seven. I had to go out. Sorry. I didn't want to wake you. Make yourself at home. I left you a key. I'll be back this afternoon. If you can, take the dog out. I didn't have time. And be careful, the door locks behind you. The dog's in the bathroom. I put him there so he wouldn't disturb you.

Hope you slept well,

See you."

She wondered whether to add "later" or "this evening" or "sometime," but she wanted the "see you" to be something that goes without saying. There was no need to go into detail. At the last moment she added: "P.S. There's no more milk." In her desk drawer she found the spare key, put it on top of the note, took her bag, and left the apartment, closing the door quietly behind her.

13

The man woke up and found himself in a dark room; the blinds were drawn and a smell of sleep hung in the air. The alarm clock on the nightstand showed that it was almost ten. He was glad he didn't have to go to work. The genius director was sick. He thought: She and I will have breakfast together, maybe we'll go out for a while, and then we'll come back here, and maybe we'll go to bed, and we'll talk a little, and then I'll go home. He hadn't

slept at home for two nights now and it bothered him. On principle. As far as he was concerned, the day was planned perfectly:
he could be with the woman and without her too.

He got out of bed, put on his underwear, and went out into the
hall. The woman wasn't in the living room. In the kitchen he found
the note and the key. He sat down to read the note and was filled
with anger. The woman had nice handwriting, round and intelligent, but his anger was too great for him to appreciate her handwriting and her intelligence. She had gone off and left him alone.
She had asked him to take the dog out for a walk, as if the dog
belonged to them both. She had left him a key.

As he saw it, he had three alternatives: To ignore the note,
the key, and the dog; get dressed; leave; and slam the door behind him. Or he could follow her instructions, but only partially:
take the dog out—he shouldn't have to suffer whether he belonged to them both or only to the woman—and then leave the
key on top of the note, exactly where it was before, and slam the
door behind him. Or he could follow the instructions in full, including the ones between the lines: take the dog out, bring him
back, leave the apartment, lock the door, and keep the key. He
told himself he would decide after he had his coffee, but then he
remembered she was out of milk. This was the thing that made
him most angry.

The man went into the bathroom to wash his face. When he
opened the door the dog leaped on him. It was the first time in
the dog's life he had been locked up and he was terrified. The man
picked him up and stroked his head and told him about the note
and the key, and wondered aloud what he should do. Suddenly he
felt full of love for the puppy, as if the dog was closer to him than
anything in the world. But then his foot stepped into a puddle. He
looked down, put the dog on the floor, dragged him by the scruff
of his neck, and pushed his nose into the urine. The dog whined
and scraped his feet, but the man went on holding him until he
was sure that the dog understood his mistake.

Afterward the man was sorry. Not for the dog, who sat chastised and trembling under the sink, but for trying to train him in the first place. What for? It wasn't his dog. He went into the living room and sat on the sofa. He hadn't decided which course of action to take, and wondered if there were any possibilities he had overlooked. He had left the dog in the bathroom, where his whining turned into jackal-like howls. I won't give in to these manipulations, he thought.

He leaned back and his hand touched something soft. He picked up the woman's black tank top and examined it. Then out of habit, he sniffed the material. He failed to identify any smell capable of leading him to the right decision, but was suddenly a lot less angry.

14

The woman sat in a café, half an hour's walk from her house. When she walked there it was still early. The air was chilly and she shivered. She had walked fast, nearly running, and had sat down in a place that seemed far enough away. She wondered whether the man was still in the apartment or had already left. She stayed in the café for nearly two hours, drinking two cups of coffee and eating a Danish.

She wondered whether the man might poke around in her drawers and closets and find things he shouldn't see. She let the thought scare her, because there was something pleasant about the fear, but she knew she had nothing to hide from him. That was the problem. Her photo albums, for example, would reveal only childhood snapshots, family photos, pictures from trips abroad taken by obliging strangers who had agreed to photograph her: the woman standing outside some museum, resting on a cliff surrounded by seagulls, holding a giant tomato in a market, sitting alone in a café. Her bookshelves contained no books with mysterious inscriptions and her desk was free of any incriminating evidence. All the man would find in her drawers were old bills, all paid on time and filed in separate envelopes.

There was nothing in her closet to provoke suspicion or jealousy. On the right the man would see dresses and skirts and jackets on coat hangers, on the left T-shirts and jeans, and in the middle stockings, panties, bras, and pajamas. If he climbed on a chair and opened the upper doors he would find coats and sweaters and winter blankets still stored away because the fall had only just begun, and as usual it was only a sequence of heat waves with the promise of relief.

The waitress asked if everything was all right, if the woman wanted anything. She smiled and said no. The waitress was a woman of about her own age, tall and heavy with reddish hair in a ponytail. From time to time she sat down at a corner table and read the newspaper and took a bite of her sandwich, until she noticed customers arriving or beckoning her. Then she got up, put her sandwich down on its plate, wiped her hands on her apron, and hurried to the table that had disturbed her breakfast, smiling brightly.

The woman looked at the waitress. There was something serene and noble about her that suited her height and her ponytail. For a moment the woman felt like inviting the waitress to sit down with her. She wanted to know all kinds of things: whether she had guessed her age right, what her name was, whether she liked her work, what kind of sandwich she'd recommend, whether she had a boyfriend.

The woman was sure this serenity wasn't something you were born with. The waitress, she thought, wasn't pretty, she was too tall, ungainly, her face and arms were covered with freckles, she worked hard, running from table to table with her pad and smiling at the customers, but in fact, thought the woman, she was smiling to herself. She had a secret. That was clear. The woman couldn't think of anything more likely than love.

The deeper she sank into the waitress's story, trying to draw strength and encouragement and wisdom from it, the more she added details—elaborating on the waitress's apartment, her boyfriend, what he looked like, what he did for a living, and whether he was asleep in the waitress's bed, waiting for her to finish her shift and come home—and the further she receded, with a feeling of relief, from her own story, from her own apartment and from the man she didn't know was hers or not, whether he was sleeping in her bed and waiting for her, whether he had left long ago and would never come back.

The waitress saw the woman looking at her and made haste to put her sandwich down again and hurry over. The woman found herself face-to-face with the smile and the serenity. Suddenly she didn't know whether they were real or whether she had made them up too, and she felt embarrassed at having disturbed the waitress. She ordered another cup of coffee.

She emptied a packet of sugar into her cup and stirred. Again she raised her eyes, carefully this time, to look at the waitress, who was now standing with her back to her and talking to a customer. Perhaps her serenity was the kind that came after a long struggle, something available to everyone, something acquired. The almost masculine height, the heaviness, the too-pale skin and the strawlike red hair, the smattering of freckles, even the breasts that were too small for the rest of her body—all these, thought the woman, moved harmoniously and naturally, as if they couldn't be otherwise, as if she needed no one else's approval.

The woman thought about the man's body: average height, maybe shorter than the waitress, average shoulders, the beginnings of a paunch, cropped black hair, average arms, average hands, bitten fingernails, a face that was hard to remember exactly, and brown, slightly doggy eyes.

In the final analysis, she thought, his looks were average, even mediocre. He was intelligent, but up to now she hadn't heard him say anything she hadn't heard before, and even though he was interesting to listen to, she knew she listened out of anxiety.

Since she had graduated from university five or six years ago, her anxiety had hidden away in all kinds of corners. It had turned into a kind of pet that had to be fed, tamed, played with, and taken out for short, regular walks, tied firmly to a leash. All those years it had never occurred to her that she was raising a monster, that her anxiety wouldn't be satisfied with anonymity, that one day it would demand a name, something catchy and banal, something like the fear of being alone. The young lawyer and the divorced painter were final attempts to put the anxiety in its place, to defeat it, suppress it, but the anxiety had won.

It was the anxiety that had led her to ask a friend whether she could introduce her to someone. It was the anxiety that had filled her up with hope when the friend said she would ask another friend, who did know somebody. The anxiety had sat for a whole day by the phone waiting for the friend to call, and less than an hour later the anxiety had dialed the man's number. It was the anxiety, of course, that had caused her to make the terrible mistake of asking the man whether he wanted to keep in touch when what she had actually been asking him was whether he wanted to keep in touch with the anxiety. And it was the same anxiety—good for it, she thought, for having so much energy—that had dreamed up the plan with the key.

Suddenly it occurred to the woman that the waitress's serenity was really despair in disguise. Each of her smiles was actually a cry for help; nobody loved the waitress and the waitress didn't love herself. She wanted a different life and a different job and a different body, and perhaps she even wished to change places with the woman.

A little before ten the woman asked for the check. The waitress, who was about to finish her shift, brought it, gave her change, and thanked her with a smile for the generous tip. On the way home the woman decided to go to the market. She set out with the calm tread of a person who has made an important decision: She wanted the man. She didn't want to be like that waitress. She didn't want anyone to look at her first with curiosity and then with pity, and to not want to change places with her for anything in the world.

15

The man was happy to find himself on his woman friend's porch. He felt he could breathe freely at last; at last, after two confusing and exhausting days, he could be himself. The friend brought him a chilled beer, noisily opened a bag of potato chips, sat down on an armchair beside him, and folded her legs beneath her. There were two old armchairs on the porch—his and hers.

He hadn't bought milk. He had taken the dog out for a short walk, and the dog, who had already forgotten the incident in the bathroom, frisked and romped all the way, chewed the man's pants, and even though he wasn't on the leash never left his side, even when the man stopped at the grocery and stood for a couple of minutes in the entrance without going inside.

Afterward the man and the dog went home. The man smoked a cigarette, reread the woman's note, as if new instructions might have been added to it, and wondered whether to take the note with him, as if it might be important evidence in a future court case. In the end he decided not to, because the woman might interpret it as an admission of guilt. He left the note on the table and walked out of the apartment, locking the door behind him and pushing the key deep into his jeans pocket, separate from his own key ring. Now he could feel the key digging into his thigh. He raised himself a little in the armchair, put his hand in his pocket, and fingered the metal. It was an ordinary key for a simple lock.

The friend asked him how the blind date had gone, and the man said okay.

"Did you sleep with her?" she asked. The man gulped down the rest of his beer and nodded.

"You want another one?" asked the friend, and before he had a chance to answer she went inside and came out with a new bottle.

"So," said the friend, "go on, tell me. How did it go?"

"It went," said the man.

"What went?" The friend laughed. "What's happened to you? Suddenly you're shy?"

"I guess so," said the man.

"So?" said the friend. "Can't you tell me anything?"

"What do you want to know?" asked the man and took out the pack of cigarettes he had bought on the way.

"Anything," said his friend and dug into the bag of chips. "What does she do? She's a teacher, right?"

"She's a translator," said the man.

"I thought she was a teacher," said the friend, disappointed. "I thought she was some kind of schoolteacher."

"No," said the man. "She's a professional translator."

The friend sensed danger. The man had been on blind dates with more impressive occupations; she herself had fixed him up with lawyers, writers, architects, actresses—so why was he defending this translator of all people? They sat in silence for a few minutes, and then the man said: "We've got a dog."

"Both of you?" asked the friend.

"She has. We found him together. But she hasn't decided whether to keep him yet. She may get rid of him."

"Or you."

"Or me."

"Or you her."

"Maybe," said the man. "Maybe I'll get rid of her."

There was something reassuring about knowing that at any minute, when his old enemies came to attack—restlessness, boredom, the feeling he'd been cheated—he could get rid of the woman. Blind dates always promised something and never kept their promise. He didn't know how to define it exactly, but he knew whatever that something was, he hadn't received it. This blind date, for example, was already full of promise, but he promised himself that he wouldn't let her disappoint him; the minute that began to happen—by now he could always tell when it was happening and it was sure to happen, it was only a matter of days—he would get rid of her. Then he'd be back on this porch with a beer and his friend and a bag of potato chips that made too much noise.

Suddenly he missed the woman. He wondered whether she had found the puddle in the bathroom, whether she was angry with the dog, whether she was angry with him, whether she had taken out her anger on the dog. He imagined the woman hitting the dog and heard him crying in his head. Then he imagined the woman and the dog sitting at home, waiting for him. He emptied the second bottle of beer and threw his burning cigarette into the yard.

16

The woman consoled herself over the fact that the man hadn't bought milk with the fact that he had taken the key. She mopped up the puddle in the bathroom calmly. She had begun to get used to the new rules. She had no way of knowing whether the man had taken the dog for a walk. The leash and the collar were lying on the table in the living room where he had left them last night. She was sorry she couldn't ask the dog, that he couldn't tell her exactly what had happened in the morning. She could have trained the dog to be an excellent spy, she thought, if only he could talk.

She stood the shopping bags on the kitchen table and arranged the vegetables, fruit, and cheese in the fridge. Then she took down the little jars of spices from the shelf above the stove, emptied them into the garbage, and refilled them with fresh spices she had bought in her favorite shop. The vendor remembered her and asked where she had disappeared to. She had bought enough spices to last for a thousand meals.

I bought something for you too, she said to the dog, who began to whine in anticipation at the sound of her voice. From one of the bags she took a bone full of sinew and marrow, and put it down on the floor next to his bowl. In spite of everything, she was in a good mood. She decided to open a bottle of beer and call the man. The drink was supposed to make her forget the dangers lurking in this phone call, but the beer wasn't cold. She put a bottle in the freezer and went to take a shower.

When she came out of the shower the house was already dark. She went into the kitchen and saw the dog crouching next to the porch door in the darkness, his back to her, gnawing the bone with his eyes closed, and suddenly she was afraid of him. She saw him in a new light. A beast of prey crouched in her kitchen and there was no knowing what it might do. She remembered reading somewhere that you should never give a dog raw meat, because the smell of the blood drove them mad. She tried to imagine the puppy attacking her. The idea seemed ridiculous, but on the other hand what did she know about him? She had taken him into her house from the street, without asking any questions, without knowing anything about his past, where he had been, and with whom. She leaned against the fridge and looked at him. He was so intent on the bone that he didn't even bother to look back at her. He wasn't hers any longer, she thought; she had lost him. The bone was a mistake. But she was afraid to try to take it away from him.

She opened the freezer and touched the bottle but it wasn't cold yet. She took the piece of paper with the man's phone number out of her diary, sat down on the living-room sofa, put the telephone on her knees, and dialed. After four rings his answering machine came on. I'm not available and it's your problem, the man's voice announced. She hung up.

She went back into the kitchen, opened the freezer, and touched the bottle again. The dog looked as if he was sleeping. She whistled to him and he turned his head toward her, the huge bone between his little jaws, his eyes half closed as if drunk.

Back in the living room, she turned on the television and turned down the sound. Again she dialed the man's number, again she heard the message on the answering machine, and again she hung up before the beep. Then she tried to call her girlfriend. There too she got the answering machine, which said: Either I'm not here to take your call, or I just don't feel like it. Leave a message. Bye.

She didn't leave a message because she didn't want the friend to return the call later, when the man was there. She hoped he would just turn up and bring a present for the dog, like he did yesterday. She heard the monotonous gnawing sounds from the kitchen—if it wasn't for the bone the puppy could have kept her company, at least. The weatherman appeared on the television screen with good news. She couldn't hear his voice but she saw his pointer dancing on the synoptic map. Fall had arrived. The end of predictions and hopes and gut feelings. It's going to rain tomorrow. The woman saw the forecaster surrounded by painted clouds and lightning, against a picture of a little boy and girl splashing in a puddle of rainwater, their arms linked and a smiling umbrella over their heads.

Again she dialed the man's number and again she got the answering machine. Again she dialed her friend's number, and again she hung up before the beep. Suddenly she remembered that her friend had gone out on a blind date. She envied her. The date with the man now seemed far away: the moments when she had stood in front of the mirror trying on her black dress, the place where they had arranged to meet, the awful table they had given her, as if the waitress wanted to punish people sitting alone in the café and spoiling everybody else's fun. And, of course, his lateness. And there were the moments when she was afraid he wasn't going to show up, which seemed quite pleasant and even nostalgic compared to what she was going through now.

Suddenly she thought of a horrible scenario: the man was her friend's blind date. When she asked the friend who she was meeting, she had said she knew nothing about him. The woman knew next to nothing about the man. Again she dialed and again she heard the answering machine. This time she didn't dial her girlfriend's number.

She remembered the key, and this calmed her a little. If he had taken the key, he would have to bring it back. They would have to meet at least one more time. Then she panicked and ran to the entrance hall to check in case he had pushed the key under the door. She went down on her knees and examined the floor tiles, but the key wasn't there.

17

A few minutes before midnight the man returned home. He had a small studio apartment on the ground floor with a kitchenette and a bathroom and a Japanese screen with pictures of snowy mountains dividing his double bed from the rest of the room. He hadn't been home for over forty-eight hours and the apartment greeted him with an offended air, punishing him with dust and stuffiness and a smell of mold and dirty socks. On the floor, under the windowsill, he saw the clay pot with the miniature tree his friend had given him smashed to pieces. The strong wind that had begun to blow in the evening must have banged the window shut and knocked the tree to the floor. The tree itself was intact, with crumbs of earth clinging to its tangled roots, but the pot was shattered.

The man picked the tree up and lay it gently on the bed, and then he turned on the answering machine. There were only five messages, and he was disappointed. After all, he had been gone more than two days. The first message was from the woman friend, who asked how he was doing and how the blind date had gone and said she was dying of curiosity. The second was from one of the production assistants, a young woman of twenty-two with whom he had had a short affair last winter, letting him know that they wouldn't be shooting tomorrow either. The third was from his best friend who asked if he would have dinner with them on Friday and told him that the baby missed him, and the fourth was from the woman friend again, asking where he was. The last message was from the woman.

It was long and muddled: she apologized for calling so late, although she didn't say what the time was, and the man concluded that she had called not long before. She said something terrible had happened to the dog and it was her fault. She had bought him a bone, which he had gnawed on, suddenly beginning to choke. He was coughing and retching and she didn't know what to do or where to call. She said it was terrifying. She thought the dog was going to die. She asked him to come as soon as he heard the message. Then there was silence. He could hear her breathing, until she put down the receiver—as if she was afraid to hang up, as if the dog might die.

He wanted to call but he didn't have her number. There was no point in calling information because she lived in a sublet apartment. He wanted to know whether the dog was still alive, and if there was any point in going over to her place. It was already quarter after twelve, and she must have left the message at least half an hour ago. The dog wouldn't have survived that long with a bone stuck in his throat. Maybe the woman had managed to find a vet. Maybe she had called a cab and taken the dog to the vet. In either case, whether the dog was alive or dead, the man knew that he had to go to her. He left the apartment, locked the door, got into his car, and drove to her place.

The woman opened the door and threw her arms around him. She smiled a big smile, but the man didn't know if she was grateful to him for coming to save the dog, or to some higher power that had removed the bone from the throat of the puppy, who was sitting on the sofa wagging his tail before he leaped on the man with barks of joy. He didn't look like a dog whose life had been in danger only a few minutes ago. The man asked the woman to tell him exactly what had happened, but she said there were no words to describe it. You have no idea what went on here tonight, she said, and rested her head on his shoulder. The man was curious nevertheless. He asked where the bone was, and the woman pointed in the direction of the kitchen. The bone was broken to bits, as if smashed with a sledgehammer. The man couldn't understand how the puppy could have done such a thing with his little teeth. He would never have imagined that such a small dog possessed so much power. The floor was covered with splinters of bone. There were big splinters and small sharp splinters. He didn't know which of the splinters was the one that was stuck in the puppy's throat.

He collected the splinters in his hand, went back to the living room, sat down next to the woman, and showed them to her, but the woman covered her eyes with her hand and said: "No. I can't look." He picked up the puppy and showed him the splinters too, but the puppy wasn't interested in them either. He wagged his tail, laid his head on the man's thigh, and closed his eyes.

"Don't give him bones again," said the man and put the splinters down on the table, disappointed, and the woman hugged him and said: "No. I've learned my lesson. It's a good thing you came."

There was a horror movie on cable television, an old black-and-white film, and they watched it with the sound turned down, looking at the actors' exaggerated expressions of horror, their mouths gaping in screams whenever the monster approached. But the monster wasn't really frightening. On the contrary. There was something cute and touching about it. The man felt the dog's breath on his thigh and the woman's heavy breath on his neck. He stroked her hair and asked her: "Whose side are we on?" And the woman murmured sleepily: "The monster's."

18

The long walks on the beach. He tried to remember them now. It was his first winter and everything filled him with wonder. The giant shadow cast on the sidewalk by their entwined bodies and his own hurrying little shadow; the last, long traffic light before the promenade where the three of them waited for the light to change; running in the sand after they had all crossed the street.

Huddled on the kennel's concrete floor, a shiver ran down the dog's spine as he closed his eyes and saw before him, sharp and clear, his puppy version running in the sand. He tripped and rolled on his back and got up and shook himself and sneezed, mad with joy. When he turned his head he saw the man and woman behind him, two dark spots keeping an eye on him so that he wouldn't run away or get lost. He was filled with wonder.

But now he was disturbed by the barking and whining of his fellow inmates. In the din of the pound he tried to reconstruct the exact route taken by the three of them from the house to the beach. There was a kiosk. Sometimes they stopped to buy something or chat with the owner, who gave him something to eat: a square of chocolate or a piece of sticky coconut candy. He had no patience in those days, and would dance around the man and the woman, imploring them with growls and jumps to go on walking. But he didn't dare move away without them. The kiosk owner would look at the three of them and laugh, and ask questions: how old is he and what breed is he and what's his name, and when they left the kiosk he would keep on watching them and feel jealous— jealous of how they lit each other's cigarettes, standing facing each other, the man's hand on the woman's shoulder, or the woman's hand pushed into the man's coat pocket; of the big umbrella sheltering them all when it rained; of the proud puppy turning his head back to look at the kiosk receding in the distance.

Sometimes the walk to the sea took a long time because the man and the woman met people they knew. They would each introduce the other to their friends, and the friends would look down and ask: "And who's this? Is he yours? What's his name?" And the man and the woman would answer: "We haven't decided on a name yet." Sometimes the friends would suggest names and the man and the woman would try the names out on him, but everything seemed too short or too long, too cute or too forbidding, too temporary or too permanent.

Once they ran into the man's matchmaking friend in the street. She hugged the man and kissed him on the cheek and said: "Long time no see." Then the man introduced her to the woman. The friend smiled and asked the woman: "So where have you been hiding him?" It was a joke but the woman didn't laugh. The friend didn't look very happy either. The man and his friend chatted a bit, and the dog jumped up and down and tugged at the man's shoelaces and jerked his head in the direction of the sea. The friend asked if they'd like to sit somewhere and have coffee. The man hesitated and looked at the woman, but the woman pushed her hand deep into his coat pocket and said that the dog was restless and they should go on with their walk. When the friend said good-bye and turned away, the man looked after her and said to the woman: "She's the one who introduced us."

"Yes," said the woman, "I know. She's the one you had an affair with."

It was hard to find a position to sleep in. The dog tried to imagine his mat but he couldn't. It was the only thing in his life he had been able to take for granted and had therefore never bothered to preserve it in his memory. In the dark he saw the big tin bowl full of dog food, but he wasn't hungry. He remembered his red plastic bowl and he missed it, even though it too had betrayed him in recent months. But it was a symbol of the beginning. In the pound the barking died down and the dog heard sounds of gnawing and scratching and the restless padding of paws on concrete.

He remembered other things: the first six months, the beach full of surprises—shells and fish bones and seaweed and plastic bags and pits full of salty water, cigarette butts, and the jellyish creatures the man and the woman carefully avoided as they walked along the shore. He himself had fallen in love with them at first sight. Whenever he saw one he would go up to it, circle it, sniff it, and bark at it, barks that grew more substantial as he grew bigger. When there was no response he would cautiously reach out with his paw to touch it. It was hard to tell whether they were alive or dead, but once one of them sprayed him with a burning liquid and he ran for comfort to the man and the woman who were busy building castles in the sand.

Later on he learned to beware of the jellyfish. He amused himself with digging and running around in circles and barking at the
waves, or else he enjoyed the quiet company of the man and the
woman, lying still next to them, moved, like them, by the sunset.

19

The man liked living at the woman's place but he didn't want to
give up his own studio apartment. The rent was low, and it wasn't
a problem for him to go on paying it and also to pay his share of
her rent. He had lived in his place for seven years. He felt that
giving it up would be like giving up the love of his life, and even
though he had never actually experienced such a love, he was sure
it would feel exactly like this. He wanted to keep in touch with it,
to visit it from time to time, to smell it, to move around in it, to
open and close the windows, to turn the lights on and off, to see
how it was getting along without him, to take something from it.

During the first month, which was also the first month of winter,
when things were not yet clear, he visited his apartment faithfully
two or three times a week, each time taking something else: books
he thought he wanted to read, tapes, shoes, clothes, sheets, a mug;
he crammed them all quickly into a big bag and hurried out of the
apartment as if he was robbing himself.

He would put the bag in the woman's kitchen on the table or
on the living-room floor and pretend that he had forgotten all about
it. A few days later he would see his things scattered around the
house as if they had always been there. The woman put them
where they would fit in with her things but also maintain their
independence in the shared space; she didn't want the man to feel
he had lost them. The books, which were mainly big books, film
encyclopedias, she placed on her bookcase, at the end of the top
shelf, leaning with all their weight on a row of poetry books in soft
covers. The little, miscellaneous things, the uprooted personal

things, she put in places where they would be sheltered by larger objects.

She didn't touch his clothes. At first they were scattered around, on the floor, on chairs, hanging on the hooks in the bathroom. She smiled to herself when she saw them making their way, one by one, to her closet. She had cleared a space on the two bottom shelves in the left half of the closet, and pushed her own clothes together in the right half of the closet leaving a few empty coat hangers on the unoccupied part of the rod. For a month she watched the man's clothes wander around the house like a flock of orphans until they found their way to the empty shelves or the empty hangers—close to her own but not touching them. The man and the woman never actually spoke directly about living together, but the things spoke for them, especially the clothes, which spoke the loudest.

Except for one Friday night, when the man went to have dinner with his friends, they spent all their evenings together—something that was equally strange to both of them but affected them in different ways. The woman was the first to panic. One afternoon the man took the dog to the vet for a checkup and immunization shots. She sat in the kitchen and leafed through a new cookbook the man had bought her because he knew that she wanted it and because he found the photos appetizing. Outside a strong wind was blowing, shaking the porch door.

She enjoyed sitting at the table, feeling the cold tiles under the man's thick socks, and browsing through the recipes. She didn't know whether she liked the book or the fact that the man had bought her a present. Almost every day she saw him showering the dog with gifts, rubber bones, a special shampoo for dogs, a hairbrush, bone-shaped biscuits that he gave the dog as a reward whenever he learned something new, and she regarded these gifts as presents to her as well.

She wondered whether she should try one of the simpler recipes in the book and quickly surveyed the contents of the fridge and the cupboards in her head. She had all the ingredients. She went into the living room, chose one of the man's tapes, and put it into the tape deck. A metallic noise filled the house but didn't overcome the wind, which buffeted the windows and slammed the doors. She checked all the windows to make sure they were securely shut, and closed the doors too. Then she returned to the kitchen, opened the cupboards, took out jars and cans, took out a chicken from the freezer, and put it on the marble counter with its legs pointing at the ceiling.

It felt strange to be in the kitchen without the dog—nobody under her feet, nobody sitting hopefully next to the fridge, nobody dragging a bowl on the floor. There was a stillness in the kitchen that reminded her of life before the dog and the man. She thought of them walking together down the street, the puppy bumping into the man's legs and raising his head from time to time to receive the man's approval for some doggy desire which she understood very well; the man striding next to him with giant steps, double steps that she too found it difficult to keep up with. She imagined them in the car, the man behind the wheel, smoking, listening to the radio, driving fast, and the dog trying to balance himself on the passenger seat, flung from side to side. She tried to imagine the vet's office, the other dogs with their owners, the vet himself, his metal table, and her puppy who didn't know what was waiting for him.

He was definitely their puppy now. The man had volunteered to take him to the vet. He wanted the responsibility, that was clear, and he even seemed to her to enjoy it to such an extent that there were moments when she felt he was appropriating the dog. This happened whenever the man tried to train him, kneeling on the floor, scolding him, encouraging him, explaining to him, dragging him to this or that puddle, locking him in the bathroom, inventing all kinds of punishment. At these moments she felt as if the man and the dog were merging, that they shared an understanding which excluded her. Sometimes they both seemed to be waiting for their meals with the same sense of expectation, with the same trust and belief that at the appointed hour their food would land in its plate. How quickly she had entered this role which gave her a feeling of control, which, although it was as temporary and fragile as the feeling she got from writing notes, had a calming effect and filled her with serenity. It was an acquired serenity, but nonetheless a serenity she had not known before.

She touched the chicken and realized it would take a good few hours to thaw. She could speed the process up by soaking it in water, but she didn't want to do anything to spoil the new recipe. She went into the living room and turned the cassette over to the other side, sat on the sofa, and listened. The music was too noisy for her taste and she couldn't catch the words, if there were any words in all that metal, but she didn't want to turn the tape deck off or change the cassette, because she was afraid of disrupting the delicate balance between the man's things and her things—a balance that now also included smells and sounds. She listened to the music and the wind and the thunder beginning to roll outside, and suddenly she was flooded with joy and restlessness. She thought of the rain about to fall, of the dinner she was going to make, of her new family—the man and herself, and the dog between them like a radiator giving off warmth—and she wondered what made her so sure. The man had not hidden the fact that he had never had a serious relationship, that he had never lived with a woman, that he had never been in love. She found it difficult to believe that this could be true, but when she thought of herself she knew that it was.

Almost everything the man possessed was already comfortably settled in her home. Everything he had accumulated in seven years and succeeded in cramming into his studio apartment, except the furniture, which belonged to the landlady. Two days ago they had driven there together to pick up the remains of his belongings. She looked around at the damp walls, at the bed covered with old newspapers, at some book the man had started reading before he met her, an ashtray, two or three disposable lighters, a miniature tree which had dried up and shed its leaves on the sheet.

If anyone asked her to give an account of her first days with
the man, she would have noted that this was the moment she fell
in love—the moment when they collected his things, the remnants
of his previous life, a moment preceded by many long moments
of uncertainty and fear delaying the actual act of falling in love,
which had perhaps come long before.

The day after the night when he came to save the dog, they sat
in the kitchen and drank coffee. Early in the morning the rain had
started coming down in floods, exactly as the forecast had promised, and the man had gone with the dog and her umbrella to buy
milk. They sat together in the kitchen and drank coffee. The incident with the bone was not mentioned again, but it seemed to
her that the man was angry. She was so preoccupied with her fear
of the man getting up, pushing back his chair, putting his cup into
the sink, perhaps washing it too, and telling her, this time in so
many words, that he didn't want to see her again that she didn't
notice another, more substantial event when the man, in a way
which he would never be able to explain to himself, began to
love her.

20

The puppy was declared a three-month-old mongrel, healthy and
full of life. He wouldn't be big, the vet pronounced, he would be
medium-sized, and the man felt disappointed for a minute, as if it
were his child they were talking about, his genes to blame for the
dog being a medium-sized mongrel.

The man had chosen the vet from a list in the phone book
because of his name, which had a foreign sound. The man imagined an experienced, elderly doctor. He was surprised when his
turn came and he picked the dog up in his arms and went into the
little office and found a man of about his own age, with nothing
foreign about his appearance, and who didn't seem particularly

experienced either. He thought the vet looked like him too: they were both average height, a little heavy, with short black hair and brown eyes. And what surprised him most of all were the vet's nails, which were bitten to the quick, just like his.

The vet asked the man to sit down, which he did, in an old iron chair, with the dog in his lap. The vet put out one hand to pat the dog and with his other hand he opened a desk drawer and took out an index card. He chose a blue pen from a glassful of pens and pencils; the dog snatched it from his hand and began gnawing it. The man apologized and pulled the pen away from the dog, wiped it on his trousers, and returned it to the vet, who laughed and patted the dog again, and then tapped the pen on the card and said: "Name?"

" 'Name?' " repeated the man.

"The dog's name," said the vet.

"He hasn't got a name yet." The man snickered.

The vet raised his eyebrows: "He hasn't got a name?"

"Not yet," said the man. "We found him in the street, about a month ago, and we haven't decided on a name yet. We're still thinking about it."

The vet explained to him that the dog had to be registered with the municipality and be issued an identity tag, and that he himself had no objections to treating a nameless dog, but the authorities wouldn't approve.

"So what do we do?" asked the man.

"We give him a name," said the vet. "Even a temporary name. In order to register him."

The man laughed in embarrassment and said: "Beats me. I can't think of a name. Could you write: 'Anonymous'?"

"Anonymous?" asked the vet. "I don't think that's possible. A dog with owners isn't an anonymous dog."

"But he was a stray dog," said the man hopefully.

"He was," said the vet, "but he isn't anymore."

The man was suddenly angry with the dog, who had put him

in an embarrassing situation. The dog set his front paws on the desk and tried to pull a pen from the glass.

"I know," said the man. "Write 'Anonymous' as a name. I can choose any name I want, can't I?"

"Yes, you can." The vet sighed. "If you want to call him 'Anonymous,' you have the right to do so. It's a little out of the ordinary, but it's possible."

"So write down 'Anonymous,'" said the man and suddenly his anger at the dog was replaced by guilt.

The vet wrote the new name in its square and repeated it aloud, stressing each of its syllables separately. The man wasn't sure if the vet was mocking him or flattering him on his original choice.

"A-non-y-mous," repeated the vet. Then he tapped the pen on the card again and asked: "Name of owner?"

"Owner?" repeated the man.

"Yes," said the vet. "What's your name?"

"My name?" asked the man. "You want my name?"

"Yes," said the vet, "unless you're also called 'Anonymous.'"

"No," said the man and tittered and blurted out his name, and the vet began to write it down in the appropriate square.

"Wait a minute," said the man. "Don't write anything yet. I don't know if I'm considered the owner."

"You don't know if you're considered the owner," the vet repeated.

"He isn't only mine," said the man. "He belongs to my girlfriend too."

This was the first time that the words "my girlfriend" had been said—not just to someone else, to a stranger, to a doctor insisting on following the rules, but also in the man's head. The words had escaped under pressure, but they came out so naturally that the man smiled to himself, a smile the vet mistakenly interpreted as a secret smile, and he said: "So that's what it's about. Am I to understand that you're a married man and that our little 'Anonymous' belongs to your mistress?"

"No!" protested the man. "I'm not married!" And again he

found himself saying, this time in a desperate tone: "I live with someone, I have a girlfriend!"

"I understand," said the vet. "You've got a girlfriend. You live with someone. I'm happy for you. I live with someone too. We have a dog too."

"Yes," said the man, and blushed.

"We could add her name too," suggested the vet.

"Yes," said the man, "I think you should add her name too," and he watched with a feeling of suspense as the pen produced the woman's name in large, printed letters, sitting in the same square as his own name, under the square with the name of the dog.

When he left, after the vet with the bitten nails had examined the dog and immunized him and written a prescription for calcium tablets to strengthen his bones, the man felt exhausted and humiliated, as if he'd been the one standing shivering on the cold metal table, as if it were his legs that had been felt and his stomach poked and his tail lifted and his eyes and ears peered into; as if he had then been held down and stuck with a needle; as if he had been so frightened he had peed on the table, which had a special drainage hole for cases like his.

Outside it was already dark and heavy drops of rain began to fall. On the way home the man stopped at a pharmacy and bought the dog's calcium tablets. Then he was stuck in a traffic jam and he used the time to think of how he'd tell the woman what happened in a way that wouldn't allow her to mark it up as a victory, even an indirect one, even though he didn't know if the woman kept a daily balance of power in her head, as he did.

She hadn't asked him to move in with her, and he hadn't asked her if she wanted him to. She needed him, that was clear, and the dog needed him too, and after two or three days of putting the woman through more agonizing uncertainty, he realized that perhaps he needed them too. He drove through the rainy streets with one clear picture in his head: him standing naked on a ladder in the woman's apartment taking down three small space heaters from the top of the closet, with both of them, the woman and the dog, standing at the foot of the ladder looking up at him, the woman's hands outstretched to take the heaters and the dog resting his front paws on the bottom rung of the ladder and barking.

It may have been a random combination of circumstances: the sudden onset of winter, the woman, thoughts of whom mingled with tender thoughts of the dog, the way his best friend looked at him at dinner Friday night, when the man told him and the baby's mother about the woman. He tried, as usual, not to go into detail, and thus to make light of the whole affair, but he found himself saying more than he wanted to, more than he thought he had to say. And thus, without even thinking about it, when he stood naked on the ladder and handed the woman the three old heaters, he told her he had a new radiator in his apartment and he would bring it the next day.

To be on the safe side, he moved into the woman's apartment in stages, small stages divided into half stages and fractions of stages that kept his mind off the overall picture which amounted—he had to admit it now, stuck in the rain behind a line of cars—to one thing: he had moved in with her. That's what had happened.

The night before last they had gone together to pick up the rest of his things from his apartment. Because of the move in stages there was almost nothing left to take, and the apartment seemed big and empty and hostile. The woman didn't say anything, but he saw the way she looked around and absorbed the little that remained of his bachelor life. He quickly packed his remaining belongings—the television set, the stereo system, his quilt, a toaster oven that didn't work but which he wanted anyway—in the cardboard boxes they had brought from the grocery. Together they crammed the boxes into the backseat of the car and drove away.

He knew the incident at the vet's was meaningless, a pretense for the sake of the city authorities, but it disturbed him nevertheless. In the past he had never experienced difficulty in defining things. Definitions seemed to him child's play, a game he was good at playing. All the women he had ever gone out with had received an immediate definition from him, according to a classification table he had been working on for years. They had names and occupations and probable IQs, they had measurements and beds and smells and sometimes tears, and they had demands, impossible from his point of view; some, whom he both hated and admired, escaped in time from his definitions and left him sitting alone with his classification table, perplexed and rejected.

There was the writer, for example. Strange, he thought, that she resembled the woman so much, but gave off a sense of mystery that she lacked. She too had straight black shoulder-length hair, she too was short and thin. But the writer was very self-centered and she wasn't shy. She talked about herself all the time, and she didn't listen to him or ask questions, which was fine as far as he was concerned, because he felt that in her company he needed to keep quiet. She made him feel like nothing and at the begining he liked it. It was easy.

The writer drove him to her house. She had a black sports car with a convertible roof and a stick shift that creaked and groaned under her hand. He had offered to drive his car but when he told her what he had she said: We'll take mine. She lived in a house with a big, neglected garden and she had two Persian cats.

They sat in the living room and sipped cognac in huge glasses and listened to some requiem or other—the man couldn't remember which—that was the writer's favorite. She adored requiems. The Persian cats—a female and a doctored male, brother and sister—stalked the carpet with their tails in the air; from time to time they sniffed the man's shoes and looked at him indifferently.

The writer picked one up—he thought it was the male—and stroked it and sat it on her lap and told the man that she wasn't interested in having a relationship. Her freedom was important to her, she said; she couldn't stand any kind of dependence. That's why I have cats, she said.

The man tried to enjoy the taste of the cognac, without success.

He felt a kind of excitement in anticipation of the humiliation he was about to endure. For a moment there was something thrilling in being a victim—the writer's incessant talking, the way she handled the stick shift, her house, the tragic music, and the cats which were clearly part of the conspiracy.

The writer was older than the man. She was nearly forty. She wanted to play a game and he was willing to take part in it, but he was a little disturbed by the thought that the attractive woman sitting next to him on the sofa, absorbed in the requiem, wanted so little for herself and he was the little that she wanted.

He had sex with her in her enormous bed, and the two cats lay on the pillows at their heads, purring. The writer refused to remove them. She said that she liked having someone watch. He tried to make a joke of it and said if they had to have witnesses he would have preferred humans, so they would at least understand what was going on. She said her cats understood exactly what was going on. They looked extremely bored, and this made the man feel embarrassed and helpless, as if he was required to perform a show, not so much for the writer, but for the cats. He knew they were testing him and he didn't have a chance, because these cats had clearly seen everything.

It was over quickly and the writer asked him to go home. Obediently he collected his clothes from the floor and got dressed; he was going to kiss her good-bye, but the writer said there was no need for such rituals. She asked him to shut the door behind him when he left. He suddenly felt a need to hit her and murder her cats, but instead he asked her if she wanted to keep in touch, and she said no.

They met a few more times anyway—always on the man's initiative, and after negotiations—and each time it seemed to him that he was improving a little, that his naked reflection moving in the four glassy blue eyes looked more encouraging. The writer, in stark contrast to what you might have expected from someone who radiated so much independence and mystery, was terrible in bed.

Apart from his own quick breathing and the incessant purring of the cats, there wasn't a sound in the room. Her chattiness, her promising driving, the words that she treated as if they too were her pets, even the tragic music she liked—there was no trace of any of these in the huge bed, and the man got lost there in his desperate attempts to prove something to himself, but mainly to the cats.

His short affair with the writer didn't end with separation or with a slow and agonized petering out, but with a brief, formal message on her answering machine. He called, as usual, two or three weeks after their last meeting, and heard her recorded voice making the usual laconic announcement: You have reached such and such a number, leave a message, but suddenly she pronounced his name and said, You, don't bother leaving a message. Right after that the long beep sounded and he hung up. He didn't know what was more insulting: that she had mentioned his name so all the other callers could enjoy his rejection, or the word *you*, which sounded even more anonymous than anything that had taken place between them.

The rain turned into a flood. The man sat at the traffic light and waited impatiently for it to turn green. Even after it changed, he knew it would still take him ages to get home. The whole city was jammed because of the rain, and because it was a bad time anyway, the hour when everyone was rushing to get home. He turned on the radio and lit a cigarette. The visit to the vet had exhausted him. He looked at the dog and stroked his head. He complained to him about the endless traffic jam and bad-mouthed the vet. But the dog had already forgotten his humiliation and was fascinated by the windshield wipers.

21

He remembered their first fight vividly. Even now, as his fellow inmates stopped pacing back and forth in their cages, lay down on the concrete floor, and fell asleep, he could still hear the woman crying. He closed his eyes and pricked up one ear, listening to the memory of the man's voice, hearing the same restrained, reasonable tone the man used with him when he did something bad and that made him hide under the sofa, ready to admit everything and beg for forgiveness; he heard the didactic voice that made the woman cry harder and slam doors—that lost voice which brought out the best in the dog and the worst in the woman.

They were alone together for six months. For six months they shut themselves up in the house, each one choosing a corner of his own and learning to navigate the territory in which they all met. The man took the area next to the entrance, which gave him enough space for a desk. He had an extra telephone line and an electric outlet installed, and next to the desk he placed a metal filing cabinet he had found in the street.

Above his desk he hung a board where he posted all kinds of photographs with colored tacks—photos of him at work, standing next to a big camera and talking to the cameraman, conferring with the genius director, lighting a cigarette for one of the actresses who pushed her hair aside and held his hand offering the match. And there were other pictures too—one of a plump baby with downy yellow hair, exposing her two teeth to the camera, held by two hairy arms; another of the man's woman friend in a bathing suit, her arms around the man's waist as he smiled and made horns over her head with his fingers.

The woman's territory was a consecutive sequence of corners. It began in the bedroom and included half the bed and three-quarters of the closet, passed through the bathroom, which was almost all hers, except for one toothbrush, shaving equipment, and a yellow rubber duck the man had bought for himself when he went with his best friend on a shopping expedition for his baby. It continued through the living room, where her desk stood and most of the man's possessions were scattered—the books, the tapes, the little things in which he had ceased to take an interest since moving in with her. The kitchen too was hers, and especially the table, which turned in the course of time from an ordinary Formica table into a fortress. From her position at the table, where she worked on her occasional translating jobs, took the phone when she spoke to her girlfriends, and placed the heater, she could see the right-hand corner of the man's desk.

The dog had a few feet of cold floor under the sofa, which were exclusively his. Sometimes the man or the woman would sweep his corner and he'd stand aside anxiously watching his accumulated property being swept away. A white sock, empty yogurt containers, shreds of newspaper, a yellow tennis ball were dragged out from under the sofa by the bristles of the broom as the dog danced around it and barked in protest.

They would sort through his things, throw most of them out, and put the things they took pity on, like the sock and the tennis ball, in places where the dog couldn't get at them. If he stared long enough at one of the objects, the yellow ball on the man's desk or the sock hanging on a door handle, if he growled at it or whined, the man or the woman would relent and give it back to him, throwing it on the floor and looking at the dog as he pounced on it and crawled under the sofa holding the prize in his teeth.

Six months, that's how long it took for everything in the house, the woman's things and the man's things and the dog's few personal belongings, to be shuffled and reshuffled like a pack of cards until they all found their places. And one day a dog license arrived in the mail; printed in small letters in the little square at the top was the word *Anonymous*, his breed and color and the names of the man and the woman. The woman asked, What's this? and the man casually told her the whole story.

The dinner party was the man's idea. He said: "Let's invite

my friends and your friends, two couples." Let's combine our two worlds, he said without saying, and the woman agreed. It reminded her of the days when she had cooked meals for couples who brought along their single friends, but now everything was different.

The man invited his best friend, the baby's father, and his wife, and the woman invited a close friend and her boyfriend. They planned the menu together, conferring and arguing and trying to combine the different tastes of each couple. The dinner was set for Thursday, and early on Sunday morning the man found the woman sitting at her table in the kitchen with all her cookbooks open, including the one he had bought her; she was wrapped in a blanket warming her hands at the radiator. He loved her. Now he was sure.

All those months he had tried not to burden himself with such thoughts. They were unnecessary and dangerous. He knew his own logic, the skill he had developed in analyzing everything to pieces only to be left at the end with satisfaction at the successful analysis and a pile of pieces. He stood at the kitchen door and looked at the woman, who smiled at him, her hair still a little flattened from sleep and her feet moving in his white sports socks that she liked so much. There was a little scratch on her neck: he had given it to her in the night and he was as proud of it as a child. She asked: "Coffee?"

He sat her on his lap, leafed through the books with her, chose the first course with her, and then made love to her on the floor. In the great feeling of love he suddenly had for her, a drowsy love, he helped her stand up, turned her around, and brushed off the threads of dust clinging to her body.

He took a sip of her coffee, which was already cold, and went to wake the dog to take him for a walk. The dog was sleeping in his usual place, on the rug at the foot of the bed. During the last few months his mischievousness had turned to laziness. The man had trained him well. His needs had become less and less urgent.

Twice a day the man took him downstairs, in the morning and at night before they went to sleep. The collar now fit perfectly, and had two silver disks attached, one with his license number and the other a heart-shaped tag the man had bought; the leash always stayed at home. From the beginning it was clear that the dog didn't need to be tied up.

Sometimes the woman took him out, but the dog preferred walking with the man. The woman was always afraid he would escape or run into the road. She didn't trust him, and whenever he left her for a moment to sniff something or stare at another dog on the opposite sidewalk, she would run over, grab his collar, and hurry him home. The man suggested putting him on the leash if she was so anxious, and once she tried, attaching the brand-new leash to the collar, but the dog sat down at the front door and refused to budge.

On Thursday morning the man woke the woman, made her coffee, and brought it to her in bed. He also brought the radiator and placed it near her. He sat down on the bed and offered her a little box wrapped in gift paper. The woman snatched it from his hand, tore off the paper, and opened the box. When she saw the necklace she jumped on him and threw her arms around him. They had seen the necklace together in a store display window near the house. She put the necklace on and the man helped her to fasten the clasp, kissing the nape of her neck. Then he bent down, scratched the dog behind his ears, and said that it would be nice if they invited his woman friend to the dinner party as well.

She was lonely, he said, and he felt a little guilty for having neglected her.

The woman didn't know what to say. She kept quiet for a minute and then said: "But it will be all couples. She might feel uncomfortable."

"Yes," said the man. "I thought of that. But I thought—and if you don't want to just say so—that maybe you could ask your friends to bring someone. My friends have been trying to fix her up for years and nothing ever comes of it. She's been through everyone they know. Maybe your friends know somebody? I thought it might be nice. Don't you?"

"Yes," said the woman. "It might be nice."

"But only if you don't mind," said the man and wound his sock around the dog's muzzle, but the dog wasn't in the mood to play. He looked at the sock which had slipped to the floor, lay back down on his rug, closed his eyes, and cocked one ear.

"So it's okay?"

"It's okay," said the woman.

"Will there be enough food?"

"Yes," said the woman.

"So do you mind calling them? Do you mind asking?"

"No," said the woman. "I'll call."

At noon the man called the woman from a phone booth, and in a babble of shouts and laughter and hooting horns she heard him saying that his friend was delighted with the invitation and that she'd come. "Well, did you talk to them?" he asked. She knew that he could hardly hear her in the noise. "Yes," she said, "I talked to them."

"And what did they say?" shouted the man. "What did they say?"

"They said they know someone but they don't know if he's free this evening. They'll try to get in touch with him."

"What did you say?" asked the man. "I can't hear, there's a lot of noise here. We're shooting outside."

"They said they'd try," said the woman.

"Are they bringing someone?" shouted the man, and the woman, who was speaking from the kitchen, standing next to the porch door, suddenly filled with anger and yelled: "What's the matter with you? Are you deaf?"

"What?" said the man. "I can't hear. Wait a second, okay?"

"Okay," said the woman quietly, to herself, and rolled her eyes, rubbing her foot on the belly of the dog who was lying on his side next to the fridge. In the background she heard honking and distant voices, and she tried to guess if the woman whose voice she heard was the beautiful actress in the picture on the board.

When the man came back to the phone there was less noise but there was static on the line. Now she couldn't hear him.

"So what did you say? That you talked to them?" asked the man.

"What?" said the woman.

"Did you talk to them?"

"Yes!" she shrieked into the phone. "Yes, I talked to them! I've already told you a thousand times, I talked to them!" And the foot resting on the dog's belly suddenly kicked, and the dog jumped up and began running around the kitchen, whining and confused.

"Sorry!" said the woman. "I'm sorry!"

And the man said: "What?"

And the woman yelled: "Forget it! I can't hear a thing! We'll talk later."

"We'll talk later?" asked the man.

"Yes!" screamed the woman. "Yes!" And she slammed the phone down.

When the man came home everything was ready: the kitchen table stood in the middle of the living room, covered with a blue tablecloth, set for eight, and wonderful smells came from the kitchen, smells that had greeted the man while he was walking up the steps. It was a cold evening at the end of winter and all the heaters in the house were on. The man took off his coat and put it and his key ring on his desk. He found the woman sitting on the sofa, with the dog's head in her lap.

He looked at the table and exclaimed admiringly. He put down two bottles of wine he had bought and said: "I brought wine. You forgot to tell me to bring some, but I remembered."

"I didn't forget," said the woman. "The guests are bringing wine. You didn't have to buy any."

He returned to the front door and examined the table from there in order to go on admiring it from a distance and see how it would look to someone coming in. Then he went into the kitchen, opened the oven door and peeked inside, lifted the lids of the three pots standing on the stove, opened the fridge door, and whistled appreciatively at the dessert waiting there, covered with Saran Wrap. He returned to the living room and sat down next to the woman, put the dog's head and paws on his thighs to warm them, and said: "So everything's ready."

The dog was the first to sense it. He had known in the morning that something bad was going to happen, and then came the kick in the afternoon. It was the first real kick he'd received since the day the man and the woman had taken him in, and it was unlike any kick he could remember. He had crawled under the sofa and watched the woman's legs walking back and forth in the living room, and he heard her crying in a low voice. The crying didn't last more than a few minutes. When he finally came out and stepped softly into the kitchen the woman tried to pick him up, but he wasn't a puppy anymore, and while the upper half of his body was clasped in her arms his hind legs scrambled in the air. For a moment they danced a strange kind of dance until the woman let him go, and a dim memory flickered in his head of that first day, when he was five weeks old— an unsuspecting stray dog.

"What's wrong?" asked the man. "Are you in one of your moods?"

The woman remained silent and held the dog's tail in her hand.

"You know," she said, and the eyes she had made up a few minutes before filled with tears, "that's a stupid question when you come to think of it. I'm always in one mood or another."

"It's just an expression," said the man. "I never really thought about it. So are you or aren't you?"

"Yes I am," said the woman and caught a big tear trickling down her cheek with the tip of her tongue.

"Are you crying?" asked the man.

"No," said the woman.

"What's wrong?" he asked and tried to put his arm around her, but she moved away, dragging her half of the dog with her to the end of the sofa.

"You take me for granted," she said. "That's what's wrong."

"What?" said the man.

"I'm not your slave," said the woman.

"What?" said the man. "What are you talking about?"

"About this dinner," said the woman. "It was your idea. You wanted to invite people, and I've been slaving over it all week, and today, out of the blue, you suddenly decide to invite that friend of yours, and it wouldn't be so bad if it was only her, but now someone else is coming too that we don't even know."

"So they are bringing someone?" said the man happily, forgetting that he was on the brink of a fight.

"Yes!" screamed the woman. "Are you happy? Yes! They're bringing someone. All day long I've been busy with these stupid arrangements! All day long!"

The man assumed his didactic tone, which made the dog prick up one ear to figure out whether the reprimand was meant for him, and said: "Look. I didn't mean for the whole burden to fall on you. I suggested having a dinner party because I thought it would be fun for both of us. I thought it was time for you to meet my friends and me to meet yours. For six months we've been at home, alone, and it's not that I don't like it, but we never go out at all, we never meet people, and I just thought that it would be a change for us. That's all. And besides, I did help you. We planned what we would cook together."

"What we would cook?" screamed the woman. "Did you cook?"

"No," said the man. "You. You cooked."

"Naturally!" said the woman, and her hand pulled the dog's tail. He woke up and looked at her, but he didn't whine. He got off the sofa and walked slowly, almost limping, to the bedroom.

"As usual! You live here like a king, three meals a day, on the clock, without lifting a finger! What have you got to complain about?"

She didn't want to say these things. They were as new to her as they were to the man, but she couldn't stop. "You moved in without even asking me. We were only together about a week, and suddenly your things landed here, and suddenly I turn into some housewife"— and suddenly the woman found herself taking profound pleasure in merely saying these things, even though they weren't true, because the outburst was more pleasurable than the truth.

But the man was interested in the truth. He said: "Are you serious?" And the woman, who felt as if she was sitting in a roller coaster, decided to test the safety bar of her seat, gripping it with both hands to see how strong it was.

"Yes," she said, "I'm dead serious."

"I didn't know you felt that way."

"Neither did I," said the woman.

"I thought there was something between us that went beyond calculations," said the man, and the woman, whose roller coaster had crossed the abyss and was at the beginning of a new ascent, said: "There's no such thing as no calculations. Everyone makes calculations, all the time. Their entire life."

"But I thought that when people loved each other they were beyond all that."

"So did I," said the woman.

"You should have said something. You should have said something before I gave up my apartment. It was a bargain. I'll never find anything like it again. You could have told me two weeks ago, if that was what you felt."

"That's what you care about?" asked the woman. "That lousy apartment? And you talk about calculations!"

And something told her—someone who had been working at the theme park for years—that this was the moment to get off the roller coaster, before it rose to the height of its arc and began a new drop, which on any serious roller coaster was sure to be more extreme than the one before. And that someone was generous enough to whisper: Listen, he said the word *love*, he said "when people love each other." But because of the other passengers shrieking she couldn't hear him.

"Look," she said, "our guests are coming in half an hour. There's no point in continuing this conversation now."

"No, there isn't," he said. "And to tell you the truth I don't know if there'll be any point later either." And all at once the safety bar opened, and the old man in charge of the roller coaster, who was disappointed in her, said: Get up, the ride's over. You weren't injured, but you can't get on again. And she burst into tears, the tears of a child who'd fallen off a swing, but the man felt no pity for her. He stood up, put on his coat, took the keys, and whistled to the dog.

The dog didn't want to go out in the cold. He pricked up one ear, raised his head a little from the rug, and wondered whether to respond to the whistle. There was always the possibility that it was a mistake, that his ears had misled him, that the man hadn't whistled for him. But the man wanted to go out, the cold didn't bother him, and he went into the bedroom, bouncing the key ring in his hand. The dog opened his eyes and wagged his tail, and when he heard the soft, rebuking, reasonable tone, the loving, disappointed tone, and when he heard the woman slamming the bathroom door, he got up and followed the man out.

22

When the man returned from walking the dog, he found the woman sitting on the sofa with his friend. He and the dog had roamed the streets for nearly an hour, going as far as the beach and filling the dog—who had loped reluctantly at his side at first, with the strange limp he had suddenly developed—with a renewed burst of joy and a feeling of adventure. When he saw the promenade spread out on the other side of the street with its brilliant lights he stood up on his hind legs, rested his forepaws on the man's thigh, wagged his tail, and barked approvingly. But the man suddenly turned around and began retracing his steps. The dog went on sitting on the curb, looking alternately at the traffic lights—at the standing figure changing to the walking figure, which he always liked best—and at the man disappearing.

A few minutes passed before the man realized that the dog wasn't at his side. He knew he was late, that the guests had probably arrived, and he began running back to the promenade, sweating inside his overcoat. From a distance he saw the dog sitting with his back to him and staring at the traffic lights. He whistled angrily, one long whistle, and the dog pricked up his ear, turned his head toward him, and limped over with his tail between his legs. He walked home with his new walk, constantly bumping into the knees of the man, who scolded him and told him to hurry up, asking: "What's the matter with you? What's wrong with you today?"

The woman and the friend sat on opposite ends of the sofa, turning their faces and necks and shoulders to each other. When the man came in his friend stood up and embraced him, and then bent down and patted the dog, jiggling his body between her hands and murmuring all kinds of nonsense into his ears. She was his first guest and he didn't know what to do. He held back a little growl in his throat and waited for her to leave him alone. When she let go he limped into the kitchen and drank a little water and then retired to the bedroom, turning his head to look at the guest, who danced enthusiastically around the beautiful table, and at the man, who gazed at it proudly. The guest asked if she could help.

The woman went into the kitchen and the man followed her, asking his friend what she wanted to drink.

"Whatever you have," said the friend, standing in front of the big bookcase, scanning the contents, and pausing in front of the man's familiar books, touching them with her fingertips.

"Does she know that we're fixing her up with someone?" asked the woman.

"Yes," said the man, and touched her chin with a finger still cold from the walk.

"Are you talking to me?" asked the woman.

"Of course I'm talking to you," said the man.

"So does that mean we're friends again?" asked the woman and glanced at the dog's full dish.

"It means that I'm talking to you," said the man. "Has he eaten today?"

"No," said the woman. "I gave him his food this afternoon but he didn't touch it. I don't know what is the matter with him. He's in one of his moods."

The man smiled. "Can I help you with anything?"

"No," said the woman. "Everything's ready, I just want to check on the potatoes. Get her something to drink, I'll be with you in a minute."

The bell rang and the man went to open the door. The woman heard the voices of her friend and her friend's boyfriend, and the man's voice introducing himself and saying: "Nice to meet you." She emerged from the kitchen and hugged her friend, and the man took the bottle of wine they had brought and admired it loudly and put it on the table, next to his two bottles. The woman went back into the kitchen and heard the man's friend asking him all kinds of questions about the wine, and the man and her friend's boyfriend answering with long explanations.

Her friend came into the kitchen, put her hand on her shoulder, and asked: "Have you been crying?"

"Yes," said the woman, "we had a fight."

"What about?" asked her friend, tossing the big salad standing on the kitchen table in a glass bowl.

"About nothing," said the woman. Then she opened the oven door and said: "Have a look and tell me if they're done."

"He looks nice," said her friend and poked the potatoes with her finger. "They're done," she said and licked her finger.

The bell rang again and again the man went to open the door, holding the bottle of wine that had sparked the discussion in the living room, and had already led to a friendly little argument between himself and the woman's friend's boyfriend.

The man's friends came into the living room, apologizing for being late and blaming it on the baby, and behind them stood the single man.

"Look what we've brought," said the man's friend, and took a bottle of French wine out of a plastic bag.

The man protested and said to the woman: "Look what they brought! You know what an amazing wine this is? What on earth did you bring it for? Are you crazy?"

"Why not?" said the baby's mother. "This dinner party is a historical event."

"Hysterical," joked the man, and took the bottle. Now he stood in the living room brandishing the two bottles, and in the middle of all the talk about fine wines the single man was almost forgotten, as he stood next to the table in his coat and read the labels of the two bottles of wine that were excluded from the competition.

Everyone introduced themselves and the woman collected their coats and took them to the bedroom. When she opened the door and entered the dark room the dog raised his head and the woman heard his tail thudding on the mat. She put the coats down on the bed. They smelled of the outside and of cold.

23

The single man was shy. He listened quietly to the animated conversation taking place between the two couples—the man's couple and the woman's couple—who immediately seemed to have found a common language, and to the subconversation going on between the man and the woman about their role as hosts. He also listened to the man's friend, who drank too much wine and tried to force her way into both conversations. He himself hardly said a word, but when he heard there was a dog in the house he asked if he could see him. The man said: "I think he's in the bedroom, should I get him?" And the woman said she thought they had better leave him alone, because he wasn't used to so many people. The single man was disappointed. He loved dogs, he said. If he hadn't lived alone in a small one-room apartment he would have owned a dog or even two. The friend stood up and said: "Come, I'll show him to you," and the single man stood up and followed her, embarrassed, to the bedroom. The three couples smiled and a silence fell upon the living room. The man put his hand on the woman's hand. He was disappointed in his friend. She was drunk and obvious.

The friend turned on the light in the bedroom and the dog woke up and blinked. He sat up and yawned and stared at the two people standing at the door. The friend said: "Let's pat him," and she grabbed the single man's hand and dragged him to the dog. The man freed his hand from hers and bent down and stroked the dog. The friend bent over him and the single man and the dog smelled her alcoholic breath. The man stroked the dog's head gently, and the dog licked his hand and the friend rested her hand on the single man's shoulder.

When they returned to the living room everyone wanted to hear about the dog, and the friend talked about him as if he were her dog. She talked about his history, his habits, and what he liked to eat, and immediately everyone started to talk about dogs. It was an excellent subject, because for a moment the single man forgot his shyness and gave them all the benefit of his extensive knowledge about dogs. He was a good-looking man, better-looking than the other men in the room. The men noted the friend's good looks. In spite of the cold weather she was wearing a thin blouse with a low neck, a miniskirt, and black thigh boots. Her lips were painted with dark, brown lipstick, most of which, the women noticed, was smeared on the rim of her glass.

The man knew her body well. Between one blind date and the next, between a one-day affair and a two month-affair, he would go to bed with her and in the morning, as he left, they would jokingly try to guess when the next time would be. The last time had been over six months ago, in the summer, a few weeks before he had met the woman. It was his birthday. Strange, he thought now as he looked at her, strange that he had never thought of her as sexual. She was his friend and he slept with her out of inertia. This evening for the first time he saw her in another light, in a dark alley, in the glare of the headlights of a police car. He thought: Six months ago, if I hadn't known her, if she wasn't a friend of mine, if I'd met her at a party, I would have taken her home and gone to bed with her. He was ashamed of these thoughts, but he was even more ashamed of his friend. He hated to see her like this, seductive and desperate. But now she was part of the past and her aggressive presence in the room was no longer a part of his life. This thought cheered him. He was glad he was at another party now, his party, which was, he felt forced to admit, a celebration of victory.

The single man sat in an armchair and gave a lecture about dogs, and the friend got up and went to the table and poured herself another glass of wine. She didn't go back to her chair. She sat down on the floor at the single man's feet. The single man tried to move the armchair back, but the armchair was too heavy. He felt the friend's back leaning on his legs, her spine and her shoulders rubbing against his knees. Slowly, so as not to attract attention, he crossed his legs. The friend turned her face toward him and smiled, holding her wineglass in the air, until he settled back in the armchair in his new position, and then she rested her head against the leg still planted on the floor. The single man told everybody about the dog he had as a child, a watchdog tied to a chain in the yard, and how the dog had guarded over him, growling at anyone who dared come close. Then the baby's father told them about the little dog he had as a child, which had been bitten to death by another dog, and the single man, who listened attentively and nodded, put his other leg down on the floor too, and suddenly parted them both, so that the friend fell backward. She said: "Oops!" He said: "Sorry!" Now she was obliged to settle for the armchair as a backrest.

The topic of the conversation changed from dogs to cars, and the single man fell silent. The friend turned her face to him and asked: "What kind of car do you have?" and before he had time to reply that he didn't have a car she said: "I love cars. And I love men who drive fast."

"You haven't even got a driver's license," said the man, who was sitting on the sofa, filling with hatred for her, his arm around the woman's shoulders.

"And he drives fast!" said the friend, pointing at the man. "You should see him. He drives like a madman! He should have his license taken away. I swear, if we weren't friends, I would turn him in."

"That's not true," said the woman. "He's a good driver. Maybe he drives fast, but he's in control."

And the single man said: "I'm a pretty bad driver. I haven't got a car. I haven't driven for years."

"You're not a bad driver!" the woman's friend broke in. "You're just careful."

"I love careful drivers," said the man's friend, standing up to fill her glass, waving it in the air, and asking: "Who else wants more?"

Nobody wanted more. It was late, and they all had somewhere to go and something to do. The man's couple had to relieve the baby-sitter and the woman's couple had to get up early to see an apartment they were thinking of buying. The single man didn't have any plans, except to get away from the friend, who sat down on the floor at his feet again, the full wineglass in her hand.

The man and the woman looked at her and regretted the fight they had had earlier. The man could hardly remember anything about it, only that it was unnecessary. As for the woman, the words "love each other" kept echoing in her mind. She suddenly felt a surge of affection for the man's friend. In her home, hers and the man's, a real home where people cooked and cleaned once a week and kept a dog and had fights—which also provided a sense of security—a spectacle of loneliness had unfolded. For the first time in her life, the woman had been able to watch the spectacle, which she knew by heart, from a good seat, comfortable and protected in the gallery.

The guests got up to leave and the woman's couple offered the single man and the drunk friend a ride home. The man and the woman felt sorry for the single man, who didn't have a car and didn't have a choice and would be forced to sit in the backseat with the friend, who jumped at the offer, going to the bedroom to bring the single man's coat, ignoring the other people and the other coats, stepping in the darkness on the dog, who finally released the growl she had coming to her—the first growl of his life.

24

Bad times had come for the dog. The man and the woman, encouraged by the success of their first dinner party, began entertaining people at home. They felt the need to see themselves in the eyes of others, and the dog, who loved them blindly, wasn't enough. Almost every evening they had visitors. Sometimes one couple, sometimes two, and sometimes one of the couples was accompanied by an aggressive little creature, who lurched through the house, screamed and rummaged in the cupboards, smashed things and dribbled and peed on the floor and provoked savage instincts in the dog, which surprised not only the man and the woman and the couple responsible for the creature but also the dog himself.

Whenever the couple with the baby came to visit, the man and the woman shut the dog up in the bedroom. Whenever the man's friend came to visit, the dog retired to the bedroom on his own initiative. It was no longer his house but theirs; he was a tenant, completely dependent on the changing moods of his landlords.

All this would still have been bearable, if the man and the woman hadn't decided one night to remove him from the bedroom and close the door. He submitted to the new sleeping arrangements, but he no longer knew if he was inside or outside. During the eight months of his life he had only known the sensation of being shut in the man and the woman's bedroom, not being shut out of it.

It was the woman's idea. It happened after their second quarrel. They had had guests, the dog didn't remember who they were, but he assumed that the baby wasn't there or the friend either because he spent the evening in the living room, in his usual spot on the sofa, between the man and the woman.

This time they didn't talk about dogs or cars. The guests talked about sex. Each of them told some amusing story from his past. None of them had anything to fear, because each of the guests, and also the hosts, had a partner to separate them from their pasts. The man talked about the writer, and his audience's laughter encouraged him to exaggerate. He described her as an aging, frigid, psychopathic spinster, and himself as a scientist conducting an experiment. He felt he was getting his revenge on the writer, who had surely had God knows how many victims since and was still alone, in her enormous house, with her ramshackle garden and her requiems and her cats.

The woman told them in the same breath about the young lawyer and the divorced painter, and as she spoke she pushed her finger into her throat and made vomiting noises. Everyone roared with laughter, especially the other women in the room, but the man was silent.

When the guests left, the man and the woman cleared away the glasses and ashtrays without saying a word. The dog lay on the sofa, pricked up his ear, and waited. The silence frightened him more than any sudden noise and even more than the music that the man played at full volume when the woman was out of the house. He lay on the sofa and listened to their footsteps going from the living room to the kitchen and back, to the faucet being turned on and off, to the rustle of the garbage bag, to the creaking of the closet door, to the little scrubbing sounds of toothbrushes. His ear twitched, but otherwise he didn't move a muscle. He sat like someone lying under a blanket waiting to pounce on a burglar moving around the house.

The man sat down next to him and turned on the television. The woman put two steaming cups of tea on the table.

"Where are the cigarettes?" she asked.

The man shrugged his shoulders.

"They were here a minute ago," said the woman.

"Well they're not here now," said the man.

The woman stood facing him, hiding the television screen with her body, and said: "Is anything wrong?"

The man was silent.

"Are you in a bad mood?"

The man nodded.

"What's wrong?" she asked and sat down beside him on the sofa. The man moved aside.

She leaned over to the man, her elbow touching the dog's back, and stroked his arm, and asked again: "What's wrong?"

"You ask as if you didn't know."

"Because I don't know."

"You don't know," said the man.

"No, I don't know," said the woman.

"But you know how to fuck," said the man, picking up the remote control and switching channels.

"Wait a minute," said the woman and burst out laughing. "Are you talking about the stories I told before?"

"What's so funny?" asked the man.

"I don't believe it! You're jealous!" said the woman and tried to tickle the man's stomach, but the man seized her wrist and put her hand back on the sofa.

"Did you have to tell everybody?"

"But everybody told their stories. So did you!"

"But your story was particularly disgusting."

"No more disgusting than yours," said the woman.

"That's different," said the man.

"What's different?" said the woman. "Tell me what's different."

"I don't know," said the man, "but it's different."

"Why? Because I'm a woman?"

"Maybe," said the man.

"Are you trying to tell me that you thought I was a virgin when you met me?"

"No," said the man in a measured voice. "I didn't think you were a virgin, but I didn't know you had those kind of skeletons in your closet either."

" 'Skeletons'?" cried the woman. "One fuck and half a blow job, you call that skeletons?"

"Yes," said the man and looked around for the pack of cigarettes.

"For three months you fucked a corpse and you talk to me about skeletons?" said the woman.

"It's not the same thing," said the man. "And it wasn't three months, and she wasn't a corpse."

"Why?" said the woman. "Why isn't it the same thing? Tell me."

"Why?" said the man and the didactic note crept into his voice. "I'll tell you why: because men and women are different. Men fuck. That's how it is. It may be disgusting, but that's the way it is. It wouldn't have been so bad if you told me that you were forced, that you didn't know what you were doing, that you were drunk, but as far as I understand, and you explained it clearly this evening, you were in complete control, you even seduced them!"

"So you would have preferred me to be raped?" said the woman. "It would have seemed more moral to you if they'd raped me?"

"You take what I say and you distort it," said the man, who got up to look for the cigarettes. "And you always do it. I say one thing and you hear another. What I meant to say was that I fucked because I was lonely."

"And me?" yelled the woman. "What do you think I was? And anyway, you know what? I take back what I said before. You didn't fuck a corpse, you're right. The corpse fucked you. She fucked you good and proper, her and her disgusting cats, and you know what? Good for her!"

"Your feminism impresses me," said the man.

"And I didn't know you were such a chauvinist," said the woman. "And I'm not in the least impressed."

He walked around the living room looking for the cigarettes, but he was too distracted to find them. The woman saw the pack and the lighter on the top shelf of the bookcase, where the man had put them when he was straightening up the room. But she didn't say anything. She watched the man turning over the cushions, bending down to look under the sofa, even moving the dog to see if he was lying on top of the cigarettes, and then she looked at the pack and the lighter mocking him from the heights of the shelf. The man sat down and covered his face with his hands. He shook his head from side to side, and then he rubbed his eyes with his fists. She didn't know if he was grieving for her or the lost cigarettes.

She stood up, went to the bookshelves, took down the packet, lit herself a cigarette, and put the pack and the lighter back on the shelf. The man raised his head and said: "Bring me one too, will you?" And the woman sat down next to him and put the pack of cigarettes and the lighter on the table. They smoked two cigarettes one after the other. They had nothing to say to each other. They didn't know how to fight. It was a technique the man never thought he might need to know one day, and the woman relied on her instincts to tell her what to do when the time came. But now the time had come, and her instincts were silent.

25

That night, and the following nights too, the woman curled up in the man's arms, caressed him tenderly, and tried to catch his eye. One minute she wanted him to console her, the next she wanted to arouse him, but the man could neither console her nor make love to her. He stroked her hair and ran a hesitant finger down her spine, and felt her body tensing toward him in the darkness.

But then he muttered something about being tired and turned his back to her.

The man was no longer angry. He was paralyzed by fear. He was afraid that if he gave in to even a single muscle he would turn into the young lawyer who did it without passion, or even worse, into the divorced painter who couldn't do it at all. He was sorry he couldn't be like the writer, that he couldn't lie on his back without moving and let the woman do what she liked to him, without knowing if he was alive or dead, and without it mattering to either of them. And one evening the woman said that maybe the dog was the problem. She said: "You can't perform with animals looking at you. You said so yourself." She said this ironically, in revenge for the weeks when he had turned his back to her, but the man, who missed her and didn't know how to turn back to face her again, listened to her and said: "Maybe you're right."

This was the first time they had laughed since their fight. They lay on their backs in bed and held hands and made each other laugh with the accusations they threw at the dog, who after five minutes of this was blamed not only for the man's temporary impotence, but also for the political situation and for the existence of wars, starving children, and earthquakes.

They lay in bed and pointed at the dog dozing on his mat, and roared with laughter. Then they began to kiss. The man suddenly felt aroused, but he didn't want to take any risks. He got out of bed, stood in the doorway, and whistled. The dog raised his head and looked at the man, and then he lowered it to his paws again and closed his eyes. The man stuck two fingers in his mouth and whistled shrilly, and the woman burst out laughing. It was funny to see the man standing naked next to the door, with an erection, and whistling like a lifeguard. The man laughed too, and his whistles shook with laughter. The dog, encouraged by the good mood that had returned to the bedroom, got up and stretched, wagged his tail, and walked to the door. He stood there for a moment, not knowing exactly what he was supposed to do now. The man seized him by the scruff of his neck and led him into the hallway. Then he retreated to the doorway, shut the door, and jumped into bed. "Poor thing," said the woman, when the gales of laughter had subsided and the man began to caress her. "Give him his rug at least." The bedroom door opened and the man went out, holding the dog's rug with the tips of his fingers. He laid it on the floor, next to the wall, and said to the dog: "Get down," and the dog lay down in his new place.

It worked. Now that the dog wasn't in the room the man could imagine that he didn't have a dog, and if he didn't have a dog that meant that he was still living in his bachelor apartment and he hadn't yet met the woman. And if he didn't have a dog or a girlfriend, that meant that the woman he was in bed with was a strange woman. It made him feel guilty, but it helped. The night that the dog was banished to the hallway, the man was like an animal. He uttered sounds that he didn't know he had in him, performed acrobatic feats he didn't know he was capable of, and hurt the woman without the faintest idea that he was hurting her.

For a week, or two or three—afterward she couldn't remember how long it went on—the woman lay beneath the man with her eyes closed, without desire, but hoping that the violence was a transitory stage to something better. She cooperated, and found herself also uttering exaggerated animal sounds, in response to his unfamiliar sounds. She scratched his back and bit him and pretended that the tears flowing ceaselessly down her cheeks were tears of happiness. Afterward she would turn her back to him and listen to his breathing until he fell asleep.

During the day they each hid in their corner. The man drank his morning coffee at his desk as he leafed through his diary, arranged appointments, and made phone calls at the top of his voice so the woman would hear that he was busy. The woman drank her coffee at the kitchen table, and sometimes, when she couldn't stand the solitude of the mornings, she would get dressed and go out, inventing imaginary meetings with friends, and going to sit alone in the café with the redheaded waitress.

She found it difficult to concentrate, but the man threw himself completely into his work. He would leave the house at noon, come home hours after dinner, and sprawl on the sofa in front of the television. When he couldn't stand the woman looking at him he would go out for long nocturnal walks with the dog, taking brisk, rapid strides, the dog dragging his feet behind him.

Sometimes the man passed his old house and wondered who the lucky guy was who had moved into his apartment. Once he walked past a little after midnight and saw two people, a young man and woman, carrying out the landlady's old closet and standing it on the sidewalk. For a moment he wanted to run up and shout at them, ask who had given them permission to throw the closet out, but he restrained himself. He stood on the other side of the street, leaning against a stone wall, and looked at them. Even after the young couple had gone back inside, he went on standing there looking at the closet and the passersby, some of whom stopped next to it, opened and shut its creaking door, walked around it, knocked on it with their knuckles, and wondered whether to take it home. But none of them wanted the closet.

On these long walks, when he wasn't busy spying on his old house, he would sometimes walk down his woman friend's street. He hadn't seen her for a while and he wondered how she was. They talked on the phone; she called him regularly once a week, mostly on Friday afternoons, when the loneliness of the week reached intolerable peaks. When the woman answered, she managed to mobilize all the cheerfulness in the world in order to make a few meaningless remarks before she asked: "Is he there?"

One night, when he saw the light on her porch, he almost went upstairs, but he was afraid of the moment when he would sit down on the old armchair, which was once his armchair, and he would have to collect his thoughts and tell her what was happening, because she would be able to see at once that he was miserable.

When he arrived home after his wanderings, the apartment would be dark. It was the beginning of spring, the windows and the shutters were open, and a pleasant breeze was blowing through the rooms, trying to banish the evil spirits imprisoned there in the winter. He would find the woman asleep, or pretending to be asleep, curled up under her comforter, from which she refused to be parted in spite of the warm weather. He would stand next to the bed and get undressed, and apart from the rustling of the leaves outside, and the lapping of the dog in the kitchen, and the soft thudding of his clothes falling to the floor, everything was quiet. A quiet broken only by the sound of the bedroom door slamming, and afterward the whispers and the demands and the grunts.

One night they did it in the bathroom. The woman was standing by the sink brushing her teeth, and the man came and stood behind her and slid his finger down her spine, and then he pulled her panties down to her ankles. He saw her face looking at him in the mirror. She put her toothbrush down, quickly washed her face, wiped her hands on her T-shirt, braced herself, and gripped the rim of the sink.

The dog passed the bathroom door on his way to his rug, and when he saw them standing there he stopped. They didn't see him. The woman's head was bowed; her hair sheltered her face. The man's cheek was pressed against her head, and his face was turned to the wall. The dog was flooded with sadness. The man and the woman looked like the dogs in the park. Sometimes he would run to join them, sniffing and filling with excitement, retreating when the big males growled at him, or squeezing in between the medium-sized and little dogs clustering around the hindquarters of the female, and sometimes, if he was lucky, if he was brave, he even succeeded in mounting her for a minute himself.

Now he stood and looked at the man and the woman, and in the silence he heard only the whimpers choking his throat, and the woman's necklace hitting the side of the sink.

26

In the middle of spring everything seemed to return to normal. Guests were invited to dinner, complaining good-naturedly about the weeks of neglect, and the house filled again with noise and people and food. The days were calm, gentle, and full of sunlight and fine weather. They were also full of the presents the man and the woman gave each other—silly little things, bought on the impulse of the moment in the wish to appease and placate, for the crisis had passed, they knew that, but bits of it still floated around the house like wisps of cloud.

They had been living together for nine months. Each of them thought this number symbolized something. The man imagined a child. The woman imagined separation. Each of their thoughts contained some plausible element, distant enough, something to play with but not actually touch—at night, before they fell asleep, in each other's arms.

One Saturday they decided to paint the apartment. They worked all day, dipping their brushes in the paint, climbing up and down the ladder, exchanging only necessary words, not wasting time. They painted in a frenzy, laboring to cover every stain, filling the little holes with plaster, plying the walls with layer after layer of paint until they could absorb no more. When it grew dark, they turned on the lights and the walls glared at them like flashing knives. They looked around, dazzled, and then they picked up the newspapers from the floor, put the furniture back, washed the paint off themselves, and released the dog from the kitchen porch. They had locked him up there early in the morning with a bowl of food and his pan of water and the sock and the yellow tennis ball.

They sat in the kitchen and ate dinner under the neon light, whose coldness and whiteness was intensified by the freshly painted walls, and whose little flickers irritated their eyes. They each followed their own thoughts, the man that he still loved her and the woman that it had been so long since she had any thoughts of her own. The man sat across from her and ate his omelette, his hair glistening from the shower. He smiled at her and stretched his hand over the table to touch her chin. She thought: He hasn't done that for a long time. She wanted to reciprocate with a little gesture of her own, but she couldn't think of one that would symbolize what they had had between them.

But what had they had? she thought, and began to crumble the slice of bread on her plate. Fear, she thought, that's what there was, I became somebody's girlfriend, and a coward. It began with the fear of being alone, and when she met the man the fear didn't disappear, but was doubled and magnified until it blinded her. And now, she thought, even if she wanted to go back to her original, independent fear, she couldn't because the fear of being alone had become something else: the fear of being alone again. Like a sick person who only becomes really afraid of his illness when he begins to recover, she thought, and raised her eyes from her plate to look at the man. He was reading the newspaper. One of his hands was lying across the table, touching hers, and the other was slowly turning the pages, while his mouth chewed a piece of bread in time to his reading, with the chewing motion stopping whenever his eyes came to rest on one or another sentence.

She sat on her chair and waited for the wave of anxiety to flood her, but it didn't. She raised her eyes to look at the man, to look at him so that she would be afraid of losing him, but she no longer saw him. On the other side of the table she saw a man reading a newspaper, his legs stretched out, his toes wriggling inside his socks, biting his nails. She saw a stranger with a familiar appearance and smell and movements, especially of rapidly nibbling his nails, which reminded her of the way birds cracked seeds with their beaks.

She had never given much thought to this gesture before. It was just another one of the man's habits, a part of him, but now that her eyes were dismantling him, the nail biting became something separate, a weakness, even a sickness. She looked at the parrotlike pecking and heard the nibbling sounds, and then went on taking him apart: first the head, the top of which peeped over the newspaper, a masculine head with hair cropped almost to the scalp. Black hair, with occasional strands of white, which the man angrily uprooted in front of the mirror as soon as he noticed them. And then there was the forehead, furrowed now with the effort of reading, and the eyebrows and the eyes, which ran over the page without noticing her, and the full cheeks, still a little red from shaving, and the nose. And under the nose the lips—the upper one thinner than the lower, both now stretched to make room for the busy teeth nibbling the nail of the little finger on his left hand.

There were the shoulders, roomy and inviting and beloved, the arms and the hairs that covered them, the hands, the thick fingers, neither long nor short. And the chest, and the little paunch, and the stripe of hair that began on the chest and parted into two separate lines on the stomach to meet again at the groin—there too the man would sometimes discover a white hair which saddened him—and then there was his penis, but when she tried to think of it separately, like the forehead, or the cheeks, or the nibbling, all she could see before her eyes were the past few weeks, the man who was a stranger.

She wanted to run to him and embrace him, to put him back together, but her gaze went on dissembling him, as if it contained active digestive juices. She saw the man's thighs, thick and solid, his knees with the big ugly scar on the left that always felt a little strange when her fingers or tongue touched it, and the feet and ankles; and last the heels—dry and rough—with toes that were beautiful and perfect. The man was proud of them and liked looking at them and rubbed them against each other inside his socks.

And then her hungry look went around the man and rested on the nape of his neck, with the little wisps of hair, and the back, and the two little cushions of fat on either side of his hips, and the buttocks, as small and tight as a child's, and the back of his thighs, and the hollows at the back of his knees, and the taut tendons of the ankles, and again the heels.

But no fear came; on the contrary. A strange calm possessed her. Not the serenity she had imagined and wished for, but a peace that was tired and even shy, that didn't know whether it should suddenly make its appearance now, just when everything seemed to be working out. Precisely now, when the house had been transformed and looked so clean and promising. She didn't want to break up with the man, but the possibility no longer frightened her. I've been so alone these past weeks, she thought, that I have nothing to fear.

The dog, who was lying quietly next to the fridge, suddenly woke up as if he sensed his master was in danger, and pressed himself against the man's legs.

What's up? asked the man. He put the paper down, stared into space, and shivered, shaking off someone else's dream in which he appeared. It's getting chilly, he said, and went to close the porch door. I think I'll put on a shirt. He was about to go to the bedroom, but then his eye fell on the newspaper, and he sat down and went on reading, rubbing his arms with his hands.

The quiet dinner, the painted apartment, the shower, filled him with satisfaction. The newspaper hid the woman from his eyes, but her presence on the other side of the table, the sound of her knife and fork, their dog rubbing himself against his legs, all these were part of a picture he had composed in his head, a family picture that merged with the information he absorbed from the newspaper, a picture hidden among the headlines in the lines of print, a picture that smiled and winked at him and told him it would be there later too, when he put the paper down and raised his eyes to look for it.

He was cold, but he was too lazy to get up. He sat on his chair rubbing his shoulders and hoped the woman would get up and bring him a shirt.

He went on sitting there, rubbing his shoulders, ostentatiously

now, but the woman didn't get up. The man peeped over his newspaper at her, sitting and staring at her plate, her fingers forming
crumbs of bread into little balls.

"Hey," he said, "what's up? Is everything all right?"

The woman said: "Yes. Everything's fine."

"It's getting a little chilly," he said.

"You should put something on," she said, and her hand reached
out to take the newspaper.

27

In the summer the man and the woman took a vacation. That's
what we need, they said, a little vacation, far from everyone, far
from our friends. They missed the first six months, when they had
been all alone. They decided to fly to Paris. Far from the big
mirror, which never stopped reflecting them, testing them, breaking their reflection, mocking them, and confusing them. The man
asked his friend if she would stay in their house for a week and
take care of the dog, and she agreed willingly.

She arrived on the eve of their departure and went down to
the cab to help them load their luggage in the trunk. The man
gave her the keys to the apartment, and the woman reminded her
when the dog had to be fed, how much to give him, and when to
take him for a walk. The friend asked whether she should water
the plants and the woman said no, she had just taken care of them.
This was a lie, but the woman didn't want any favors from the
man's friend. If the plants died, it was too bad. The dog was another story.

The friend kissed the man on the cheek, wished them both a
pleasant trip, and waved to them as the cab drove off. She went
upstairs and inserted the key in the lock. She heard the dog whining and his disks rattling, but when he saw her standing in the
doorway with her big knapsack he retreated and jumped onto the
sofa, where he curled up in the woman's place.

The friend took her clothes out of the knapsack, went into the bedroom, threw them onto the bed, and opened the closet. The man had promised her they would clear a shelf for her, but all the shelves were full. She stood in front of the open closet and she didn't know what to do with her things. She opened all three doors. The right side was packed tight with dresses, skirts, and coats, the two upper shelves on the left held the woman's shirts and pants, and the two bottom shelves were full of the man's things. Folded up at the bottom of the pile were the black jeans she had bought him, and which he had never worn. She tried the middle door, where she found a jumble of socks and underwear and various soft and undefined items of clothing belonging to both the man and the woman. She put her own little pile on top of them.

Afterward she went into the kitchen and filled the electric kettle with water and turned it on and read the long list of instructions about the dog in the woman's fine handwriting. At the bottom the woman had written, in her name and the man's name: "We hope you'll feel at home."

She went back to the bedroom, sat on the bed, and took off her shoes. She lay on her back, unzipped her jeans and wriggled out of them, and then took off her shirt. She went on lying on her back, on the man's and the woman's bed, wearing her bra and panties. She turned over onto her stomach and laid her head on one of the pillows, and suddenly she found herself sniffing, breathing in the pleasant smell of detergent, but seeking a different smell.

The dog walked down the hallway, peeped into the room, and returned sadly to the living room. He was ten months old. The friend lay on her side and fingered the clean sheet drawn tightly over the mattress. She thought about the man. She thought: I haven't slept with him for ten months now.

She got up and looked for something to wear, pulled a tank top and a pair of shorts out of her pile, and put them on. She heard the kettle hissing and closed the closet door, but she immediately opened it again and pulled a big white T-shirt with long sleeves out of the jumble of the man's and the woman's clothes. She didn't know which of them it belonged to. She took off the shorts and the tank top, crammed them into her pile, and put on the big T-shirt.

Then she made herself a cup of coffee and looked for something to eat. In the fridge she found a pot with leftover rice and two meatballs. She put the pot on the stove and lit the flame, but suddenly she was too hungry to wait. She took the cold food off the stove, put it on the table, and sat down to eat.

The man told her about the meals. Whenever she asked him how things were going with the woman, if he didn't regret moving in with her, if he thought their relationship had a future, what he felt about her, he would tell her about some meal the woman had cooked, as if this was the answer to all her questions. He never told her about their sex life.

Afterward they had invited her to their dinner party, and she had tasted the woman's cooking herself, but she was so drunk that the next day, when she sat at home and tried to reconstruct the menu, she couldn't remember it. All she could remember was the taste of the single man's rejection. She remembered how she had fawned on him in the car, and she remembered herself writing down her phone number for him before the three of them dropped her off in front of her house.

She ate the cold rice and meatballs greedily, scraped the leftovers from the bottom of the pot with a fork, and gathered up bits of rice with her fingers. The dog, whose hope was still automatically aroused by the sound of food, got off the sofa and presented himself shyly in the kitchen. The friend looked at his bowl. It was empty. She studied the list again, to see when she was supposed to feed him. The woman had written eight o'clock, and it was already after nine. The dog sniffed the air. The friend stood up, held the pot close to his nose, and then put it in the sink. She glanced at the bagful of dog food standing on the fridge, a new bag which the man and the woman had bought before they left to save her the trouble. The note assured her that it would be enough to last all week. She took it down and stood it on the table, and the dog began to wag his tail. She picked up his bowl and put it on the table next to the bag. They could have cleared a shelf for her. They could have filled his bowl before they left, but no. They left it up to her.

She found a pair of scissors in a drawer, and was about to open the bag, but suddenly she changed her mind and returned the scissors to the drawer. She lifted the heavy bag and put it back on top of the fridge. She put the empty bowl down on the floor, and when the dog approached it and stopped next to it, stared at it, and then looked at her inquiringly, she stuck out her tongue at him.

She went into the living room and flopped onto the sofa. She picked up the newspaper which was lying on the table, and when she began to read it she noticed a stain of tomato sauce on the collar of the white T-shirt. She sprang up and ran into the bathroom, took off the shirt, put it in the sink, and rubbed the stain with soap. She stood there for a long time, rubbing the material between her fingers, afraid to lift the shirt out of the water and foam in order to see if the stain was gone.

The dog walked down the hall and stopped to look at her. Then he went up to his rug, lay down on it, curled up into a little ball, and closed his eyes. The friend took the wet T-shirt out of the sink and held it up to the light, but there was no need for light to see that the stain was still there. It had spread and changed its shape, from a little spot surrounded by splatters into a huge amoeba dividing and multiplying itself in the fabric. She rushed around the apartment looking for bleach. She looked under the kitchen sink, in the cupboards, on the kitchen porch, in the bathroom, and even in the bedroom closet, but she couldn't find any. She threw the wet shirt into the bathtub and hurried to the living room to look for a pen and paper. She found a notebook on the woman's desk, tore a page out of it, and wrote a memo to herself, in big letters: "Buy bleach!" She put her frantic note on the kitchen table, next to the woman's calm note.

In the morning, after sleeping in the man's and the woman's bed, she went into the kitchen and found the dog dozing next to his empty bowl, his head on his paws. Then she saw her note, made herself coffee, drank it quickly, and washed the cup and the pot and fork standing in the sink. She got dressed, went down to the grocery, bought two bottles of bleach, milk, beer, and rice, and went back upstairs. She crammed the shirt, which had begun to smell bad, into the pail she found on the kitchen porch, and poured in the two bottles of bleach. She heard the phone ring and the answering machine saying: "We're not at home. Leave a message and we'll get back to you," and then the beep, and someone leaving a message: "Where are you? What's happening? How are you? Call us."

She gave the dog water, but his bowl remained empty. She didn't want to kill him. She wanted to see him suffer. After she hadn't taken him out for three days the dog peed and shat on the bathroom floor, next to the pail which gave off a terrible stink.

Most of the time he lay on his rug in the hallway and slept. From time to time he got up and walked slowly to the kitchen, his tail between his legs, his pelvis lowered, as if he couldn't make up his mind whether to sit or stand. He stood for a long time at the kitchen door, in this new posture, looking like a big, old rabbit. He looked at his bowl from a distance, too hungry to beg, too well trained to try to snatch something from the hands of the friend, who greedily devoured everything in the fridge.

It was a week of heat wave and the apartment blazed. Every day the dog drank his water, and at night, when the friend went out and left him alone in the house, he went to the bathroom, squatted next to the pail, and peed. During the day she closed the shutters and lay on the sofa in her bra and panties, and in the evenings she went out. She came back very late, long after midnight, and took off her clothes on the way to the bathroom where, ignoring the sharp smell of the bleach and the urine, the puddle on the floor, and the rotting T-shirt in the pail, she took a cold shower. Then she wrapped herself in a towel, opened the shutters and the windows in the bedroom, and lay down on the bed. She wondered what the weather was like in Paris.

And she wondered how she would celebrate her thirty-fourth birthday in three months' time. For five years she had celebrated her birthdays with the man, who always brought her some silly present—kitschy earrings, heart-shaped soaps, dolls. On his birthdays she gave surprise parties for him in her apartment. In three months' time he too would be thirty-four, she thought. All these years she had seen the fact that she and the man had been born in the same year, one week apart, as another sign that they were meant for each other. There were a lot of other signs she invented, but the birthdays were the main thing.

Two weeks before he had met the woman he had celebrated his birthday. He was depressed, he said, he was already thirty-three and still alone. She had made a party for him on her porch. It was a pleasant summer evening, not hot and stifling like this one, and you could breathe. She had invited all his friends, everyone she had invited in previous years, and made sure to tell the couple with the baby a few of weeks in advance so they could find a baby-sitter. Nevertheless they turned up with the baby, who was six months old and turned into the attraction of the evening. The man played with her, held her in his arms, and hugged and kissed her, and after he had blown out the candles on his cake with her help, he took her to the bedroom and changed her diaper, on the bed, as if she were his baby.

The friend had bought him a pair of black jeans, which she knew he liked, and after the guests left and the man remained sitting in his armchair on the porch she said to him: "Try them on." He went into the bedroom, took off his pants, and came out to the porch wearing the new jeans, which were tight. "Never mind," he said. "I'll wear them a bit and they'll stretch." But he never wore them. Afterward he returned to the bedroom and got undressed, taking off his shirt and underwear as well as the new jeans, lay on his back on the mattress, and called her to come to bed.

She quickly cleared away the empty bottles and the ashtrays and the paper plates with the remains of the expensive cake she had bought, the beautiful, multilayered cake, which didn't taste as good as it looked, and she collected the thirty-four little pink candles, which the baby had pulled out of the cake and scattered all over the house, and then she hurried to the bedroom. The man made love to her, kissed her on the cheek, and thanked her for the party and the present and going to all that trouble, and then turned his back to her and fell asleep. Now, as she lay in the middle of the man's bed, she couldn't remember what had made her think those days had been happy.

She fell asleep crying into the pillow. In the house the air stood still, hot, and heavy, full of the dreams she dreamed in her sleep—in which she saw herself as a big gray pigeon gathering crumbs in a rainy European square—and the waking nightmares of the hungry dog.

On the morning of the fourth day the friend hurried to the butcher's and bought a pound of fresh meat. She ran home, sweating in the heat, and filled the red plastic bowl. She sat at the kitchen table—the woman's note was still there, stained with coffee and tomato sauce—and looked at the dog. He stood next to his bowl and stared. His legs trembled and she thought that perhaps it was too late, perhaps he was already too weak, perhaps he was dying, perhaps he had forgotten how to eat.

She encouraged him with kind words, urged him to eat, she pleaded, but the dog went on standing next to the bowlful of meat, the trembling spreading from his legs to his back, his tail hanging between his legs, making weak whimpering sounds.

Suddenly he began to howl. It was a long jackal howl which split the air and caused the shutters in the opposite building to open. He stood with his back to her, his head raised to the ceiling, his eyes closed, and his howls tore the silence of the hot, dry morning.

She pressed both hands against her ears and began to cry. I've killed him, she thought, and tried to think of what she would say

to the man and the woman when they returned, in three days'
time, refreshed and in love, looking for their dog. What would she
do with his corpse? But suddenly the dog fell silent. He turned his
head to her and she smiled at him and whispered: "Eat." He circled
the bowl, sniffed it, looked at her again, then picked up a piece of
meat daintily between his teeth, and ran to his rug. He ran like this,
back and forth between the rug and the kitchen, until the bowl was
empty, and a pile of red meat rose on the mat. The dog lay next to it,
his head resting on his paws. He pulled one piece after the other into
his mouth and chewed the meat slowly, as if the act of eating hurt,
and his face was twisted in a strange, crooked smile.

28

In Paris the woman was the man's translator. He didn't understand
a word of French, and the woman, who spoke French fluently, was
happy to be his teacher, his interpreter, ordering for him in restaurants, consulting the waiters on his behalf, chatting with strangers in the street, asking them for directions. In the mornings she
would slip out of their hotel and return with big breakfasts. They
ate sitting on the bed, and the woman told him enthusiastically
about the adventures she had had on the way. Everything was an
adventure for her that week. The whole week it didn't stop raining.

She made friends immediately, with the unfriendly shop assistants and the old neighborhood barber, to whom she entrusted her
hair one morning on the way back from the delicatessen. When
she returned to the room she jumped onto the bed and tossed her
cropped head in the man's face, splashing him with cold raindrops.

For a week she dragged him through the streets, his hand
clutched in hers, and he tried to keep up with her, holding over
their heads the big umbrella they had bought at the airport. She
was full of joy and he had never seen her like this. At home, even
when she was in a good mood, there was always a cloud of unhappiness floating above her head, liable to burst at any moment and

shower them both with tears. He liked that cloud. He liked the tears. He didn't like seeing the woman unhappy, but he liked the permanent presence of her tears, the fact that it was easy for him to make her cry. Here in rain-swept Paris the cloud had vanished. Now and then he tried to see whether it still existed, sticking imaginary pins into it, provoking, sulking, but nothing happened. The cloud and the woman he knew had stayed at home, and he ran after this strange woman in the street.

In the plane on the way back she told him that she loved him. All the way they had been silent, he sullen, she pensive. A little while before landing she took his hand in hers, turned her face to the window and looked at the white floor of clouds and the wing of the plane gliding above them, looked back at him, and said: "I love you."

He thought that he was going to cry. He wanted to cry out of relief, because he believed her, and he wanted to cry because he was afraid that she was lying, but mainly he wanted to cry because he had never felt so lonely as during the past week. He fastened his seat belt and then fastened hers and said nothing. He put his hand back in hers, which had remained waiting in her lap. He waited for her to ask if he loved her too, but the woman looked out of the window. He waited for her to ask at least why he hadn't responded to her sudden declaration of love, but the woman pulled him toward her and said: "Look! Land!" And like a little girl she was filled with excitement in anticipation of the landing.

They arrived home in the middle of a scorching day and found the shutters closed and the dog sleeping in the hallway on his rug. He heard their footsteps on the landing and their voices and the key turning in the lock, but he remained slumped on his side, one ear cocked and listening. They came up to him, surprised and concerned, and bent down to stroke him. He raised his head and looked at them, and then lowered it to the rug again and stared at the wall.

The house was tidy, and there was a smell of cleaning products in the air. On the kitchen table there was a bunch of flowers in a glass jar. The dog's bowl was full. On the table was a note addressed to them both. "Welcome home," it said, with a row of exclamation marks. "I hope you had fun. Everything here was more or less as usual, except for one little accident: I ruined a white T-shirt of yours. I'll buy you a new one. I bought some food and cleaned up a bit. We'll talk later. Hope you had a good flight. We missed you."

There were eighteen messages on the answering machine. Seven for the man, five for the woman, and six for both of them. They sat in the living room, their suitcases still in the hall, and listened to the messages. Then the woman went to shower and the man made iced coffee. They drank it in silence, smoking, parting from their vacation. In the afternoon they wandered around the dim apartment, careful not to bump into each other or to step on the dog, who remained motionless on his rug. When evening fell the woman opened the shutters and the windows and went into the bedroom to unpack. The man whistled to the dog.

They went to the beach, because the man thought there would be a breeze there, and sat on the sand looking at the last bathers coming out of the water, drying themselves with their towels. Most people on the beach were elderly, a few families with children, and a few youngsters hanging around doing nothing. There were a few dogs too, rushing around and barking and dashing into the sea and running back to the shore, shaking off the water.

You couldn't really call what had happened in Paris a crisis, thought the man. A crisis was something that was easier to deal with, defined, known, but what had happened in Paris was worse than a crisis: for the first time in his life, thought the man, he was afraid of being alone. He remembered sitting naked on the bed and waiting for the woman in that depressing hotel. He remembered the rain pouring down outside, the dirty brown color of the curtains, and someone shouting something down below, in the street, in the foreign language he had come to hate.

He had paced restlessly up and down the room, from the window to the bed and back to the window again, parting the curtains and looking down to see if the woman was coming. In his boredom he began to pick things up from the floor—her stockings, her bra, panties, hairpins he found scattered all over, not knowing if they were hers or if they belonged to some other woman who had been in the room before them. The hairpins annoyed him. He picked them all up, crawling over the carpet and examining it thoroughly, which kept him occupied for fifteen minutes, and then he put the handful of pins on the little table next to the woman's side of the bed.

He wasn't hungry, but he wanted his breakfast. He lay in bed and smoked and waited for her. He suddenly heard the sound of a woman laughing and the tapping of heels running up the stairs, and he stiffened and pulled up the blanket, ready to scold her as soon as she burst into the room, but it wasn't her. He heard a man's voice climbing up the stairs after the woman and continuing up the next flight to the floor above. It was another woman. With another man. Not his woman, who had disappeared without even leaving a note.

It never occurred to him that something might have happened to her. It was clear that her disappearance was deliberate, aimed against him, and even though it was only eleven o'clock it seemed to him that he hadn't seen the woman for hours, even days, that she had vanished long ago.

This was the first time in his life that he was afraid of being alone. This was the first time in his life that he took off his watch and held it in front of his eyes and watched the minutes passing. It was humiliating, but it distracted him from his thoughts and kept him busy for an hour, and when he suddenly heard her running up the stairs, and this time it was definitely his woman, he quickly put the watch down on his bedside table, and leaned back against the pillows.

A strange woman entered the room. It wasn't the hair that made her so strange—now, on the hot beach with the quiet dog at his side, he had to admit that the new haircut suited her—it was a jigsaw puzzle of female parts, all of which he knew, but whose composition made up a different picture, not the familiar picture that was born in their kitchen, but the picture of a beautiful woman in a foreign magazine.

"Where were you?" he asked, and now too, on the beach, he heard his hoarse voice in that room in France.

"Where were you?" he asked again, and his eye, which had become addicted to the watch hands moving, glanced at it quickly on the bedside table, as if another whole hour had passed between her entering the room and him repeating his question for the third time in the same two minutes: "Where the hell were you?"

She turned and smiled, jumped on the bed, and shook her head, splashing him with drops of water: "I had my hair cut."

"Yes," he said. "I see. But where were you?"

"At the barber's," she said and ran to the mirror. "Do you like it?"

"All morning?" he asked. "You were at the barber's all morning?"

"No," she said. "I wandered around a bit. I bought things. I had my hair cut right near here. I found a place. It looks pretty, don't you think?"

"No," said the man. "I don't like it. It doesn't suit you."

"It doesn't?" she asked.

"No. Definitely not."

He sat leaning back in bed and lit another cigarette, slowly put his watch back on his wrist, and waited for the tears. She stood in front of the mirror with her back to him, quickly rearranged a few strands of hair, turned to him, and smiled again, but he shook his head and muttered: "No, it doesn't suit you."

He looked at his watch—he couldn't stop doing it now—and waited for the woman to burst into tears. "But it'll grow back," he said, "so it's not so terrible. It'll grow quickly."

She jumped onto the bed again and, kneeling, shook her head at him and said: "It won't grow, because I want to keep it like this. I'm going to have it cut again in two weeks, when it begins to grow. It won't be a problem to find someone to do it, it's a simple haircut." And then, as if remembering something, she hurried back to the mirror and said: "That's the only problem with this hairstyle, that you have to have it cut every two weeks." Then she asked him what he wanted to do that day, and he said he was hungry and asked her what she'd brought to eat. She spread a big towel on the bed and laid their breakfast on it.

29

The summer was almost over and the man had not yet told the woman that he loved her too. At first he didn't say it because he was waiting for her to say it again, so that his "I love you" would be moderated, a response rather than a declaration. He continued to keep quiet because he was afraid she had lied to him in the plane, since after they came home she did nothing to prove her love. On the contrary, it seemed that she was a little cold, and in the end he stopped believing that he really loved her.

During the entire week of their vacation he had felt tired and irritable; he didn't know the language; he was completely dependent on her. For the first three days the woman was sure that the foreign city, the sights, the food, even the interminable rain, were the reasons for her happiness. On the fourth day she had woken up very early and looked at the man sleeping. He lay on his side, his knees raised to his stomach, one hand flung out to the side of the bed, the other clenched into a fist close to his mouth. Even in his sleep he looked worried. She looked at him until he suddenly turned over and his forehead touched her knee. He frowned, as if in thought, his eyelids fluttered over his darting, dreaming eyes, and his thumb touched his lips. She looked at him and thought: When he's sleeping he expresses more feeling than when he's awake.

She got dressed quietly and made up her face and took the big umbrella and left the room and descended the old wooden stairs and planned their day: she would come back with their breakfast and wake the man, they would eat together, chat a little, maybe they would make love, and afterward she would ask him to come on a walking tour of the city. He would refuse, he would say that he didn't feel like it, she would protest, but not too much, and then she'd leave him in the hotel. She reminded herself to buy him a newspaper in English, maybe a film magazine, so that he wouldn't be bored in her absence. In the evening they would meet again and go out to a restaurant. So she would be able to be with the man and also without him. She felt a surge of joy as she stepped out into the street and began to run in the direction of the delicatessen. He wasn't going to spoil it for her, she said to herself as she stood in front of the counter and pointed to the things she wanted, two of each. He couldn't spoil things for her, she thought, and suddenly it occurred to her that his unhappiness was the reason for her happiness now.

She remained standing in the entrance to the shop, thinking, deliberating whether to run back to the hotel, shake the sleeping man awake, hug him, and feed him, or whether to wander around the streets a little longer. If her happiness now depended on his unhappiness, returning to the room would make her unhappy. It seemed strange that it had to be this way—either her or him— and she wondered if it was the same with other couples, if all the men and women had to take turns being happy and unhappy. How did they keep it up for so many years? Perhaps the more time passed, the easier it became, because each of them knew when it was their turn, and perhaps they even learned to be happy when it was the other person's turn. It's either swings or seesaws; she suddenly remembered one of the first things she had said to him on their blind date.

She went into the first café she came across, put the delicatessen bag down on a chair, and ordered an espresso. She drank the coffee and smoked a cigarette, peeking at the watch of the person sitting at the next table because she had forgotten hers in the hotel room. It's already eleven o'clock, she thought. The man must have woken up long ago. She felt as if her whole body contracted to double its weight, as if rising from the chair the man's own weight would send her sailing through the air, over the rooftops, through the mist, right into the hotel room. The man was right: the room really was depressing.

She ordered another espresso and lit another cigarette, and glanced at the bag of goodies sitting on the chair, suddenly looking almost human, swollen and erect, with grease stains spreading over it: What will they decide? Where will they take me? And from moment to moment its contents were losing their freshness.

The woman looked at the bag and remembered the croissants and baguettes, the breakfast drying up before her eyes, and she stood up, paid, picked up the bag, and opened the umbrella—with the new skill she had acquired over the past few days—with one hand, and began to run in the direction of the hotel.

She could already see the green tiled roof and the pediments with the little gargoyles protruding into the street, and then the window of their room on the second floor. She noticed the little barbershop, three buildings away from the hotel. She turned her head to look at the window of their room, and then she went inside, pushing the glass door with her shoulder and stopping for a moment in alarm when the bell rang.

The place was empty; there was a smell of shaving cream in the air. There was something very masculine about it that did not welcome the dramatic entrance of the young woman with the huge umbrella and the decomposing paper bag. She sat down on a high chair, put the bag on the floor, and, when the old barber approached her and asked politely and with an air of surprise what she wanted, she said: "Short!"

He explained to her that this was a men's barbershop. He told her he had no experience in cutting women's hair, that he didn't know what she wanted, that he was afraid of disappointing her, that perhaps she should go to a ladies' salon, where they would be able to help her. He pointed with a long finger to the window, trying to explain to her how to get there, but she smiled at him and said. "Short. That's all."

The barber sighed, touched her hair hesitantly, threw a white cloth over her, picked up his scissors, and began shuffling around her, examining possibilities, grumbling to himself. Slowly and cautiously, lock by lock, he snipped and pruned, stepping back to inspect his work after every snip. When he was finished the big clock on the wall said twelve o'clock. It was the longest short haircut of his life.

The woman remained seated in the high chair and smiled at herself in the mirror. The old barber stood behind her, resting his hands on the back of the chair, accepting her praise with a bowed head and curious little glances in the mirror. He was seventy-five years old, and he had never cut a woman's hair before. Sometimes he cut the hair of little girls who came with their fathers, but that was easy. This was the first woman who had ever sat in his chair and demanded, with a strange and charming impudence, that he cut her hair. It was a challenge, it was scary, and it had worked.

When the woman left, the barber opened the door and stepped outside with her. Her arms were wrapped around the bag, which filled the air with buttery smells mingled with peppermint and soap. The barber took the umbrella from under her armpit, opened it over her head, and placed the wooden handle in her hand. Then he went back inside and began sweeping up the black hair scattered over the floor. He gathered it in his hands and threw it into the garbage can, and suddenly he was filled with sadness at the thought that he might never have another opportunity to cut a woman's hair.

At the hotel the man was in a foul mood. He kept at her all day long. He had never tried so hard to insult her, to undermine her confidence, and he had never failed so completely. The more he insulted her haircut, the more she liked it; the more she saw how hard he was working to cover up the injury of her desertion the more she deserted him, and the rest of their vacation turned into a series of dozens of little desertions.

All week the woman looked at the man sleeping curled up on his side, his thumb touching his lips, and suddenly, on their last day in Paris, she panicked. She thought: Perhaps I've gone too far. Perhaps it's already too late. She had never seen him so lifeless, so defeated, and, above all, so silent. On the last night they went to an expensive restaurant. The food was bad, but the man, uncharacteristically, said nothing. He didn't even bother to remind her that the restaurant was her choice, that he had been against it from the beginning. Afterward they wandered the streets a little. It was the first night without rain. The man looked around him and swung the furled umbrella back and forth. The woman prayed for him to say something insulting, to criticize her, to say that he wanted to go back to the hotel, but the man was silent. The next morning when they packed their bags in silence, it occurred to her that perhaps she had killed something in the man. They sat in the airport cafeteria and drank coffee from paper cups, and when the woman talked, trying to sum up with him their shared impressions of the trip, even though she knew there were no shared impressions, the man smiled with bitter commiseration, as if to say: I'm sorry that you've lost me.

30

In August, a month after they had returned from Paris, the man and the woman talked for the first time about splitting up. The woman raised the subject, and she did it gently and compassionately. You're not happy with me, she said to the man one night and turned off the television, which he had been staring at all evening with empty eyes.

He looked at her in surprise.

"Yes," said the woman, "I know you're not happy with me. And you're right. I'm not good to you."

He went on looking at her, and then turned his eyes back to the blank screen.

"I want us to talk," she said. "I've been thinking about it a lot lately. Actually, it's almost the only thing I think about."

"What else do you think about?" asked the man.

"Why do you ask?" she said.

"No particular reason," he said. "It's just that we haven't talked much lately. I'd be interested to know."

She said: "About myself. I think about myself. I think," she whispered, "that maybe I'm not happy with you."

"You're not happy with me?"

"No." The woman panicked. "I didn't say that. I said that I think about myself in the context of our relationship. And that perhaps, I'm not always happy with you. I don't know. I don't know what I think," she said. "What do you think?"

"About what?" said the man.

"I don't know. About us. About everything."

"You're asking me if I want to break up?"

"No," said the woman. "Of course not! I'm just asking, in general, because we haven't been talking to each other lately, as you said."

"And before that we did talk?"

"Yes," said the woman. "I think that we used to talk. Not exactly heart-to-heart. Somehow we never had those. Things happened naturally. We didn't feel the need to talk. Do you think that's a bad thing?"

"I don't know," said the man. "I never thought about it."

"No," said the woman. "Neither did I."

"You're playing games," said the man.

"No I'm not," said the woman. "I'm trying to have a conversation."

"You're not trying to talk," said the man. "You're trying to make me say that I want to break up. To make it easy for you."

They both looked at the dog, lying between them on the sofa.

"Look at him," said the man. "Look how ugly he's grown."

"He isn't ugly," said the woman. "Don't say that."

"But it's true," said the man. "You remember how cute he was when we found him?"

"Yes," said the woman and looked nostalgically at the dog.

"Did you think he'd grow up to be such a monster?"

"He's not a monster," said the woman. "Maybe he's a little ugly, but he's not a monster."

"Did you ever think that one day you'd hate him?"

"I don't hate him. Why on earth should I hate him?"

"I do," said the man.

"That's not true. You love him," said the woman.

"I love him and I hate him," said the man.

"And me too."

"Yes," said the man. "Right now I do."

"And was there ever a time when you only loved me? Without hate?" she asked.

"I think so," he said. "At the beginning."

"And when did you start hating me?"

"In Paris," said the man.

"I thought so," said the woman.

"And you?" asked the man, and felt tears welling up in his eyes—the tears of Paris that had not yet completely ripened.

"What about me?"

"When did you begin to hate me?"

"I don't know," said the woman, and the man burst into tears. The woman tried to put her arms around him, but he shook her off, rose from the sofa, and went to stand next to the window. The outburst of weeping was short. The woman lit a cigarette and leaned back and threw the match into the ashtray. The man sniffed and raised his arm to his face and wiped his eyes with the sleeve of his T-shirt. Then he took a deep breath and looked out of the window. The woman put out her cigarette, stood up, and went to stand behind him. She put her arms around his waist and pressed her cheek to his back, and felt an insulted little jerk of rejection. Afterward she rubbed her chin in the hollow between his shoulder blades, kissed the fabric of his shirt, which was warm and damp with sweat, and stood next to him, groping with her hand for his, which was pushed deep in his jeans pocket.

They both stood at the window. They looked at the ugly apartment buildings. Some of the windows were already completely dark; in some the lights were still on, especially in the kitchens. Then they looked at the dog who was sleeping on the sofa.

"If we break up," said the man, "who'll take him?"

"But we're not splitting up," said the woman.

"But if we do?"

"I don't know," said the woman.

"Because I don't think I'll want him."

"No," said the woman, "neither do I."

"It would complicate my life," said the man. "My life's complicated enough as it is."

"Let's not think about it now," said the woman gently.

"Let's be on our own for a while," said the man. "Like we were in the beginning. I don't feel like having dinners and going out all the time. I'm sick of everybody."

"So am I," said the woman.

"Let's hide in the house," said the man and turned his face to her, and the woman looked into his eyes which were still wet.

"Okay," she said and kissed him on the lips.

They kissed, and in the middle of the kiss he went on mumbling: "Let's be on our own for a while."

The phone rang and they disengaged themselves. They couldn't decide whether to answer. After six rings the dog raised his head in surprise. The man picked up the phone.

"They want us to come to the bar for a drink," he said to the woman. "You want to go?"

"It's late," she said. "Isn't it too late?"

"It's a bit late," said the man and covered the mouthpiece with his hand, "but still, we could drop by for an hour."

"But you just said that you don't want to see friends anymore, that you want us to stay at home for a while."

"I know," he said.

"I don't mind going," she said, "if that's what you want."

"Whatever you like."

"All right," she said. "I don't mind."

"I think it wouldn't do us any harm to go out tonight, even if it is late, just for an hour. Okay?" said the man and sniffed again.

"Okay," said the woman. "If you feel like it."

When they came home at three o'clock in the morning the man was drunk. The woman had to drive home. She hated driving and she was angry with him, but when she looked at him sitting next to her, strapped in the seat belt which she had fastened for him, staring out of the window and singing children's songs, she burst out laughing and bent over to kiss him on the cheek. The man, she thought, was at his best when he was helpless. When they went upstairs she supported him. The man climbed up one step and down two, loudly singing "Three Blind Mice," changing the words of the refrain to "I love you."

She put him to bed, took off his shoes, stripped him of his shirt and jeans, and covered him with the blanket. "I feel nauseous," he said, and let his head fall to the side.

"You want to go to the bathroom? You want to throw up?"

"No," he mumbled, "I just feel sick."

"Should I make you a cup of tea?"

"No. Did you hear what I sang to you?"

"When?"

"On the stairs."

"Yes," said the woman. "I heard. So did the neighbors."

"And what do you think?"

"About your singing?"

"No," the man mumbled into the pillow. "You know about what."

"I think you're drunk, and I'm glad you love me. I've been waiting a long time for you to say it. Ever since we came back from Paris I've been waiting for you to say it."

The man tried to get out of bed. He didn't know what he wanted to do: to embrace the woman standing in front of the open closet and looking for a T-shirt, or to go to the bathroom and throw up. He began lurching in the direction of the door, emerged into the hallway, and stood there for a moment, swaying and holding on to the walls. He looked down at the dog lying on his rug, and suddenly he felt dizzy. He called the woman. She came out into the hall and looked at him, standing with his legs apart, his hands leaning on the walls, and the sleepy dog looking up at him from below.

"He's growling at me," said the man.

"No, he isn't. Come to the bathroom."

"You didn't hear him," said the man. "A minute ago he growled, he bared his teeth at me and growled."

"Come on," she said gently, "come to the bathroom with me."

"I don't want to go to the bathroom," said the man, "I want him out of here. Take him away. He's dangerous. He's going to attack me."

"Stop it," said the woman. "You're totally drunk. You're talking nonsense. If you don't want to go to the bathroom, then come to bed."

"No," said the man. "I want him out of here. I don't want him here. He scares me."

"So what do you want me to do?"

"Get him out of here."

"Where to?"

"I don't know. Just take him away from me."

"I'll put him out on the landing," she said. "Go to bed. I'll take him out. Don't worry. He won't hurt you." She went up to the dog and stroked his head. The dog rolled over onto his back. He raised his bent legs in the air and his ears fell back onto the mat. The woman was surprised. She had never seen him lying like this before. It was a position most dogs liked, but not this one. The fur on his stomach was soft and pleasant to the touch. She tickled him and giggled when she saw one of his hind legs beginning to dance in the air. His eyes were closed and his nose was wrinkled, and from his dark gums his teeth stuck out. He seemed to be smiling.

She took hold of his collar and pulled him to his feet. He shook himself and followed her to the front door. The woman went out to the landing with the dog behind her. He looked at her curiously as she pointed to the straw doormat. She stood there in her panties and T-shirt and pointed. "Get down!" she said and retreated into the apartment. For a moment longer she stood there looking at him looking at her, and then the light went off on the landing and the door closed. When she returned to the bedroom she found the man lying on his side on the bed and calling her in a low voice. He had vomited on the floor. She brought a rag from the kitchen porch and cleaned up the mess, and then she held the rag with the tips of her fingers and threw it into the pail standing in the bathroom, and filled the pail with water.

31

In autumn the dog's appearance changed. His hindquarters sagged and his walk turned into a kind of crawl. The man and the woman took him to the vet, and the vet said it was a problem with the pelvic bones. "Our little Anonymous is suffering from a genetic disease," he said. But the doctor was wrong.

The dog spent most of his days and nights on the doormat. After recovering from the insult, he found something consoling in it. Twice a day the man and the woman would open the door and he would go inside, drink a little water, eat the dog food in his bowl quickly and efficiently, making a crunching noise which broke the silence in the house. Then he would go out to the landing again, with the residents going up and down the stairs, the children who bent down to pat him, and the solitary old lady from the top floor who felt sorry for him.

Sometimes, when the man left the house, the woman would open the door and invite the dog in, as if he were an old lover. She would sit down on the sofa and pat the seat beside her, but the dog remained standing in the entrance hall, or sometimes, against his will, he'd be drawn by some longing into the living room and lie down hesitantly on the floor. At night he could hear the voices of the man and the woman rising from the apartment, quiet voices. There were no sounds of clattering pots, metallic music, or crying.

Nobody took him out for walks anymore. He went out alone, once or twice a day, for a short and purposeful walk around the neighborhood, sometimes going into the park and looking from a distance at the dogs playing together or at some lucky dog racing after a stick somebody threw him. When the stick flew through the air, his body would tense in participation, his head and front legs would spring forward, but his sagging, broken hindquarters would always remain rooted to the spot, as if to say: The stick isn't for you.

Sometimes he would accompany the woman to the grocery and sit outside, displaying the calm indifference of a dog waiting for its master. When she'd come out he would follow her home and climb the stairs behind her, stop on the last step before the second floor landing, wait until she went inside and, sending him an apologetic look, closed the door. Then he would lie down on the doormat. He had his food, his water, and his mat, and he was free. He was neither a street dog nor a house dog, He was a kind of in-between dog, a temporary pet.

And then there was the birthday party, the procession of people climbing the stairs carrying bottles and plastic bags. They rang the bell, bent down to pat the dog's head, and disappeared into the apartment. The stairwell was flooded with music, cheerful voices, bursts of laughter, and whistles. At midnight the man's friend came out, bent down, swayed on her heels for a moment because she was drunk again, and then kissed the dog on his nose and shoved a piece of birthday cake into his mouth.

She had organized the party and paid for almost everything. She called the woman one day and asked her in her cheerful voice: "So what are we doing on the thirtieth of October?"

"I don't know," said the woman. "I haven't thought about it."

"You didn't?" the friend asked in a tone of rebuke. "But you know what the thirtieth of October is, don't you?"

"Yes," said the woman. "Of course I know. It's his birthday."

"And today it's mine," said the friend, an accusing sadness stealing into her voice.

"Really?" said the woman. "Happy birthday! I didn't know."

"Never mind," said the friend. "I thought that maybe we could do something together. We always celebrated our birthdays together. If you like, we can have it at my place. Or yours. Whichever is more convenient."

"Our place," said the woman. "I think we've got more room here. But I'm not sure he wants a party."

"So what?" shrieked the friend. "He's not supposed to know anything about it. It's a surprise. I throw a surprise party for him every year. He expects it."

"He does?" the woman asked hesitantly.

"Yes he does! And listen, you won't have to do a thing. I'll bring everything."

"But I can do something too."

"No, don't do anything. Really. I'm an expert. I'll buy the cake, I know a good place, I always buy there, and if you like you can make some dips and buy crackers or something."

"Okay," said the woman. "I'll make dips. I'll buy crackers."

"And everybody'll bring wine and beer, so you don't have to buy any."

"Who will we invite?"

"You invite whoever you like and I'll invite whoever I like."

"So you'll invite friends of yours too, right?"

"Absolutely!" said the friend and laughed loudly.

But she arrived alone. She was carrying a huge cake in a cardboard box and there was a plastic bag holding a parcel wrapped in pale blue paper hanging from the fingers of her right hand. The woman opened the door and took the cake and made room for it in the fridge. "I brought decorations too," said the friend, and stood a chair in the middle of the living room. "Let's do the balloons. When's he coming?"

"He should be here in an hour. When did you tell people to come?"

"Now," said the friend and blew up a giant balloon. "I told them to come at nine. And you?"

"Nine," said the woman. She took the balloon from her mouth and tied it.

The man's friends and the man and the woman's friends arrived, and the woman waited for the friend's guests to arrive, but when the man arrived, at half past ten, and pretended to be surprised, there were still none of her guests there. The man embraced the woman and kissed her on the mouth, and squeezed the friend's shoulder. "She does this to me every year," he said to the woman.

Then he sat down to open his presents, and someone put a new cassette he had bought the man into the tape deck—another metallic horror to which the man listened with a kind of guilty childish smirk, looking around the room for the woman. She had bought him a shirt. It was a denim shirt that she knew he wanted, and everybody immediately urged him to try it on. At first he protested, but then he gave in, took off his T-shirt and threw it on the floor, and put on the denim shirt which suited him and was the perfect size. Whistles of admiration rose from the men and women who were standing around drinking beer.

He looked at the friend and said: "I'm sorry. I haven't had a chance to buy you a present yet."

"Never mind," she said. "I haven't had a chance to buy you one either," and the woman glanced quickly at the entrance hall and the plastic bag leaning against the man's desk.

"The shirt's great," the friend said to the woman.

"Yes," said the man, "I've wanted one like it for ages."

"I know," she said.

The friend had paid a lot of money for the shirt she had bought, and for a moment she wondered if she and the woman had gotten their gifts at the same place. "Where did you buy it?" she asked the woman, who told her the name of the shop. It wasn't the same one, and suddenly this made the whole thing even worse, as if the two women, sometime during the week, had set out in different directions, for different parts of town—one known for its expensive boutiques and the other for its sidewalk bargains—and had each bought the same shirt for the same man. One of them would hang up one shirt later in the closet, smelling faintly of his sweat, while the other would take hers back the next day, wrapped in its pale blue paper, to the awful, pretentious shop uptown, and ask them to exchange it for something else.

The woman disappeared into the kitchen and returned carrying the cake with its seventy candles. Thirty-four for the man and thirty-four for the friend, and one each for the next year. She set it on the table, and the man and the friend, who were sitting side by side on the sofa, filled their lungs with air and blew out all the candles with one long breath. She started to pull out the candles and to lay them, smeared with white icing, on the table, but the guests stood over her impatiently and demanded their slice of cake. The friend hurried to the kitchen and got a big knife and smiled at the woman. "May I?" she said, and the woman stepped back and watched her sticking the knife into the middle of the cake.

32

The man took her home. It was strange to turn into her street and park next to the familiar building. She asked if he wanted to come up for coffee, and he found himself apologizing. The woman didn't like being left alone at night, he said.

"But she's got the dog," the friend said. "What's she afraid of?"

"The dog"—the man smiled—"isn't a watchdog. He's a terrible coward."

"When are you going to give him a name?" she asked, and took her keys out of her bag.

"Yes," said the man, "it really is about time. Imagine if we have children someday. What will we tell them when they ask what the dog's name is?"

"Your children probably won't have names either," she said.

His heart contracted. Not because of what she'd said, but because the possibility that the woman would be the mother of his children now seemed very remote to him. He lived with her, he went to bed with her, he had practical conversations with her, and recently he had even found himself spontaneously and somewhat savagely making dinner for her. The cooking took his mind off the silence that pervaded the apartment, and the woman who spent all day slumped in front of the television, the remote control lying limply in her hand, too apathetic to change channels.

He cooked like a madman, and she didn't protest. She sat down at the kitchen table when he called her, and the food he had cooked with imagination and rage was inedible. Either he added too much seasoning or he forgot the seasoning altogether, either he burned the meat or he served it almost raw and sat and watched her struggling, bolting it down and ignoring the blood dripping onto her plate. She hoped he would leave. He hoped she would ask him to leave.

His love for her had gone through so many metamorphoses that when he looked at her eating or emerging from the bathroom after a shower, fully dressed, suddenly shy, he felt all that was left of his love was fear, that this was the love of his life and it was over, and therefore there was no point in leaving and moving on, because he had already received the ration of love he had coming to him.

He found himself following his friend upstairs. "Just for coffee," she said. He looked around at the familiar apartment, he even went into the bedroom for a minute to see if everything there was the same, the bed, its thick, scratchy cover, the two pillows, and then he went out onto the porch.

"It's a little chilly," said the friend. "Should we go inside?"

She brought the two armchairs in from the porch and stood them in the living room. Then she went into the bedroom, taking with her the plastic bag she had been holding in her hand all this time, and came out in a T-shirt and panties. The man sat in his armchair and glanced at his watch. Exactly two o'clock. He wondered if the woman had started to worry yet, or if she had already lost her capacity to worry about him, just as she had lost the capacity to yell at him and scold him and fight with him and cry because of him.

"So we're thirty-four years old," he said.

"Yes," she said. "And we're both still single."

The last time the woman had cried was the night they had spoken about breaking up and afterward they had gone out to meet friends at a bar. Even though he was very drunk, before he fell asleep he had heard her crying in the bathroom. Since then they had gone on with their lives as if they were still a little drunk. There was a kind of dull heaviness between them accompanied by a faint queasiness. And every morning it seemed that one of them would wake up sober, look around and take fright, drag himself into the kitchen, and drink a couple of cups of strong coffee. When the other one shuffled in, they would look each other in the eye and say: "Enough."

The friend gave him a cup of coffee and sat down on the floor at his feet. "You still take sugar?" she said. "Yes," he said and closed his eyes.

"You too, right?" he said.

"No," she said. "I don't take any."

"Right," he said. "I forgot. You don't."

And suddenly she burst into tears. The man opened his eyes and listened for a moment to her sobs, to her sniffling, and he touched the hand covering her eyes. He bent down and whispered: "What's the matter?"

"Nothing," she said, "nothing."

"Tell me. What's the matter?"

"It's nothing," she said, "I just feel a little down."

"I've never seen you cry before, you know? Is it because I forgot how much sugar you take in your coffee?"

"I don't take any sugar," she burst out and began to sob again. She laid her head in his lap. He put his hands on her shoulders. "Stop," he said, "Please don't cry." And he glanced at his watch again.

"Are you all right?" he asked.

Her head nodded in his lap.

"Are you sure?"

She sniffed and raised her head and looked at him. She stared at him with her wet eyes and began to undo his fly buttons. The man held her wrist and said: "Stop it! What are you doing? Don't do that."

"But why not?" she wailed. "Tell me why?"

"You know why," he said.

"You were never so faithful before," said his friend. "Never!"

"I never had a girlfriend before," he explained in a fatherly voice.

She listened to him, her face turned to the side, her eyes still full of tears, her fingers holding one of the metal buttons on his fly.

"Why do you stay with her?" she asked. "You're not happy."

"I don't know," he said and stroked her hair. "Because I love her, I guess."

"You don't love her," she said. "You don't even know what love is."

"Look who's talking," he said.

He touched her chin, his fingers groping for a little scar, and he raised her face and smiled and said to her: "You know that I'll always love you."

"Yes," she said, "like brother and sister."

"Yes"—the man smiled—"like brother and sister."

She laid her cheek on his knee. He felt the wet warmth of her tears soaking through his jeans. He ran his fingers absentmindedly through her hair, looked up at the ceiling, closed his eyes, and sighed. "Life sucks," he said.

He thought about the children he wanted to have with the

woman. A girl, and then a boy. He tried to think of names for
them and he couldn't come up with any he liked. He stroked the
friend's hair. He tried to think of all kinds of names. He brushed
his fingers over her tense neck and felt the little hairs bristling
under his fingers. He felt comfortable in his old armchair.

He sank into a daydream about the daughter he would have.
He saw his little girl running around the house in a diaper. He saw
her sitting in a high chair in the kitchen. He saw himself sitting on
the bathroom floor and bathing her. He thought about how happy
he would be. He heard her shrieks of joy, her feet kicking in the
water, he even succeeded for a moment in feeling her little body
pressing against him through the white terry-cloth robe with the
hood. It was perfect. The sponge and the yellow rubber duck and
the baby soap. He enjoyed the vision so much that he didn't even
notice the woman wasn't there. She wasn't in the picture. Warmth
enveloped his body, and suddenly he had an erection. He opened
his eyes in alarm. His friend's face was buried in his lap. He wanted
to get up, but he didn't try. He whispered, and he didn't hear
himself whisper: What are you doing? He didn't hear her answer
him either. He gripped the arms of the chair with both hands and
bit his lower lip and sighed: Stop it. His feet moved on the floor
as if they were going somewhere without him. He racked his brains
and tried to grasp when the moment had begun, when he had
abandoned himself like this, but there were no thoughts in his
head. There was no baby there, and no bathroom or white terry-
cloth robe with a hood, and the woman wasn't there, and suddenly
he was absolutely alone. His feet stopped moving on the floor and
his hands let go of the chair arms and hung suspended for a moment in the air until they landed on the friend's head and pressed
it down.

He sat paralyzed in the armchair. The friend stood up and went
into the bathroom and came back with a towel soaked in warm,
soapy water. She knelt down and wiped him with it. He looked at
her, and closed his eyes again. Then he looked at his watch.

33

When he got home, a little before three, the lights were still on in the apartment. There was a pile of paper plates on the living-room table and next to it a tower of disposable cups. On the floor was a big garbage bag with half the chocolate cake peeping lopsidedly out of it. The broom was leaning against the sofa, and lying next to it was the dustpan into which the birthday candles had been swept. He went up to peep into the garbage bag and saw his name written in white cream on the cracked chocolate icing.

He walked around the house turning off the lights and then he went into the dark bedroom. The woman was lying in bed with her face to the wall. At the foot of the bed, on her side, on the little rug which had been stored all these months in a plastic bag on the kitchen porch, lay the dog. The man stood in the dark and looked at him. The dog didn't move. Then he looked at the woman curled up under the blanket pretending to be asleep.

He decided to take care of it in the morning. He felt too guilty to make a scene now. He got undressed, threw his clothes into the laundry hamper in the bathroom, and got quietly into bed. He put his arm on the woman's waist. He knew she was awake. He prayed she would say something, mutter something resentfully, but the woman said nothing.

In the morning he found her drinking coffee in the kitchen with the dog lying on his side next to the fridge.

"Why is he here?" he asked, but the woman didn't answer.

He turned on the electric kettle and leaned against the marble counter.

"Why are you here?" asked the woman.

"What's that supposed to mean?"

"Why are you here?"

"Where do you want me to be?" he said, moving the dog aside with his foot and opening the fridge. "Where's the milk?"

"It's all gone," said the woman.

"But I bought milk yesterday. How can it be gone?"

"Because it's gone," said the woman.

He knew where the milk was, but he was afraid to look. He glanced down at the floor, at the two tiles next to the porch door. On one of them stood the bowlful of dog food. On the other the dog's aluminum pan, brimming with milk. He looked at the woman, who was sipping her coffee and reading the paper.

"Why did you give him all the milk?" the man asked and stared at the dog. The dog averted his eyes.

"Because he likes it," she said.

"Why did you bring him inside?" he asked. "Why did you bring him into the house?"

"Because it's his house," she said.

"What are you trying to tell me?" he said.

"What are you trying to tell me?"

"Stop it!" yelled the man. "That's enough. Let's talk. Let's really talk."

"Go ahead and talk," said the woman. She folded the newspaper and put it down on the table, and took another sip of coffee.

The man sat down at the table and lowered his eyes to the floor. Between the legs of the table he saw the dog's thin legs trembling. He's got strange legs, that dog, thought the man, legs like a deer. He had never noticed them before. Come here, he said gently, but the dog ignored him.

The man whistled, and the dog ran to him. He put his front paws on the man's thighs, and began to whimper and wag his tail. The man stroked his head. "Come here," he said to the dog and grabbed him by the scruff of his neck. "Come here, you little idiot." He stood up and led the dog to the front door.

"You're not putting him out," said the woman quietly.

The man opened the door. He tried to drag the dog outside, but the dog sat down in the doorway and began to cry.

"Don't you dare put him out!" the woman screamed from the kitchen. "Don't you dare!"

The man took hold of the dog's forelegs and pulled. He was stronger than the dog. The dog slid forward, his forelegs trapped in a scissor grip by the man's hands and the paws of his hind legs scratching the floor.

The woman ran to the door and yelled: "Leave him here. He's mine. I want him here." But the man didn't hear her. He looked deep into the dog's eyes, and the dog looked into his eyes. Only his tail now remained inside the house. The rest of his body was trapped in the man's hands, in a kind of violent embrace, with the man kneeling in front of him, their heads touching. Both of them suddenly had the same look in their eyes. Later, when he tried to reconstruct what had happened, the man thought that it was strange, the way the dog looked at him, because dogs, he had once read somewhere, were incapable of looking you in the eye.

The woman put her hand on the man's shoulder. He hadn't sensed her coming up behind him; he startled and stuck his elbow in her thigh. She put out her hand to stroke the dog's head, but his lips trembled, and she heard a noise that sounded like a distant generator, a low, deep growl, coming from his throat. She drew back, but the man and the dog went on squatting there, face-to-face, trembling, as if caught inside an electric circuit.

The man let go. Suddenly he raised his hands and fell backward and sat down on the landing. The dog too sat down and looked at him. The man rested his elbows on his knees and buried his head in his arms. The dog raised his head and looked at the woman, stood up, and went outside onto the landing. Then he pressed himself against the wall and walked along it, up and down.

The woman bent over the man and whispered something in his ear. The man shrugged his shoulders and then he stood up and went inside with her. At noon the door opened and the man came out again. He was showered, his hair was wet, he looked relaxed, and he was smoking a cigarette. He hopped over the dog, who was lying on the mat, and ran down the stairs. A few minutes later the door opened again, and the woman, whose hair was wet too, said to the dog: "Come and eat."

34

Winter set in. It was cold on the stairwell, and the wind whistled to the dog from the bottom of the steps. Every morning the old lady from the top floor climbed the stairs and stopped next to him, transforming her loneliness for a moment into a modest act of giving. "Here's a cookie," she said to him in a breathless foreign accent. "Here's a slice of turkey." She started to take him into account when she did her shopping in the market.

Every day the dog watched the slow procession of objects going down the stairs. Books, tapes, a toaster oven carried in the man's arms, its electric cord dangling after it like a tail. And finally, on a rainy morning in the middle of November, the dog saw a colorful pile of clothes floating past him like a big cloud, and one sock, a white sport sock, which was left lying on the stairs.

The dog missed the man. At night his shadow appeared before the dog's eyes and in the mornings the memory of his voice pierced the silence of the stairwell, the silence of his daily march to his bowl, the silence of his new routine—the memory of the didactic, explaining voice. But above all it was the man's smell that flooded him with waves of longing. He didn't know what to do with them. When they came, he would close his eyes tightly and lay his head on his paws.

The smell was everywhere. The smell of his bare feet on the kitchen floor, the smell of his muddy heels on the doormat, the faint and painful smell of his sweat, still lingering in the stairwell, diluted over the weeks and fading into the other smells of the building—frying and cooking, small children, the smell of rain brought in by people going up and down the stairs, the fur of a wet cat seeking shelter, the bad smell given off by the old lady.

Sometimes when he went out for a walk he thought he saw the man's car passing in the street. His heart beat hard when he saw the back of the car turn quickly into another street, its white color flashing in the dark. He wanted to chase it, but something always stopped him and rooted him to the ground: the hindquarters of his body, where his nightmares were stored.

The woman wanted him to come back and live inside the house, but he preferred to remain outside. She tried to coax him to stay, but the dog set clear limits: he ate and drank, allowed her to pet him a little, but then he walked to the door and sat down next to it until the woman let him out.

And one day, at the end of winter, his body began to straighten out. His pelvis, as if a small crane had come to its rescue, rose a little, and his gait grew less apologetic. His tail still hung down, sheltered between his legs, but now and then it too showed timid signs of life; it would wag for a moment, against his will, at the sight of another dog.

Seeing the park and the dogs and their owners no longer hurt so much either, and sometimes the woman accompanied him. The dog would take her out for a walk; she followed in his footsteps, straining to keep up with his new and energetic pace. Every now and then he would stop and turn his head to make sure that she hadn't run away or gotten lost. Sometimes she would sit down on a bench, take a book or a newspaper out of her bag, and try to read, but her eyes would always wander, lingering on the old people sitting on the other benches, on the couples crossing the paths, or sitting on the lawn and eating together, a towel or a blanket spread out between them. When he saw her sitting like this, like a sad, heavy air balloon rising in the wind, he would rush to her and gently dig his teeth into her ankle, trying to catch hold of the string that would bring her back to earth. He wanted to make her happy with the things that made him happy.

And one day he brought her a stick. He laid it in her lap and waited. The woman took the stick in her hand and looked as if she didn't know what to do with it, and suddenly she threw it far and smiled when she saw the dog racing off with a speed she didn't know he possessed. He came back to her panting with the stick between his teeth and, bowing his head, laid it in her lap. They played like this for an hour—the woman inproving her throws and the dog, as if some spring had been released inside his body, stretching out and growing straighter as he ran. At noon, when the woman tired, the dog who lay down at her feet was no longer the doormat dog she knew, but a proud hunting hound with an invisible brace of pheasants.

And there were new friends too. At first they treated him with suspicion and were afraid of coming close, because in spite of his confident posture and his tail which now wagged constantly, they could still smell the residue of sadness and sickness. There was a big black dog who looked dangerous at first but proved to be good-natured and a faithful friend. And there was a little bitch who scampered around all the time and courted him, and there were people too, who sometimes came up and spoke to the woman.

And one night, at the beginning of spring, the man returned. He was a little thinner; there was a black-and-white beard on his chin. He had a new coat, not the big, soft coat the dog remembered from the previous winter, but a short leather jacket that gave off a sharp animal smell. He was glad to see the dog; he bent down and patted him and then straightened up, smoothed his new beard with his hand, and took his key ring out of his jacket pocket. He chose the middle key and was about to insert it in the lock, but then he changed his mind, put the key back in his pocket, and rang the bell. The dog closed his eyes and pricked up his ear. The woman opened the door and the man went inside.

THE HAPPINESS GAME

A few minutes after he left, a strange thing happened: hundreds of black birds appeared out of nowhere and swooped down on the old palm tree across the street and polished off the dates hanging from it in bunches—the dates he said had to be picked because they were no good for the tree, they weighed it down and they suffocated it, and that little by little they would kill it.

We stood on the balcony, leaning against the stone ledge and looking at the passersby. We looked at the cars turning into the street and disappearing around the corner, at the building opposite, at the balconies and open windows, we looked at the palm tree, we looked at everything it was possible to look at in order not to look at each other.

We had just finished fighting. It was our first fight. I started it and did most of the fighting. Nathan kept quiet and muttered briefly only when I said something that was, in his opinion, factually incorrect, or particularly insulting. But it was more of a mumble than an utterance, something muffled he said in a low voice to the floor, his mouth full of quiet facts.

I never thought I would be that kind of woman, an accusing, hysterical woman who put her hands on her hips when she made her accusations, but as I stood opposite Nathan sitting on the sofa, mumbling to the floor, my hands suddenly landed on my hips and stuck there. I felt as if I'd grown little wings that would help me to take the fight to some other place, higher and more civilized. That's how I felt when I stood in the middle of the room with my hands on my hips and tried to save our relationship.

We stood on the balcony and looked at the street. I asked if I should cut up a watermelon and Nathan nodded. I went into the kitchen and took the watermelon out of the fridge. I cut it in half and cut one half into cubes and arranged them on a plate and stuck two forks into the top two cubes. I picked out a sweet watermelon this time, and I saw it as a good sign, because I didn't know how people were supposed to feel after a fight. It was our first and last fight. I put the plate down on the ledge, between us, and we ate in silence and went on looking at the street, and then he turned my attention to the palm tree and its burdens.

He pointed to the tree with his fork and with his mouth full of juice he said: "It's about time those dates were stripped from that tree."

I asked why and he said that they were weighing it down.

I didn't want to talk about the tree. I wanted to talk about our relationship. But I'd already said everything I had to say a few minutes before, and now I was standing on the balcony and eating watermelon and having a polite conversation and feeling sorry for a tree and knowing that it was all over.

He said: "If the dates aren't removed, the tree will die."

I asked: "So what should we do?"

And he said: "Nothing. There's nothing we can do."

The plate was emptied and I took it back to the kitchen. I put it in the sink and turned the water on and let it run and in the meantime I tried to think quickly about what to do next, if there was anything it was possible to do. When I returned to the balcony Nathan was already standing with his back to the street, one knee bent and his shoe resting on the stone ledge, crumbling dry geranium leaves he had picked from the flowerpot between his fingers.

I asked if I should cut up more watermelon and he said no. I knew that these were our last moments together and I wanted to buy time. I said it was no problem, that there was a lot more, another whole half, and he said that he already had enough and he thinks he's going to leave now. I asked if this was it, if he was leaving, and he said yes. He stood a minute longer with his big shoe resting on the ledge and said: "I think I better go now." I said: "Yes." He threw the handful of geranium flakes into the street and rubbed his palms together and took his foot down and said: "I'm leaving." I thought: The last thing we did together was eat watermelon.

At the door he said he was sorry. He said he was sorry it had to be this way and I said he didn't leave me any choice. He put his hand on my shoulder and said he didn't understand why it had to be this way and I said there was no alternative. He said again that he was sorry and took his hand off my shoulder and slid his fingers down my arm and looked at me sadly. I closed the door behind him and when I turned the key in the lock I heard his heavy steps going down the stairs and then the intercom door slam shut. I went into the kitchen and saw the half watermelon on the marble counter, wrapped it in a plastic bag, and put it in the fridge and I knew that in a few days I would take it out again, still wrapped in the plastic, and throw it away.

Then I went out onto the balcony. I stood and leaned against the ledge and stared at the street, which looked completely different from the way it looked a few minutes ago, though nothing in it had changed. I looked at the cars turning into the street and disappearing around the corner and at the building opposite with the balconies and open windows and I looked at the palm tree and then the birds arrived. They darkened the sky, came down to perch on the TV antennas and the treetops, and screeched excitedly, sending commands to one another, and then they massed in black bodies on the palm tree and pecked at the dates with hammerlike pecks until they polished them off.

They vanished suddenly and it was impossible to tell if the tree was relieved. The dry, yellow boughs didn't rise, grateful and liberated, and the stooping trunk didn't straighten up after the birds had gang-raped it, hysterically flapping their wings. I was sorry Nathan didn't see it. I was sorry it happened a few minutes after he left. I went inside, closed the shutters and the windows and the balcony door, and said to myself: It's over. I made a clean break. Then I lay down on the sofa and started crying. The phone rang and I didn't pick it up. I counted four rings and the machine answered. My parents invited me to come for lunch on Saturday.

2

I met Nathan at a Purim costume party last year. He was wearing a clown's hat on his head. It wasn't one of the cardboard cones you can buy in a toy shop, but a real jester's cap made of different-colored pieces of cloth, crowned by horns stuffed with some soft material with silver bells sewn onto their tips. It was touching and childish.

I wasn't wearing a costume, because I couldn't imagine anything I really wanted to be that evening, except happier. I was thirty and I wanted to be in love and I wanted self-confidence and peace of mind, and I wanted a home. I assumed that the perfect costume for a woman who had all these things was to go as she was, so in a way you could say that I was wearing a costume.

My last one was a failure. I was five years old and I dressed up as Queen Esther. There were characters I liked better than Queen Esther, who always seemed too biblical and boring to me, but on the other hand I wanted to be like everybody else.

The dress was okay, layers of rustling white satin which I wore over white woolen tights, but there was a problem with the royal shoes. I wanted glass slippers, but my mother, who like a veteran traffic policeman knew how to direct my fantasies into roads that were clear that morning, explained that I had mixed things up. Glass slippers belonged to the story of Cinderella, she said. Queen Esther wore ordinary queen's shoes. I said: "But why can't we buy two bottles of soda and break them in half and I'll go to kindergarten in them?" And she said: "Because it's dangerous and impossible." I said: "But nobody else will have shoes like them." She said: "You don't need what nobody else has. You need what everybody has." I said: "But I'll be the most beautiful." And she said: "Queen Esther wasn't beautiful. Cinderella was beautiful," and relying on my short memory she promised: "Next year you can go as Cinderella."

This sounded logical to me, and since I was the last child in the world who would want to get her fairy tales confused, I proudly put on my sandals, whose straps my mother had covered with silver foil. But that morning it rained cats and dogs—one of the usual disasters that strike children on Purim—and on the way to kindergarten, while my mother held my hand and assured me that everything would be all right and said that it was a pity that at my tender age I should be so sad and sulky, like my father, I stepped in a puddle and the silver foil came off my left sandal. I have a black-and-white photo in my album in which I'm standing and holding up the hem of my dress with my fingers, one sandal regal and the other not, and accordingly, a half smile on my face.

It didn't rain on Purim last year. It was a clear, cold night and I drove to the party in my car. I was wearing a black sweater and jeans and boots. I liked the confident tapping sound they made on the floor. A friend who knew the hosts was supposed to meet me there. I walked into the noisy apartment and looked for her. She said that she'd be dressed as a fairy. I saw a lot of fairies there, but my friend wasn't among them. I went into the kitchen and looked at the rows of beer bottles perspiring on the counter. In the music playing in the living room I heard the soft, intermittent tinkling of bells. I took a bottle and opened it with the bottle opener tied to the handle of the door of the fridge with a long pink ribbon of the kind used to decorate gifts. The bottle opener was disguised too. Someone had covered it with shiny stickers shaped like stars and crescent moons.

The kitchen was crowded with two fairies, a Superman, a Queen Esther, and a tall bald man wearing a cat's mask. I said to myself that if my fairy didn't show up in fifteen minutes, I was going home. I hated parties. They intensified all the feelings that parties are supposed to expel. I thought of pouring the rest of my beer down the sink and leaving, but then I heard the tinkling of the bells coming closer. The clown came into the kitchen looking for the bottle opener.

He was very tall and he had blue eyes, and whenever he moved his head there was a soft tinkling sound. He opened himself a beer, leaned against the counter next to me, and took big gulps from the bottle, staring at the dark living room with a bored expression on his face. I looked at his cap, at the horns bending over his forehead and his ears and tinkling softly. He looked as if he had put the cap on years ago and felt so comfortable in it that he forgot it was there.

The loud music was suddenly replaced by a children's song. The hosts were playing "Little clown, full of glee, you dance with everybody," and the dancers were adjusting their steps to the simple tune and words. They hopped up and down and made questioning gestures with their hands, and cocked their heads from side to side at the "Won't you" of "Won't you dance with me?"

"Would you like to dance?" asked the clown.

I nodded and put my beer down on the counter and followed him into the living room, to a little clearing in the crowd. I found it difficult to perform childish steps in front of a stranger, but the clown skipped and hopped opposite me with a naturalness that seemed almost cynical. He twirled his hands and cocked his big head from side to side, and at the "Won't you" shrugged his shoulders stubbornly. The other dancers looked at us—at the clown shrugging his shoulders and ringing his bells, and at me, treading on the spot and smiling a half smile. He wasn't pretending to dance like a child. That was the way he danced.

I was attracted to him immediately. I was attracted to him even before I saw him. At first I was attracted to the sound of the bells and then I was attracted to the dance which took me back twenty-five years, to that rainy Purim, to the big roomful of children, steeped in the smell of mud and damp poppy-seed cakes and urine, and the strains of this same song, reverberating an awful disappointment. "She cried all morning," the kindergarten teacher told my mother when she came to pick me up at noon. "I didn't know what to do with her, Mrs. Lieberman," she said. "She took off her sandals and sat in the corner. I begged her to put them on and come and dance with the other children, but she only pouted and shrugged her shoulders. I wouldn't let her walk around in her stockings. It's cold today, Mrs. Lieberman. What could I do?"

The song ended and we stood facing each other for a moment and I didn't know what to do. The clown looked abandoned and betrayed; even his cap looked as if it had suddenly wilted. Without a word, he turned his back to me and walked heavily back to the kitchen.

Again we stood leaning against the counter. He introduced himself and said: "Nathan." I said: "Maya," and he said it was a pretty name. "So is Nathan," I said. And he said: "You think so? Actually, I don't like my name." I asked him why, but he only shrugged his shoulders. My eyes were still looking for my friend the fairy, but I didn't care anymore if she came or not. Another Queen Esther arrived instead, and a tiger with red hair, which matched the color of the stripes on her costume, with a long tail bouncing behind her. They embraced Nathan, and he opened beers for them with the costumed bottle opener and then left to dance with them. He didn't say excuse me, or I'll be right back, or see you later.

I watched him dancing with the tiger and the Queen Esther, and thought that it was time to go home. I thought of my bed and the weekend papers strewn over it. I thought of my apartment, of the bathroom, of its moldy smell in winter when the windows are closed, and the damp towels, I thought of my toothbrush, which was old and needed replacing, and I thought of the stained mirror above the sink, and the way from the bathroom to the bedroom, feet shuffling in socks and hand groping along the wall to turn off the lights: the toilet, the light in the bathroom, the fluorescent light in the kitchen, and last the light in the hallway, until only one light remained on—the reading lamp next to the bed which cast a yellow spotlight on my pillow.

I went downstairs and got into my car. I warmed up the engine and melted the vapors on the windshield. When I drove out of the parking space, I looked in the mirror and saw him coming out of the building. I waited for the huge figure in the blue parka to get into a car, but the clown passed my car and the other cars and went on walking with broad strides toward the main road. He stood there for a minute, my headlights illuminating him, the jester's cap on his head and his hands in his pockets. I honked my horn, a short, hoarse honk, and he turned around, surprised. Despite the closed windows, and the humming of the engine in neutral, and my heart beating in anticipation and self-reproach, I could hear the bells coming closer.

He came up to the car, bent down, and stared inside, looking for the faceless honker. I opened the window and asked him if he didn't have a car. "No," he said. "Are you going to get a cab?" "I don't know," he said. "Do you want a ride?" I asked. This was the first time in my life I had offered a strange man a ride, but I thought that someone dressed as a clown couldn't be dangerous. He didn't say a word, went around to the door on the passenger's side, opened it, and squeezed into the seat next to me. The cap got squashed against the ceiling of the car and he took it off and held it rolled up between his hands. I noticed he was going bald. As if he too had only just noticed it, he touched his head apologetically.

My car was too small for him. His long legs were spread out, one knee touching the door and the other pressed against the glove compartment, his body was thrust against the back of the seat which he pushed back as far as it would go, his bare head touched the ceiling. He mumbled his address and the whole way there we didn't say a word. He smelled of wet fur and crushed leaves and the smell flooded the car, drowning out its usual smell of fake leather and plastic and a horrible smell called "Evergreen" dispersed by the air freshener in the shape of a fir tree that hung over the mirror. I got it as a freebie at the gas station, and though I couldn't stand the overpowering chemical smell, I was too lazy to get rid of it and waited for the odor to eventually evaporate. Now the car filled with a different odor, perhaps the one the air freshener was trying to imitate.

I looked at Nathan out of the corner of my eye. He was staring out the window. His enormous hands were resting on the crumpled cap, and I saw that there was dirt under his fingernails, reddish brown dirt that looked like soil. There was something touching about his appearance, something big and slow, with a kind of hostile indifference, and that smell and the little wisps of hair on the nape of his neck. He looked out the window with the same unselfconscious childishness with which he had danced, examining the empty streets and the buildings and the bus stations and the street signs, absentmindedly crushing the cap between his hands and breathing heavily. I drove slowly, with deliberate care, like a forest ranger driving a lost bear back to its lair.

3

A month before I met Nathan my parents got divorced. Since they were already old, my father seventy and my mother sixty-seven, they couldn't do it alone. I had a married sister who lived in Florida. Tali was three years younger than I and she had a one-and-a-half-year-old baby. When I told her on the phone that they were getting a divorce she said: "But I'm pregnant." A few weeks later she really did get pregnant, perhaps to make it clear that she couldn't help us get divorced, because she had a family of her own.

Today she has a boy and a girl and we all have pictures of them on our fridge. Two American children smiling on the doors of three refrigerators.

My parents weren't healthy, and I wondered where they got the courage, or the innocence, to separate, with the decade ahead of them likely to be difficult and ridden with illness, and probably their last. I asked my mother if she wasn't afraid of being alone, if it didn't frighten her that there would be nobody to take care of her when she needed something, a cup of tea in the middle of the night, or if she slipped in the bathtub, and she said no, she wasn't frightened at all. "What's there to be afraid of? I'm independent," she said, "and I have got you."

One scorching Saturday at the end of last summer, we were sitting in the kitchen and she suddenly asked me if I knew a good lawyer. "Maya," she said, "do you know a good lawyer?" My father was standing next to the stove frying an omelette. From the minute she decided on the divorce, a few weeks earlier, she had stopped cooking for him. This was a form of protest she got from a movie she saw on TV, and because of it they now had to take turns frying their eggs.

She offered to make me breakfast but I said I wasn't hungry. I didn't want her to get up and take an egg out of the fridge for me and stand next to the marble counter with one hand on her hip and the other holding the egg waiting for my father to finish with the frying pan. It was ridiculous, this business with the private omelettes. I said that I wasn't hungry, and she asked if I knew a good lawyer and I saw my father's shoulders stiffen, prick up like ears, with the spatula waving and trembling in his hand.

"What do you need a lawyer for?" I asked.

"I don't know," she said. "Don't you need a lawyer when you get divorced, Jack?"

My father shook his omelette in the pan in order to disguise the trembling that began to spread through his body. He stood there frying and shaking, his shoulders talking to us, the spatula scratching the bottom of the pan. When he was angry he trembled, when he was sad he trembled, when he was afraid he trembled, and sometimes he trembled when he was happy, although it was a long time since I'd seen him trembling with happiness. Not even when my sister called from Florida one Saturday a year and a half ago and said: "Congratulations, Daddy, you're a grandfather now." And he didn't look happy a week ago either, when she called to say that there was another baby on the way, and that they hoped that this time it would be a girl.

"So what's this I hear, Daddy?" her voice echoed over the transatlantic line. "You're getting a divorce? What's come over you all of a sudden? Have you gone mad?" "We'll see," my father said. "We'll see. The main thing is that you should take care of yourself." Then my mother snatched the phone from him and asked Tali if she was feeling nauseated. When she was pregnant with the first child, she vomited for nine months. But Tali had been a born vomiter, so it was hard to know with her.

When we were kids, we had to take plastic bags with us everywhere. My mother was relaxed about her throwing up, Tali was a little martyr, but my father couldn't stand to see her suffer. He would hold her forehead and tremble when she threw up. When we were driving in the car and Tali began to wail "Daddy, stop the car!" he would hit the brakes and jump out and open the back door, grab Tali by the arm and drag her to some corner or traffic island, and when she felt better and they returned to the car and she sat down beside me on the backseat, with a content expression full of suffering and satisfaction, I would lean forward and look at my father's feet dancing on the pedals. Tali would press up against me and she too would look at our father's trembling legs, stifling giggles that smelled of puke and a healthy sense of humor, but I was worried. I was afraid that he would lose control of the car and kill us all.

I sat in the kitchen and looked at him standing at the stove and trembling and ruining his omelette.

"I don't think you need a lawyer," I said. "Tali and I aren't minors anymore, you don't own the apartment, you don't have a car or any property to fight over. What do you need a lawyer for?"

She put out her cigarette in her favorite round tin ashtray and sighed. She seemed a little disappointed that she didn't need a lawyer. She was disappointed that her divorce, like her marriage, wasn't particularly dramatic. My father transferred the torn omelette to a plate and sat down across from her. Her cigarette continued to send up spirals of smoke from the depths of the ashtray. They had an annoying tendency, my mother's cigarettes, never to go out completely, especially when my father was sitting opposite her, reading secret messages in the smoke signals like an old Indian chief. "Those cigarettes," he muttered to himself, "twenty-four hours a day," and a drop of oil trickled down his chin.

"You see!" my mother shouted and pointed at my father stooping over his plate. "That's what I need a lawyer for! So he won't nag me all the time!"

"That's why you're getting a divorce," I said. "He won't nag you anymore about your smoking after you're divorced. You don't need a lawyer for Dad to stop nagging you about the cigarettes."

It seemed to me that my mother didn't understand the real nature of her divorce. She thought that the divorce would be a remedial stage in her marriage—a transition from a dull marriage to a thrilling one. She didn't take into account the fact that she would have to separate from my father. She assumed that he would still be there even after he gave her the divorce, that the divorce would hang, framed like a diploma, in the little kitchen, where my father would also be, sulkily frying himself an omelette and trembling, or maybe she thought that she would begin to cook for him again after they got divorced.

"So what are we going to do?" she asked gloomily, staring at my father sitting opposite her and eating without appetite. "How do you get divorced without a lawyer?"

"You go to the Rabbinate," I said.

"The Rabbinate? Where's the Rabbinate? I don't even know where it is."

"The same place you got married," I said.

"Didn't they move?" she asked. "They must have moved by now."

"I don't think so," I said.

"Can you find out for us?" she asked. She pulled another cigarette out of the pack and held it between her fingers, but when she saw my father's gray eyes looking at her over his plate she didn't light it. Maybe she didn't light it because his look no longer begged her not to smoke while he was eating. It was a look that said that he had given up all hope of enjoying his food or anything else long ago, and that he knows where the Rabbinate is. "Jack," she said quietly, "wipe your chin."

"I'll find out for you," I said.

"And find out when they're open and what we have to bring, maybe we need photographs, and how much it costs. Maybe we need witnesses, we needed witnesses when we got married didn't we, Jack? Remember? I hope it isn't going to be too complicated. And ask if you can testify for us too."

"She can't," said my father.

"Why not? Why can't Maya testify? Because she's our daughter? She knows us better than anybody. Her testimony will be the best. Nobody else can testify as well as Maya."

"Because she's a woman," said my father, standing up to put his plate in the sink. "Women can't testify."

"Ah," said my mother and lit her cigarette. "I didn't think of that."

My mother suffered from high blood pressure and she was thirty pounds overweight, but according to her she had a calm and optimistic personality, which was in itself a kind of health, and Tali always said: "I'm not worried about Mother." And in fact she had no reason to worry, because most of the time Mom worried about her. She was surprisingly mature in everything concerning my sister. They were similar, although Tali inherited her thin build and

short, almost dwarfish, stature from our father. They had the same
wavy, auburn hair before Mother's went gray, and the same round,
brown eyes. There were times when they wore the same clothes
and shopped together in the mall and sat in cafés, and smoked
cigarettes together and Tali consulted her freely about boys, although there wasn't much to consult about, because she married
her first boyfriend.

Mom was sorry when Tali went to Florida with her husband,
because she lost her best friend. I felt sorry for her and tried to
fill the gap, but it didn't work out. She made faces when we stood
in front of the display windows in the mall, shuffled her feet when
she was tired, turned down my suggestions to sit down to have a
cup of coffee and rest, and if I did succeed in persuading her, she
would agonize for ages over which cake to choose, pacing back and
forth in front of the display case, until I was forced to order for
her, to put her out of her misery. She let me pay for her when I
offered, she always agreed graciously, without protesting, and I
always offered, because something about her screamed, in addition
to everything else, economic helplessness.

"You'll forgive your mother," she said to me on one of those
exhausting shopping expeditions when we didn't buy anything.
"You'll forgive your mother for being so spoiled, won't you?" I
hugged her when she said that.

"One day, I hope, you'll also have a good man, to pamper you
the way you deserve," she said when we stood on the escalator in
the mall. She always sank into a reflective mood on the escalator.
"But you'll be careful who you choose," she said, her fingers gripping the moving rail, "and find yourself someone strong. He doesn't
have to be too brainy, Maya—you don't need an intellectual. You
need someone to take care of you and love you. A guy with a big
heart. And make sure he's faithful. He shouldn't be a womanizer,
and he shouldn't be thin, Maya!" she said and tripped, as usual, on
the last step. "You listening?" she said as I helped her up, sup-
porting her arm. "Stay away from thin men!"

"But Tali's husband's thin," I said. "Yes," she said, "but Tali is a different story, and Yossi's not so thin anymore, anyway. Tali says he's got a belly on him like a pregnant woman." "And Dad's thin," I reminded her. "Yes," she said, "your father is really very thin, and lately he's been losing weight too and I'm a little worried about him." I never imagined that one year later, one spring day after Independence Day, on the very same escalator, she would tell me, a second before missing the last, sly, step again, that she decided to get a divorce.

I took her to a café and sat her down opposite me and refused to let her hesitate over the cakes. I ordered a Danish for her, although I knew she didn't like them, and I said to her: "You won't last one minute without Daddy." She took a little bite of the pastry and said: "You don't understand." I said: "What, Mother, what don't I understand?" And she said: "It's my last chance." "Your last chance for what?" I whispered, and my mother, her eyes welling up with tears and her mouth spitting crumbs, shouted: "To be happy!"

I was silent, and she sniffed and tried to wipe away her tears with the paper napkin, one of those flimsy napkins you pull out of a metal container that are incapable of absorbing anything. Her lipstick shone with confectioners' sugar. I asked: "But what about Dad?" And she said: "Dad is Dad. You know he doesn't like changes, but he'll manage." She took a little mirror out of her bag and looked at herself, and then she pushed the plate aside and said: "Why did you order me a Danish, Maya? You know I hate them."

We sat in the kitchen. My father washed the frying pan and put it on the rack. My mother began to ask him to get her a pack of cigarettes from the drawer, but she changed her mind at the last minute. Obviously she realized that she couldn't bring a lawyer into our lives and in the same breath, in the stifling air of four eggs

fried in pairs, ask my father to do her a favor and bring her cigarettes. She didn't exactly know what she was doing, but she had a
sense of timing.

She stood up heavily and sighed, went to the top left drawer
next to the stove, and took out a new pack. My father dried his
hands on a towel and replaced it on its hook, and looked at my
mother struggling with the drawer, which refused to close. There
were always problems with this drawer, because it had too many
things in it. He waited in silence for her to say "Enough, Jack, I
can't take it anymore," and when she said "Enough, Jack, I can't
take it anymore," and resumed her seat at the table, peeling the
cellophane off the new pack, he went up to the drawer and closed
it quietly, with one deft little push.

My father bought her the cigarettes. Every Friday he brought
home two cartons from the market. He knew a shop where they
sold them at a reduced price. When my mother asked him for the
address—she had prepared a notebook with essential phone numbers and addresses for after the divorce; it was a child's exercise
book with pictures of Barbie dolls on the cover that she bought in
a stationery shop—he didn't know how to give her directions. "It's
complicated," he said. "You won't find it. I'll get them for you."

"What do you mean?" she asked suspiciously.

"I'll get them for you. Every Friday I'll bring you your two
cartons, as usual. You're not going to quit smoking after we're divorced, right, Deborah?"

"Right," she said. "Actually, maybe I will. After the divorce I'll
quit smoking."

"So write that down in your notebook too," he said. "So you
won't forget."

She gave him a bitter smile, and he said: "But in the meantime,
can I get you your cartons? Would that be a problem?"

"No," my mother said, confused and defeated, and suddenly
her eyes lit up and she said: "But how will you get into the house,
Jack?"

"With my key," he said.

"But I might change the locks," she said. "I think you'd better give me the address of that place anyway. Just in case. Because maybe I'll change all the locks in the apartment."

There was only one lock in our house, which she started referring to as "the apartment" after announcing the divorce. I think she got that from some movie too. Lately she had been watching a lot of American melodramas about women who escaped from their husbands who beat them, or who were alcoholics, taking their little blond children with them, wearing sunglasses and racing over the continent in old cars, realizing their true strength on the way. My mother had never been to the States, and she didn't have a driver's license either. My father had never hit her, and the only time he drank was wine at the Passover Seder. And nevertheless, last summer, with a sad, romantic determination, she began calling our house "the apartment."

Ever since then the house started behaving accordingly, and turned into a three-room apartment with a long narrow kitchen and a rectangular living room with a closed-in balcony, separate toilet and bathroom, and two bedrooms: my parents' room with its huge built-in closet, and mine and Tali's old room, where over the past few weeks all my father's things were piling up on the two single beds.

4

I was disappointed when I dropped Nathan off in front of his building and he didn't invite me in or ask for my phone number. I watched him go inside, pushing his cap into one coat pocket and taking his keys out of the other.

A friend once told me that I frightened men. "You frighten men," Noga said, lighting a cigarette and blowing the smoke away from her. She was one of those smokers who hated cigarettes but liked the habit. "It's a kind of pattern," she went on analyzing my problem, her left hand, with big silver rings on each finger, absentmindedly touching her neck, looking for the huge hickey she showed me when we met. "You see?" she said. "At first they think you're really sweet, and then they freak out."

"So maybe it's their pattern," I said.

"No," said Noga. "I know what I'm talking about. I've seen you in action. I've seen you at school. I've seen you at parties. I've known you for a long time. You just don't know how to play the game."

"What game?" I asked.

"There are a lot of them," she said and tapped her cigarette nervously on the edge of the ashtray, "but in your case I mean the happiness game."

"What's that?" I asked.

"You have to act as if you're happy, okay with your life, even though we both know you're not. And then, at the right moment, and there are no rules about this, so don't ask me how you know when that moment arrives, only then, you start unloading your unhappiness, but in small doses. Not too much at once."

We were sitting in a new café that had just opened next to her house. She liked inaugurating new cafés and then abandoning them. She was hyperactive, and beautiful. Not beautiful in the usual sense; she was short and plump and she had dry, frizzy hair that she had struggled with all her life, wasting money and hope on treatments that only made her hair rebel and frizz all the more, but Noga loved herself, and she did it so wholeheartedly and enviably that the world apparently had no choice but to love her back. I always argued that she loved herself because men had always loved her, but Noga said that it was the other way around. We agreed that it was a classic case of the chicken and the egg.

"This is a nice place," she said and looked around with a bored expression. "Let's make it our hangout." I said, "Okay," even though I knew that the next time we met she would suggest we go somewhere else. "You see?" she went on. "They run away from you because they realize that you're very smart and very sad. For men, brains and sadness are a lethal combination." And in the same breath, impatiently grinding out the half-smoked cigarette, clutching my hand in hers—I felt both the warmth of the hand and the coolness of the rings—she said: "Maya, I promise you that one day you'll see how wonderful it is to come home after a lousy day, the lousiest day in your life, to someone who's waiting for you with a big hug and dinner." And of all her sentences, this was the one that saddened me the most, because for me it was a cliché but not for Noga, and she squeezed my hand in hers and said: "I promise you."

Noga was always involved with men who asked her to come live with them after they'd known each other for a month or two, maybe because she seemed needy to them, as if every day of her life was the lousiest day of her life, or maybe because she was a wonderful cook. For the last year Noga had been alone, because she was in love with someone who had a girlfriend. She was very calm for someone in love with somebody who was in love with somebody else. She was sure that everything would be all right, and she waited patiently.

It was my friend Noga who was supposed to dress up as a fairy. She never made it to that party. What happened, she told me a few days later, was that she was just about to leave home, dressed in a white satin dress she had sewn herself, with layers of tulle and ruffles, and white shoes she had once bought for the wedding of some childhood friend of ours, shoes that were useless except for weddings and costume parties, and she even had a pair of little wings she had worked on for a week, bending wires and attaching transparent parachute silk to them, and a wand she got at a toy shop.

She was just about to put on her coat over her costume and leave, when Amir arrived. He stood in the doorway and announced that he had broken up with his girlfriend. He was on the verge of tears. Noga stood in the kitchen in her fairy costume, with her wand in her hand, and made him tea. The next morning he suggested that they move in together.

She said to me: "You see? You have to be softer, a little more helpless. I know it's not really you, but try. Don't be sad. I already told you, sadness is no good. It frightens them. Too much strength isn't good either. A little strength is okay, it's even sexy, but not too much. You have to find the balance. Try to be a little pathetic, if you can, and you'll see how it works. Like a charm."

I said: "But Amir came to cry on your shoulder. He was the pathetic one. What exactly is the charm here?" And she smiled mysteriously and said: "You don't understand how it works." I said to her: "No. How does it work? A minute ago you told me I had to act happy."

"Sure," she said, "but you shouldn't overdo that either, because then they think that you don't need them. Sure I let him cry on my shoulder. I made him tea and stroked him, gently, nothing sexy or anything, I put my hand on his, and I listened to him talking about his disgusting ex, he talked for about three-quarters of an hour without stopping, and then you're not going to believe what I did."

"What?" I asked.

"I burst into tears!" said Noga and burst out laughing.

"You burst into tears?"

"Yes," she said, "you know me, I can turn the faucets on and off whenever I feel like it. So all of a sudden, when we're sitting there in the living room, and he's telling me how miserable he is and what's going to happen to him now, the tears started pouring out of my eyes. At first he didn't even notice, he was so busy feeling sorry for himself, and then he suddenly looked at me and said: 'What's wrong?' He panicked, you should have seen him. I said: 'It's nothing. I'm sad for you. It hurts to see you like this. I'm sad that in the end we're all so alone in the world.' "

"You said that?" I asked. "Are you serious?"

"Yes," she said. "Something like that."

"But that's such a horrible cliché!" I said.

"Clichés are good," she said. "Horrible clichés are excellent. And you have to learn not only how to say them but also to live them."

She said this and signaled the waitress. She said that she was in a rush. She had to meet Amir at his place. They had made plans to meet at noon and redecorate the kitchen together.

5

The last man I slept with was tall and thin and better-looking than Nathan. Micky also had blue eyes but had thick black hair, and he wrote bad poems. We sat in my place, on the couch, and he showed them to me, poem after poem, holding the pages with the tips of his fingers as if they were fragile or wet. I felt sorry for him when I read his poems. I met Micky at the university. I was working on my Ph.D. in comparative literature and I shared an office with a teaching assistant who would use the room to take naps or fight with his girlfriend on the phone. Micky studied economics and business administration. I found him wandering the corridors of the arts faculty one evening, looking for a pay phone. His battery was dead, he said, and he had to call a tow truck. I told him he could call from my room. We sat in the room for two hours waiting for the tow truck. We talked about cars and poetry. With the same anger that he spoke about the battery that betrayed him, Micky spoke about a woman he had once been in love with. He said it was infuriating because it was a new car. Then he asked if I would like to read his poems sometime.

I told him that they were touching. I even dwelled here and there on an image, and when I saw how flattered he was, I felt even sorrier for him. He sat sunk into the sofa, the pages piled on his knees, and I noticed that he had drawn little pictures on some of them, mainly birds and musical notes. He wrote about rainy streets and unrequited love. Rinat appeared in every line, surrounded by birds and musical notes and fingerprints. She was his girlfriend in high school, his first girlfriend, and she was the inspiration for all this crude sorrow.

My parents' divorce was finalized that morning, and I was glad when Micky called that afternoon and asked if I remembered him, "the guy with the dead battery," and I said: "Yes, of course I do. How are you? How's the car?" "Okay," he said. "Got a new battery," and he asked if he could come over in the evening with his poems.

We sat shoulder to shoulder with the terrible poems between us. When we finished analyzing them he laid them in a pile on the floor and sighed. For a moment longer he went on staring at them, leaning forward, his head bowed over, reading them upside down even though he knew them by heart, and then he put his hand on my shoulder. Even through my sweater I could feel his cold fingers and their feeble weight. I was disappointed that his fingers were so light.

"I still miss her," he said. "Funny, I haven't seen her for fifteen years, but I still have feelings for her."

"What kind?" I asked.

"Sadness," he said, "and a sense of a missed opportunity."

"But you were seventeen," I said. "It was your first love."

"And I guess my last too," he simpered, and his thin fingers tickled my neck. "I've had girlfriends since," he said. "I even lived with someone for a year. I don't know, maybe one day something will happen."

"What will happen?" I asked.

"You'll probably think it's childish."

"No," I said. "Tell me."

"I'm waiting for someone who'll be so different from her, so much the opposite, so much Rinat's antithesis, that maybe because of that I'll manage to fall in love with her. Do you understand?"

"I do," I said.

"I'm dying to fall in love with someone. It would be great to fall in love with someone right now."

"So where is she today?" I asked. "Are you still in touch?"

"No. Not at all," he said. "I hear about her sometimes, through friends. She's already married. She has a child."

"And you're sad that it's not your child," I said.

"Yes," he said. "How did you know?"

"Because I'm smart," I said.

"You really are," he said, "and I really appreciate you reading my poems. It's important to me to know what you think. It's hard to find people who can understand you," he said, "really understand you, I mean. And also let you lean on them a little sometimes. My friends all study economics and business administration. You know what I mean?"

"Yes," I said and laid my head cautiously on his shoulder. "I know what you mean. You can't really lean on them."

"So I hope you don't mind my crying on your shoulder tonight," he said and tapped his fingers on my shoulder, in time to some tune he was humming to himself. I wondered what it was, maybe something he had liked listening to in high school. He cleared his throat and said: "You know what? Sometimes I feel as lonely as a dog," and then the phone rang and I got up to answer it.

It was my father. He had gotten mixed up. He wanted to call my mother and dialed my number instead. He apologized and said: "Oh, it's you, Maya? I was going to call your mother"—this was the first time he had ever called her "your mother"—"Do you know where she is?"

I told him that I thought she was at a lecture at the university. For months she had consulted me about what she should take, what I thought would suit her, leafing through the catalogs as if they were fashion magazines and pointing with her fingernail at all kinds of bizarre courses. This evening she finally took the plunge.

"She told me that she was going to a lecture," I said.

"At this hour?" he asked.

"I don't know, Dad," I said. "Sometimes those lectures go on till late." He said: "Oh, I see," and we hung up. I could hear him walking around the apartment, which didn't have any furniture yet. I wondered if he was sitting on one of the chairs I lent him, the ones I took from their apartment ten years ago, when I left home. I wondered if he was listening now to PBS public radio on his little transistor radio. I wondered if he was crying.

Once in my life I had seen my father's shoulders heaving with sobs. This was a few days after my mother had consulted me about a lawyer. I went into their apartment, opening the door with my key. I didn't expect to find him at home. These were the hours when he ran his errands, the time of day he liked best. Every morning, Monday to Friday between eight and twelve A.M., he roamed the city, getting on and off buses, going in and out of office buildings, holding a shabby cardboard folder under his arm, chatting with drivers and clerks and doormen, making jokes, waiting patiently, happily, on long lines.

He had retired two years earlier. His colleagues in the accountants' office where he worked gave him a farewell party. For months before his retirement he had prepared himself to swallow the insult of the gold watch. "What do I need a gold watch for?" he grumbled, but eventually he managed to persuade himself that he needed one, and on the morning of the party he said: "All right, so a gold watch it is," and before he left for the office he took off his old watch and put it in the drawer of his bedside table. But they didn't give him a gold watch. One of the two partners in the firm, Ofer Horowitz, a man my age, presented him with a fancy executive's diary with an artificial leather cover and an envelope containing two hundred shekels worth of vouchers at a household goods and gift shop. The three typists in my father's department collected money to buy him flowers. There were also cakes from the bakery across the street. With the vouchers my mother bought a wok and began practicing Chinese cooking, but the fancy diary remained closed and appointmentless, lying in its gift wrapping on top of the heap of his old suits that piled up on my childhood bed during the months of that summer and fall.

That morning he didn't go out on his errands. Maybe he saw the crying as an errand in itself, something that had to be done in order to get it over with. My mother was at the hairdresser's. Thursday was her day at the hairdresser. He was sitting on a chair in the living room, facing the balcony. The shutters were closed, but one ray of sunlight entered the room and illuminated the place where he was sitting in a square of light. I don't know if he heard me come in. He didn't make a sound and his shoulders heaved, and I wanted to go up and lay my hand on his shoulder, but I knew that it would be like shutting him up. I stood behind him and waited and when I heard him sniffing I asked if it was because of the divorce that he was crying. He shrugged his shoulders and said nothing.

"It's sad," I said.

"I'm tired," he said. "I'm not sad so much as tired. All this running back and forth to the Rabbinate, at my age. Who's got the strength for it?"

"I'll go," I said. "I'll try to spare you as much running around as I can." But I knew that this wasn't what he meant. He liked going on errands, but he liked errands that had a point, ones that he initiated, and he didn't see any point in this divorce, and it wasn't his initiative, and he was afraid of being alone.

He was a great believer in marriage, my father. He wasn't familiar with anything else. Before he met my mother, who worked for a few years as a switchboard operator at the accountants "Horowitz and Amit," he had another wife, Violet. He never showed us any pictures of her, because he had burned them all. Violet was hit by a bus. My father was married to Violet for ten years and they never had any children. Violet, so Mother told me, was never in a hurry.

It was my mother who poured water over my father when he fainted on the morning he was informed of Violet's death. Violet, who was never in a rush, ran across the street to try to catch her bus, and was hit by a bus coming from the other direction. "Number four," was all my father volunteered when Tali and I expressed a healthy girlish curiosity, and to this day we don't know whether number four was the bus that hit her or the bus she was trying to catch. Mother says: "Both." She doesn't like talking about Violet either.

Mom was sitting at the switchboard when it happened. She saw my father coming downstairs, passing the glass aquarium where she sat, hesitating for a moment at the entrance, touching the wall with his fingers, and then collapsing on the floor. She was the one who had transferred the call from the police to him a few minutes earlier, and she knew it was bad news. When she saw him collapse, she took a jar of flowers—every morning she would buy herself a few flowers on her way to the office in order to make her aquarium seem like home—and rushed over to him. He woke up in her arms, wet and surrounded by daisies, and that's where he stayed.

I promised him I would make some initial inquiries at the Rabbinate, and the next day I drove there, but I was told that my parents had to come themselves. I asked the clerk if it was because I was a woman. "No," he said, "that's got nothing to do with it. The mother and father have to come themselves," he said, "and the daughter can accompany them if they need help." He said "the daughter" as if it was some hypothetical daughter he was talking about. Then he explained where to find parking. "Let the husband and wife come!" he shouted after me as I thanked him for the information and started down the stairs; like a master of ceremonies he cried: "Let the parents come!"—let the royal parents enter the stage.

"Who was it?" Micky asked when I sat down again on the sofa, trying to remember exactly where my head had been. He put the poem he was reading back onto the pile.

"My dad," I said. "He got mixed up. He was trying to call my mom."

"They don't live together?" he asked.

"They got divorced this morning," I said.

"Don't ask, I have terrible problems with my parents too." He sighed.

"Really?" I asked.

"My father broke his leg last week skiing. They were in Switzerland. They go every winter."

"How old are they?" I asked.

"I don't know exactly. Fifty something, fifty-five? Something like that, I think. Wait a minute, my father's fifty-five, he had a birthday recently. And my mother's a little younger, maybe fifty-three, or - two," and suddenly I envied him, not because his parents were so young, but because he didn't know how old they were.

"So your parents got divorced this morning?" he asked.

"Yes," I said, and laid my head on his shoulder again. "I was at the Rabbinate with them. It was a nightmare."

"Yes," he muttered. "You know what? I think she's there too now, with her husband and kid."

"Who?" I asked.

"Rinat. She married a lawyer. Every year they go to Saint Moritz to ski. I think they go to the same place as my mother and father. My mother told me that she saw her there two years ago, with the kid. Never mind," he said sighing. "So now father's home all day and he drives my mother crazy. We got him a Filipino nurse and he drives her crazy too. He's so spoiled. My big brother and I have to go and visit him all the time and be nice to him and to the Filipino nurse and play chess with him. They're not taking the cast off until next month. It's a nightmare."

"It is," I said.

We had sex on the sofa. It was too narrow for both of us, so at some point we slid onto the floor, all worked up, but not enough not to feel we were crushing the pages; not enough to really damage them. When I got up I had a poem stuck to my behind. I peeled it off carefully and apologized, and gave it to Micky who was sitting cross-legged on the floor, horrified by what had happened to his poems. He crawled around on his hands and knees collecting them, smoothing out the corners and blowing on the pages. We drank tea and I saw him hesitate, trying to decide whether to stay the night. I told him that I liked sleeping alone and he was relieved. When he left, I too suddenly felt like writing a bad poem. I knew I was capable of it, but before I had time to start writing I fell asleep.

6

My parents got divorced on a fine day at the beginning of February. I drove them to the Rabbinate, let them off outside the building, told them I'd meet them inside, and went to look for parking. My mother, who was sitting on the seat next to me, got tangled up in her seat belt and couldn't get out, and my father leaned over and tried to extricate her. She fell out of the car, groaning and gasping, clutching his shoulder. Her bag had come open and the contents were scattered over the seat. My father and I tried to put everything back quickly, but someone was already honking behind me and I had to drive off. I saw them in the mirror, standing on the sidewalk, hesitating, my mother waving at me and my father looking at a window display of electronic equipment and watches.

There was no parking in the place where the clerk had promised there would be; apparently a lot of people were getting in and out of marriages that morning, and I had to drive around the block five or six times. On the seat next to me lay a broken cigarette and a mint that had escaped from its wrapping. I wondered whether my mother was sucking one of those mints now, whether she was rummaging in her bag to find my father his sugar-free candies, whether he was sitting next to her, his open palm lying limply in his lap, waiting for her to find the candy while she said "Hold on," even though he wasn't pressing her. I wondered whether they were sitting on a bench in the corridor, waiting for their turn, quietly sucking their candies.

I found parking in one of the side streets and ran back to the Rabbinate. I was afraid I would find them still standing on the sidewalk and waiting for me, but they weren't there. The clerk told me they had already gone inside. I waited outside, on the bench. I took out a book of crossword puzzles I'd bought at the newsstand outside my house that morning, but I couldn't concentrate. I tried to hear what was going on inside, the sound of the marriage ending, the quill squeaking on parchment, a wooden gavel banging on a table, the judges' stifled laughter at the sight of the elderly couple who'd suddenly decided to get divorced one fine winter's day. But no sound escaped from Hall number 2. My parents, who always made such a racket together, got divorced in silence.

When the doors opened they stepped out, dazed and blinking as if they'd emerged from of a movie theater. My mother said that the divorce had made her hungry and suggested that we all have some breakfast. My father shrugged and took his wallet out of his pocket to see if he had enough cash.

We went to a café not far from the Rabbinate. The three of us sat at a small table, round and unsteady, and had nothing to say to each other. My father waited for my mother to take the last cigarette out of her pack. He wanted the pack so that he could use it to steady the table. When she pulled out the last cigarette and lit it, he took the pack, flattened the cardboard with his fist, folded it, and pushed the square under the rocky table leg. As he straightened up, he was flushed and out of breath. He hadn't taken off his coat. Nor had she. He picked up one of the big laminated menus that the waitress put on the table, and hid behind it. My mother smoked pensively. Then she glanced at the menu and asked him whether she should order the large breakfast or just coffee and a croissant. He said he didn't know, and ordered the large breakfast for himself. This included an omelette made with two eggs, salad, cream cheese, swiss cheese, jelly, rolls, fresh orange juice, and coffee. I don't think he was that hungry, but he didn't know where his next meal would come from.

I had no appetite. I never had an appetite in the morning, and never in my parents' company, and especially not now, because of how early it was and the circumstances and the intimacy of the little table, which was still wobbly. They never pressed me to eat.

Tali was the problem child, but this morning they looked at me anxiously when I put the menu down and asked the waitress just for coffee. Their eyes pleaded with me to eat something. Even something small. "Just a little something," my mother urged, to give me strength.

My father paid, my mother behaved naturally. He calculated the tip exactly and left the waitress a stack of ten-cent coins on the saucer. I was embarrassed, but I didn't want to say anything, an hour and fifteen minutes after his divorce. My mother went to the rest room and he stood up, swaying, and put his wallet in his coat pocket together with the little containers of jelly that came with the full breakfast.

We stood outside and waited for my mother. A cold wind suddenly began to blow and all at once the sky clouded over. I tightened my father's red woolen scarf around his neck and pushed the ends into his coat collar. He smiled shyly at me. Then I wiped a crumb from his chin. I was glad to have something to do so I wouldn't have to make conversation. This was the first time we'd been alone together since they had separated. Through the glass front of the café I saw the waitress going over to our table and collecting her tip with irritable, jerky movements; then she pulled the folded cigarette pack from under the table leg and threw it into the ashtray.

My mother came out, a fresh layer of lipstick smeared over her mouth and her thinning gray hair combed back, and smiled at us. She had a radiant smile, my mother, and I wondered whether it was the first thing my father had seen when, thirty years earlier, he had opened his eyes, soaked to the skin and in a state of shock, surrounded by flowers and his coworkers' legs.

We walked to the car where my mother said to my father: "You sit next to Maya, Jackie. I'll sit in the back." It was a long time since I had heard her use his pet name. My father sat next to me and fiddled with the car radio, looking for public radio, his faithful friend. My mother spread out in the backseat, looking from right to left and lightly touching her hair. Maybe she was trying to view the shops, the streets, the buildings, the signs, and the trees through the eyes of a free woman. I think she was disappointed to find that they looked the same as they always had.

I drove her home. She got out of the car, leaned through my father's window, and said: "Okay, drive carefully now. Bye, Jack." My father nodded without looking at her.

I drove him to the place he had rented, not too far from where I lived. It was a two-room apartment on the first floor, and his rent was lower than mine. The former tenant was a film student who'd gone out with Noga, which was how I'd heard about the apartment. It was a real bargain, but my father thought it was highway robbery. For thirty-five years he had been used to paying a ridiculous rent to an elderly landlord who spoke Yiddish and waited patiently for him and my mother to die so he could get the apartment back. My father thought that three hundred and fifty dollars a month was outrageous. I paid five hundred, and to cheer him up I'd suggested we change places. "I'd be happy to change places with you, Maya," he said.

I watched my father going into his new home; he passed a row of overflowing garbage cans and glanced out of habit at the mailbox, which still had the name of the guy who had lived there before stuck to it on a big label. When I got home there was a message on my answering machine from my mother, telling me how happy she was with her new life.

7

He left me a note on the windshield of my car. I was parked next to a hardware store facing his building, and when I came out, carrying rolls of kitchen paper for lining my father's cabinets—I had arranged to meet him at noon to help redecorate his kitchen— I saw a piece of paper folded in two peeping from beneath the windshield wipers. It was a flyer advertising something and I almost threw it away without looking, but then I saw something scribbled on the back: "Regards from the clown," it said, followed by a phone number.

I wondered what Nathan would have done if he hadn't seen my car parked by chance, across the street from his house. Two weeks had gone by since Purim, and I should have forgotten about him by now; nevertheless, just as I was about to go to my neighborhood hardware store, I remembered there was a smaller, more expensive one near where he lived. Luckily I had found a parking space right at the entrance. I stood in the store trying to decide whether my father would prefer flowers, birds, stripes, or a solid color, which I liked, but I couldn't concentrate, because Nathan's image loomed before me and kept multiplying until it became a pattern itself— a huge white sheet printed with his big body, his hands with their dirty fingernails, and his jester's cap.

I stood in the store and remembered the advice single people are always given: Love comes when you're not thinking about it, suddenly, in a moment of distraction—advice that is as depressing as it is encouraging, but mainly full of contradictions, because even if you manage to distract yourself from being obsessed about love by concentrating on *not* being obsessed, the result is that the distraction and its object are one and the same, so what's the point— especially when love is supposed to be the ultimate distraction and the greatest obsession of all.

I bought the striped paper and went out to the street, where I saw the note sticking out from beneath the windshield wipers. I stood and read it two or three times. I tried to guess whether Nathan had seen me getting out of the car or remembered the license number. It didn't make sense that he would remember something like that. I got into the car, turned on the ignition, and read the note again. I put it down on the passenger seat, and at every traffic light studied it again, four words and a number. I hurried home and read the note again on the stairs, then went inside and called Dad to tell him I'd be late.

"How late?" he asked.

"A little," I said. "I have a few things to do. Do you need to go out?"

"No," he said. "Where would I go? I'm waiting for you. I bought grilled chicken. It's good. From the place where your mother always buys."

"I'll be there soon," I said. "But you go ahead and eat. Don't wait for me. I've already eaten."

"You have?" he asked with a kind of despair in his voice.

"Maybe I'll have a bite with you," I said, reading the note again.

"Then I'll wait," he said. "I'm not so hungry either."

I knew Nathan's number by heart. I called him and we arranged to meet in the evening at a little café next to his house. He didn't sound surprised to hear from me so soon. I drove to my father's place and, stopping at the traffic light, I drummed my fingers on the steering wheel even though the radio wasn't on. My father opened the door, holding a chicken leg in his hand.

We had a nice afternoon. Encouraged by my good mood, he did his best to entertain me in his empty apartment. We still hadn't bought any furniture. Every Friday, when I suggested that we look for garage sales in the newspaper, he made some new excuse and said that he could manage, that he didn't need much. He had a single bed and a closet and an old fridge left behind by the previous tenant, and the two chairs I had lent him standing in the living room.

He made coffee and opened a bag of imported cookies filled with white cream and ate four or five of them, one after the other. He lowered his eyes when I gave him a rebuking look, the kind of look he was well used to, although it was less severe than usual today. My father suffered from a dangerous combination of diabetes and an immense, almost infantile, craving for sweets.

He asked me how I was, how much I had paid for the paper, and then looked for his wallet to repay me. I said: "Forget it. It's a present for the new house," and he said, "What do you mean a present? Why should you buy me presents?" and began rushing around the apartment looking for his wallet, holding the bag of cookies in his hand. He found the wallet on the counter in the kitchen, next to the dismembered chicken peeping out of the silver foil.

I sat on the chair and nibbled cookies and gave my father advice on interior design, where we'd put what, whenever we bought it, and I reminded him that it was time to buy some furniture, that he couldn't go on living like this, maybe this Friday we'd go, and he said: "Yes, on Friday. I'm free," his chin full of crumbs. When I got up to leave he saw me to the door, the bag of cookies in his hand, and said: "I'm glad to see you in a good mood, Maya. Don't be annoyed with me for saying so, but you seemed a little depressed lately." As I walked past the broken mailboxes he suddenly called me. I went back to him; he raised the hand holding the cookie bag, stroked my hair, and said he wanted to give me some advice. He hoped I knew that he only wanted what was best for me. I said I knew. Then he blushed. Perhaps it wasn't a father's place to say this to his daughter, he said, perhaps it would be better coming from a friend, but a young girl shouldn't be sad all the time. It made a bad impression. In any case, that's how it was when he was young.

8

Nathan worked in a plant nursery. Every morning he got up at five-thirty and took two buses to the nursery outside the city. "It's a long way," he said, "nearly an hour's trip," but he didn't care. He dozed on the bus, or read the paper. He'd been working there for three years. This is what he told me when we sat in the café that evening, at one of the tables outside, even though it was cold. He said: "I prefer sitting outside, if you don't mind," and I said that I didn't.

He was thirty-four. He had studied at the university for a few years, seven or eight, he said, political science and history, and then philosophy and theater. He had wanted to study law too, but not for money, for justice, even though it sounded silly and romantic. I told him that it didn't sound silly and romantic, and asked why he hadn't been accepted.

"I didn't apply," he said. He'd never finished his B.A. because he didn't believe in degrees. "Neither do I," I said.

"Yes," he said, "but you already have three."

"Two and a half," I said. "I haven't got my Ph.D. yet. And I'm not studying for the sake of the degree."

I had no idea why I was still in school. I wasn't interested in research, I hated libraries, I didn't want to teach, I didn't know what I was going to do after I got my Ph.D., but the university gave me money to carry on so I did. I told all this to Nathan, casually, mocking myself and the university, but he looked at me sadly—perhaps he was already familiar with this female ploy, women putting themselves down so he would like them—and said: "Nobody ever offered me anything like that."

"Maybe you never asked," I said.

"So who did you suck up to?" he asked without looking at me, and dipped the tip of his thumb into the foam on his coffee.

"I didn't suck up to anyone. I had a professor who for some reason thought I was gifted."

"I never had a professor like that," he said.

"Maybe you never stayed long enough in one department," I said.

It was clear that Nathan didn't particularly like me. I thought he would like me more if he knew that I was unhappy, but I remembered what Noga had said about unhappiness and how you had to introduce it carefully, in small doses. "School is depressing," I said.

"Yes," he said, "I think so too."

"Sometimes I just don't understand what I'm doing there."

"Getting a Ph.D.," he said.

"Yes," I said, "but sometimes it seems like a total waste of time."

"Some people waste their time on less important things," he said and licked his thumb.

"It doesn't sound so terrible to me, working with plants," I said. He snickered bitterly and said nothing.

"No, seriously. It sounds relaxing. I wouldn't mind doing work like that."

"Yeah," he said, "sure."

"You know what?" I said, to change the subject. "I thought it was cute, the way you danced."

"Cute?" he said.

"Yes," I said. "Like a child."

"That's the way I dance," he said. He looked insulted. "So what will you do after you get your Ph.D.? Teach some boring course?"

"Yes, I guess I'll teach some boring course," I said.

"Maybe you'll write a book," he said, with a kind of pent-up mockery in his voice.

I said: "Maybe I'll write a book."

"What about?" he asked without raising his eyes from the table.

"About men who dress up as clowns and ask women with Ph.D.s to go out with them, and spend the evening making them feel guilty."

He smiled and said: "I didn't ask you to go out with me."

"No," I said, "you just had an urge to write something and leave it under my windshield wiper. Maybe you're the one who should write a book."

"Yes," he said, "except that I'm not the talented one."

He signaled the waitress to bring the check, and it was clear I wouldn't see him again. I tried to summon Noga's calm voice. Noga would have asked herself what she saw in this guy in the first place. Noga would have stood up and walked away, but I went on sitting there.

We both leaned back in our chairs and stared at the empty mugs and waited for the check. He looked very surprised when he raised his eyes and saw me crying.

He said nothing. He sat and looked at the empty mug and then back at me again, but he said nothing. Then he cleared his throat, leaned forward, and touched my hand with his thumb. I let my hand rest on the table, under his thumb, consoled. He asked me what was wrong, and I said I didn't know.

Nathan took his thumb off my hand and said: "If you like, we can go to my place. I don't like sitting too long in cafés. I get restless."

"Yes," I said, "me too."

He paid for me, even though I'd worked out my share before I burst into tears, but when the waitress came and looked at me with concern and then at Nathan with a questioning face, he hurriedly took out his wallet and pushed my hand away gently when I reached for my bag. He seemed to find it impossible to take money from a crying person, and I liked this. We squeezed into my car, where I stopped crying and was only sniffling a bit, and now and then I took my hand off the wheel to wipe my eyes on the sleeve of my coat. He said I had a nice coat. Like at the party he said I had a nice name. He said it in the same tone, as if he had a limited vocabulary and made the most of it. "Nice coat," he said. "Thank you," I said. "Your coat's nice too." He said: "Really? I don't like it." I said: "At least it looks warm. Mine isn't warm at all." He was about to take off his parka and put it around my shoulders, but I said: "I'm fine," even though I was freezing.

He lived in a small apartment on the top floor of an old building that looked as if it was about to collapse. He made me tea in his kitchenette and then we sat down in the room on a mattress covered with an old velvet cloth in a faded shade of orange. It began raining hard. The rain beat on the tin sheets that covered part of the roof, on the water tanks and solar reflectors standing on it, and heightened the sense that a real storm was raging outside. Our mugs of tea stood on the floor. We sat side by side on the mattress. Nathan leaned his back against the wall and pressed his knees toward his chest. He wore jeans, an old blue sweatshirt spattered with white bleach stains, and work boots with army socks.

He stretched his hands out to the space heater and rubbbed them together. I saw them glowing in the red light of the electric coils; he brought them so close that I bit my lip in sympathetic pain, but Nathan made the little smile that children make a second before doing something naughty, and then he put his hot hands on my cheeks.

My face absorbed the heat instantly. He left his hands there even after the heat had passed from him to me, and then took them away and put them close to the heater again, then put them on my hands and did the same thing again until the whole cycle took on the rhythm of a game. He put his hands against my neck, gathered heat from the heater as if cupping water in his hands, and quickly put them on my thighs. He asked if I could feel the warmth through my skirt and I said yes; my eyes were closed, he was the mediator between me and all the warmth in the world, and when he stopped I felt cold until he took off his blue sweatshirt and draped it over my shoulders.

We spent the night on the mattress. I wanted to tell him about myself but he didn't seem interested, and I too, after formulating a few sentences in my head, lost interest in what I had to say. I was worried about what would happen in the morning, when the magic of the tears and the rain and the game with the heat and the sex had vanished.

At five-thirty in the morning the alarm clock standing on the floor went off. Nathan kicked off the blanket, got up, put on his clothes—the ones he had worn the evening before—and began moving around the apartment. Without saying a word, he washed his face, brushed his teeth, filled the electric kettle with water. I sat on the mattress and picked up my clothes from the floor. He put on his work boots and asked how many spoons of sugar I took in my coffee; I said one, and he put the coffee on the floor, next to the the mug of tea from last night, which was still full. He drank his coffee in big gulps and walked around the room, fastened his watch around his wrist, tied his laces, opened the blinds, shoved his wallet into the back pocket of his jeans, turned off the heater, and stood next to the front door waiting for me to put on my coat.

"What time do you have to be at the nursery?" I asked as we ran down the stairs.

"Six-thirty," he said.

"Do you want me to drive you?"

"No," he said, "it's too far."

"It's no problem," I said. "It makes no difference to me once I'm in the car. And there's no traffic yet."

"Thanks," he said, "but I'm used to taking the bus."

The car was standing outside, gleaming from the rain, a wet flyer stuck beneath one of the wipers. I pulled it out and threw it in the street. I opened the door and before getting in I said: "Last chance!"

He didn't say a word. As on the first night when I offered him a ride, he opened the door and squeezed into the seat next to me.

He stretched out his legs and yawned and rubbed his eyes and the car filled up again with that smell of his. Then he mumbled directions and stared out the window. We drove in silence for ten minutes until we left the city and turned off the main road into an industrial area, driving along a narrow road with small garages on either side, still closed. Then the orange groves began. "We're almost there," he said, stifling a yawn, and pointed ahead, "right at the end of the road," and I felt that time was running out, time in which I had to do something, I didn't know exactly what, but I knew I couldn't let whatever it was slip away. A couple of tears crept into my eyes. They surprised me, and I wondered if I might have harmed myself yesterday by bursting into tears like that, because maybe now I wouldn't be able to stop. I dried the tears, pretending I was just rubbing my eyes, and I yawned.

The sex had been good, but I knew that it wasn't just because of that; this wasn't the first stormy night to dissolve into a morning of fatigue and embarrassment and self-hatred. I was full of dread. The good sex and the weariness and the embarrassment were all familiar, but the dread was completely new.

I turned off the dirt road and Nathan said: "This isn't the turn."

I said: "I know," and stopped the car behind a low concrete building covered with graffiti. I pulled on the hand brake and stroked
his neck and opened his jeans' fly. We moved to the backseat and
fucked. Then we got out of the car, each from his own side, and
slammed the doors and looked, separately, at the view: Nathan
stretched facing the orange groves and I stared at a brown field.
We got back into the front seat, I started the car, and we continued
our journey. When I let him off at the entrance to the nursery,
whose huge tin sign was painted orange and decorated with plants
and birds, he said: "So, good-bye," and walked heavily to the gate.
He took the keys out of his coat pocket and then turned around
and came back to the car—I was still sitting there with the engine
in neutral, yawning and rubbing my eyes to buy time—and leaned
through the window, stammering: "You want to come over tonight?"

9

One day at the end of spring, in the week between the Holocaust
memorial day and the Independence holiday, my mother had a
heart attack. It was mild and it embarrassed her more than frightened her. What good was her freedom, she said, if her heart
couldn't take it? The attack came late at night, in front of the
TV. It was ten to one. Channel One had signed off and she wanted
to go to bed. She stood up to turn off the television. The national
anthem was playing in the background and she suddenly felt pressure on her chest and the famous stabbing in her left arm. She
thought it was heartburn, or gas, because she'd eaten a lot of french
fries that evening, but to be on the safe side, and in a panic which
she found hard to admit even in her hospital bed, she called an
ambulance.

My father was the first to be notified. He told me afterward in
an accusing tone that they had tried to call me from the emergency
room but I wasn't home. I was at Nathan's. When I got home early

in the morning—after that first time, Nathan no longer allowed me to drive him to work; he said he could sleep in the bus, but I knew that he didn't want to owe me anything—there was a message from my father on the answering machine: "Maya, it's Daddy. Your mother had a heart attack," and there was a note of triumph in his voice.

I drove to the hospital in frantic haste. I didn't know how serious it was. My father wasn't at home when I called back, and I assumed that he must be at the hospital, that he had been with her all night. I tried to prepare myself for the sight of my mother in intensive care, surrounded by monitors, pale, perhaps unconscious. Perhaps she had tried to call me when she felt bad, and I wasn't there. Perhaps she thought something had happened to me, perhaps she wondered whether to leave a message and what to say in it. I imagined her standing in the living room between the armchair and the television, between confusion and panic, pressing her hand to her chest, dialing the number for an ambulance while I was only a few streets away in a room on the roof of an old building, lying naked on a mattress covered with a velvet cloth smelling of dust and sweat, relatively happy. I sped through the empty streets and waited for stabbings in my own chest, for the first pangs of guilt, but they didn't come.

I parked in the empty hospital lot, went into the entrance lobby, and waited for the elevator. Next to me stood an orderly leaning on his elbow on a white metal trolley piled with bedpans and kidney-shaped bowls. The smell of disinfectant hit me and challenged the smell I still had on my skin. I stood next to the orderly in the elevator and sniffed my fingers and thought that sex could make a person calmer, wholer and stronger, that it beat anything: death, heart attacks, and all kinds of tragedies happening in every room, on every floor, at every minute—as if it were a big cross being waved by priests and nuns to scare off the devil.

The elevator stopped on the eighth floor and I went into the cardiology ward. I passed an old woman shuffling her feet in terry-cloth slippers and dragging a pole with intravenous bags swaying back and forth like transparent fruit. Next to her, a young woman held her elbow, trying to match her steps to the impossibly slow gait of the old woman. It was hard to tell if the young woman was a daughter, granddaughter, or hired help. And I thought: Mom has exactly the same slippers. And maybe later this morning I would take her for a walk in the corridors, and hold her elbow and crawl along by her side. I looked at the two women disappearing at the end of the corridor and thought of the night before.

Every morning when I came home—Nathan always insisted that we meet at his place—I would lie down in bed and go over every detail and the day would pass quickly. I checked papers and exams and gave everyone high marks, in the lazy haze and sudden generosity I felt toward the world. And when evening began to fall I tried to guess if Nathan was on his way home, if he'd changed buses at the central bus station, if he'd found a seat, if he'd reached his building, and if he was climbing the seventy-five steps to his apartment, standing in the kitchenette, drinking water from the bottle in the fridge, glancing at the note stuck to the door with a magnet, where I had written my phone number which he hadn't learned by heart, dialing and saying: "Hi, I'm home." And I would ask: "So how was work?" And he would say: "The usual," and I'd be sorry I'd asked, because we didn't ask each other questions, especially not the mundane kind couples asked each other—and he would say: "So do you want to come over?" and I'd hear him swallow a big gulp of water and say: "Yes."

We had been seeing each other for two months every night except for weekends, which he wanted to keep for himself. I had no idea what he did on the weekends and I didn't ask. I didn't tell anyone about Nathan, except for Noga, who of course took a dim view of the whole thing. "You can't build a relationship on sex," she said, when we sat in her and Amir's kitchen on Saturdays, and I said: "I know," and she said: "You don't give a damn about what I say."

In the mornings, when I came down the seventy-five stairs in Nathan's building—I always went up fast and came down slowly—

I thought about Nathan getting dressed in his little room on the roof, rubbing his eyes and splashing cold water on his face, searching for his wallet because he always forgot where he'd put it during the night, standing at the deserted bus stop, dozing or reading the paper on the bus, looking out at the garages and the orange groves, the landscape that could have been part of my daily routine as well if we'd been a real couple. But there was an element of quiet bravura in me which said everything would be all right, that you couldn't go to bed with someone almost every night with such passion for such a long time without something happening in the end, good or bad. So I waited. I stood in front of the nurses' station and asked about my mother and the nurse said: "Mrs. Lieberman is in room number two," and pointed the way.

Room number 2 was quiet and bathed in sunlight from the eastern window. My father was sitting next to her bed, on an orange plastic chair, reading a newspaper. My mother was lying on her side, facing the door. When she saw me, she sat up in bed and smiled and said: "You can go now, Jack. Maya's here. Thank you very much for coming. I appreciate it very much." My father stood up, folded his paper, and looked at me, confused and embarrassed, as if he wanted me to intervene on his behalf and prevent his banishment from the room.

"Tell your mother to stop smoking," he said as I got into the elevator after him and rode down to see him to the bus stop. "There's no need," he said. "Go be with your mother. Don't leave her alone," but I said that it was all right, that I'd keep him company for a while. In the entrance lobby he stopped at the kiosk and scanned the rows of candy. I wanted to remind him that they were forbidden, but I said nothing. He bought a chocolate nougat bar and slid it into his coat pocket. My father had a gray woolen coat that he had worn every winter for as long as I could remember. I don't know what he saw in this coat, which was bulky and ugly, and in any case it was already too warm for a coat. Perhaps he liked it because of the big pockets where he could hide things.

When the bus came I kissed him on the cheek, and promised

to call and fill him in when I got home. He hadn't shaved and had prickly stubble on his cheek. I went back to my mother's room, which she was sharing with an old woman who was lying with her back to us with her face to the window, and all I could see was a mop of white hair sticking out of the blanket like mattress ticking. I thought: Maybe it's the old woman I saw in the corridor, exhausted from her walk. I asked my mother if they'd already told Tali.

"Why worry her?" She smiled at me. "It's nothing. The doctors say it's nothing. In two or three days I'll be back home."

"Still," I said, "I think we should let her know."

"There's no need, Maya," she said. "It's really not worth it. Do me a favor, don't call her. I don't want to worry her. The little one has an ear infection and Tali hasn't had a good night's sleep for a week. Leave it. In a day or two I'll be back home and we can call her then."

She was sent home after a week. My father didn't visit her in the hospital again, but he called me twice a day. I don't know if he was really concerned, or just bored. The doctors gave her a list of strict instructions. She wrote it all down in her notebook, which she asked me to bring to the hospital. In the car on the way home she read the list aloud to me in a resentful voice. She had to stop smoking, lose weight, give up fried foods, and start doing moderate exercise, walking or swimming, for example. "I can't make so many changes at my age," she said, cramming the notebook into her bag, opening the window, and lighting a cigarette.

I asked if she wanted me to stay for a few days. She said: "Absolutely not!" I said: "Mom, you need someone with you." She said: "Don't start making a fuss, Maya. I'm not dying." I said: "Still, I'll feel better if I know you're not alone at night," and she said: "Okay, if it will make you feel better, then okay."

I stayed with her for four nights. I left Nathan a message saying that my mother had had a heart attack and I couldn't come for the next two days, and that I'd see him on Sunday night. That night, and the next, and over the weekend, I checked to see if I had any messages. There were a few from Noga and from my father. On the last night, after I got up to turn off the television, my mother leaned back in her armchair, sighed, lit a cigarette, and said: "I envy your generation of young women." I asked her why. She was silent for a moment and said: "Because it's easier for you. You're more liberated." Then she confessed that she had never enjoyed sex. "Daddy wasn't a very good partner," she said, and he was the only one she'd had. I didn't know if she felt the need to confide because she was afraid of dying, or because she didn't want to go to bed. It wasn't too late, I said, even though it was clear to us both that it was.

10

It was pleasant sitting in Noga and Amir's kitchen. There was always a breeze coming in from the balcony and plants everywhere. On a Friday afternoon at the end of June the air was as sticky and humid as usual, but in their kitchen, for some reason, it was always pleasant. Amir walked around the apartment in shorts, bare chested and barefoot, holding a bunch of grapes and dropping them one by one into his mouth, throwing his head back and catching them in the air; Noga jerked her head at me as if to say look at that clown. When Amir came close to her, dangling the bunch of grapes between his fingers, she sprang to her feet and plucked one and pulled the elastic of his shorts open and threw the grape into them. Then she began running around the apartment shrieking and laughing and Amir made a face at me as if to say look at that baby; he chased her and suddenly it was quiet and I heard them kissing in the living room.

They invited me to stay for dinner; they were thawing frozen hamburgers, but I said I had plans and left. I got into the car, turned on the air conditioner, and began driving around the streets. The sun was already starting to set, too slowly, and was still blazing. The radio was playing quiet Hebrew songs. I had no plans.

I thought of stopping to call my father, to ask if he wanted to look for furniture. I knew he didn't want to furnish his apartment, that the two chairs I had lent him only served to emphasize the emptiness, which was the most powerful emotional statement he had ever made, more effective and sophisticated than his trembling. But I also knew that if I called to say I was free and offered to go bargain hunting, he would jump at the chance not to be alone on Friday night, even at the price of a few pieces of second-hand furniture.

But I didn't call. I drove aimlessly until I found myself on Nathan's street. I parked and got out of the car and walked around for a while. The stores were already closed, including the hardware store, whose locked shutter filled me with sudden longing for that winter morning, for the note beneath the windshield wiper— regards from a clown and a phone number, that was all—and especially for the moment when I could have chosen not to call.

A candy store was still open, and I bought a Popsicle. This must be the place where Nathan bought his newspapers. On Sundays I would find them scattered around his apartment, on the kitchen table or the bathroom floor, on the mattress and the carpet, a few pages blowing around the roof, the crossword puzzles always solved in a red marker, which seemed a little strange because he'd once said that he hated crossword puzzles.

I had climbed thirty steps before I realized what I was doing—I was going up to his apartment on a Friday afternoon. When I reached the roof and knocked softly on the tin door I was bathed in perspiration. Nathan opened the door. He was in his underwear and looked as if he'd just come out of the shower. He kept a tight grip on the edge of the door, which was boiling hot in this weather, as if he was trying not to open it but also not to shut it in my face, and said: "What are you doing here?"

"I thought I'd surprise you," I said.

"You did," he said.

"Are you in the middle of something?" I asked.

"Not exactly," he said. "But I'm expecting someone."

"Guests?" I asked.

"Sort of."

"It's boiling hot," I said.

"Yes," he said and shifted his weight from one foot to the other. The whitewashed floor was blazing too.

"It's a scorcher outside," I said and noticed that I was still holding the Popsicle stick in my hand.

"You want something to drink?" he asked.

"Yes," I said, "water. I'm dying of thirst."

He opened the door and said: "Okay, come in for a while."

The apartment looked different. It was tidy, the clothes were all put away, the dishes were washed and stacked on the rack, the fridge, I noticed when Nathan opened it to pour me a glass of water, was full of food: cheese and all kinds of yogurts. In a big plastic bowl on the top shelf there were peaches, grapes and apricots, and a mango. Nathan hated fruit.

I asked: "Is everything okay? You seem a little nervous."

He said: "You shouldn't have come without calling."

I sat down on the mattress and drank my water. Nathan leaned against the wall and, drumming his fingers, he said: "Someone's coming any minute."

"A friend?" I asked.

"Sort of," he said.

"Not a friend?"

"No," he said. "But you shouldn't have come, Maya. You should have called first."

Sigal lived on a kibbutz. Every Friday she'd leave her kibbutz in the north, spend three and a half hours on two buses, get off at the central bus station, buy flowers, and take another bus, her bag hanging from her shoulder, near the black ponytail and long earrings made of colored birds' feathers. She would get off at the stop next to the hardware store, cross the street, climb the seventy-five steps to the apartment on the roof, knock on the tin door and go inside, and stay till Saturday night.

They had spent the weekends together for five years. He said:

"There's someone I've been seeing for a few years now." I asked: "How many?" And he said: "Five." And I asked: "What's her name?" And he said: "Sigal." And I asked: "Where's she from?" And he mentioned the name of her kibbutz and explained where it was, sketching a map of the country in the air. I asked what she looked like, and he said: "What difference does it make?" And I said that it made a difference and he said: "She's about your height, she's got long black hair in a ponytail."

I invented the earrings, but not the flowers. When I came on Sundays and saw the flowers standing wilted in a jar on the marble counter, I had been touched, as I was touched by the down on Nathan's back. I liked the fact that he was a man who bought himself flowers.

I asked: "So the flowers are from her?" And he said: "Yes," and I asked: "And is she the one who does the puzzles?" And he smiled and said: "Yes. Sigal's addicted to crossword puzzles."

I asked whether he loved Sigal and he said he didn't know. They had been together for such a long time, he supposed he loved her. He stood in his underwear leaning against the wall, drumming on it with his fingers, and glancing at the clock.

I asked if he loved me, and he shook his head. I asked why he and Sigal didn't get married, and he said it wasn't that kind of relationship. "So what kind of relationship is it?" I asked. "Different. There's no obligation," he said. "That's why it was okay for me to be with you, too. I didn't feel I was cheating on her, or anything." "And me?" I asked. "Did you feel you were cheating on me?" "I don't know," he said. "Does Sigal know about me?" "No," he said, "I didn't tell her." "So you're cheating on Sigal," I said.

"I didn't lie to you, Maya. I never lied."

"No," I said, "you didn't lie. You just didn't tell me that on the weekends you were fucking somebody else."

"Don't talk like that," he said. "I understand that you're angry, you have a right to be angry. But that's not the way it is."

"Sigal's late," I said. "Shouldn't we be worried? She's late."

"I guess you don't want to see me anymore," he said.

"I didn't say that."

"So you want to?"

"We don't really have time to talk about it now. We're expecting company."

"Right," he said, "but I'm willing to go on as before. I like you, Maya. I like being with you. I have no problem with going on as before."

"Sure you haven't," I said. "Enjoying the best of both worlds."

"It's not about enjoyment. Things just worked out that way."

"No," I said. "It's not about enjoying yourself. You're really suffering. Anyone can see how much you're suffering. Sunday through Thursday you screw the city girl and on the weekends you screw the country girl."

"Don't talk about her like that. You have no right. You don't even know her."

"But she's your girlfriend. So maybe it's time I got to know her."

"She's not exactly my girlfriend."

"Like I'm not exactly your girlfriend?"

"Yes," he said. "Exactly."

"So who's the other woman: me or her?"

"I don't know, Maya. Why does it matter?"

"It matters. Who? Me or her?"

"Neither."

"Neither?"

"Both of you."

"Both of us are the other woman?"

"No."

"So who?"

There was a loud, confident knock at the door, the knock of someone who had come a long way and knew she was expected. Nathan detached himself from the wall and gave me a frightened look. I heard the door open and Sigal say: "Hi! What a scorcher!" and then the sound of a little kiss. She came into the room, with her backpack and her ponytail, shorts and a tank top. There were no earrings and she wasn't wearing a bra. Her breasts were as small as an adolescent's. She put the flowers on the bookcase. She said a hesitant "hello" and looked at Nathan, who said: "This is Maya, she's a friend of mine."

Sigal dropped her backpack and said: "I'm Sigal," and I said: "Nice to meet you, finally. Nathan's told me so much about you." And she said: "Really? What did you say?" and she hugged him and tickled him and he wriggled out of her embrace and asked us both if we would like some fruit. He said there was some washed fruit in the refrigerator.

11

I had promised to make a salad to take to lunch at my mother's on Saturday, but I forgot and arrived empty-handed. My mother said there was plenty to eat anyway, and at the last moment she had invited Dad too. "We're not enemies," she said.

My father arrived, sweating, too warmly dressed, holding a bottle of rosé wine which he handed to my mother. She thanked him and asked if she should put the wine in the fridge. I told her to put it in the freezer, and she told my father that everything would be ready in a minute—he should sit down and relax. He sat down hesitantly on the sofa, testing it for comfort, as if he were sitting on it for the first time.

"I didn't sleep all night." He sighed. "The mosquitoes were killing me." He leaned back, took a handkerchief out of his pants pocket, and wiped his forehead. "So, what's your mother cooking?" he asked. I said I thought she was making her pot roast with potatoes, with cold soup for starters. "Yogurt soup?" he asked hopefully. "Yes," I said, and he said, "Good! Perfect for this weather." I was supposed to bring a salad, I told him, but I'd forgotten, and he said never mind, there was plenty to eat.

I hadn't slept all night either. After leaving Nathan and his guest I drove around aimlessly till it got dark. I considered calling Noga and Amir and asking if their dinner invitation was still on. I knew they'd be happy to feed me and discuss my situation, but I didn't know what my situation was. Sigal was much prettier than I, and she looked younger too, and she radiated the serenity of someone who didn't know she was being cheated on. I did know, and even though I hated her I began to feel sorry for her too, because she didn't. She came in all innocence from the kibbutz, three and a half hours on the bus, with those flowers she bought at the bus station, and she knew nothing. I couldn't stop thinking about her breasts, which looked as if they'd stopped developing at a certain stage and stayed small and perky. I parked outside my house and sat in the car for a few minutes longer with the air conditioner on. I didn't hate her and I didn't feel sorry for her. I was jealous of her. Not only for her breasts, but also for not knowing.

I could have not known too. I could have stayed with Noga and Amir for dinner, helped them cut up the salad, eaten a hamburger, and then watched TV, gone home, and still not have known. I could have taken my father shopping for furniture and one more weekend would have gone by not knowing, like the one before and the one that would follow.

I sat on the sofa and watched my mother setting the table. I looked at my father standing up and sitting down, standing up and offering to help, my mother declining his offer as he sat down and stood up again, not knowing what to do with himself, taking out his tattered handkerchief and wiping the sweat off his face.

The night before, after I got home, I stared at the TV for a few hours, switching from channel to channel, all the time the thought flickering in my mind that I'd promised to make a salad. I said to myself: You're too practical, the salad isn't important now, but at a certain moment I jumped up from the sofa and ran to the kitchen to see if I had salad stuff. Of course I did—I'd bought it that morning at the vegetable stand. The visit to the vegetable stand seemed like an event from the distant past, and suddenly my previous situation of not knowing seemed to me even better than the situation I wanted to be in with Nathan in the future because up until a few hours ago the not-knowing had at least been mine. Nathan had never been.

A little before midnight I considered calling Noga, but I knew she would insist on my coming over right away. And while I was hesitating on the other end of the line she would make a face at Amir to say: "Maya's having a crisis and she's coming over," and he would nod to say that it was fine with him. I hesitated until it was too late to call. I knew I could wake them. They'd understand. They'd come to get me in Amir's car, explaining that I shouldn't drive in my present state, but I didn't want to declare a state of emergency. I wanted to think about things logically and calmly. I wanted to be practical.

I opened a bottle of beer and dragged a chair onto the balcony, sat down, put my feet on the rail, and looked at the sky, covered with hazy clouds. I closed my eyes and let my head fall back and tried to convince myself to relax because nothing terrible had happened. But I couldn't relax and I couldn't convince myself that nothing terrible had happened. On the other hand, I said to myself: What do I actually know about him? After all, we'd hardly talked. We'd had sex for five months. I'd never asked him what he did on the weekends. If I had asked he would have been forced to lie. It was too bad I hadn't asked, because then at least he would have lied, and he hated lying, and it would have made him suffer. On the other hand, maybe he wouldn't have lied, and what I now knew I might have known five months ago. Since I had been relatively happy for the past five months, I was glad I hadn't known, because five months of happiness, even a relative happiness that turned out to be groundless, was still nothing to sneeze at.

I returned the chair to the room, closed the balcony door, got into bed, and tried to read the paper. The weekend papers were strewn across my bed, and I thought that doing a puzzle would be the best way to calm down. I got up to get a pen and went back to bed, cheered up by having something to do. I solved three definitions easily one after the other, but my thoughts strayed back to Nathan's apartment, effortlessly climbing the seventy-five steps.

I looked at the clock next to my bed. It was ten to one. I wondered if they were screwing. Although the thought was unbearable, I tried to visualize it to the bitter end so I could get rid of it, and at the same time filled in some more definitions in the puzzle. I bit the pen and tried to guess: Who was on top and who was underneath? Sigal didn't seem the type to be on top, but what did I know? You can't tell what people are like in bed by the way they look or talk, or just because they have innocent-looking breasts.

I got out of bed, took the puzzle and the pen, grabbed another beer from the fridge, dragged the chair back to the balcony, and turned on the light, around which moths clustered frantically. I went on with the puzzle and thought: Tomorrow Sigal will get up and they'll drink their coffee at their leisure, not the way we drink ours when Nathan's in a hurry to go to work. And Sigal will wash her face, maybe she'll take a crap, and then she'll sit down at the kitchenette table, eat fruit from the big bowl, take the red marker out of her backpack, and solve all the puzzles in a flash; I'll come on Sunday and see the papers strewn all over the apartment and the flowers—I couldn't remember what she'd brought this time, carnations I think—wilting in the jar.

Again I felt uncomfortable on the balcony. I left the chair outside in case I wanted to go back there; it was already two o'clock and hard to tell how the night was going to develop. I closed the door, got into bed, and turned off the light. Again I thought about Sigal's breasts. Noga had the same kind of breasts. A second before I fell asleep I reminded myself that I had to make a salad tomorrow.

My mother, father, and I sat around the kitchen table and ate in silence. We never used to eat in silence, and now it was like a powerful spice that made the soup and the roast and the potatoes inedible. My father was sweating heavily, and my mother moved the fan closer to him. He crammed a little potato into his mouth as the sweat dripped from his forehead onto his plate. Mom asked if he was feeling all right and he said yes. He complimented her cooking. She took a clean kitchen towel out of the stubborn drawer, which now opened and closed without difficulty, wet it, and gave it to him. She said: "Jack, wipe your face. You're sweating like a pig."

When we finished eating, he stood up to help clear the table, but my mother took the stack of plates he collected and said: "Sit down, Jack, you're a guest."

He went into the living room, dragging the towel and the fan with him. He plugged it into the TV socket and sat down in front of it, in my mother's armchair. "You really don't look so good, Dad," I said. "You're a little pale. Are you sure you're okay?"

"I'm fine," he said. "It's just so hot today."

Mom brought out ice cream and cake. She apologized for not having time to bake, so she had bought a Black Forest cake. She said: "It's for Maya, Jack. You shouldn't eat it. It's got tons of sugar."

My father looked at the cake in disappointment. Mom said she'd wash some fruit for him. She went into the kitchen while he cut a big slice for me and a smaller slice for himself. I forgot to scold him, or perhaps I was just too preoccupied with my new situation, the state of knowledge, which demanded a new mindset. Maybe I just didn't care; my father was a grown man, let him eat what he liked, let him enjoy himself.

I heard my mother washing the fruit, and I looked at my father sitting in the armchair, gobbling cake.

My mother returned carrying a glass bowl full of fruit: apples, apricots, and peaches glistening with water, and a cut melon with three little forks stuck in three of the cubes. My father's face was glistening as well, from the sweat and from what looked almost like happiness. The cake was delicious, and he gathered up the crumbs with his fingers and popped them into his mouth.

Mom held the bowl of fruit in one hand and the melon plate and forks in the other, and turned from him to me with an accusing look. "Eat the melon, Jack. Eat the melon instead of the cake," she said, lifting the bowl and the plate as if raising them in the air would elevate their status, but my father didn't answer. He smiled apologetically and his wet face turned pale, his head flopped to the side, and he passed out.

My mother stood there a moment longer with the fruit, not knowing what to do, and I hurried over to my father who, although he was unconscious, was still gripping the edges of his plate with both hands.

By the time the ambulance arrived he had regained consciousness and was mumbling all kinds of apologies. The paramedic took his blood pressure and said he was all right. "He's got diabetes," I said. "It's nothing," my father said. The paramedic asked a few questions, how old he was, if he had had other fainting spells recently. I said that he was seventy; my mother corrected me and said: "Seventy-one, he had a birthday in May." My father looked around apathetically. The paramedic asked again if he had fainted before, and my mother said: "No. He hasn't."

"I have," my father mumbled.

"You have, Jack? When?"

"I have," he said.

"When, Mr. Lieberman?" the paramedic asked and suddenly decided to take my father's pulse, and while he was kneeling next to him and holding his wrist my father mumbled again: "I fainted."

"Maybe we should take him to the emergency room?" said my mother.

"No need," said my father.

"There's no need," said the paramedic. "His blood pressure's normal. I want you to keep an eye on him, Mrs. Lieberman. You and your daughter should monitor his condition. See that he takes a lot of liquids. Especially in this heat. And maybe you should go and lie down, Mr. Lieberman."

"Yes," said my father, "I feel a little tired."

"Come along, let's help you up," said the paramedic and bent over him, raising him by his armpits. Dad and the paramedic walked together with measured little steps to the bedroom, the paramedic holding him gently by the elbow. My mother whispered to me to follow her to the kitchen. She dug her nails into my arm and said we couldn't leave my father alone at night.

I said I knew that, and I would stay with him. She said she'd gladly let him stay in her apartment, but the sofa was very uncomfortable, you sank right into it. "And in the room with me"—she turned her head in the direction of the bedroom with a panicky movement—"isn't such a good idea." I said I understood, but we should let him sleep for a while because it was too hot to go out. She said: "Of course," and the paramedic came in and gave us instructions. He told my mother to keep an eye on him, he was sleeping now, but when he woke up he had to drink, by force if necessary. During the night, he had to be woken up and given liquids, and my mother said: "Yes, thank you very much, I'll see to it that he drinks."

She saw the paramedic to the door, thanking him all the time, and I went to see Dad. He was lying on his side, covered to the waist with a floral sheet, his mouth open, one hand under his head and the other lying limply on his thigh, the fingers trembling in his sleep. The paramedic had rolled up his sleeve to take his blood pressure, and there was a row of insect bites on his arm. I went out on tiptoe but he called me.

"Aren't you asleep?" I asked. He must have heard us talking in the kitchen.

"I'm just dozing," he said. "Maya, you don't need to sleep at my place."

"You'll sleep at my place, Dad. You'll be more comfortable."

"There's no need," he said. "I don't want to be a burden."

"It's no burden, Dad."

"Don't you have plans?"

"Not today."

"You sure?"

"I'm sure, Dad. It's all right. You'll rest at my place. We'll watch TV and have something light to eat. I have lots of vegetables in the fridge. And we'll see how you feel tomorrow."

"I'm not ruining your plans for Saturday night?" he mumbled into the pillow.

"No," I said, "you're not ruining anything." And I bent down to kiss him on the forehead. "I have no plans."

"You're a good girl," he said in a sleepy voice.

"Go to sleep, Dad," I said and let down the blind.

"An angel," he said, and I tiptoed out of the room.

12

At the end of summer Tali told us she was pregnant again. "My sister's pregnant," I said to Nathan one night, when we stepped out onto the roof for a breath of fresh air. We stood barefoot on the whitewashed floor which was still hot; he looked down at the street and asked if it was her first child. I said no, it would be her third, and he asked how old Tali was. I said she was three years younger than I, that she had a child for every year between us; he nodded and went on looking down at the street and I realized how little he knew about me.

"Tali has a boy of two and a half and a girl of seven months," I said. "Her husband, Yossi, is a computer whiz and makes a lot of money. They went to America seven years ago." Suddenly I wanted to talk. "They live in Florida," I said.

"The boy's called Michael, and the girl Jennifer. If they have another son they're going to call him Jonathan," I said. "That's what Tali said. If it's a girl, they haven't decided yet. They can't make up their minds between Kim and Naomi, pronounced the American way. Nay-oh-mi. They'll never come back here," I said. "How can they come back to Israel with a daughter called Jennifer?"

Nathan said he liked the name Jennifer. Then he asked if I wanted children. I said yes, very much, and he said that Sigal wanted children too.

Since that weekend we had begun talking about her freely.

When I showed up at his place on Sunday night, after taking my father home, I sat down at the table in the kitchenette and picked up one of the puzzles to see if there was something she hadn't solved, but she'd done it all, and I said to Nathan: "Sigal's a whiz." He didn't know what to say. He smiled shyly, as if I'd complimented him, and not the girl he loved. He hadn't called me during the day and looked a little surprised when I showed up as usual around nine. He opened the door, placed a consoling hand on my shoulder, and asked if I wanted a beer; I nodded and sat down at the table facing the pile of newspapers.

I asked about their weekend as he handed me the bottle. He said it had been terrible. Sigal had come down with food poisoning and they'd spent Saturday in the emergency room.

"We went to some fish restaurant," he said. "It was her birthday."

She must have eaten something bad. At one in the morning she began to throw up. At first they thought it would pass, but it didn't. "Poor thing," he said, "all night long I held her head." At five in the morning he called a cab and took her to the hospital. Sigal was dehydrated and had a fever, and Nathan said that she could have died. "You should have seen her," he said, "the shape she was in." They gave her an intravenous and kept her under observation until the evening. She only went back to the kibbutz this morning. He refused point-blank to let her take the bus last night, even though she was feeling much better. "Even so," he said, "it's a three-and-a-half-hour journey." He had wanted her to stay tonight too, to be on the safe side, and for his own peace of mind, but she had too many things to do on the kibbutz. She had promised to call the minute she got home. I might have found her here tonight too if she hadn't had so much to do on the kibbutz, and I thanked her in my heart.

We had sex as if nothing had happened. While we were in bed, I imagined him and Sigal together. It comforted me to think that at least this weekend they hadn't slept together because of Sigal's food poisoning. Then Nathan got up and went naked to the kitchenette to get a bottle of cold water; he took big gulps from it on the way back to bed. He lay next to me on the mattress and kissed me on the shoulder. His lips were cold. He said he was glad I'd come. He was sorry about Friday and the way it had happened. He put his hand on my shoulder and squeezed it a little and said he was glad I'd decided to come back.

When we stood on the roof for a breath of air I told him about Tali and her pregnancy. I told him about her vomiting and how we would take bags with us everywhere when we were children. He said that Saturday and going to the emergency room with Sigal he realized how awful it was to throw up, and that you had to be really careful with fish.

"Yes," I said, "especially in summer."

We stood on the roof because it was stifling inside. I said I couldn't wait for the summer to end. He said he felt the same. I loathed the summer; he said this summer had really been unbearable. I asked him how old Sigal was, and he said twenty-six. I said: "Yes, that's right, you were celebrating her birthday, at that fish restaurant." I asked him when she planned on having children, and he said she wasn't in a hurry. Now that we'd started talking, we had to go on. It was more exhausting than anything else we'd done. He was silent for a few minutes, trying to find something interesting to talk about, and he asked if Tali and I were alike. I said no. He asked who I looked like, my mother or my father, and I said neither, but there were people who found some resemblance between me and my mother. Then he asked what my parents did.

I told him they were both retired. My father had been an accountant, and my mother never had a career. She worked for a few years as a switchboard operator in my father's office, which is how they met. He said it sounded romantic. I told him it was less romantic than it sounded. I asked him if he thought summer would ever end. He said: "Sure, it has to end."

I thought that maybe I should ask him about himself, a couple of questions about his family, his parents, if he had brothers or sisters, where he grew up. I thought: Here we are standing on the roof at night, making polite conversation, but I didn't want to ask him anything. I knew everything I wanted to know, and had no desire to know more. He'd had a girlfriend for five years and he apparently loved her very much. He worked at a nursery and he didn't have a lot of ambition. He didn't like fruit or crossword puzzles. He had blond down in the small of his back and on his behind. I too had little ambition; he had never seen my apartment, where I lived, and he didn't even know my address. He knew my phone number, but not by heart. Had I come down with food poisoning, he would have let me take the bus home if that was what I wanted to do. I knew there were two kinds of women in the world: the kind people always want to take care of and the kind they don't. I knew I was one of the second kind, and suddenly this saddened me. I knew it was only a matter of time until one summer evening, maybe in a year or two years, a cartful of hay drawn by a weary horse dressed up with ribbons would convey Nathan and Sigal to their wedding ceremony, which would take place under the open sky, on the dining-hall lawn in the kibbutz in the north, and I knew that I was the other woman.

13

My mother said she wanted to buy me a present. She called me one morning, waking me up, and said she wanted to go to the mall to buy me something. "Why?" I asked, and she said: "I just feel like it, Maya. I don't need a reason. I'm your mother." We drove to the mall and wandered around the stores I hated. She told me to pick whatever I liked. "Anything," she said. "Let's splurge!" It made me laugh, the way she said "splurge."

We walked slowly past the display windows and looked at the clothes and the shoes; household goods were a possibility too, and my mother stood next to me, patient, watching me out of the corner of her eye, watching me searching for the one thing that would make me happy. "Well?" she whispered from time to time. "There are so many nice things. Don't you like anything?"

I suggested we sit and have a cup of coffee. I was confused by all the choices and couldn't make up my mind. I said my feet hurt. She said: "Your feet hurt? At your age?" I said maybe it was because of the heat, and that this summer was unbearable. She had suffered terribly from the heat this summer too. We rode up the escalator. I got off before her and waited to catch her arm, but this time she didn't trip. She set her foot down firmly, shod in its orthopedic sandal, and smiled at me provocatively, as if she had been practicing getting off the escalator secretly. She looked at me and said: "And you thought your mother was hopeless." "I never thought that," I said. "Yes you did, but never mind, let's sit down and I'll buy you a cup of coffee."

We sat in the café with the bad cakes and the bad memories; my mother ordered a slice of apple strudel and I wanted just coffee. She said: "You're doing this on purpose." I said: "Doing what?"

"You never order anything," she said.

It wasn't true, I just wasn't hungry.

"So when do you eat?" she asked.

"I eat, don't worry. You can see that I eat."

"I'm not worried," she said. "I just wanted to treat you and you won't let me."

"If it matters so much, I'll order something," I said.

"What's the matter, Maya?" she asked. "What's wrong with you lately? You seem a little depressed to me," she said.

"I'm not," I said. "I'm tired and hot, and I hate the summer, and my feet hurt." I called the waitress and ordered a cheese Danish.

My mother said she couldn't understand how I could eat it, that the Danish tasted like soap, it was the worst thing in the café, why did I have to pick that of all things? "Why do your feet hurt?" she asked, and I said again it was the heat, that I had walked to Dad's place today because my car was in the garage.

"What's wrong with it?" she asked.

"Nothing. An oil change."

She finished eating her strudel and asked for a glass of water.

She told the waitress to bring me one too. "Drink, Maya," she said. "In this heat you should drink all the time."

She said that she hadn't asked me out today just to buy me a present. That was an excuse, she said, for us to get together. She wanted to consult me about something urgent, and after that we would go on looking for my present. She said: "I won't let you out of it. You'll leave here today with something."

"What did you want to ask me about?"

"I've been seeing a therapist," she said and blushed, lifting the glass of water to her lips to drown the words just out of her mouth.

"You're in therapy?" I asked, raising my own glass of water.

"I go once a week."

"Who is it?" I asked.

"Never mind, Maya. Someone recommended her."

"Who?" I asked.

"Tali, when we were talking on the phone, after Dad and I got divorced . . ."

"Tali?" I asked.

"Yes," she said and asked the waitress for another glass of water. "Tali thought I should go for counseling, that's what she called it. She said everyone in the States goes, that it was nothing to be ashamed of. She said divorce was a big step and I should have somebody to talk to."

"So you went?"

"Yes," she said. "It's someone Tali's friend Michal knows, someone she studied with."

"Someone young? Michal's age?" I asked.

"Yes, why not? Age doesn't matter."

"Your therapist is a girl of twenty-eight?"

"I can't see why it's a problem," she said. "Tali said she was very good. And she really does seem very sympathetic and mature."

"Why didn't you tell me?" I asked. "You've been in therapy for six months and you haven't said a word."

"I don't know," she said. "Maybe I was afraid you'd think I was depressed. I didn't want to worry you."

"So why are you telling me now?" I asked.

"Ah! That's exactly what I wanted to talk about," she said. "Orna and I have been talking . . ."

"Orna? That's her name?"

"Yes," said my mother. "Orna thinks that maybe I should reconsider the divorce. She doesn't say it in so many words, but maybe I was a bit hasty."

"Are you unhappy being alone?" I asked. "Is that why you're in therapy?"

"No. God forbid. I'm getting along nicely. You can see I'm getting along just fine."

"So what's the problem?" I asked. I imagined a young psychologist, younger than I, sitting opposite my mother with her legs crossed, in some air-conditioned clinic she shared with two or three other young psychologists, nodding at her from time to time and squeezing insights out of her, which my mother hurried to write down in her notebook on her way home so she wouldn't forget.

"Why are you so hostile, Maya?" my mother said. "I'm just trying to talk to you. You're my daughter, aren't you? If I can't talk to you, who can I talk to?"

"I'm sorry," I said.

"I could see you were in a bad mood," she said. "I know you well enough."

"Yes," I said. "Forget it. Tell me what Orna said."

My mother was glad to get back to her therapist and said: "She thinks that maybe what I did, the whole divorce thing, was just to get revenge on Dad."

"Revenge? What for?" I asked.

"Her," she said and again pressed the glass of water to her lips.

"Violet?" I asked.

"Yes, her, Violet," she said and her shoulders shrank in pain.

"You told Orna about her?"

"We talk about her a lot," she said.

"But she's dead, Mom. She died over thirty years ago. What's the point in revenge? What did he do?"

"That's what we're talking about, just yesterday we talked about it, Orna and me. I'm telling you, she's really good. Very mature. There are a lot of things I've never really thought about. All kinds of things I swept under the carpet, like Orna says. Your father didn't always treat me right. I felt very bad in the first years of our marriage. Because of her, Violet. She died suddenly like that, such a tragedy for your father. But it was a tragedy for me too, being with him like that. He didn't talk about her, but she was there all the time, in the background, like a picture on the wall, but I had enough on my hands, I had you and Tali, and I was busy taking care of you, and I tried not to think about it."

"Think about what?" I asked.

"Your father and her, Violet." It was hard for her to say the name. "I know he loved her very much. But then you grew up and left home, and I had more time to think, and I realized that all the time I'd been a compromise for Dad. Just a compromise."

"Is that what Orna told you?" I asked. "That you were a compromise?"

"No. God forbid. Orna didn't say it. She just points me in the right direction. She's very sympathetic."

"So the divorce was all an act?"

"No! Of course not! Do you think your mother's completely mad? Of course it wasn't an act. I really thought I'd be better off without him. All those years I was his compromise, and he'd become mine too. From the love of my life, your father turned into a compromise. See how sad it is? But that's life, I'm not complaining. So I thought: Maybe I'll be better off on my own. What do I need him there for all the time, to remind me what a big compromise I was? I thought it was better to be alone."

"So what's changed your mind?"

"Nothing," she said and stared at the strudel crumbs on her plate. "Dad's not well."

"Neither are you," I said.

"No, neither am I. We're not young anymore."

"No," I said. "You're not young."

"So maybe we should act like adults."

Neither of us spoke for a few minutes. My mother went on staring at her plate and squashing the crumbs with her finger. I looked at the people sitting around us, men and women with bright shopping bags, shiny plastic bags bearing the logos of boutiques and shoe stores and bookstores and gift stores. My mother sighed and lit a cigarette. The waitress cleared away my cup and plate and asked if she should leave the water. "Leave it," said my mother, "it's so hot today," and she smiled apologetically at the waitress.

"Are you scared of being alone?" I asked.

My mother was silent.

"A little," she said. "Maybe I am a little scared of being alone."

"And you want me to tell you if you should go back to Dad?"

"I thought I'd talk to you about it."

"I'm sure Dad will agree."

"Yes, I know that. But I'm not sure what I want."

"You say you don't want to be alone."

"No," she said and took a last sip of water. "I don't want to be alone. Not at my age."

"And what does Tali think?" I asked.

"I didn't ask her," my mother said. "She hasn't got time for these things."

"But she's got time to send you to a shrink," I said.

"Maya," said my mother, "you have to stop talking about Tali like that. She has her life and you have yours. You're different. And we love you both, Dad and I love you both."

"So go back to him," I said. "Talk to him and tell him how you feel."

"Yes," she said. "I'll tell him. We'll go and visit him and talk to him. I'm glad I spoke to you, Maya. Now let's get the check. I'll pay. Take your hand out of your bag."

Mom paid the waitress and left her a generous tip. I told her it was too much, and she said never mind, the waitress was very nice, even though the waitress wasn't particularly nice, but my mother was acting as if she'd just discovered that the world was a good, friendly place, full of potential for happiness—it was just too bad she hadn't known this before.

We walked out of the café into the air-conditioned mall and took the escalator down. I had to pick up my car from the garage. We said good-bye at her bus stop and I set off in my direction. Mom called after me: "So we'll talk to Daddy. Right?" I said: "Yes," and ran to catch my bus. I sat behind the driver and looked out the window. We hadn't bought me a present after all. My mother sat down on the bench at the bus stop, next to an old woman who moved aside to make room for her.

14

They broke the news cautiously. The three of us were sitting around the table in the kitchen with the plants and the pleasant breeze. We were eating a light meal because it was too hot for anything cooked. We had cheese and bread and an onion omelette. Amir chopped the onion and whistled to himself and wiped his tears. Noga said that it was his job to cut up onions and make omelettes and whistle silly tunes he invented while he cooked. Once again I was sitting in Noga and Amir's kitchen on a Friday afternoon and eating with them. Once again it was sweltering outside yet pleasant in the kitchen. Noga and Amir had a theory about getting the right exposure, but I thought it was just luck. They were lucky with their apartment.

Noga sighed and said she'd eaten too much, and she lifted her tank top, Amir's tank top, patting herself on the stomach. Amir cleared the table and put the dishes in the sink. He filled the electric kettle, stood behind her chair, gripped the backrest, and rocked it back and forth. Noga told him to stop. Amir kissed her neck, took his hands off the back of the chair, put them on her shoulders, and massaged them. Noga said again that she'd eaten too much, raised her eyes and looked at Amir and asked him why she had eaten so much, and Amir kissed the tip of her nose. The kettle boiled and he asked us what we wanted to drink; Noga said that she didn't want anything, she was too full, and I said: "Iced coffee." Amir said iced coffee was a good idea, that he would have iced coffee too, and asked Noga if she didn't want to change her mind. She said no, he put his hands on the back of the chair again, rocked it back and forth, and said: "We're getting married."

"Amir!" Noga shrieked.

"What's wrong?" he said, rumpling her hair.

"I wanted to tell her," she said, and shook her head. "Stop that! I don't like it," she said and Amir took his hand away and poured a little boiling water into two cups and mixed it with the coffee. "If I'd waited until you got up the courage to tell Maya, we'd be on our way to get divorced." Noga massaged her stomach and said: "Don't exaggerate." I said: "Congratulations."

Amir opened the fridge and took out the milk. "She's been trying to make up her mind how to tell you for a month."

"Stop it!" she wailed.

"It's true," he said laughing. "She's been agonizing over it for a whole month."

"Why?" I asked.

"Because she was afraid of your reaction," he said.

"Will you please stop talking nonsense?" said Noga with real anger. Amir pushed his hand into her hair and rumpled it again.

"Stop it!" she yelled and grabbed his wrist. "You know I don't like it. Why do you keep doing it?"

"Because I like it," he said. "I like annoying you."

"Were you really afraid of my reaction?" I asked.

"It's not the way it sounds. It's not like there's a conspiracy. I just didn't know how to tell you. We just decided. About a month ago. It was quite sudden, and we haven't told anyone yet except our parents."

"She was afraid you'd be jealous," said Amir. "She was afraid you'd get depressed about it."

"Bullshit," Noga said.

"I'm glad," I said. "Truly, with all my heart. You don't have to feel uncomfortable."

"Really?" she said and looked at Amir who was standing behind her still rocking her chair. "Do you mean it?"

"Yes." I said. "I mean it."

Noga lit a cigarette and threw the match into the sink. Amir took a tray of ice cubes out of the freezer and said: "And she's going to quit smoking after we get married."

"That's why we're getting married," she said, "so I'll quit."

"So when is it?" I asked.

"September," they said together.

Amir banged the tray of ice on the counter and said: "If you're still with that asshole you're going out with, you can bring him so we can finally get a look at him." An ice cube came free of the tray and landed behind the fridge, and Amir bent down and groped for it with his hand.

"I'm not going out with him," I said.

"Yes, they never leave his house," said Noga.

"Why, is he stingy?"

"Emotionally," said Noga and laughed and blew out smoke. I laughed with her. Amir crawled on all fours looking for the ice cube. Noga told him to forget about it, it would melt anyway, and he said he didn't want a puddle under the fridge. I looked at him in his short pants. He too had downy hair in the small of his back. I thought that maybe this was why I had fallen in love with Nathan, this hair, that you fell in love because of the small things. Amir was short and thin, and the hair on his back was black. I wondered whether I could fall in love with Amir, with his skinny legs and hollow chest and protruding ribs, Noga's Amir with the black hair in the small of his back, and I knew that I could.

"So when in September?" I asked. "Before the holidays?"

"Definitely," said Noga. "After that it's already winter."

Amir said: "We're looking for a place with a garden."

"I've heard of a few," I said. "I can find out for you."

"We're going to look at a couple of places tomorrow. You want to come?"

I said no, that I had work to do at home. I had tons of stuff to read, but thanks anyway.

"If you change your mind," said Noga, "we won't leave before four. Right?"

"Four, five," said Amir, "when it's a little cooler. Maybe we'll go to the beach first."

We sat in silence for a few minutes. Amir gave up on the ice cube and told Noga there would be a puddle under the fridge. He put the two mugs of iced coffee on the table and stirred them rapidly, making the ice cubes tinkle. He stood next to the table between Noga and me and stirred the coffee, until Noga told him to stop because it was giving her a headache. She said, "That's enough," and stroked the small of his back. Amir threw the spoon into the sink and took his coffee to the living room. Noga went on rocking her chair and smoking and patting her stomach.

I drank the coffee, swirling the ice cubes from side to side. Noga looked at me, troubled, and I smiled at her. "You're not really happy for me," she said, but I told her that I was. She said she would understand completely if I wasn't, but I said again: "I am. I really am." She said they were expecting guests, friends of Amir's she couldn't stand, but that's the way it was when you lived with someone. You made all kinds of compromises. You've got no idea how many, she said, and she asked me to stay, because these friends depressed her. "They're so boring," she said. "They got married two months ago, but from the way they behave you'd think they'd been married for fifty years. Stay," she said. "We'll gossip about them in the kitchen," but I said I had to go because of all the work waiting for me at home. I leaned toward her and took her hand in mine—her left hand with the silver rings. There were three new rings: one from Amir, one from her mother, and one from Amir's mother. I squeezed her hand in mine and said: "Congratulations, really, with all my heart," and we stood up and hugged, and her curly hair touched my cheek. It was soft and smelled of shampoo and onions.

15

I waited for my mother outside Orna's clinic, which was located on the ground floor of a new, marble-covered apartment building uptown. I sat in the car and waited. It was four in the afternoon. We had told my father we'd be coming around four. He had insisted on holding the meeting at his place. My mother wanted him to come to her. She said on the phone: "Why don't you come to the house?" But he was firm and said he preferred us to come to him. When I told him Mom wanted to talk about their getting back together, he said: "All right. I don't mind talking if she wants to, but at my place." He wanted her to see him in the rented apartment he hated so much, still without any furniture. I don't think he wanted her to feel sorry for him. I think he wanted to let her settle the score. He didn't need Orna to explain that Mom had divorced him out of revenge for Violet. He wanted her revenge to be complete. He wanted her to know he had served his sentence.

My mother came out of the building. I honked and waved at her. She got into the car, fastened the seat belt, lit a cigarette, and didn't say a word. I wondered what they'd talked about, my mother and Orna, in the air-conditioned clinic on the ground floor of the marble building. Mom was wearing one of her nice dresses—a sleeveless dress with a triangle pattern. She sighed and looked out the window. She was in the pensive mood that people sink into when they come out of a therapy session.

When we reached my father's street, she noted that it was nice. I parked outside his building and she asked: "Is this it?" I said: "Yes." His building was ugly, old, neglected. She walked up the path, looking at the gas balloons and garbage cans and the broken mailboxes. She asked if there wasn't a tenants' committee and I said no. She stood and examined the mailboxes until her eyes stopped at my father's. "Jacob Lieberman" was written on the label in print letters, in childish writing, under a label which said: "Nitzan Alon. Zoom-in Productions."

"Why doesn't he remove it?" she asked and touched the previous tenant's label with her fingernail, as if she was asking my permission to peel it off. I knocked lightly on my father's door, and my mother asked why there wasn't a bell. I said there was, but it didn't work, and she said that you should fix things, that you shouldn't leave things too long, because they take their revenge on you. I knocked on the door again. Mom stood behind me, clutching her little handbag. "Why doesn't he answer?" she whispered at the back of my neck. My father opened the door. He was pale and unshaved.

We went in, he closed the door behind us. My mother stood in the entrance hall, examining the few bits of furniture in the living room. She pointed with her chin at the two chairs and said: "Those are ours, aren't they? Didn't you once take them from the house, Maya?" and my father said: "She loaned them to me, until I get settled."

I went into the kitchen to make coffee. My mother and father remained in the living room, staring at the chairs, until she came into the kitchen and said: "What's taking so long?" I said: "It's this electric coil. You have to boil each cup separately." She said: "It's too bad he hasn't got a table and chairs in here. We could have sat in the kitchen. Why doesn't he buy a kettle? He can take one from our place. We have two. He knows there's an extra kettle. I told him he could take whatever he wanted. Why didn't he take it?" Then she asked if I'd noticed that Dad hadn't shaved today. She said he did it on purpose, to annoy her. To look more pathetic than he really was. I told her he hadn't been paying too much attention to shaving lately. She tasted her coffee to see if it was sweet enough, and said that I didn't need to give her lessons on my father, that she knew him better than I did.

We returned to the living room, my mother holding her cup with the tips of her fingers, and me holding mine and my father's. He was sitting on one of the chairs with his face to the window. On the western wall there was a high, rectangular window, which was closed most of the time because it overlooked the entrance path and the garbage cans and gas balloons.

My mother sat down on the other chair. She moved it closer to my father, out of habit, but stopped halfway. She put her cup down on the floor, rummaged in her bag, and took out her cigarettes. She took one from the pack, then took out her lighter, lit it, and brought it up to the cigarette, but suddenly she removed the cigarette and, still pressing the lighter spring with her finger, held the flame out to my father and asked: "Is it all right if I smoke, Jack?" He nodded and said: "There aren't any ashtrays," and I said: "I'll find something," and my father said: "There are some empty cottage cheese containers under the sink. You can use one of them." My mother, happy to have obtained permission to light her cigarette, took a deep drag, exhaled, and said: "Why do you keep empty cottage cheese containers, Jack?" He said: "For ashtrays."

I brought one, and she put it on her lap, balancing it against her bag. "Should I open the window a little, Dad?" I asked. "I don't think so," he said. "It's noisy outside and it smells of gas." "Isn't there a tenants' committee?" my mother asked. "I don't know," said my father. "Apparently not," I said. "That's no good," she said and bent down to pick up her coffee from the floor. I said: "But it has advantages too. There's less to pay. Less hassle." "Oh, Jack, I forgot to tell you!" My mother snatched at the conversational tidbit. "Our tenant committee's changed! Did Maya tell you? You know who's the head of it now?" My father didn't answer, shrugging his shoulders like a child who doesn't want to appear too interested. The committee had always been my father's favorite chore. For years he had volunteered as chair, to the relief of the entire building. He had kept the accounts and the receipts and had taken them with him when he moved. Now they were packed in a manila envelope at the bottom of his suitcase in the bedroom, and my mother said: "Gottlieb!"

"Gottlieb?" he asked.

"Yes, Jack. Gottlieb! Can you believe it? It's a disaster! We don't know what to do."

She was trying to butter him up, prodding his soft spot. Telling my father that the tenants' committee was a disaster, that Gottlieb didn't know what he was doing, that he forgot to collect the dues, that he didn't give out receipts, that the water supply had been nearly cut off twice, was like telling him that she missed him, and not just her, but everybody. The whole building missed him.

My father digested the news in silence. I sat on the floor and leaned against the wall and drank my coffee. I hugged my knees and said: "Okay, enough small talk."

They both looked at me with sorrow and surprise.

I said: "Dad, you're not well."

My mother said: "Maya's right. You have to take care of your-self."

I said: "You're not well either. You know you could have another heart attack."

"Yes," she said, "but I don't think about it. You have to live your life Maya, and not think too much."

"In any case," I said, "we're here to solve the problem. We're here to find a practical solution." Suddenly I felt as if I was Gottlieb, a failed chairman, facing two quarreling, obstinate resi-dents, the only ones in the building. I said: "Dad, Mom says she's ready to think about getting back together."

"But only for a trial period," she said, and burned a hole in the cottage cheese container as she tried to put out her cigarette. "Only for a trial period, Jack." Suddenly my father rebelled—I should have seen it coming. I had seen his shoulders charge like batter-ies—he turned to her and said: "I don't need any favors, Deborah. Please don't do me any favors."

I stood up and opened the window because it had become

unbearable in the room, and the smell of the garbage and the gas seemed preferable. I leaned against the wall and said: "Stop it, both of you. It can't go on like this. You're behaving like children, both of you. We came here to talk, not fight. You've fought enough. You've been fighting for thirty years. Aren't you sick of it?"

They were silent for a minute and then my father said: "We didn't fight."

My mother, who had fallen into the trap of believing he was on her side, said: "That's true, Maya. Your father's right. We never fought. That's one good thing you can say about us, we never fought."

"We didn't fight the way we should have," he continued, and she frowned and said: "What do you mean, 'the way we should have'?"

"We didn't fight the way we should have," he said, "and you know what I mean."

"No," she said angrily, "I don't know what you mean. I didn't know we were supposed to fight at all. Where does it say that we were supposed to fight? But you tell me how we should have fought. Go on, since you're such an expert, tell me how we were supposed to fight."

There was silence. My father stared out the window I'd opened. Outside we could see the roofs of parked cars and the heads of passersby. Suddenly a car alarm went off, wailing without stopping, or perhaps we had only just noticed it. The smell of the garbage and the gas filled the air, and my father turned to face my mother, turned his head and neck and shoulders toward her, and whispered: "With passion, Deborah. That's how people should fight."

I stood with my back to the wall and stared at the floor. I was witnessing one of the few intimate moments in my parents' lives, maybe the only one but certainly the most solemn. It was like catching them in bed together. But it was worse. They sat on those two ugly chairs, dressed in their familiar clothes, my mother in the dress with the triangle print, and my father in brown pants and a white long-sleeved polyester shirt, and both of them more naked than I had ever seen them.

"With passion. People should fight with passion," he said again, and looked back at the window. "We always went through the motions," he said to the window. "We always behaved like a couple who knew when they should fight and when they shouldn't. I never heard you scream at me, Deborah, really scream from your guts, from your heart, not just getting little digs in and criticizing me about this and that."

"You're not such an innocent either," my mother hissed and lit another cigarette. "You're not innocent at all, Jack! You know it very well. As if I'm the only one to blame. 'Passion'! You throw out these words, where do you come up with them? Where does he come up with them, Maya?"

"You're talking?" he said. "You, whose whole life is some Disney movie? Big words are your specialty, Deborah, that and a few other things."

"What other things?" my mother pounced. "Tell me Jack, what other things?"

"You want me to tell you," he said. "You really want me to? Do you think your weak heart can take it?"

"Tell me! Stop trying to be clever and tell me!" she screamed and rose to her feet, dropping the scorched cottage cheese container and her patent leather bag, which also had a little hole in it from the burning cigarette that had passed right through the plastic container. "Well! Tell me already!" she yelled and put her hands on her hips. "Get it all out, Jacob, all of it! Now that you've finally learned to talk."

My father stood up—I thought he was about to walk out of the apartment—but he bent down, picked up the chair, turned it around, and sat down again, with his face to my mother, who paced back and forth in front of him, the way she always did in front of the cakes when we went to a café together.

He cleared his throat again and again, as if each cough was an opportunity to rephrase his words and take them back, and then he said, in a quiet tone: "First of all, Deborah, you didn't even love me when we got married."

"Jack"—she sounded horrified, as if she had only just noticed that I was with them in the room—"what are you talking about, Jack? Tell me, what are you talking about? Perhaps our oldest daughter would like to know why you're suddenly saying such terrible things and talking such nonsense, Jack, nonsense! Maya, you want to know, don't you?"

I stared at the worn floor tiles in silence. I tried to count them.

"Deborah," he said, "I don't want to hear all your stories again, about how you were in love with me for years, how it thrilled you every morning to see me coming into the building, how you waited for the moment when you could put through a call to me, how you prayed for my wife to disappear, how you bought flowers every day so I would pay attention to you. It used to flatter me, Deborah, I admit, but I don't need lies anymore."

"I wasn't lying, Jack," she said and her eyes filled with tears. "I really loved you."

"No," he said. "You wanted to get married, I can understand that. But you didn't love me. You were thirty-two years old and you wanted a family. I can understand that, Deborah. You wanted a family."

"But I loved you, Jack! I swear I did! You can ask the typists in the office. Ask Judith! She knows! Ask Malka! Malka was my friend. You can even ask Mr. Horowitz. Even he knows. Ask Maya. She'll be my witness."

"Deborah," he said quietly, "you're fantasizing. Stop fantasizing, a woman of your age."

I felt my flesh crawl and a childish instinct urged me to put my hands over my ears. To hear my father say: "fantasizing." There was a kind of embarrassing exposure in the word and he spat it out as if it disgusted him. There was something blunt in his voice, something masculine and sexual, which didn't suit him, like the stubble on his cheeks and chin, which in contrast to the white hair on his head was coarse and black.

Mom was sobbing now. She sat back on her chair, which was set at right angles to his, and cried with her face to me and the wall. She didn't even bother to look for a tissue in her bag, which was lying on the floor, with the burn mark on it like a tattoo. Then she said in a submissive tone which contained a touch of flirtatiousness: "But I'm sure I loved you, Jack. That's how I remember it, anyway. I didn't marry without love. I would never have done such a thing."

My father said: "It doesn't matter anymore."

She sniffed, trying to decide whether the moment had come to be consoled, but then she turned to face him and said: "Look who's talking, Jack, look who's talking."

"But at least I never lied to you."

"No, you never lied," she said. "That's the problem. You told me many truths, Jack. Do you know what it felt like living with you all those years and knowing that you didn't love me? It was worse. I at least told you that I loved you. And you, you were only interested in the truth. Only the truth! Not my feelings."

"There was no point in lying," he said. "There was no point. You know it."

"What does it matter if there was a point or not? You could have made my life a little easier, Jack. A little, for the sake of my ego. What does it matter if there was a point or not?"

"I'm sorry," he said. "I know it wasn't easy for you, but you know I hate lying. I can't do it."

"No? Then you should have tried a little harder. You know what it was like living in Violet's shadow? You know what torture it was? Chinese torture. And I didn't even know what she looked like, you burned all her pictures. Everything! Like a little boy you went and made a bonfire in the yard."

"I didn't burn them because of you," he said.

"Of course not!" she said. "Not because of me! Not for me.

Because of you! Only you! Because you're an egotist. Because it didn't occur to you that I might be suffering, tossing and turning in bed at night trying to guess what she looked like. I had to humiliate myself and ask around the office, in case somebody had seen her coming in one day. Maybe she came to visit you, to bring you a sandwich, but nobody ever saw her. Why, Jack? Why didn't she come to visit you? You were married for ten years. Isn't it strange, Jackie? Isn't it strange that she never came once?"

"Drop it," he said. "I'm asking you. Let it go."

"I don't want to!" she said. "I won't drop it! I deserve to know. I have a right."

"You don't have any rights!" he yelled. He wasn't trembling anymore. He was just yelling. "You don't have any rights anymore. We're divorced. Remember? You wanted us to get divorced, so now you haven't got any rights, you can forget about your rights!"

"I do!" her voice pleaded. "I have a right to know."

My father was silent. Outside the alarm went on wailing. Someone walked on the path and crammed a bag of garbage into the can. We heard the bag rustling and the lid closing. "Gorgeous, Deborah," he said. "She was gorgeous."

My mother sniffed, took a tissue out of her bag, and wiped her eyes.

"She had a Slavic beauty. A noble beauty. She had blond hair she used to put up with two combs, like this." He demonstrated on his bald head. "And high cheekbones, and she was tall, much taller than me, maybe even a head taller. At first it embarrassed me, but later on I got used to it and I liked it"—I had never seen my father so dreamy and full of joy—"and she dressed very elegantly. And she didn't understand Hebrew too well. I tried to teach her, but she laughed and shrugged her shoulders, like a little girl. Like this: don't want to, don't want to, and she had a smile, Deborah"—he demonstrated the smile to my mother—"I fell in love with her smile."

My mother stopped crying. She looked straight at my father and her eyes were dry now. "Why didn't you tell me all this till now?" she said. "Why?" And my father kept quiet. He was very calm. His shoulders were slumped and relaxed. "There, you see, you could have made things easier for me. Much easier. Look, your poor ex-wife has taken on flesh and blood. A human being. Not a ghost. A human being! It's easier to cope with a human being, Jack. What would it have cost you? What would it have cost you to tell me this thirty years ago?"

But my father was somewhere else. He sat quietly and limply on his chair, carried away on the wings of a smiling vision that didn't speak Hebrew.

I asked if they wanted more coffee, but they didn't answer. They looked at each other. I asked again: "Should I make more coffee?" but my voice didn't penetrate the wall. "I'll go and make some for me," I said and went into the kitchen. "Let me know if you change your minds."

I waited for the water to boil. The electric coil leaned on the rim of the glass, and there was some perceptible movement in the water, little bubbles clustering around the coil. I went back into the living room and saw my mother and father sitting exactly as they had been a few moments before. Staring at each other. I told them I had to leave, but they ignored me. I picked my bag up from the floor. "Can you take the bus home?" I asked my mother. "I have to run. I have a meeting at the university." I went into the kitchen, unplugged the electric coil, opened the front door, and said: "I'll talk to you later, okay? I'll call," but they still didn't answer. They turned their heads for a second and my father nodded, but not at me, as if he were responding to someone else. I slammed the door behind me, and when I walked up the path I could see their heads through the rectangular window.

16

That night both my parents tried to reach me. Each one called me separately to tell me they were getting back together. I was at Nathan's and didn't bother to check my messages, even though I knew they'd both call. When I got home at six-thirty in the morning, there were six messages on the answering machine.

The first was from my father: "Maya, it's eight o'clock and your mother just went home. Please call me." The second was from my mother, who announced that she'd come home and she had to talk to me. She sounded excited and out of breath. In the background I heard the weather forecast on the television. The third message was from my mother, asking where I was and saying she wouldn't go to bed before twelve o'clock. The fourth was from my father, who said he was worried about me, and the fifth was my mother again: "Maya," she said, "it's nearly twelve o'clock and you're still not home. Call me the minute you get in, okay?" The sixth message was from her as well, to tell me that she and Dad were getting back together and she was going to bed now.

It was early and still cold. I made myself coffee and sat down to drink it on the balcony. I looked at the geranium, which had dried up even though I watered it all the time. There was something wrong with these plants. They looked dry and thin and they never bloomed. I thought of throwing out the pots together with the soil and the sickly plants, but I left them hanging from the rail out of laziness and in the hope that the geranium would recover by itself, because they say that geraniums are impossible to kill.

I drank my coffee and picked at a few leaves which crumbled and turned to dust between my fingers. Yesterday afternoon, after I'd left my parents sitting in the empty room staring at each other, I sat in the car and didn't know where I wanted to go. Nathan wasn't back from work yet and I had a few hours to kill. I didn't want to go home because I knew my parents would soon emerge from their trance into a reconciliation as draining and hostile as the fight itself. They would wake up and call me to tell me they had decided to move in together; neither of them would sound happy, and all of us would immediately begin discussing the technical side of the reconciliation, which was the easiest, and we'd all be glad that my mother hadn't changed the lock after all, that my father still had a key, even though he hadn't used it because in the end he'd forgotten his plan to buy her cigarettes at a discount store, and we'd all be glad he didn't have any furniture, only a suitcase he hadn't even unpacked and a few kitchen utensils my mother would tell him to throw away, the electric coil, and the two chairs.

I drove to Noga's. I knew Amir would still be at work and we'd be able to sit in the kitchen while I told her about my parents and then about Sigal. I'd listen to her scold me for not telling her before and ask why I hid things from her, what kind of a friend was I, why did I destroy myself, where was my self-respect?

When I got to Noga's street, I saw Amir's car parked near their building. I assumed he had left her the car, as he often did when Noga needed it. I parked behind it and peered inside. On the backseat were cardboard boxes stamped with the name of a printer—wedding invitations, probably—and in the front, a pair of Amir's shorts and Noga's flip-flops and newspapers turning yellow in the sun.

I went up to the apartment and rang the bell. Nobody answered. I rang again and waited. Afterward I heard footsteps and Amir asking softly: "Who is it?" I said: "Me," and he opened the door, tightening a sheet around the lower half of his body.

"You're home?" I said.

"Uh-huh," he said, "I didn't go to work today. I was sick."

"Really?" I asked. "What's wrong?"

"Nothing," he said, "nothing serious." Noga shouted from the bedroom, "Who is it, Amir?"

"Maya!" he shouted back and Noga shouted: "Hi, Maya!"

"Were you sleeping?" I asked, but before he had a chance to

answer Noga came running out of the bedroom and stood behind
Amir, threading her arms into a long sleeveless T-shirt.

"Why are you standing outside?" she asked.

"Did I catch you in the middle of something?" I asked, hating
myself for asking.

"No," said Amir and walked back into the bedroom, holding the
sheet up behind him. "We were just having sex."

"Amir!" said Noga.

"Really?" I asked as I walked into the kitchen. Noga filled the
electric kettle and scratched her foot with her other foot and said:
"Forget it, Maya. What's up?" She took some grapes out of the
fridge. "Is something the matter?"

I said no, I was in the neighborhood. I thought Amir was at
work.

"He didn't go to work today," she said.

"What's wrong?"

"Nothing," she said. "He just didn't feel like it. We had a lot of
stuff to do. We had to get the invitations from the printers. Oh, I
wanted to show you how they came out. Amir!" she shouted.
"Where are the invitations?"

"I don't know!" he shouted back from the bedroom. "Where
are my pants?"

"Which ones?" she shouted and washed the grapes under the
tap. "The green ones?"

"Yes," he said.

"Didn't you wear them to the beach yesterday?"

"I don't remember," he said, "but I can't find them now."

I didn't say anything. I didn't want them to think I was in the
habit of peeking into their car with the boxes from the printers
and Noga's shoes and Amir's green pants, and the newspapers yel-
lowing in the sun—at that moment the car represented an intimacy
and happiness so great that peeping inside it was worse than catching its owners having sex.

We talked a bit about the invitations, and Noga told me about
the hassles they'd had with the printers and how many mistakes

they'd made. She sat opposite me and stretched and ate grapes and yawned. She said she would never get married again. Even if she got divorced from Amir she would never get married again. She said the whole thing was one big hassle.

Amir came into the kitchen in his underpants, and Noga looked at him and giggled. He said: "What's the big deal? I'm not shy in front of Maya. She's family, and I can't find my green pants."

"They're in the car," I said. "I saw a pair of green pants in the car and your invitations as well."

"Go get them, Amir," said Noga. "Before anyone steals them."

"In a minute," he said. "I'm starving. Sex makes me hungry."

"Amir," said Noga.

He winked at me and opened the fridge and bent down to look inside and pushed his hand into his underwear and scratched his behind. "There's nothing to eat," he said.

"There's grapes," said Noga.

"I don't feel like grapes," he said and sat down next to me. He smelled of sweat and of the perfume I'd given Noga for her birthday.

"Come on, go down and get the invitations. I want to give one to Maya," said Noga. "And bring my cigarettes from the car."

"You promised you're quitting," he said and stood up and left the kitchen.

"After the wedding," she said. "I have one more month, so get off my case."

Amir came back into the kitchen wearing jeans, took the keys, and said he was going down to the car. He asked if they needed anything at the grocery and Noga said no. He asked if I wanted anything and I said I was leaving in a minute. Amir said that he'd buy chicken breasts and we could make schnitzel. Noga said that she was sick of schnitzel; they ate it every day. Amir said he was dying of hunger, and he opened the fridge to see if they had eggs. Noga said: "Stay for dinner, if you're not sick of the menu. We've become a boring couple," she said. I said I had an upset stomach and I wanted to go home. Noga told Amir he couldn't go to the grocery without a shirt, and he said he could. He went out and shut the door and Noga shouted after him: "And don't forget my cigarettes."

I wanted to tell her about my parents. I wanted to tell her about Sigal. I wanted to take advantage of Amir's absence to unload everything, quickly, and hear a few words of rebuke and comfort, and I wanted her to force me to stay for dinner, but I said nothing. Noga asked what I'd eaten to upset my stomach, and I said I didn't know. She asked if she should make me a cup of tea and I said no, it was too hot, and she said she was hot too. She lifted the T-shirt from her stomach and stretched it and her childish little breast popped out of the armhole, and she said she was sick of summer and of life in general, and sometimes she was even sick of Amir too, though she loved him, and suddenly I hated her.

Amir came back with the green pants and the cigarettes and the invitations and the groceries. He asked if I wouldn't change my mind and stay to eat with them, and Noga said: "She's got an upset stomach." Amir asked if I'd like a cup of tea, and Noga said it was too hot for tea. "I'm hot and I'm sick of everything," she said, and Amir leaned over her and put his hand into the armhole of her T-shirt and touched her breast. I stood up and said my stomach hurt and I thought I'd better go home and take a nap. Amir and Noga said they would go and take a nap too, until the chicken thawed.

17

I turned off the highway into the industrial area. I passed the rows of garages, which though I had only seen once now looked familiar and beloved. On the left I began to see the orange groves I remembered from the winter, from the morning after, the first in a series of mornings that even after six months still had the frightening feeling of the morning after.

I passed the low concrete building with the graffiti, the building behind which we had sex in the car that morning. I saw the right

turn and turned slowly into it, and then I saw the nursery and the
huge, orange tin sign with pictures of birds and flowers. I had come
to tell Nathan that I didn't want to spend the weekend alone.

There was nobody in the nursery. Apparently the owner—
whom Nathan occasionally talked about—had already gone
home. It was almost closing time. I walked along the dirt road
that led to a round structure with plastic walls tacked to a
wooden frame, through which I made out Nathan's silhouette. I
walked around the back, found a gap in the plastic sheeting, and
peeked through it.

I saw him bending over a big clay pot with a lemon tree. He
stood huddled over it, without moving, looking at a worm. He held
it between his big fingers, careful not to crush it. He didn't see me
standing there. He was concentrating on the parasite he had
extracted from the soil. He stopped, his blue work pants slipping,
exposing the soft hair covering his lower back and his behind. I
loved him so much at that moment that I didn't know what to do.
I thought maybe it was a mistake to have come here and broken
the rules.

Through the gap I saw his fingers stroking the worm. He put
it on the back of his hand and slowly got up. He examined it in
the shaft of sunlight penetrating the plastic sheeting, breathing on
it, tilting his head from side to side as he studied it. I thought of
turning around and going home and waiting for him to call and
ask me if I was coming, and I would say yes, and get into the car
and park next to the hardware store and quickly climb the seventy-
five steps and we would have sex. But I didn't want to go to bed
with him today; I wanted to fight.

He stood up suddenly and turned his head toward me. He was
startled and shook the worm off his hand and it dropped to the
ground. He walked toward me, wiping his hand on his pants. He
asked me quietly what I was doing there.

He pushed the torn plastic sheeting aside, bent down, and came
out through the gap. He asked: "What happened? What are you
doing here?"

"Is there somewhere we could sit down?" I said. Of all the things I could have said, that's what came out.

"Can we sit somewhere?" I asked again.

"The office is closed," he said. "I don't have the keys." I said that I had to sit down. "We can sit in the car," I said.

"No," he said, as if the car was a trap, and sat on the ground. "We can sit here, if you want."

I sat facing him on the ground and pulled at some strands of grass. "I wanted to talk. I thought I'd pick you up and we'd go to my place," I said. "I could make some dinner. I've got all kinds of things at home. There's a watermelon."

He stared at the ground in silence.

"I need to talk," I said again, like a robot.

"What about?" he asked.

But this time I didn't answer.

"So you want to go to your place?" he asked.

"Yes," I said.

"You're sure you don't want to come to my place?"

"I want you to come to me," I said. "You've never been to my place."

He considered it. He weighed my proposal as if we were talking about some fatal step. For a second I thought of taking it back. If he came to me he would see where I lived. He would see the living room and the bedroom, the bed covered with books and newspapers and half-solved puzzles, he would see the evidence of my mundane occupations. He would see what I did to pass the time, he would see the kitchen, the watermelon in the fridge, the watermelon I hadn't opened yet and which I would probably throw out whole. He would see the bathroom, the terry-cloth robe hanging from a hook on the door, all my makeup, rows and rows of bottles, he would see my toothbrush, not the one I kept in my bag, the other one, standing in a plastic cup on the edge of the sink.

"I want you to come to me," I said again. His face softened and he said: "Okay, I'll close up here and we'll go."

I waited for him by the car. I leaned against it and played with

the keys. I bounced them in the palm of my hand and looked at
Nathan's silhouette moving slowly around the hothouse, behind the
opaque plastic sheeting.

We drove in silence. Nathan looked out the window. I concen-
trated on driving. I told him he could turn on the radio if he liked.
He didn't. He stared out the window and occasionally glanced at
my profile out of the corner of his eye. I felt like a warden driving
an escaped prisoner to jail.

We went up to my apartment. I dropped my bag on the floor
and asked if he wanted something to drink. I poured two glasses
of cold water. He took his glass and stood embarrassed in the living
room. He inspected my bookcase. I stood next to him and asked
if there was anything he'd like to read. He ran his thumb over the
rows of books and asked if I had read them all. I said no. Then he
took a book and leafed through it and said that he'd read it. That
it was good. I said that I'd read it too and also liked it a lot.

He sat down on the sofa and put his glass on the floor. I asked
if he wanted more water, he said no. "A beer?" I asked. He shook
his head. He said it was a nice apartment. I said it was expensive.
He said that his was a real bargain, and he was scared that one
day he would be thrown out. I said that was scary.

Nathan lowered his eyes again, and it looked as if he was counting the tiles. He took a deep breath and exhaled through his nos-
trils. I asked if he was sure he didn't want anything else to
drink, and he shook his head again. I said: "How can you go on
like this?"

I said: "Nathan, how can we go on like this?" and he was silent.
I said: "I can't go on like this. Can you?" But he didn't answer, so
I continued: "You have two girlfriends. Do you realize that? Me
and Sigal. Any way we look at it, you have two girlfriends," and he
said: "That's not true."

I said: "What's not true?" And he said again, softly, to the floor:
"It's not true."

"You don't have two girlfriends?"

"I already told you," he said.

"What did you tell me?"

"Then," he said.

"When?"

"When you met her."

"What did you tell me then?"

"I told you," he said.

"What did you tell me?"

"I told you," he said slowly, "that it wasn't like that. It's not how you say."

"So tell me how it is." My voice rose again, along with my left hand which stretched out, like a tray, to collect the answer.

But he was silent. I stood in front of him with my hand stretched out, and I suddenly no longer saw myself as someone waiting for an answer but as a beggar.

"Look," I said, "the way I see it, you're having two affairs. One with me and one with Sigal. It makes no difference to me that you've known her for five years and me only six months. I don't think that means anything. It's a lame excuse. And you should know that I often thought of telling her. But don't worry," I said, when I saw him raising his eyes for a second and looking at me and dropping them to the floor again, "you don't have to worry, because I won't. But you should know that sometimes, on Fridays, I go past your street in the afternoons."

"What for?"

"I just drive past, and sometimes I see her getting off the bus, with those flowers she always brings you. And there are times when I want to get out of the car and run and catch her before she goes upstairs. And I feel like telling her that there's something she should know. That I'm not a friend of yours, like you said when you introduced me. Or maybe I am? Do you see me as a friend?"

"No," he mumbled.

"And I feel like telling her that I'm your girlfriend."

"That's not true."

"What's not true, Nathan?"

But he was silent.

"Why won't you talk to me?" I said. "Why? Just tell me how you feel."

"I don't know," he said.

"How do you feel about me? Tell me."

But he only took a deep breath again, and blew it out.

"Because I love you. That's how I feel. As much as we pretend that it's just sex, that's not the way it is. I love you."

"Stop it," he said.

"Stop what?" I said. "What were you thinking all these months? That I don't feel anything for you? Is that what you thought?"

He said, "No." He said it quietly. He spoke to the floor: "That's not what I thought."

"So tell me what you did think—that it could go on like this forever? That it would go on until you made up your mind? It's pretty clear that you love Sigal. It's clear that you're going to marry her."

"Stop it," he said again.

"And if that's what's going to happen, and I'm pretty sure it is, if not now then in a year or two—then I should know where I stand. If it's true, then I should know. And if it isn't true, if Sigal is just someone else you're fucking, then I want to know that too. Because I can't go on like this, because with every day that passes I fall more in love with you. And I hate you too. And I can't go on, I can't, because in the end I'll hate myself."

But he shook his head from side to side. He rested his arms on his knees and leaned forward, and shook his head from side to side, and took those deep breaths.

"Nathan," I said. "I know that it sounds like a terrible cliché, but what it comes down to is that it's either me or Sigal."

He didn't answer. I took two steps toward the sofa. I could already smell him from where I was standing, from where I was standing and saying, "Make up your mind," from where I was shouting, "Now. Make up your mind now." And I took another step, until there were only two tiles separating us, and my body wanted to collapse and fall onto Nathan and say: "Don't decide," and a strange tremor crept up my back and stopped at my shoulders, and then my hands came up and set themselves on my hips and I yelled: "Decide!"

He had a tortured look in his eyes when he finally raised his head. I don't know how long it took until it happened and how many more times I said "Decide," but he had a tortured look in his eyes, and this gave me hope. He looked at me without saying a word, he looked at me with those suffering blue eyes, and the more I looked into them the more I understood that it wasn't pain in his eyes but panic, plain and simple panic. And afterward he dropped his head again and stared at the floor tiles, and it seemed to me that I heard him mumble something. It seemed to me that he mumbled to the floor tiles: "I can't decide."

"You can't decide?" I said. "Is that what you just said?"

He nodded.

"Do you want to think about it?" I asked. "You want to think about it for a few days and talk to Sigal?"

He shook his head.

"So what do you want?" I asked. "You want to go on like this? You want to go on being with both of us?"

He nodded again, but this time heavily, doubtfully, and my hands gripped my hips, and I took another step toward the sofa and I could already touch his knee with mine. I could have sat down beside him on the sofa and hugged him and said: "Let's forget it," but I stepped back and said: "So let's break up."

He went on nodding heavily, and I went on standing in the middle of the room with my hands on my hips and mumbling: "Let's break up." Afterward I went to the toilet. I didn't need to go, but I hoped that by the time I returned Nathan would have decided that he wanted us to stay together. I sat on the seat and felt a huge lump of tears forming in my chest. I sat on the toilet without pulling my pants down, and when it seemed to me that enough time had passed, I flushed the water and returned to the living room. Nathan was standing on the balcony, leaning on the rail, and looking down. I stood next to him and stroked his back. I touched the down on the small of his back. It was wet with sweat.

I asked if I should cut up the watermelon. He nodded. I went into the kitchen, took the watermelon out of the fridge, split it in half, cut one half into cubes and put them on a plate, and stuck two forks into the two top pieces. I tasted a little piece that fell onto the marble counter. It was sweet. It was the sweetest watermelon I'd ever tasted in my life.

I went out to the balcony and put the plate down between us, and we both ate in silence, watching the street. Even though it was the sweetest watermelon I'd ever tasted in my life, I couldn't enjoy it because of the lump in my throat mingling with the sweetness, and because I knew that it was the end and we wouldn't see each other again. Nathan ate heartily. He was relieved he could eat a watermelon and didn't have to talk. He stuck the fork into the big cubes and crammed them one after another into his mouth, and the juice trickled down his chin, and he suddenly began talking to me about some tree that I'd never noticed before.

It was an old palm tree in the yard across my building, with bunches of dry dates hanging from its fronds. He pointed at the tree with his fork and said that someone should pick the dates, because they were suffocating the tree, and if the dates weren't picked the tree would die.

The plate was empty, and I asked if I should cut some more and he said no, he had eaten too much. He said he thought he should go. I said okay, and walked him to the door. I heard him going down the stairs and the entrance door slamming. I went into the kitchen and wrapped the second half of the watermelon in Saran Wrap and put it back in the fridge. Then I went out to the balcony and hundreds of black birds suddenly landed on the tree. Within a few minutes they had polished off the dates. I was sorry Nathan hadn't seen it and I realized I would never see him again.

I went inside and closed the blinds and the balcony door and lay on my stomach on the sofa and the lump of tears burst and it was a great relief. All kinds of sobbing sounds came out of my mouth, and there was a mixture of sugar and salt on my tongue.

The phone rang. I didn't pick it up. For a moment I hoped it was Nathan calling from the pay phone around the corner to tell me he had decided. I let the answering machine take the call and raised myself on my elbows to hear if it really was Nathan calling to say he had decided and was on his way back. I counted four rings and waited for the click and afterward the silence and afterward the beep and for a second I was full of joyful expectation and I sniffed. After the long beep I heard my mother's voice. She said: "Maya? It's Mom. Dad and I want you to come for lunch on Saturday, if you're not busy." She was silent for a moment and I heard her light a cigarette and blow the smoke into the mouthpiece. Then she burst out laughing and said: "Your father is learning to cook."

MATTI

On May fifth, 1990, which was a lovely spring day, a man came in with his wife who complained that he was suffering from headaches. "Terrible ones," she said and shook her head, "terrible headaches," as if they were her own, and then she squeezed the hand of the tall shy man who within minutes became our patient.

We let her describe the symptoms, enriched by metaphors full of distress and imagination, and when she finished, leaning toward us and whispering, "My husband's not the same person he used to be," as if he weren't there, we nodded and asked: "How long has this been going on?" and she said: "About three months."

"Since February?"

"Yes, February," she said.

"Pain since February," we wrote down, and the woman—who rose from her chair to glance at the brand-new medical chart, which might have contained something that cheered her up, with its look of importance, its possibilities, and in the creative freedom the patient was about to ruin for us all—said: "Yes, February. He had a bad case of the flu and then it started," and we wrote: "After a flu, the patient began to complain of pain." "A bad flu," she emphasized, so we wrote: "After a bad case of influenza the patient began to complain of pains." "Terrible pains!" she insisted and pointed at our pen, so we wrote down "terrible," too, and the woman put her hand back in her lap and nodded approvingly, as if we had jointly finished composing the first, indifferent sentence of a fairy tale, immediately after which the horrors would begin.

She quickly picked up the style and began dictating the case history to us, adding to "terrible"—"sharp," "blinding," "para-lyzing," "unbearable," "monstrous," "inhuman," "indescribable"— and when she felt that the description of the pain was over-shadowing the pain itself, she looked at her husband who was staring at the carpet scratching his head, asking him with her eyes to contribute something, just one word to sum it all up, but the man mumbled: "No."

"No?" she asked.

"Not three months."

"Two months, then?" she scolded him. "What difference does it make, Matti, you've been in agony for two months now."

"Don't exaggerate," he said quietly. "I'm not in agony. It hurts a bit, but I'm not in agony."

"Oh really?" she said and dropped his hand. "So why are we here? Tell me: why are we here?"

"Because you wanted us to come," he said. "You wanted to."

We are familiar with this dialogue. The patient and his wife sit here, in a well-lit room with large windows and a comforting view, probably aware of the fact that they'll look back on this day with hatred, and maybe they'll long for it, too, because it was the day when, as far as they were concerned, everything was still possible, a different diagnosis, for example. And in the meantime, in order to buy time, they argue about the details: how long and how bad, and why not admit it, and who's lying, and who's angrier and who's more right and who's more frightened, and who hurts more—this is the ritual.

"And these pains," we asked Mr. Rosen in the tone that

specialists concoct from even doses of sympathy and impatience, "are they severe?"

"No," he said, but Mrs. Rosen immediately corrected him: "Yes!"

"Any dizziness?" we inquired, and the woman, who knew that he was about to deny the dizziness as well, quickly said: "Yes, put down 'yes.'" "Nausea?" we asked and jotted down "yes" before the man had time to answer: "No." "No?" the woman protested. "Did you forget what happened at the Passover Meal?" "That was from the food," he said. "No it wasn't," she said, "we were all fine. And at *Lake Kinneret*? Don't you remember what happened at *Lake Kinneret*?" He kept quiet, remembering what had happened at *Lake Kinneret*, and we wanted to ask: "What happened at *Lake Kinneret*?" but we asked if there were any visual disturbances, and he looked at her and nodded, and she took his hand in hers again.

"A virus, perhaps?" we suggested.

"Yes, a virus!" Mr. Rosen snatched at the opportunity we gave him to recover, because after all, that too is our role, to give hope, or at least the hope of hope, or at least, not to diagnose death before we are sure.

But the woman kept shaking her head from side to side in sorrow and disbelief. She had short hair, a metallic gray, a round face and round glasses and thin lips compressed in a nervous smile and the promise of tears that indeed burst out a few weeks later, when we told her that her husband's condition was hopeless.

She was very pale when she brought him to us that first time, surrounded by a fidgety aura of anxiety that accompanied her every movement—from the moment she knocked on the door and apologized for disturbing us even though they had an appointment made five weeks in advance, and motioned him with her head to come in, and waited for him to sit down before taking the chair next to him—until the moment she folded the forms for the tests we had ordered—enough to keep them busy for another five weeks—and pushed them into her bag, thanking us as she did so, and all the time shaking her head.

Birds were chirping outside in the tops of trees planted many years ago on the grounds of our hospital, with little bronze plaques bearing the names of the donors who had made the trees possible and the lawns, the benches, the entrance lobbies, the cafeteria, the elevators, the state-of-the-art operating rooms, the wards, the beds, the tables and chairs and the pajamas and the diagnoses and the windows, and the pen with which we tapped on the chart of Mr. Rosen, who wasn't interested in the view and whose eyes were fixed on the carpet.

We looked at the woman who now appeared ten years older than she had the first time, we watched her develop a new kind of loneliness that spread through her body with the lightning speed of a malignant tumor. A loneliness we can easily diagnose, for instance in the way she absentmindedly plays with the paper clip that fell from one of the patients' files on our desk: she picks it up and opens it and winds it around her finger and turns it back into a paper clip and puts it back where she found it, and suddenly she's embarrassed because she realizes that it's no longer usable, that she's twisted it out of shape, and all the time she's listening to us with that silent nodding of hers that we were no longer sure if we found touching or irritating.

And it seems to us that our patient wants to say something as well, and maybe behind our back he steals a glance outside and thinks: What a beautiful view, what a beautiful day, and wonders how many more days like this he will see. But Mr. and Mrs. Rosen were silent and all that could be heard in the room was the unnecessary chirping of the birds and a printer spitting out the results of other patients' tests.

"No one ever prepared me for such a thing," the woman told us on a humid day in June, sobbing into a handful of tissues, when we told them that the tumor was malignant and inoperable. The patient stood up and looked straight at us—this was the first time we noticed the color of his eyes, a bitter green full of life—and said: "That's impossible," and to her he said, "I'll meet you in the cafeteria," and walked out of the room. And though it was unprofessional of us, we couldn't help thinking, when we heard his footsteps receding on the linoleum floor, that like the argument over the details, the anger, in Mr. Rosen's case, was a luxury, too.

Mrs. Rosen apologized for her husband and burst into tears again. Nobody had prepared her for such a thing, she said, to see him like this. Ill. Dying. Dead and leaving behind two small children. Ill yes, we said, but not dying yet, and certainly not dead, and as for the small children—we put out a hand to touch her fingers but withdrew it at the last minute—yes, this is very sad.

She already knows what's going to happen: she'll fuss around him when he vomits and moans and deteriorates faster than anyone can imagine but also slow enough to drive her out of her mind, and she doesn't deserve this. Her enemies don't deserve this. Nobody does. But who are her enemies? And will he be in pain? Yes, we say, but he's already in pain, she says, real pain. Yes, we say sympathetically, but it won't be the same kind.

And his pillow will be covered with hair that fell out, the black, frizzy, problematic hair he always hated and fought with every morning in front of the mirror. Stupid battles, they'll think, armed with the proportions imposed on them by the disease, which will only make things worse, because they will make them feel sad not only because of what's ahead but also for what's past, and who has the strength to deal with the past now, on top of everything else?

And their bed already smells of medicine, and the few days he has left, and the endless days in which she'll try to inspire him with false hope, when all she'll want to do is get out of the house for a while and sit alone in a café. And we want to say something encouraging to this woman, something that will save her from the terror of guessing and the loneliness, something along the lines of: Sometimes death is the easy part, but we keep silent and plan how to bring this ritual, which we need to cut short because we have no time to spare, to a dignified conclusion, how we'll get up from our swivel chair and walk over to our patient and lay our hand on his shoulder, which always tends to droop a little after receiving such news, and raise him to his feet and walk him to the door, behind which wait, anxious and submissive, patients who are paying us fees they cannot afford in hopes that we won't tell them what we've just told this nice couple, who are already disappearing into the elevator and who have eight floors in which to digest the news before they land in the parking lot.

But Mr. Rosen is now roaming the hospital corridors in search of the cafeteria and ruining our plans, and we look at the woman who is crying and flooding our office with something violent and physical that, like her husband's tumor, we don't know how to deal with, and blowing her nose and asking: "How long does he have?" And before we have a chance to remind ourselves that we must never become too involved in one person's sad story, the patient reappears in the doorway, holding a sandwich wrapped in cellophane.

2

He smiled at me. It was August 1979, a hot, disgusting day, I was wearing black jeans and a boring white tank top, I was sitting in the inner courtyard of the Café Milano practicing being a woman. I must have looked ridiculous with my elbows leaning on the table, drinking one espresso after the other, smoking Nelson cigarettes and writing poems with feigned feverishness, 'cause I thought then that inspiration was sexy, absorbed in myself and the paper napkins full of horny, rhymed reflections piled up under the glass I set on top to prevent them from flying away, not that they could have flown anywhere in the dead heat of eleven o'clock in the morning, but not too absorbed in myself and my serious, childish poems to notice that a sad-looking man was sitting next to the wall smiling at me.

Which encouraged me to go on writing and order another double espresso and emphasize to the waiter and for the benefit of the stranger, whom I hoped was listening, the words "without milk"—because the woman I planned to be was a dangerous and mysterious woman, with caffeine and nicotine and promise flowing in her veins—and to light another cigarette with the end of the old one, and to wipe away the perspiration from my upper lip from the heat, or as I believed then, from the heat of creation, because I thought that maybe I was finally being discovered by a talent scout, or at least some other kind of hunter.

I was fifteen, and I was sorry I wasn't wearing something more poetic in honor of the unexpected encounter with the stranger, a long black dress, maybe earrings, or dark glasses hiding adventurous sadness.

The stranger was dressed like someone who had nothing to say in particular: jeans and a belt with a big, shiny buckle, like Superman, and an ordinary white shirt with the sleeves rolled up to his elbows. He looked, at first sight, like some kind of clerk.

There was nobody else sitting in the courtyard of the Café Milano that morning, because the umbrellas didn't provide much relief and the regular customers preferred the ceiling fans inside which moved as laboriously as the waiter, and like him were more symbolic than efficient. We were alone, myself and the man with the clerk's appearance, sitting with his back to the stone wall which was covered with dusty ivy and swarming with insects, smoking a cigarette and smiling at me.

I put down my pen and opened two packets of sugar, one of which tore, spilling its contents on the table, immediately inviting two bees to start buzzing aggressively around the mug, the ashtray, and the sticky poems. The man stood up, put his cigarettes and matches into his shirt pocket, and I thought he was going to pay and leave me alone with vague plans that could no longer materialize, but he stopped next to my table, scratched his head, and said: "It's impossible to sit over there. It's full of chiggers."

"Yes," I said, "but this place is more dangerous, because of the bees."

He sat down on the chair opposite me and began sweeping up the spilled sugar with his hand, blowing the grains away and lifting the paper napkins with the poems and waving them gently in the air. "They'll be gone in a minute," he said and watched the bees hesitating and bumping into the umbrella until they took off, buzzing angrily, and flew over the ivy-covered wall in search of some other sweet location.

He called the waiter and asked him to transfer his things to my table, which was apparently ours now: a glass of water, a cup of café au lait, and a half-eaten cheese sandwich.

Within ten minutes I learned that he despised insects, that he hates the summer, that he dreams of making movies, that he spoke in a bored, lazy tone that matched his apologetic smile, that his car was parked right around the corner and that he didn't know why he had mentioned it at all, he didn't mean anything by it, and that his name was Matti Rosen. What it was possible to learn about me in ten minutes, even though I didn't say anything, not even my name, could be seen in the reproaching eyes of the waiter, who suddenly began hovering around us, like the bees, like some strict father, both intruding and chasing away intruders.

He emptied the ashtray before the stubs went out and brought it back wet. He took Matti's glass of water away and asked him if he was going to eat his sandwich and Matti put his hand over the half-eaten roll and said yes he was, and the disapproving waiter disappeared into the café with a look on his old face that said: I did what I could.

3

Twice a week I drive him half alive to the hospital and half dead back, for the radiation treatments, and the awful medication he gets, and lately the car has been giving me trouble but there's nobody to take it to the garage, and I don't understand why they don't give him chemotherapy, and maybe it's better this way, because he throws up all the time anyway, and the doctors say that it's because the tumor's pressing down on something, and I have to restrain myself from not bursting out and screaming: "Yes, on me!"

My mother comes every day to help with the children who walk around him suspiciously, like little animals, sometimes retreating and sometimes jumping on him as if they already miss him. They hug him and climb all over him and insist that he play with them, as if they want to put him to some kind of test, and maybe, from their point of view, the whole thing may seem like a temporary nightmare and they're waiting around impatiently hoping for it to end. And as if in spite, this summer is particularly hot, one heat wave after another, and I have to see to it that he gets enough to drink, because that's what I was told by the doctors whom I hate, whom I couldn't stand from the moment I saw them because of their cruelty and because of their lies.

And the radiation, that's a joke too, they didn't say so but I know very well, it's just to show that they're doing something, "giving it a chance" as they said with the little smile that covers up big lies. "We're doing everything we can, Mrs. Rosen," they say with the nonchalance of plumbers and with that phony smile of theirs, because they have to say something, you can't diagnose a huge malignant tumor in somebody's brain one fine day and send him home to die without an explanation.

How I cried in their office that day, when they told us, but they must be used to this by now. Matti heard the news and said he was going to the cafeteria, and he left me alone as usual with all the responsibility. And the truth is that I too, at that moment, wanted to go downstairs with him, stand on line with him, take a tray and get something to make me forget everything, to bring us both back to where we were before the pains began, and the dizziness, and the nausea, and the blurred vision—something healthy, a big salad—but someone had to stay and hear what else the doctors had to say, because as much as you despise them, you find yourself believing them all the time.

But what is enough to drink? I ask myself as I stand in front of the fridge—it's kind of pleasant standing like this in the heat, I wish I could go on standing here until it's all over—and I think: So what am I going to make the kids for dinner? And what difference does it make how much he drinks when he throws it all up anyway?

My mother takes them downtown and buys them expensive toys as if they're the ones who are going to die, and I don't have any strength left to tell her that she shouldn't do it. When they come back, beside themselves with excitement, and begin unpacking their gifts, she sees the look on my face and says: "Leave them alone, Mira, they're fatherless children." "But they're not fatherless yet, Mom!" I say, because who does she think she is, that she buried him already? And she clutches my hand with her nails and says: "Shhhh . . . Mira . . . shhhh . . . don't let them hear."

From the first moment, I knew that something was wrong. "You have to go and get yourself a checkup," I said to him, because I thought it was a virus, but Matti looked at me as if to say, What do you want from me? You go get yourself a checkup. Three months, until one night he woke the whole house with his screaming: "Mira, my head hurts! Mira, I'm dying!" He held his head, and kicked savagely, even though I know he didn't mean it, at the children who came running from their beds frightened.

My mother brings Uri and Shahar back from their shopping expedition and I ask them: "So what do you want for dinner?" And maybe because I asked a little too enthusiastically—their little dinners have been my salvation lately—they ignore me. Uri shuts himself in his room with a new computer game and Shahar runs to the kitchen, climbs on a chair, and without asking permission, taking advantage of the fact that all the boundaries in the house have been breached, opens the cupboard, takes a chocolate bar, sits down in front of the television, and asks: "Where's Daddy?"

"Daddy's sleeping," my mother says with that forced nonchalance of hers that drives me up the wall, and Shahar hears the toilet flushing over and over again and takes the chocolate milk she brings him—he's been eating too many sweets lately but I don't have the energy to say no—and without taking his eyes off the screen he asks: "Grandma, is Daddy sick?" And in the middle of the noise of the cartoons and the computer-game beeps I hear Uri shouting from his room: "Daddy's dying!"

And suddenly I feel like crushing the eggs I took from the fridge in my hands, and throwing them at the wall, or throwing them from the balcony on the heads of anyone passing by, like the children used to do with their toys, just to let someone down there know there's a woman up here on the verge of a breakdown.

My mother runs into the kitchen horrified and says: "He said 'dying'! What should we do?" And I say: "Nothing, ignore it. He doesn't know what it means anyway," even though he knows very well, because in addition to everything else he inherited his father's brains and pessimism, and he looks exactly like him too, his hair and his eyes, and the bitter smile that doesn't look good on a child his age, and our friends always say: "You can see that Uri is Matti's boy and Shahar is Mira's," and it terrifies me to think that soon both of them will be mine.

4

"Alona," I said, "my name is Alona," and he called the waiter and paid for both of us, and I didn't object because I thought that this was the way these things were supposed to happen, that he was the man and I was his adventure, so he should pay, and we got up, and I followed him to his car, and sat next to him and looked straight ahead, and we didn't talk the whole way, but whenever we stopped at a light he looked at me and asked: "How old are you?" And at the first light I said: "Seventeen," and at the second light he asked: "So how old are you?" and I said: "Sixteen," and at the last light, so that he should know that he was my adventure too, I said: "Fifteen, and I swear that's the truth."

5

He lies to the doctors like a child. As if that's what will save his life. But he was never good at it, he always told the truth, even when I didn't ask him to, even when I asked him not to, to spare myself pain.

At first, days would go by without us exchanging a word, till Uri was born and provided us with a topic that may not have been fascinating, but which we at least had in common. And in spite of the anxieties and fears he always had about various disasters that could strike the child every minute of the day, even when he was sleeping, he was a model father.

He was the one who got up at night and stood by the crib long after Uri had fallen asleep. I would find him there at all kinds of strange hours of the night, leaning against the wall, or sitting on a little plastic stool, looking at the baby in the darkness and counting his breaths. When he diapered him I wasn't allowed to come near, as if I was disturbing some mysterious ritual. But the really bizarre thing was to see Matti feeding him: pushing the spoon into his mouth and immediately pressing his lips to the baby's face to lick up anything that dribbled out, even if it was Gerber's baby food or a soft-boiled egg, until one day I couldn't stand it anymore and I said: "Why don't you use a towel?" He looked at me and said: "My method's better." It was an intimacy that embarrassed me. Everything that didn't exist between us existed between them, between Matti and this baby who looked exactly like him.

One night, when Uri was two—a child with a full head of black hair and the smile of someone who wasn't sure if it was okay to smile, I was at the end of my pregnancy with Shahar—Matti was playing with him in the living room, throwing him up in the air and catching him, and singing a song, and suddenly he missed and Uri fell on the floor and cut his head open. He screamed and he was bleeding, but Matti pushed me aside with his elbow and picked him up, grabbed the keys from the kitchen table, and ran barefoot with him to the car, and before I had time to catch up with him he had already started the car and driven off, as if I didn't exist, as if it wasn't my child he had almost killed, and I didn't know what hospital he took him to, but I took a cab and searched emergency rooms before I found him in the third one, sitting on a bench by the pay phones with Uri in his arms, a big bandage on his head and one eyelid swollen, orange iodine stains all over his face, and Matti was hugging him and rocking him, and when he saw me he put his finger to his lips and whispered: "Five stitches. They gave him five stitches! Can you imagine?" And the truth is that I didn't know then if five stitches was a lot or a little and I didn't say a thing, and on the way home I drove because he said his legs were trembling.

6

And afterward, the instant coffee he gave me in a mug he quickly rinsed, and for himself Turkish coffee with milk, and the memory of the two mugs standing on the counter when I went into his room with him following me, scratching his head all the time as if something was bothering him, and neither of us came out again until dark.

There was an old stereo system on the floor, a plastic box from the supermarket holding records, a bookcase made of red bricks and wooden planks, a small TV with a twisted coat hanger for an antenna, an ashtray full of stubs, a mattress covered with an Indian cloth, and a glass lying on its side next to a dry stain of coffee residues. He wasn't expecting guests.

Next to the wall was a closet with a yellow T-shirt and a towel hanging from the door. It was one of those rooms where life takes place on the floor, and which give you the feeling that you're too tall, and so I sat down on the mattress, put my bag down beside me, and looked at him. He remained standing next to the door for a moment, and then he went into the kitchen and brought a chair whose seat and backrest were made of sky blue Formica, stood it in the middle of the room, sat down, and lit a cigarette as if he was about to interview me for a job, or remain silent for the rest of the afternoon. I rummaged in my bag and pulled out my cigarettes.

"You smoke a lot?" he asked, picking up the glass from the floor and dropping his ash into it.

"Yes," I exaggerated, "a pack and a half a day."

"You started early," he said in a reproachful voice and stroked the rim of the glass.

"When did you?"

"Me?" he said. "A long time ago. But I'm a lost cause."

He said "lost" as if it were true and as if he enjoyed saying it, and I felt pleasant tingles of danger running up my back, even though it was obvious that this man wasn't dangerous, and then I noticed that his shirt collar was too big and looked like the wings of a plane, and that under his armpits there were perspiration stains, which may have started before, in the café, or this morning, when he left the house, before he got into trouble, before we got into the car which was parked in a no-parking zone, and which had a ticket stuck on the windshield that he didn't even look at before he shoved it into the glove compartment which was already full of tickets, and then his skillful parking outside the house, the parking of a bank robber, with the nervous clicks of the steering wheel, and the way he ran up the stairs, leaving me a few steps behind, and opened the door with two turns of the key that shook the silence of the staircase, and waited for me, and closed the door behind me, and locked it twice, and immediately asked if I wanted coffee, and I immediately said yes, and only when I looked at his back as he stood at the sink and washed the mugs and I smelled his sweat did I begin to be afraid. But it wasn't exactly fear.

"Nice place," I said, because it seemed a grown-up thing to say, and went into the room. "It's a little small," he said and I felt his breath on my neck as he stood behind me and examined the room with me, as if he too was seeing it for the first time. The shutters

were closed, and the room smelled of shade and dust and there
was a silence about to be disturbed, and the premonition of a crime
that was about to be committed.

I wasn't afraid of the man sitting on the chair and smoking, or
of the room that was as crammed as an old suitcase. But maybe I
don't really remember the room. I'm pretty sure about the darkness, and the T-shirt and towel hanging from the closet door, because the towel became mine and I wore the shirt sometimes at
night, but maybe the TV with the coat hanger, and the bookcase,
and the spilled coffee are borrowed from other, later rooms, which
it saddens me to remember, as if the memory itself is a betrayal
of Matti, which is a betrayal of a chance to find out something
about myself, something innocent and far and forgotten, and
maybe a little boring.

But I remember the two mugs standing and getting cold on the
counter, brown mugs with a pattern of yellow and orange splashes,
and the chair he sat on, and how he smoked and talked quietly
and suddenly got up in the middle of a sentence and went to wash
his face, and came back, and dried his face and hands with the
thoroughness of a surgeon, and threw the towel back onto the
closet door and said: "It's hot as hell today."

7

At the end of June they called me into their office and said that
the tumor had grown to the size of a tennis ball, or a Ping-Pong
ball, I don't remember which, but it was definitely a ball. Matti
stayed home, and when I got back from the hospital he didn't even
bother to ask. Only at night, before we went to sleep and he lay
with his back to me, his fingers drawing circles on the wall, did he
mumble: "Did they say anything?"

"Yes," I said, and I was glad that I couldn't see his face, "they
want to stop the radiation. They don't think there's any point continuing."

"That's what they said?" he asked.

"They didn't actually say it. They hinted."

And then, for a while, I only heard his breathing and the hum of the electric fan, and I couldn't even bring myself to stroke his back. And suddenly Shahar came in crying and said there was a monster in his room, the same monster we had been trying to get rid of for a long time, and I got out of bed and went with him to chase the monster away and I thought: If there's a monster in the house it's me, because, how come I was so relieved when Shahar stormed into our room, into our silence, into our disaster, and I was so happy that I could take him in my arms and hug him and comfort him.

We've been together for eight years and there haven't been too many ups and downs in our relationship, and I don't know if it's because we're so different, or because from the beginning we didn't have too many expectations. And now that he's going to die, I don't feel anything for him. Not even the need to take care of him that I felt when I met him. And maybe this lack of feeling is normal, too; maybe it's something I should ask the doctors about. Because maybe they know. And if they don't, maybe they'll invent something. A theory. Like one of those theories they offer you like a shot in the arm, to give you hope for at least five minutes, so God forbid you won't pass out in their office.

I courted him as one courts a wounded man: gently, without pressure, but with persistence and the unspoken promise that I was the answer to his pain. He always said: "Mira, there are a lot of sides to me that you don't know about," and I always said: "Whatever's not related to our life together I don't have to know." And now I regret it.

But I don't regret the fact that he gave up his childish ideas of being a film director, or that thanks to me he found a steady job in computers, because how long can you go on dreaming at our age, and I'm not sorry either that I married a man who was in love with somebody else. I knew that things would work out, and they did, after Uri was born and Matti cried at the hospital and said that it was the excitement of being a father, but I knew it was really grief for that young girl, and that Uri's birth had shaken him out of the illusion that our marriage was just a first-aid station.

He loved her. And so insanely that at first I wasn't even jealous, because I couldn't imagine him loving like that, or myself loving like that, and I couldn't imagine anyone loving like that. And it was only later on, when I realized that because of this insane love he couldn't give me even the little, normal love I wanted so much, that I began to be jealous.

This is a small town, and the people here are generous with the information they offer. During our first year when he left me every other day and in the end begged me to marry him, because he'd gotten used to the comfort of a home and cooked meals and a sympathetic ear, I would meet people in the street who knew him and who told me what she was like, and what he was like with her, and how they broke up.

It was a blind date. A mutual friend gave him my number and told him that he just had to get over it. We arranged to meet in the Café Milano, even though I hate that place because it's always deserted and the only people who go there are old men and perverts, but I didn't want to sound too choosy.

He was waiting for me inside, at a corner table, and he looked haunted and unhappy about the whole thing. "There's a courtyard outside," he said, "if you're not cold we can sit there," but I said that it was all right inside and I sat down opposite him. He was wearing a big gray sweater with moth holes in the sleeves, and I immediately fell in love with his hands, which were delicate but not too small and were busy all the time with his lighter and cigarettes. He called the waiter, and when he arrived, a very unfriendly type, he asked me what I wanted and I said tea.

"Earl Grey, herb tea?" Matti asked.

"Regular tea," I said.

"With lemon?"

"No, nothing. Just tea."

"Milk?"

"No," I said, "just plain tea."

"Would you like a piece of cake? A sandwich?" he asked in a hostile tone, clicking his lighter on and off, and I said: "No, just tea."

I had been warned not to expect too much. I was told that after she left him, his cynicism, which had once had a certain charm to it, became sharp and nasty. Maybe that's why I felt that everything I told him about myself on that first date would be erased before he even noticed that he was listening to the mundane talk of someone who wasn't much to look at either. Though he didn't look at me all evening, I knew that he was taking in my appearance and that he was disappointed: the tailored jacket and narrow skirt and brown high-heeled pumps and the blouse with the Chinese collar and the pearl necklace, which was a present from my mother for my thirtieth birthday, and even my perfume, which was so floral and subtle.

When the waiter gave him the check he pushed his hand into his coat pocket to find his wallet, and left the lighter lying on the table. It was a silver Zippo, without any inscriptions, but apparently it had sentimental value, because when I picked it up and looked at it, he snatched it from my hand and said: "I have a tendency to forget things."

After not hearing from him for two weeks, I called him and asked how he was and whether he'd like to meet again. "No," he said, without even trying to lie, "I'm sorry."

And one night, at the end of winter, he called and woke me up and said: "I know I have a nerve calling after such a long time, but try to understand, I'm trying to get over a very complicated and painful relationship," and I cut him short and said: "But I heard that it was over. A year ago or something like that," as if it hadn't been two long months since we'd last spoken, and after a short silence he said: "Yes. But I'm not completely over it yet," and I said: "I see," and he said: "You don't, but forget it. You want to get together?" And I said: "Yes."

"Are you free now?" And I said: "No. It's late," so that he would know there were limits.

"Tomorrow," I said, "but try to call at a reasonable hour," and the next day he called at six and we made a date to meet at eight, and at ten he showed up, drunk.

8

"Did you ever do it?" he asked.

I blew out perfect smoke rings, which I'd practiced for hours sitting alone in cafés, or in the tool shed outside my house, where I'd forced myself, with lots of suffering and tears, to learn to smoke.

"Do what?" I asked.

He threw his cigarette into his mug and we both watched it send up smoke spirals. He put the mug on the windowsill and looked at the closed shutter and said: "Go home with men you didn't know."

"No," I said, "this is my first time. And you?"

"What?" he asked.

"Do you always bring home young girls you pick up in cafés?"

"Pick up?" he said. "Did I pick you up?" I nodded and he said: "Maybe. And no, this is the first time."

"So you've never done it?" he asked and lit another cigarette. "With someone older, I mean?"

"No," I said. "I've never done it with anyone younger either."

"So maybe," he said after a silence, which made the room even darker, "maybe I'd better take you home. Where do you live?"

9

"In a faraway country, full of jungles and lakes and white clouds speeding like racing boats in the sky and a sun dripping like a Popsicle onto the roofs of the houses, which were made of straw, and where happy and healthy families lived and raised intelligent monkeys that knew how to talk and tigers that could play the piano and elephants that liked to cry, lived a cruel wicked wizard who liked eating children."

And I beg him: "Matti, enough with that story already. You know that it gives them nightmares." But the children are riveted.

"You didn't say 'tigers that could play the piano' yesterday," says Shahar and his eyes light up.

"Yeah," says Uri, "you added that now."

"Are you sure?" Matti asks, but he doesn't hug them and tickle them as he used to when he tried to fool them, and the children nod together, enthusiastically, and I feel sad for them sitting there on the sofa, on either side of him, waiting for the hug and the tickling—which are the prize for anyone who spots a new detail in the story—but mainly I'm sad that they didn't notice that in yesterday's story he only said "happy families."

"Are you positive?" he asks again, this time in a worried tone, as if he really doesn't remember, as if it really matters.

"Yes!" they shout and rub up against him, and Shahar's hands steal under Matti's T-shirt and tickle him, but their father, all mixed up and swollen from the medication, just stares into space.

"You didn't say it! You didn't say it!" Shahar shouts into his ear.

"It's time to go to bed now," I say, and Uri gets off the sofa and goes to his room, looking back at Matti, but Shahar refuses to give in.

"But he didn't say it!" He begins to wail and rocks back and forth on Matti's knees. "Daddy, you didn't say it, right? Say you didn't say it!" But Matti doesn't say a thing and his hands lie still on Shahar's shoulders, and the boy hugs him and whispers in his ear: "You didn't say it. Say you didn't say it," but Matti is silent and the child bursts into tears.

I pick him up and take him to the bathroom, and wash his face, and walk him to the toilet and stand next to him as he pees, and pull up his pajama pants and tuck in his undershirt, and slowly his whimpers turn into a sleepy mumble and as I put him to bed he yawns and turns over onto his stomach, and before I turn off the light he suddenly sits up and says: "I want Daddy to come and say good night."

I go back to the living room and see Matti sitting in the same position, his hands suspended in the air, resting on the imaginary shoulders of a child, trying hard to remember if he mentioned the tigers yesterday or not, as if his life depended on it.

"You could have told him you didn't say it," I say and start picking up toys from the floor. "It wouldn't have cost you anything." And then it occurs to me that these arguments are ridiculous now, and with a pile of Lego bits in my hands I run into our bedroom and burst into tears.

10

What I really wanted was to go all the way, and I even had an exact picture in my head of what this going all the way should look like, with beauty and details that I can no longer remember, and for a year or two I rolled the words around in my head, and I walked down the street and said to myself: "Go all the way, all the way, all the way," until I must have been so in love with the words that I no longer cared whom I would go all the way with, but I had no idea it would involve negotiations that I didn't know how to conduct, and I didn't know what to do with this man who was sitting on a chair in the middle of the room and holding his car keys in his hand and staring at the floor, and who had no idea what to do with me either.

11

Mrs. Rosen called this morning and said that Mr. Rosen was incontinent, and asked if this meant that he was dying. Every time this happens we find ourselves envying the simplicity with which the patients and their families put into words what for years we practice not to say.

"What happened?" we asked, ready to repulse a new outburst of tears which our short acquaintance with her taught us to expect.

"This morning I took him out for a walk, because it wasn't too hot so I thought it would be okay, and I took water for him and a hat and we sat on a bench in the park and talked, and suddenly I saw that his pants were wet. He peed in his pants! What am I going to do?"

We suggested that she move him into a hospice and there was a silence on the other end of the line.

"A hospice?" she said, sniffing.

"It's not what it sounds like," we said, even though it is.

"A hospice?" she said. "So that means that he's dying, doesn't it? It means that he's dying!"

And again we found ourselves maneuvering between our obligation to medical jargon and the huge temptation to use simple human language in order to communicate with this woman whose husband had just peed in his pants.

"Your husband," we said, "needs nursing care now. You could keep him at home, but in most cases it's more convenient, both for the patient and the family, to get appropriate care in a hospice. The hospice belongs to our hospital," we said, "and Mr. Rosen will be able to receive proper care there. You have two small children, don't you?"

"Yes," she said, "seven and five."

"It would be better for the children if he went into the hospice. And for you, too, Mrs. Rosen. Matti now needs care twenty-four hours a day, and with two small children at home you can't take it all on yourself."

12

"You're crazy," he said and took off my sandals, "but obviously I'm even crazier than you are, I don't know what I'm doing and if anyone finds out they'll put me in prison for having sex with a minor. You know what the punishment is for having sex with a minor?"

The kisses started on the knees, soft kisses through thick denim, which surprised me a little because this wasn't what it said in the books and magazines I read in the toolshed or what the boys in my class did, with their blind hands groping all over the place. I lay on my back with my knees bent and looked at him crouching next to me kissing my knees, which amused me and excited me, and I thought: This is where my childhood ends. In a dark room, at the height of the afternoon heat, with a man who looks like an insurance agent and smells of sweat.

"Maybe," he said, suddenly straightening up as if he'd seen a policeman peeping through the shutters, "maybe you should wait." He began pacing back and forth in the room. "I don't know why I brought you here in the first place."

"You didn't bring me here," I said. "I came because I wanted to."

"What did you want?" he hissed. "Do you know what you want? Do you realize I could be your father?"

"How old are you?" I asked.

"Thirty," he said.

"Then you couldn't be my father. Maybe biologically, but not mentally."

13

And this was the exact moment, if there are exact moments in these kinds of things, when he gave himself to me, the moment when I was angry with him for showing up drunk and stinking and pathetic, standing in the doorway, in a blue parka and muddy shoes, with a goofy smile on his face, as if he were testing me, to see if I would throw him out or if I was desperate enough to let him in.

14

And then he got off the chair, put the keys on the floor, lay down next to me on the mattress, and said: "What am I doing? What in the world am I doing?"

He took my hand and kissed it and opened my fist and spread my fingers out like a fan and looked at each of them separately, like a doctor or a piano teacher, and said: "Even your fingers are childish," and I felt the edge of his weird collar tickle my cheek.

I took his hand and looked at his fingers, which were not those of a child but the long slender fingers of a man, covered with a fine black fuzz on the knuckles, and I noticed that his fingernails were in better shape than mine, which were always bitten and ugly, hiding eraser bits and sugar granules underneath them.

"Do you bite your nails?"

"Sometimes," I said, "when I'm nervous."

"And are you nervous now?"

"No," I said, "not at all."

"I would be nervous in your place."

"But you are nervous."

And for a long time we examined each other's hands, counting the fingers, bending and straightening them, sniffing them, pondering them and making remarks that grew more and more obscure, and kissing their tips, as if this activity both brought closer and postponed the moment when those fingers would be free to do what they wanted.

When I undid his shirt buttons, in the slow motion of films, he went on mumbling: "What am I doing? What am I doing?" but I knew that he didn't really mean it anymore. He wriggled out of his sleeves like a snake without letting go of me, maybe so I wouldn't change my mind and run away, but I had no such intention, had nowhere to go. Except home, to my parents.

15

I sat on the sofa and listened to him puking his guts out. It didn't disgust me so much as it frightened me, because I felt that at that moment, hunched over the toilet bowl and retching and coughing and maybe crying too, out of sorrow or shame or a drunken longing for her—I had to decide: to wait for him to feel better and then ask him politely to leave, or wait for him to feel better and make him stay.

Again and again the water flushed and I sat on the sofa, all dressed for our date, less formal this time than last, in a new dress with a low neck that I bought that morning without any hesitation, for a fortune, in a teenager boutique, and I tried to concentrate, to detach myself from the sounds and the smell that suddenly spread through the house, I tried to forget that he was there, puking in my bathroom—a stranger who had been given my phone number and called without wanting to.

He shut himself in the bathroom, washing his face and drying it with the clean towel I handed him through a crack in the door, and before I could decide what to do with him I went into the bedroom and took a clean sweatshirt out of the closet, in case he wanted to change. I put the kettle on and took a lemon out of the fridge and as I stood at the stove waiting for the water to boil he came and stood behind me, smelling of vomit and soap.

"I don't want anything to drink," he said. "I think I'd better go. I've caused you enough trouble already," and I turned to him and said: "Have a cup of tea with lemon and see how you feel afterward. And there's a clean sweatshirt on the bed in the bedroom. Maybe you should change, you got your sweater dirty."

"I'm disgusting," he said, with the smugness of self-pity, and looked at the stains on his sweater, and then he went into the bedroom and came out again wearing my sweatshirt, holding his sweater with the tips of his fingers.

"Where should I put it?"

"On the floor," I said, "in the bathroom. I'll wash it for you in the morning, and in the meantime you can wear my sweatshirt home."

He drank the tea without saying a word, without apologizing, without explaining, without thanking me, and at eleven o'clock I called a cab, even though he said he could drive. "Tomorrow," I said, "when you pick up your sweater, you can take your car."

But the next day I didn't hear from him, and when I went down to check, the car wasn't there.

16

The milk was spoiled. He got out of bed and went to the kitchen, groping in the darkness which had already stolen into the room from outside, and I heard him cursing: "Fuck, the milk's spoiled," and I thought: This is the first time I've ever seen a naked man walking around next to me so naturally, and the naturalness frightened me more than the awkwardness that attracted me in the morning.

He came back to the room which was messy and secretive as a cave, and leaned against the door, illuminated from behind by the fluorescent light in the kitchen, scratching his leg. "Shit!" he said. "I got bitten all over. Did you?" and I thought that he was losing the mysteriousness of who he had been an hour ago, and maybe I was too.

"The milk's spoiled." He bent down and caressed my cheek. "I'm an idiot. I left it out. Are you okay?"

And I already began to feel pangs of guilt for things that happened only a year later, one summer evening, when I left him, deep asleep with a worried look on his face, wrapped in a floral sheet.

"I have to go to the bathroom," I said and got up, shaking off his hand which was gripping mine and trying to pull me down to the mattress.

"Stop it," I said, "I have to pee."

I sat on the toilet and heard the fridge door slam, and a spoon stirring in a glass, and a faucet opening and closing, sending shudders through the pipes and down my spine, and I imagined him walking around naked in the fluorescent light of the kitchen, and suddenly I felt sad and it burned when I tried to pee.

17

My mother said: "You're marrying a good man, but watch out," and I don't know if it was one of her general warnings, or if she had seen something in him, because she didn't like the way he never looked me in the eye, she said, and also he didn't hug me enough—"He respects you, and that's good, but he doesn't hug you"—and I said that as far as hugging was concerned, I wasn't perfect either.

I wanted him to know that I knew that with every hug we were hugging her too. When he turned to me in his sleep and drew me toward him, and held me in a scissorslike grip, I didn't hug him back, because I hated that young girl of his, who haunted our bedroom like a ghost.

And maybe with all those hugs in his sleep he was asking me to help him free himself of her and all the time he was sending me a message that his suffering would be my suffering too, but I didn't help him, because I was afraid of losing him altogether, which in the light of present circumstances seems stupid. But how could I have known then, at the beginning, in the era of infinite health, when I was so busy setting the rules, that those rules would be worthless in the end, because I planned that after the rules would come the love, which would keep us together until we were eighty?

I saw her once at the gas station. It was about three years ago, when Matti and I were waiting in line and she was standing there and filling her tank by herself, without help, as if she was born in a gas station, and without looking at me or at her, with his eyes staring at the dashboard, he whispered: "That's her."

I wanted to get out and go up to her to see her from up close, maybe even introduce myself and say: "Matti's in the car," but I didn't dare. I sat and breathed in the fumes of the gas and tried not to look upset, and behind the shoulder of the boy who was cleaning our windshield I saw her standing there, two cars in front of us, with the pump in her hand, looking at the gauge, her other hand on her hip, with a kind of self-assurance, wearing jeans and a T-shirt, chubbier and shorter than I imagined her, because I imagined something boyish, and Matti suddenly lit a cigarette and I said: "What are you doing? Are you crazy? You can't smoke here," and he put it out and I said to myself: At least she doesn't have such a great body, and her hair looks dyed, and I wanted to ask Matti if it was her real color, that faded orange, but all I managed to say was: "I thought she left the country."

And then I noticed that her car was rented, and I was glad, as if this was proof that she would no longer bother us, not even in our dreams, and I said to Matti: "It's a rented car," and he said: "Maybe she's visiting her mom and dad," as if she were still a little girl.

18

"Do you want to take a shower?"

"Why are you wearing that sheet?"

"Are you okay?"

"You want to take a shower?"

"Are you sure you don't want something to drink? You want me to go down and get milk? There's a minimarket here that's open till nine. When do you have to be home? Does it hurt you there?

There's hot water if you want to shower. I hope your parents don't show up here. Take off that stupid sheet already. Are you embarrassed in front of me? Me? Did I hurt you? Are you sure? Let me show you, the faucets are tricky. Here, take this towel, it's clean. You want me to shower with you? So let me show you how to regulate the water because you won't be able to do it on your own. You'll burn yourself, I'm warning you. Will you come tomorrow? I'm putting the towel here, on the chair. Look: the faucets are the wrong way around. You see? Look! You have a bruise on your thigh. Did I do that? Did you fall? This is the hot and this is the cold. The other way around. But what will you tell your parents? Are you sure I didn't do that? Tell me, are you going to shower with the sheet on? Does it hurt? Here's the soap and be careful not to lean against the faucets. They're boiling. So you'll call me if you need anything? Okay, okay, I'm leaving, I'm leaving."

But he didn't. He kept standing there and looking at me and suddenly I was too tired to be shy but still I didn't know if I should stand with my back to him or facing him, so I sat down in the tub, and I turned my head to him and saw that he was sitting on a stool, by the door, with his legs crossed, and the look of a contented observer on his face.

When did I get that bruise, I thought, but I couldn't remember. It looked pretty new and I'm always bumping into things, and I thought that maybe he was expecting me to put on a show for him, a striptease or something, but on the other hand I was already naked, so what was I supposed to do? And he said: "Get up, so I can look at you," and I said: "I'm too tired."

"But I want to see you," he said, and suddenly he sounded like a whining child.

"You already saw me," I said and soaped myself carefully because I felt sore all over, as if I was coming down with the flu.

"Then let me soap you."

"No," I said, and I brought the showerhead to my mouth and drank the hot water because I was really thirsty.

"Why not?"

"Some other time."

"But will there be another time?"

"Sure there will. What's the matter with you?"

"What's the matter with me? What's the matter with you? Suddenly you're acting like a child." He sat on the floor next to the bathtub, touched my shoulder, and said: "I can't believe I just fucked a child."

"What's that?" I asked and pointed at a bottle of shampoo with its lid open and black hair sticking to it. "Is it for dandruff?"

"Yes," he said. "But it's good. You can use it."

"You have dandruff?"

"Yes," he said. "Sometimes. Not lately."

"Don't you have any regular shampoo?"

"No. But I'm telling you that you can use it. It makes your hair really soft."

"But I don't have dandruff."

"You don't need to have dandruff to use it. Don't be a baby. Should I wash your hair for you?"

"No."

"Do you want me to leave?"

"Yes," I said, but he just sat there and looked at me, as if the side of the tub were the railing on a balcony and I was the view, and when I finished showering I got up quickly and bumped into the faucets and burned one shoulder. To this day I still have a little scar.

19

Just because he peed in his pants once doesn't mean it's the end. I gave him a lot to drink, because they told me to, but maybe I overdid it and that's what happened. But the next morning, when he opened one eye and the other one stayed shut as if it had been stitched with invisible thread, I realized that they were right, the doctors, and I thought: But why does it have to happen so fast?

The thing with the eyes didn't bother him but it frightened the children. They went in to say good-bye before they went to school and saw him lying on his back in bed like a cyclops and it was impossible to tell if he was awake or asleep. Shahar ran to me but Uri remained standing next to the bed. "Daddy," he said, "why do you have one eye open and one eye closed?" but he didn't expect an answer because for a few days now Matti hadn't answered them, or talked, only mumbled orders when he needed something.

Uri covered the open eye with his hand. "Can you see now?" he asked and Matti shook his head, as if Uri was another one of the countless doctors who had examined him over the past few months.

"And now?" he asked and took his hand away and Matti nodded.

"Daddy," he said, "I can help you if you want. I know what to do. We have to close the open eye so that too much light doesn't get in, otherwise it'll get tired. You want to sleep now, right?" And Matti nodded.

"So do you agree? Do you agree to let me make you better?" And Matti nodded seriously, like an obedient patient.

Uri put his school bag down, climbed onto the bed, bent over Matti, and gently pulled the lid down over the open eye. "There, I fixed it," he said but the eye opened again, like a rebellious shutter, full of curiosity and anger, and patiently the child tried to close it again, and again, until I came up and said: "That's enough. You'll be late for school. Let Daddy sleep."

"But he can't sleep like that!"

"Yes he can," I said. "He doesn't need to close both eyes to fall asleep, one's enough," and Uri picked his bag off the floor, disappointed and doubtful, and said: "I'll fix it when I come back," but when my mother brought them home from school they found me trying to raise Matti from the toilet.

Shahar went into the kitchen and I heard him dragging a chair to the cabinet to get candy, but Uri remained standing in the hallway looking at me as I led Matti to the bedroom, with one arm around his waist and the other hand holding the elastic of his pajama pants—growing up there all by himself, holding the strap of his brightly colored bag.

"Go to the kitchen," I shouted to him from the room. "I'll just put Daddy to bed and I'll come and make you something to eat in a minute," and I heard him going into the bathroom, and then I heard him flushing, because I'd forgotten.

20

He massaged my shoulder with margarine. "It's the best cure for burns," he said. "I told you to be careful." I sat leaning forward on the stool in the bathroom and his fingers stroked my shoulders, the one without the burn too, with the devotion of a nurse and the guarded lust of someone who doesn't want to go too far, because after all I was wounded.

"Poor thing," he said. "I bet it hurts like hell. I keep on burning myself too. Maybe I should change the faucets for plastic ones but fuck! It's a rented apartment, why should I invest money in it?"

He had no money, he told me. He worked occasionally in film productions, sometimes as an assistant director, sometimes helping with the sets or the lighting, or as a driver, and sometimes he volunteered to work as an extra: "I have the kind of face they're always looking for in movies. I look like the man on the street," he said and ran his hand apologetically over his hair. But there was no work now, so he sat in cafés and spent the time thinking. He didn't go anywhere in particular, because he didn't like any café in particular, and this morning he went to the Milano because it was cheap there, and because it had the atmosphere of old movies, "that you're probably not familiar with: small tables, large ashtrays, wallpaper, and old waiters who sometimes own the place and sometimes they're only there because the owner feels sorry for them. Eternal extras."

"Why not heroes?" I asked. "Just because they're old?"

"Maybe," he said. "It depends how you look at it. You're a little optimistic." He thinks it would be terrible to be old and unwanted, though it seems to him that being young and unwanted is even worse. He hopes it doesn't sound like self-pity, but he feels that his life would be a lot easier if he hadn't chosen a career in film. Maybe not easy, but more secure and stable, and sometimes he thinks: What does he need this for? He doesn't have an apartment of his own or a steady job, and up until a few hours ago he didn't have a love life either.

"And now?"

"Maybe not a love life, but at least a chance of something good. Or a change. You probably have no idea what I'm talking about, but lately my life's been more or less at a dead end. And it's not that I don't meet women. I do. And it's not that I don't go to bed with them. I do. And it's not that I'm lonely or desperate or anything like that. Because I'm not."

"My life's at a dead end too," I said.

"Maybe. But it seems to me that you're a little too young for that. I don't want to sound patronizing, but you have to travel a certain distance before you reach a dead end. That feeling that you've already seen everything and that nothing can surprise you anymore or provide you with a real challenge. And yes, in a way you were a challenge for me. You still are. And I don't mean getting you in bed, even though I know that you think you seduced me. You know what a challenge it is not to play games?"

"We didn't play games?"

"You have a lot to learn," he said.

He stood by the sink and washed his hands, soaping them thoroughly to get the margarine off, and then he looked at himself in the mirror, turning his head from side to side, raising and lowering his chin. "I need a shave," he said and bent down to me. "Feel. Here, isn't it horrible?"

The stubble, which hadn't been there before when we were in

bed, made a weird sound when I passed my fingers over it and gave him a sinister, criminal look. "I'll shave later, when I shower," he said, and dried his hands. Then he looked at himself in the mirror again, smiled, and said: "Do I look old?"

21

I met his mother at our wedding. He hadn't told me much about her, only that she lived for many years now in France and that she was old. "My mother's old," he said when I asked him about his family, "and my father died when I was a baby. As you see, I don't have much of a family background."

And because my father died a few years earlier, and left my mother alone, but also thriving and independent, I thought that maybe we had something in common after all, but he read my thoughts and said: "At least you have a mother."

"What do you mean?" I said. "So do you."

"No," he said. "What I have is a French passport."

And yet she came for the wedding and sat alone all evening— even though my mother tried at first to cater to her—a woman of about seventy, obese, wearing a black widow's dress and a strange hat. She smiled at me whenever I went up to ask if everything was all right and apart from the apologetic smile, which Uri inherited, there was no other resemblance between her and Matti.

"A very unfriendly woman," my mother whispered, "very un- pleasant," and I almost felt insulted for her, because she looked so out of it, sitting there on the chair with her black patent-leather bag, taking out a little mirror from time to time and looking at herself, or popping some cake into her mouth from the plate stand- ing on the chair next to her. That's all she did all evening: stared into the mirror and ate cake that my mother kept bringing her.

"What's it like to grow up without a father?" I asked him one evening, a few weeks after he moved in with me. "Like you'd imag- ine," he said. "What do you expect me to say?"

We were sitting in the living room waiting for guests to arrive. This was the first time I dared to invite people, because even though I wanted to show off my new status, to reassure my friends that things were working out for me too, and maybe get confirmation of the fact that we were together, because if we invited people over, if we played hosts, then we really were a couple. But I was afraid of the encounter, of his moods, or his aggressiveness, and of the fact that we looked like we weren't right for each other.

I apologized for being nosy and promised that I'd never ask him about his father again. "Or my mother," he said, and I said, "or your mother, if you don't want to talk about her." But when I danced with him at our wedding, I couldn't take my eyes off the woman sitting in the corner, eating cake and looking so lost.

When he called to tell her that we were getting married, he said to me: "You'll see, she won't come but she'll send a check. You can bet on it, and I want you to know, Mira, that I don't want her money. If she sends a check, I'll send it back. I don't need any favors from her." But she didn't send a check. She came. Maybe because she was already too old to send checks, something that Matti overlooked in his anger.

They came that evening and brought gifts, as if the fact that I was living with someone was an occasion for a housewarming: Eli and Hagit, and Dan and Liora, my friends, ready to accept Matti as a member of the family, to pat him on the back, and guide him through the intricacies of bourgeois life.

"So he's the child rapist?" Dan said to me in the kitchen, when he came to get soda for the Scotch they'd brought us from their trip abroad. "He looks pretty normal." And Liora, who drifted into the kitchen, because Dan had forgotten the ice, said: "He's sexy."

"Really?" I said. "You think so?"

"Wow!" she said. "I can see why that little girl fell in love with him."

And I couldn't explain to them that Alona was not yet part of the past, because it would have undermined the pretext for the housewarming, and I couldn't tell them that Alona wasn't going to turn into a banal subject of conversation in the kitchen so quickly, between filling bowls of peanuts and taking ice cubes out of the tray. I saw her in his eyes when he watched me coming in and out with trays of refreshments like a perfect hostess, and I didn't know if he was proud of me or ashamed, and I could feel her breath in his silence which continued all evening and I wondered: How come nobody else hears her little wings flapping against the furniture? How come they don't see her sitting with her legs crossed on top of the bookcase, laughing at all of us?

22

And for no special reason—maybe because I was so tired, maybe a delayed reaction to the burn, or maybe because of the stubble which suddenly made him look dangerous—I burst into tears.

He was frightened. Maybe he hadn't seen too many women sobbing in his bathroom without any explanation or advance warning, while he was standing in front of the mirror, half admiring and half disgusted by himself. He turned around and bent down and held my hands and shook me and asked: "What's wrong? What's wrong?"

I said: "I don't know."

"But what's wrong? What's wrong with you, Alona?"

"Nothing," I said.

"Let's go to the room, okay? It's too hot in here. Let's go back to the room and you'll tell me what happened."

"I want to be alone for a while. I'll come in a few minutes, okay?"

"But I want us to talk. We have to talk!"

"Yes," I said, "but in a little while."

"I knew this would happen," he said and looked at the mirror again, as if something had changed there in the meantime.

"What?"

"Forget it now. Maybe we shouldn't have."

"Shouldn't have what?"

"Gone to bed."

"But that's not why I'm crying."

"So why are you?"

"I don't know. I swear. I don't know."

"You must be traumatized. Did you ever see a dick before?"

"Sure I did. Don't flatter yourself."

"I'm concerned about you."

"Do me a favor, don't worry about me. Okay? I swear I've seen dicks before."

"Where?"

"It's none of your business."

"In pictures?"

"No. In person."

"But where? I want to know."

"Why? What's it got to do with you?"

"I'm just curious."

"Boys, at school. Boys I fooled around with."

"How old?"

"What a stupid question!"

"Why, is it a secret? Do you have secrets from me?"

"Fifteen, sixteen, maybe. Seventeen."

"Seventeen! And you want to tell me that they didn't try to fuck you?"

"There was only one who was seventeen."

"And?"

"He didn't try."

"I don't believe it."

"You think everybody only wants to fuck all the time? Like you?"

"So that's what this is all about, Alona? You think that all I want to do is fuck you?"

"No."

"So why did you say that?"

"I don't know," I said and burst into tears again. "You said you'd

leave me alone for a few minutes and you're just standing here
and arguing with me."

"But I want to know if that's what you think: that all I want is
to fuck you."

"No."

"Then tell me why you didn't sleep with that guy. That
seventeen-year-old."

" 'Cause I didn't want to."

"Why not?"

"I wasn't attracted to him."

"And you're attracted to me?"

"I don't know."

"So why did you go to bed with me?"

"Because I wanted to."

"But how could you want to if you weren't attracted to me?"

"I was."

"So before you were attracted and now you're not?"

"I don't know."

"You gotta know."

"But I don't."

"But you knew that you wanted to go to bed with me."

"Yes."

"Did you want to go to bed with me, or did you just want to
go to bed with anyone?"

"With you."

"You can tell me the truth."

"But I am telling you the truth."

"Maybe you just wanted someone to rescue you from your virginity."

"No. And that's disgusting. Don't say it."

"What: 'To rescue you from your virginity'?"

"Stop it!"

"So do you want me to leave you alone so you can decide
whether you want me or not?"

"No."

"So what do you want? You want me to take you home and we'll end it there? So you can run to your best friends tomorrow and tell them that you finally got fucked?"

"I don't have best friends."

"That's impossible. All girls have best friends."

"I'm not a girl."

"Oh, sorry. All young women have best friends."

"But I don't."

"You want to go home? I'll take you."

"I don't want to go home."

"So what do you want? Do you have any idea what you want?"

"No."

"Then let me tell you something: Maybe I'm a pervert and I really should go to jail but it's been years since I was so attracted to someone and it's been years since I had such a hard-on, like that seventeen-year-old of yours, and then you come on to me at the café . . ."

"I didn't come on to you."

"Yes you did. Your eyes were begging: Take me, take me, fuck me . . ."

"Stop it! That's not true!"

"So I take you home with me, and believe me I'm shitting in my pants the whole way, and we go to bed, and it's amazing, better than I thought it would be, because I had doubts, and you should know that it's my first time with a virgin, not that it excited me or anything, and I saw that it wasn't such a big deal either, all those stories about blood et cetera, unless I'm not the first, Alona, but forget it . . ."

"You are!"

"Never mind. As far as I'm concerned, it makes no difference to me if you've been fucking since you were ten. I'm just not sure what happens next, Alona, but I want something to happen, I don't know what, but I don't want it end as a one-night stand, and I want to teach you things, and I want to be with you, but I also don't want to get hurt, and all this time I'm thinking: Maybe she likes me, too? Maybe she's enjoying it, too? And I saw your face in bed and I thought that you enjoyed it. . . ."

"I did! I really did!"

"And you don't have to pretend, either. Do me a favor and don't start faking orgasms for me; you're too young for that. If you're not enjoying it, then tell me."

"But I was! I swear I was!"

"How do you know if it was your first time? You were so quiet. You didn't make a sound. I looked at your face and I thought: Yes, she's enjoying it. It's good for her. And now I think that maybe you were in pain. Did it hurt?"

"No."

"And now?"

"A little."

"And is that why you're crying?"

"No."

"You promise? Because that's the last thing I want, to hurt you. I think I was a little too violent."

"You weren't. It was good."

"Now you say that you don't know if you're attracted to me. . . . I'm sorry," he said. "I went too far. I don't know what I want from you. I have no right. . . ."

It saddened me when he wiped my tears with the back of his hand and then my nose and even kissed the snot. "I apologize," he said. "I won't put any pressure on you. Do whatever you feel like. I just keep forgetting how old you are."

"But it's not important how old I am," I said.

"It is, but I should have thought of that before."

"It isn't," I said. "It's not important."

He stood up, washed his face, and turned back to me, drying himself with a towel and mumbling into it: "You're still a child."

So I went down on my knees and pressed my cheek to his thigh and with one hand he held the towel and with the other he stroked my hair and I closed my eyes and he dropped the towel and lifted my chin with his hand and looked at me and smiled and said: "Your hair's still wet. I don't want you catching a cold." And I wiped my eyes on his thigh and felt it tensing and his hand dug into my hair. "Don't you dare catch a cold on me now," and he closed his eyes and held my face in both his hands and pressed it to his thigh, and I knew what I had to do.

23

Lake Kinneret was as crowded as usual during the Passover vacation, but this time it was also raining, and Matti, who was horrified by the idea of sleeping in a sleeping bag, got into the car and announced that we were going home. But he forgot the way. The children fell asleep covered with the towels we threw over them because we hadn't thought of bringing coats, and Matti, driving fast, in the dark, confused, cursing, couldn't remember how to get home.

"What's the matter with you?" I yelled.

"Nothing! What do you want from me?"

"I don't understand what happened to you!" I said, because this was the first time in my life that he had managed to really scare me. "What is it, Matti, don't you feel well?"

"I'm fine," he said, but when we hit a dirt road and the car sank into the mud and the children woke up, at first excited by the adventure but then petrified, I said: "That's enough! Let me drive!"

"Why?" he said. "You think you know the way better than me?" And the wheels skidded as he tried and tried to get us out of the mud but only sank deeper.

"At least I can see. I can read signs. You can't see well. Yesterday you complained that you couldn't see."

"I can see very well, thank you."

"But why? Why are you being so stubborn, Matti? Do you want to kill us all?"

And there was nobody to turn to for help. It was dark and cold and deserted and the rain beat down hard on the roof and the children began crying and it was clear to me that we weren't going to get out of there.

And suddenly he seized his head in his hands and began to shake and said: "I'm dizzy, I don't feel well," and when I said: "See what I mean?" he passed out.

I was trapped in a freezing car buried in the mud on a dirt road with two hysterical children and an unconscious husband whose head was leaning against the window with the seat belt choking his neck and I hated him.

I yelled at him to wake up and he rubbed his forehead on the wet window and opened his eyes for a second but closed them again and mumbled: "I don't feel well." "Matti!" I screamed. "You have to wake up!" He opened his eyes again and in the dark I could only see the whites of his eyes and he said: "I feel really sick." The children tried to climb over the back of the seat and reach me, and Shahar held out his arms in a panic.

"Matti," I whispered and slapped his cheeks. "Wake up!" I screamed. "Wake up!"

I got out of the car and opened the door on his side and unfastened the seat belt and tried to push him over to the other seat, but he was too heavy and he didn't budge, and I slapped him on the face because what else could I do? But it didn't help and his body slumped and slid halfway out the door and I could hardly keep him from falling into the mud.

I don't know how much time went by before he woke up. Maybe it was the cold and the rain that woke him, and I shouted quickly: "Move to the right, Matti, please! Move to the right! Just a little! Try to move just a little!" And he dragged himself over to the passenger's seat and let his head fall back and Shahar wound his arms around his neck so as not to lose him again, and Uri looked at his father's dead face and asked me what we were going to do now.

I didn't answer. I asked Shahar to take his arms off his father's neck because I could see it was hard for him to breathe and I said: "Uri, tell Shahar a story." And Uri said: "I can't. I don't know any, I'm scared." I put the car into reverse and said: "Then tell him the story that Daddy always tells you before you go to sleep, the one with the elephants and monkeys and rhinos." And he said: "There aren't any rhinos." I said: "Then tell it without rhinos, Uri, it makes no difference." And he burst into tears and said: "Yes it does!" So I said: "Then tell it however you want." "But I don't remember!" he wailed. "Yes you do," I said and pressed down on the gas pedal, and my foot slipped off it because the sole of my shoe was wet. "Do your best!" I yelled.

The wheels spun around and the car didn't move and out of the corner of my eye I saw Matti staring into space with a drop of spittle dribbling from his mouth and I said: "Tell him the story Daddy always tells you. You remember. Don't say you don't remember." "But I'm scared," he said, and it seemed that the rear wheels were moving a bit but it was only my imagination. "I can't remember any stories when I'm scared," and I pressed the pedal again, this time all the way, because I didn't have anything to lose anymore, and the car leaped backward with a terrible screech.

Matti and the children fell asleep and I tried to find the way to the hospital. First the main road, I said to myself, and then the hospital, and when we finally got onto the highway I felt my whole body trembling and I felt nauseated, and cold, and I thought that in a second I was going to pass out too, but of course that was out of the question, so I went on driving and the rain stopped and signs which suddenly looked so friendly began appearing at the sides of the road and Matti woke up and asked where we were.

"Near Tiberius," I said. "We're going to the hospital."

"There's no need, Mira," he said. "I'm feeling better now."

"Yes there is!" I said. "It could happen again."

"I'll go to the doctor tomorrow," he said, "okay? I promise. Let's just go home now."

"No," I said. "We're going to the emergency room. We must, Matti. You haven't been feeling well for a long time now. Maybe it has something to do with what happened on the night of the Passover meal."

"But I already told you, it was the food."

"You almost killed us all just now. You realize that? You can't see properly, you get dizzy spells, and now you passed out. Why are you so stubborn?" And I reminded him that a week before he had woken up in the middle of the night in agony. "You remember that?" I asked. "Yes," he said. "And you were in such pain that you didn't even know what you were doing." "What did I do?" he asked, worried.

"You kicked Uri. You pushed Shahar away and you kicked Uri. You kicked him in the stomach. He had a large bruise." "I didn't kick Uri," he said. "Don't talk nonsense." "You don't remember," I said, "you just don't remember!" And he turned his head and looked at Uri, who was sleeping wrapped in a big towel, with a tearful expression on his face and Shahar curled up next to him, his back rising and falling as he breathed, and I said, this time without anger, because I knew that nothing would ever be right again: "You really don't remember?"

He took off his sweater and spread it over the children, arranging the sleeves so that they would cover as much of both of them as possible, and said: "I remember," and promised me that tomorrow we'd go to the doctor together. "But let's go home now, I'm exhausted and I don't want to spend the whole night in the emergency room, and anyway doctors don't know anything. When did it stop raining, Mira? It hadn't rained so hard on Passover for a long time," he said and touched my cheek, and my eyes filled with tears. "Yes," I said, and he said, "Years," and I had no idea yet that this was our last Passover, and the whole way home we were silent and the children slept soundly and when we arrived he took Uri in his arms and I took Shahar. We left the luggage and the wet sleeping bags in the car.

24

"It's dark," he said. "You have to go home."

I lay on my back on the bed in the towel he had wrapped me in and listened to the sounds of the neighbors' dinners, the clatter of spoons and forks, and I didn't know what time it was but my hair was already dry. "It's dark," he said. "They must be worried about you by now. We don't want to get into trouble. You can come again tomorrow. We'll see what happens tomorrow. Why don't you come first thing in the morning?" And the strange thing is that I had no fear that by tomorrow he might forget me, this fear was acquired later on, with other men in other rooms, and maybe this is what made him fall in love with me, just this—when he looked at me as I tightened the edges of the towel around me and got up to look for my clothes and said: "So I should be here first thing tomorrow morning?"—because of my innocence.

"What time can you come?"

"Seven."

"Seven? Then I better give you a key."

And that was it. It was that simple.

He got up and went to the closet to look for a key, bending down and searching through the drawers, piling little boxes and envelopes on the floor, talking to himself, naked and busy. He stood up and looked around and mumbled: "Where could it be?" and scratched his head, and the insect bites on his legs, and he went into the kitchen, opened and closed drawers again, and asked: "Where are you where are you where are you?" singing to himself, and then came back to the room where I was standing all dressed holding my bag in my hands.

"I remember seeing it somewhere," he said, and glanced at his books. "It couldn't have just disappeared. . . . Here it is! It was on the dictionary." And he opened my hand and put the key in it and said: "Close your eyes and I'll give you a surprise," and

I closed them and felt his lips on mine, and his tongue inside my mouth, and his hands pulling up my tank top and unzipping my jeans, and we did it again, and all the time I was clutching the key in my hand.

25

The next morning I called the hospital and made an appointment. It was for May, but if it hadn't been for the secretary whom I went to high school with we wouldn't have gotten May either. "You're lucky to get this appointment," she said, and asked me how things were in general and what I'd been up to all these years. "You're very lucky!" she said and was impressed with the fact that I had two children. "How many do you have?" I asked. "Me? I'm not married. Do you know any single men?" "I'll think about it." I laughed. "What are you looking for?" "Handsome, rich, I don't care if he's old and dies and leaves me all his money. So May fifth, three o'clock, okay? I put you down," and I curse the day I made the appointment.

26

Because who knows? Maybe, if Mrs. Rosen hadn't called us, her husband wouldn't be lying now surrounded by tall trees and the stillness of terminal places. Two women are sitting on the lawn, each on her own side: one has short, steel-gray hair and the other dyed orange hair. Mrs. Rosen is sitting on a bench drying her eyes with a tissue which she then shoves back into her handbag, and the other woman is sitting on the grass making a chain from pine needles. For two weeks now Mr. Rosen has been lying next to an old man, and when he occasionally wakes from a restless sleep he complains that his neighbor is filling the room with the smell of death.

Every morning Mrs. Rosen changes the flowers in the jar standing on the night table, but he says it doesn't help and she doesn't
argue with him anymore. She takes a bottle of perfume from her
bag and sprays it around the room. "Is that better?" she asks with
the restrained gentleness of someone trying not to fall to pieces.
"No," he groans, and falls back to sleep.

The other woman doesn't dare go in. She waits until noon, when
Mrs. Rosen goes home, she steals into the building, walks quickly
past the nurses and doctors who know her face but don't know
who she is, stands outside the room for a few minutes, and then
retraces her steps. Sometimes she returns to sit on the same spot
on the lawn, and smokes a cigarette or two, and sometimes she
gets into her car and drives away. The other day both cars—the
Rosens' white sedan and the other car—were parked side by side.

Mr. Rosen is sinking fast, and they both know it. The wife from
what she sees for herself and her long conversations with our colleagues, and the other woman by the appearance of Mrs. Rosen.
When she came to us a month ago to arrange for his transfer to our
hospice, she made one more desperate attempt to negotiate his dying with us. We showed her the results of his latest brain scan, as if
we were showing a child learning to read a book with big letters. She
nodded and bit her lower lip, but this time she didn't cry.

"So, this is it? There's nothing more to do?"

"No," we said. "Only to make him as comfortable as possible."

"So he's dying?" she asked and again we couldn't bring ourselves to answer this simple question, and this time we felt a sense
of failure.

"Because if he goes into the hospice, it means he won't come
out again. It means he's dying. Doesn't it?"

"Yes," we said, and she seemed relieved.

And on New Year's Eve there was a vacancy and an ambulance
that wasn't in a hurry to go anywhere was sent to pick up Mr.
Rosen. He spent the holiday sleeping, his right eye permanently
closed and his left eye open in what might look, to anyone unfamiliar with the phenomenon, like an expression of terror. Patches

of thin black hair cover his head and his hands are gray and swollen. When his blood pressure drops, there is also a reflexive trembling of the fingers. During the last week he has also begun to lose
his ability to speak and the only word he manages to pronounce
now is: "no."

Sometimes this "no" is aggressive and childish, and sometimes
whining and old, sometimes there is a whole string of "noes" and
sometimes just one long drowsy one, but in any case it's a definite
"no" which comes with increasing frequency, and the medical per-
sonnel as well as his wife by now regard it as one more meaningless
detail in Mr. Rosen's disintegrating personality, the patient being
no longer conscious of the fact that he's negating everything, and
whose "no" means no more than the tremor in his fingers. Next
week, we assume, the foul odor coming from his roommate will
also stop bothering him.

27

It's horrible how much I've changed. He probably wouldn't recognize me anyway. And maybe it's better this way. I haven't seen
him for ten years, except once, three years ago, at the gas station,
when I was here visiting my parents. At first I didn't recognize
him, because he'd gotten another car, and the new one didn't go
with his old image, but suddenly I realized that it was him sitting
there in the white car, underneath the black hair, next to his wife.

If he'd been alone I might have approached him, but then again
I probably wouldn't have. So I pretended that I didn't see them.
I was afraid of him. I was afraid of what I did to him, even though
to this day I'm not sure exactly what it was, and if it was really so
terrible. I've left men, and men have left me since then, but maybe
there's something extra cruel about the first time, before you learn
how to do it right. On the other hand, there is no perfect way. I
didn't know what to do then, except pretend I was sleeping, and
when he fell asleep, sometime after midnight, pick my clothes up

quietly from the floor, put them on in the bathroom, take the lighter I bought him out of my bag, a plain silver-plated lighter without any inscriptions or monogram, because I thought it might seem ambivalent: How can you give someone a good-bye present hoping that he'll forget you, and at the same time inscribe your name on it? And I left it on the kitchen table, next to my key, and went out and closed the door quietly behind me, without locking it.

We were together for a year until he lost his nature's child, which I, apparently, never was. A year till that morning when I opened the door and heard the water running in the shower, and I went in and said a tired hello, and he turned to me with the nudity I already found boring, and saw me with my face all made up and said: "What's this? Take it off. You don't need it. Wash your face. You look like a slut." Because I really overdid it, with the exaggeration of sixteen-year-old girls, which makes them look like a scary cross between an aging nymph and a clown, and what's more, removes them from the custody of the guy who loved them in his own particular way, the love of old men.

And at the gas station, even though it was summer, I suddenly felt cold and I tightened my grip on the handle of the pump, as if that would speed it up, and I listened to its clicks and hoped that he wouldn't see me because the embarrassment would kill me, and I looked awful too, with messy hair and jeans that made me look fat and without any makeup.

If I'd only known, I would have gone up to the car, smiled, kissed him on the cheek, and said to his wife, "Nice to meet you, I'm Alona," exhibiting maturity and nonchalance, oblivious to the past—if only I'd known that in a few years' time I would find myself hiding in the corridor of the hospice without the courage to say good-bye.

When he dies, in a matter of days, maybe even hours, he'll take part of me with him. The uncensored version, like the lost draft of a short story that got too complicated—a whole suitcase filled with old belongings that someone had lovingly kept for you all these years, and now didn't want to give back. And I would have liked to ask him: But what was I like then? What did I look like? What did I sound like? And why me? It's a small town, and bad news spreads here as fast as gossip. Only a month ago I came back from Boston, and on the way from the airport I could already sense it in the air: "Have you heard?" said the girl whose apartment I rented, who was in high school with me and with whom I'd never exchanged a word, "Have you heard?" whispered the grocer in his old neighborhood, who remembered me even though I never bought anything in his store, because Matti forbade me to go in there so as to avoid suspicion, "Did you hear what happened to your boyfriend?"

28

"Pee pee!" he yells. "Pee pee! Mira. Pee pee!" And even though he's hooked up to a catheter, he keeps wanting to get up, yelling: "Take me to the bathroom, Miraleh, I have to go pee pee!" And I'm surprised that he still recognizes me.

At first I was ashamed for him, for both of us, and for all the people whose relatives were dying in different ways, quietly or noisily, in the other rooms. Whenever the nurse or the doctor walked down the corridor and he began screaming "pee pee," I'd try to shut him up, but the nurse or the doctor smiled at me understandingly and walked past the room.

"Pee pee!" he yells and tries to pull out the catheter. "Take me to make pee pee!" And I already miss last week, because last week he wasn't as restless and the only thing he said was "No." And now it's as if he's suddenly remembering other words, like "pee pee" and "take me" and "have to" and my name, and he yells them all the time, maybe so he shouldn't forget them again.

The children have also become difficult lately. Uri's in the third grade and Shahar's in first, and everyone at school looks at them with pity. I don't know what I'd do now without my mother, without her help, it's strange how she doesn't get on my nerves anymore, and what am I going to tell them when he dies?

"Tell them the truth, Mira." I was surprised she should say this, 'cause it would have been more like her to say: "Tell them he went away on a trip." She brings them back from school and cooks for them and cleans and does the laundry, and yesterday she even took our car to the garage and came back crying because the mechanic said: "Please accept my condolences."

"What a nerve!" she said. "Offering his condolences when Matti's not even dead yet?"

"He was only trying to be nice."

"He's not nice at all," she said. "He's a crook! Did you know he was a crook?"

"Yes," I said, "but at least he's a polite crook," and we both smiled for the first time in months.

"Remember what you said about Matti when you first met him?" she said, a little embarrassed, seizing a moment of intimacy between us which would soon disappear into the general tragedy.

"What, what did I say?"

"You said he aroused your maternal instincts."

"Really? I said that?"

"That's what you said, Mira, that's exactly what you said. And I knew you were in trouble."

"Why?"

"I just knew it, I had a gut feeling. You'd been dying to meet someone for so long, you poor thing, so many blind dates, all your girlfriends trying to fix you up, and nothing ever came of it, and I knew that you'd fall in love with the first man who even smiled at you."

But he didn't smile at me. Not even when he showed up at my door two weeks after the time he arrived drunk. He had a plastic bag in his hand and said: "I brought back your sweatshirt. I even washed it." I invited him in and waited for him to apologize for the other night, but he said nothing, so I took a sip of my tea and said: "Why are you here?"

There was a long silence, the kind that I got used to later, and then he said: "I was thinking, that if you have enough patience, maybe we could see each other after all, but I wanted to warn you that you might get hurt, with no intention on my part." And I said: "There's no such thing, 'with no intention,' and I'm not at the age when I can play games."

"But I'm not playing games," he said.

"You're not serious," I said, "and you're not even attracted to me. Why do you want to waste our time if you're not attracted to me?"

"Are you attracted to me?" he asked and for a moment there was a kind of childish curiosity about him that wiped out all his anger.

"It doesn't matter. Besides, it's hard for me to be attracted to someone unless I know that he's attracted to me."

"Now you're playing games."

I was attracted to him the minute I saw him. I was attracted to his face, even though he wasn't good-looking, and to his hands, which started playing with that lighter again, the silver-plated Zippo from the café, and his fingers stroked it so lovingly that I couldn't resist and asked: "Is it from her?"

"From who?" he asked.

"From the girlfriend you used to have."

"Yes," he said, "Alona gave it to me."

And I didn't ask about Alona anymore and I didn't want to know about Alona, and three months later he moved in with me, and brought Alona with him, and clothes which I knew Alona had worn, because whenever I threw them into the washing machine I saw it caused him grief, as if I were destroying fibers of Alona, stains of Alona, and her shadow followed me around the house, kept me company in the kitchen, and made me feel older than I was every time I did something like cook or bake—especially bake—or wash or clean, and the shadow slept in our bed, as our children did later on, and there was nothing I could do about it except set limits, wherever I could, for the shadow and for Matti.

And after we got married, when I went with him to sign up for a computer programming course, and when I set up job interviews for him, he hated me for arranging his life, but he said: "That's life. We all become middle class in the end," and sometimes, in his sleep, he smiled, and I knew that it wasn't intended for me.

29

It occurred to me that maybe I was his brain tumor. There was a weird expression on his face after the second time, when he stared at the ceiling and said: "I'm in trouble."

"Why?" I asked.

"Because I'm falling in love with you."

"So why are you in trouble?" I said, flattered in a way only little girls can be.

"Because I'm fifteen years older than you, and in a month's time you'll probably realize it and you'll leave me and find someone your own age, some horny, pimple-faced boy who won't be able to keep his hands off you."

He was really sad then, staring at the ceiling and lost in thought about the terrible future awaiting him. "Yes," he said, "it's clear to me that you'll leave me," but he was already embracing me as he said it, and then he said: "Too bad you have to go home."

"I can call my parents and tell them I went away. To *Lake Kinneret*, or somewhere."

"Lake Kinneret?"

"Sure, why not? People go there."

"And they'll believe you?"

"And if they don't, so what? At least I'm letting them know I'm not sleeping at home. At least I'm responsible."

"But I don't want us to get into trouble."

"I'll say I went with a friend."

"And what if they check up on you?"

"They won't. They wouldn't dare."

"And what if they do?"

"They won't."

"But are you allowed to just take off like that and go to *Lake Kinneret* without asking their permission?"

"I've never done it before, so I don't know. I hate *Lake Kinneret*."

"Me, too," he said. And in the dark I found the phone and dialed, pulling a cigarette out of his pack, feeling his fingers stroking my back, speaking to my mother in a hushed voice charging the room with a new tension. She said, of course, that I was irresponsible. "It's after dark," she said. "We were terribly worried about you. How can you do this to us, tell me: taking off like that without telling us? And where have you been all day? You're totally irresponsible." And when was I coming back? And who was this friend who she'd never heard of before?

"Matilda? What kind of a name is that? Is she an immigrant? Where is she from, Russia? Holland?! What's going on, are you lying to me?" And when are we coming back? When tomorrow? Before dark? And where are we going to spend the night? "And what about Matilda's parents, do they know? And what do they have to say about it? How, how can you do such a thing? We really thought that something happened to you, Alona. And who is this Matilda anyway?"

And it was strange sleeping with someone for the first time in my life, and suddenly I wanted us to go out somewhere, because it was stifling in the room with the shutters closed, but he said, "No. We can't be seen together," and wouldn't even open the shutters.

30

And I didn't know how to tell him that I spoke to the doctors and saw the scans, and that they explained everything to me, and all we're waiting for now is a bed. He was lying on the sofa watching TV, his legs covered with a thin blanket, one eyelid drooping and the other open, and the room smelling of shit.

He actually had a good day, no pain or nausea, and I said: "Move over a little, Matti, I want to see if you need changing." And he tried to raise himself but couldn't, and I said: "Please, Matti, make an effort, I can't do it alone." And he tried again, staring at the screen the whole time holding the remote control in his hand, and he managed to raise his hips a little, but before I could look into the diaper he sank back onto the sofa, and I said: "Forget it, Mother will be here soon and she'll help us."

Because I couldn't do anything without her. She helped me lift him from the bed and put him in the wheelchair and transfer him to the sofa, which had become his small territory, with the big tin ashtray he liked so much and the cigarettes he forgot he lit and left burning in the ashtray, two or three at a time, turning into heaps of ash.

He spent his days in front of the TV—with the children ignoring him, making detours around him careful not to bump into him while they played—and when it became too difficult to take him to the bathroom, my mother said: "That's it, Mira. He needs diapers." And when I said: "I can't do it," she said: "I'll help you." "No," I said, "I can't emotionally," and she said: "Patience, Mira, until there's a vacancy in that place. In the meantime think of him as a baby."

But he wasn't a baby, and when my mother came back from the drugstore one day with a package of disposable diapers and said: "I got the biggest size," I started crying so hard that she grabbed my hand and dragged me into the kitchen, holding the diapers under her arm, and said: "That's enough, Mira! It will be over soon. You can cry then."

But I wouldn't let her help me, at least not the first time, because I wanted to leave him a little self-respect, and even if he had to be my baby, he didn't have to be hers. I dried my tears and took the package from her, and we waited for the children to fall asleep, and in the meantime he lay on the sofa in his soiled pajamas staring at the TV and I said: "Let me change the channel for you," because there was a soccer game on and he hated soccer, but he shook his head and said: "No!" And that's where that business with the "No" started.

I went back to the kitchen, and I saw my mother sitting at the table and smoking a cigarette she took from Matti's pack, and I said: "Mom? You're smoking? Since when do you smoke?" And she said: "Sometimes. Lately I get the urge. I guess it's because of the stress." And I said: "I didn't know you smoked," and she said: "Daughters don't know everything about their mothers," and with an amateurish flurry, she blew out a couple of smoke rings, coughed, and said: "But these are too strong for me."

I went to look at the children, and then I kissed them and shut the door, even though I never do because they get frightened when they wake up in the dark and the door's shut, and I went back to the kitchen and said to my mother: "Don't come out now, okay? You promise?" And she said: "Yes," and put out the cigarette and said: "Disgusting!"

"I'm going to make myself a cup of coffee. You want one, too?" "No," I said, and opened the package with a knife, and took out a folded diaper, and looked at it as if there hadn't been millions of these in the house only a few years ago, and she said: "I bought wet wipes too," and I thanked her and took the wipes which were in a blue container shaped like a teddy bear out of the shopping bag and went into the living room.

"Matti," I said, "I think you need a diaper," and he didn't answer, just went on staring at the players running around the soccer field silently, because I'd turned down the volume when I was putting the children to sleep. "Okay, Matti? It's not that bad. It's a little difficult for us to take you to the bathroom. You're getting too heavy," and all that was missing was for me to say: "God, you became such a big boy!" But he didn't react, not even when I pulled down his pajama pants and his underpants, and he didn't see the look on my face when the smell suddenly hit me, and it wasn't at all like a baby's smell. "Raise yourself on your elbows a little, Matti, just a little," I asked him and he obeyed, and then I remembered that I'd forgotten to bring a towel, and what was he going to lie on now? But I didn't want to call my mother, so I whispered: "Just stay like that for a minute. Keep your behind up," and that was the first time I'd used that word, but I couldn't say butt, or tushie either.

I took off his pants and underpants and rolled them up, trying not to get anything on the sofa, and with my other hand I pulled a bunch of wipes from the teddy bear and wiped him quickly and threw them on the floor, and spread the diaper underneath him and it was too small, and I could hardly close the stickers, and the whole time he did his best not to let himself drop to the sofa and his thighs trembled, and the whole time I didn't see a thing, nothing, not even what he had in front, which wasn't like a baby's but like an old man's.

31

I began to feel suffocated that night. I tried to find a position to sleep in, to escape the big arm that lifted up like a crane to pull me to his side. It was hot in the room, and it was still early, outside I could still hear TVs and bits of conversation and the horn of a passing car and a child or two who were still awake. I missed my bed with its hard mattress, and my mother's cross-examinations, not really wanting to know but afraid not to ask, and my desk with the crowded drawers, and my secrets, and the window that was always open in summer, not like this window with the shutter that didn't let in a bit of light or air.

I got up to go to the kitchen, and on the way I pulled his T-shirt off the closet door and put it on, and I took my bag too, and my panties which I found rolled into a ball on the floor, and the cigarettes and matches and ashtray, as if I were going on a trip, and in the ugly fluorescent light I tried to work on the poems I'd started in the morning, which seemed like such a long time ago, as if this would turn the wheel back, to the time when I thought I was the seducer, but nothing came, not a word, and the buzz of the fluorescent reminded me of the bees in the morning, but it was much scarier.

And at one o'clock in the morning he woke up to go to the bathroom and said: "Alona? Where are you? Why did you get up?" and he came into the kitchen with his hair rumpled, stroking his chest which was damp with perspiration, blinking and smiling a drowsy, sensual smile, took a drink of water from the bottle, and asked: "Is everything all right? You can't sleep? What's happening?"

He sat down opposite me and yawned and stretched his legs, and his toes, still warm from bed, touched mine and his toenails pricked me. He looked out through the balcony door into the neighbors' kitchen and said: "I hope they weren't spying on us, those perverts. They're always spying." He got up and stood behind me, to look at what I was writing, and when I hid the paper napkins with my hand he laughed: "You have secrets from me? From me?" And I thought: Yes. You.

What was the meaning of that hatred I felt, and the fear, and the desire to be alone so I could digest my new maturity like a python digesting a mouse, whose shape you can see clearly in its stomach, and Matti's shape was on me too—all kinds of red marks and little scratches. I know I should have been happy, but I was sad.

"I taught you everything you know," he yelled at me through his tears a year later, when for the first time he dared to call me at home, because I was always the one who called him: he wasn't allowed to call me. He cried and said: "You can't just leave like that, at least come over and we'll talk." But I said: "No." "You think you can leave me a lousy lighter and walk away? Is that what you think?" And I said: "No." "We'll just talk," he said. "No," I said. "I taught you everything you know!" he said, and I heard him light a cigarette and take a deep drag. "Everything! You knew nothing when we met, nothing! Nothing, Alona, not even how to fuck!" I kept quiet, and he saw this as an encouraging sign and said: "Come on, Alona, please. We'll just talk," and I said, quietly: "No, Matti, no," and he shouted: "So that's it? Is that all you have to say?" And I hung up.

Sometime during spring I started not to want him, because the winter passed quickly and it was very cold and rainy, and allowed for cuddling and playing hooky from school and stealing into his bed early in the morning and I had my own key, and maybe I mistook all this for love.

He tried to repair the damage and seduce me all over again, and sometimes he begged. But I came over less and less, and I didn't call him from pay phones anymore to chat, and he sat in his apartment and went out of his mind worrying where I was and who I was with, and if I was suddenly growing up behind his back. And when I came over I would take the little gifts he started buying me—earrings, bright plastic rings, pens and pencils and notebooks, and socks—and put them in my bag and ask: "You want to have sex?" And he would look at me suspiciously and say: "But you don't want to." But I said that I did, and from the minute I lay down on the bed, it made no difference.

But that night there were only the beginnings of love and suffocation, and suddenly he was hungry and said: "There's nothing in the house," and he opened the fridge and looked inside. "Not a thing," he said. "The house is totally empty," and he opened the bread box, and then searched the cupboards. "And there's nothing open around here. All the stores are closed. I'm dying! What are we going to do?"

32

On New Year's Eve they called to say there was a bed. They asked if we could get there on our own and I said no. Not with all the stairs. They said they would send an ambulance in the afternoon and that we should be ready. "Yes," I said, "thank you very much," and when I put the phone down I went into the living room and saw him sleeping like a baby, covered with a floral sheet, the TV flickering, the pictures lighting and darkening his face. The children went downtown with my mother, and I could sense the holiday in the building, the tension, the hysteria, and I thought: How can we be ready?

Because except for his left eye it looked like he was just finally sleeping quietly after so many nights of agony, long sweltering nights when he didn't shout anymore, just lay groaning on the sofa, because there was no longer any point in moving him to the bed, and I would lie awake and listen the way you listen to a baby, to catch the crying before it really starts, I would go to him and try to make him more comfortable with all kinds of nonsense like raising his pillow, or lowering it, or adding another one, or taking them both away, and removing the sheet, or bringing him a blanket if he was cold, or moving the fan closer if he was perspiring, and making all kinds of suggestions in a voice I tried to keep as calm as possible, and hear him whispering all the time: "No, no, no."

The children had gotten used to sleeping with their door closed. They preferred waking up in the dark to hearing him groan or seeing me walking up and down the hallway not knowing what to do. And all the time I was waiting for this call, for them to tell me there was a bed, and only when the woman with the pleasant, practiced voice called did I really understand what it meant, and that when Matti died the same woman would call another woman and say the exact same thing to her.

I opened the closet and took out the duffel bag, which was still full of the dank smell of *Lake Kinneret*, and I shook it out the window, and stood it on the bed and I didn't know what to pack. There was no need for clothes, or for books, so I took a few pairs of socks and underwear from the shelf and put them into the bag, which only made it look larger and emptier.

I went into the living room to check on him. He was still sleeping, and his breathing was quiet and peaceful, and I don't know if it was because he didn't know what was going on, or because he knew that I was in the other room, packing his last bag.

I felt like a traitor and I couldn't go on. I sat in an armchair and looked at him and at the weekend papers strewn over the table, and at a few pieces of the children's jigsaw puzzles that they forgot to put back in the box, and at the banana-flavored yogurt I had tried to feed him this morning with the spoon still in it, and at the layer of dust on everything—I hadn't dusted there in ages because I was afraid to disturb him. The sofa and the table and the carpet underneath were now part of his illness and they looked contagious, and I asked myself if I would have the courage to exchange them for new ones, because I couldn't imagine myself and the kids sitting on this sofa of Matti's, which looked like a stretcher now. I heard the children running up the stairs, followed by my mother's slow steps, and the door opened and suddenly the house filled with the holiday atmosphere, and the children ran straight to their room, even Uri, who was finally learning how to ignore the situation, and my mother remained standing outside and I heard her saying to a neighbor who asked if we needed anything: "No, thank you very much." "Then Happy New Year," said the neighbor, "and wish Matti and Mira a Happy New Year too."

33

He called it "pigging out," the cheese omelette and the canned soup and the radish salad and the one yogurt he found in the fridge, which looked spoiled anyway.

He cooked cheerfully. He stood at the gas stove and stirred the soup with the impatient movements of a hungry man, and broke two eggs into the pan, and stood on tiptoe to take down a rusty grater from the shelf and grated a little piece of cheese he found in the fridge door, wrapped in plastic, after peeling off the green parts, and he looked at me and said: "Sure you don't want any?" and I said no, and tried to smile and look just tired.

"Are you in a bad mood?" he asked and shoved a forkful of radishes into his mouth. "You look sad. Don't you want to eat? It's delicious!"

"I'm not hungry," I said.

"But you should eat something," he said. "It's really good."

"But I'm not hungry," I said.

"You are."

"I'm not."

"Start eating and you'll get an appetite. Here," he said, and put some yogurt on a spoon. "Open wide!"

So I ate, unwillingly, with a sour face, spoonful after spoonful, and suddenly, with an appetite, the radish salad too and the cold remains of the omelette. "See?" he said. "You were hungry. Now you'll sleep like a baby."

And I really did fall asleep, under his arm, and because I was so young it took me a year to realize that what seemed to me like giant steps into a wonderful adulthood were actually steps backward, into a new childhood even worse than the old one.

And when I came home in the morning, my mother didn't have to ask to know that I hadn't been on a trip with the invented Matilda, because I had nothing with me except for my bag with the paper napkins she found later in the garbage and said to me quietly: "Alona, these are your poems. Why throw them away?" and some change, and cigarettes, and in the inside pocket the key he gave me.

All day long I lay in bed and thought about him, and my room which I missed all night suddenly seemed to be mocking me, and the thought about his room, with its darkness and the closed shutters and the life conducted on the floor, seemed like home, not the kind you live in but the kind you take refuge in, like a shelter, and in the evening I lied again and went to him again and at the door my mother grabbed my arm and said: "Do what you want, just be careful." "And you won't say anything to Dad," I said. "You promise?" "I won't say anything," she said, and pressed her finger to her lips, as a gesture of discretion or maybe to hold back a sigh of anxiety—and I ran all the way to his house.

34

Our daily life was so banal that our nights were almost macabre. We both dreaded the moment when darkness would fall signaling the end of all the chores and tasks and small things that kept us busy during the day separating us, and we'd end up sitting together in the same living room, on the same sofa, staring at the same TV set and sharing the same silence.

And I wonder now whether it was really her fault, because you can't lay so much guilt on the shoulders of one little girl, and only now, when he's almost gone, do I dare to think that Alona was my excuse.

He didn't court me. He simply appeared at my door—one time drunk, one time sober, and the third time he showed up one night without warning, and I thought that I was tired of the whole thing and I should just throw him out, but then I noticed that instead of the silver lighter he had a disposable one, and when I asked if he lost the other one, he said: "No. But I know it bothers you, so I bought this one on the way here."

I knew that this couldn't mean a turning point, or that he's falling in love with me, but it touched me, even though I knew that the silver lighter wasn't really out of our lives, but safely stashed away in his house, or maybe in his pocket.

And at that moment it also didn't bother me that I was caught wearing a sweatshirt and sweatpants and socks, not wearing any makeup, because I realized that my role here was not to be an object of desire—that was hopeless—but to be a refuge, something that I know how to do. He said: "I prefer you like this."

"Like how?" I said.

"Like this. Sloppy. Not all dressed up."

"Sloppy? This is what I wear around the house."

"It suits you. And you look good without makeup too."

"Really?" I said. "You think so? But I would never dare leave the house like this."

"So maybe you should start daring," he said.

And I asked: "Dare to do what?"

"Things," he said. "All sorts of things you wouldn't do if you had too much time to think about them."

"Like what?" I asked.

"Would you like to take a shower with me?"

"I just took one," I said.

"That's not the point, Mira. But never mind. Forget I said it."

"What's going on?" I asked. "Are you testing me?"

"No," he said, "I'm not," and he stood up to go, forgetting the plastic lighter on the table, and I knew that I had to do something, fast, so I said: "But if you like, you can take a shower. There's plenty of hot water left."

"And will you keep me company?" he asked.

"Yes," I said. "I'll keep you company."

35

Alona, I said, my name's Alona, and she said: I know. She was standing there in the corridor and she looked so alone that I felt sorry for her and went up to her and said: I've seen you here before. I know, I said, it was stupid of me not to introduce myself, but I didn't have the nerve. I told her that I understood, that it was hard for all of us, and I asked if she wanted to go in and see him, because there wasn't much time left. I don't know, I said. You think he'll recognize me? No, I said, I don't, because he doesn't recognize me anymore. And I thought: What's one thing got to do with the other? Because I don't know what's worse, I

said—and looked at her short hair, so soft and spiky that I wanted
to touch it—if he recognized me or if he didn't.

So you're Alona, she said and smiled. I'm Alona, I said, like it
was a confession or a sudden sigh of relief. I heard about you, I
said and thought how intimidating that statement was, and I looked
at her face, which was long and soft-featured, and said to myself
that she has a good complexion. It was hard for me to look her in
the eye and she took off her glasses and wiped them with the tissue
she had in her hand, a tissue soaked with tears. I think you should
go in anyway, I said, because you won't forgive yourself if you don't.
And I thought: How does she know what I'll forgive myself for and
what I won't, but I knew she was right. Because you've been hanging around here for two weeks trying to make up your mind, and
I wanted to tell you long ago: I'm Mira. I'm his wife. But I didn't
have the nerve. Yes, I said, I understand. It's an awful situation.

For all of us, I said, to console her a little, because after all she
was the outsider and she wasn't part of the family, but at least he's
not suffering like before, or so the doctors say. And you believe
them? I asked and regretted it immediately, because what did I
want from her and why put her through more torture, and I said:
No. I don't believe them. Do I have any other choice?

And the boys? I asked. Where are they? At home, I said. They
haven't seen him for two weeks. There's no point. No, I said,
there's no point. You're right. But my mother's with them. She's
an angel, my mother. Mine too, I said, maybe all mothers are when
you need them. Yes, I said. You're right. How long have you been
in the country? A month and a half, I said. I came back a month
and half ago. Five years in Boston were enough. It's a pretty boring
place when you think of it. Yes, I said, like here. And you're not
married yet? I asked and immediately regretted it, because what
right did I have to pry into her personal life? No, I said. I haven't
found anyone. And are you interested in meeting someone? I
asked, and I thought what the hell am I doing playing matchmaker
in this corridor, and who am I going to introduce her to anyway,
when the man who loved her most in the world, who's going to

die still loving her, is lying there in the room next to his neighbor's empty bed.

I'm not exactly looking, I said, surprised at the conversation we were having, but I'm open to suggestions. You're still young, I said, there's no rush. I got married when I was thirty-one. I wondered what would have happened if Matti and I had been the same age when we met. If anything would have happened at all. If it was me or my age that he wanted. So you haven't seen him in ten years? No, I said. I can't believe ten years have passed already. It's really a long time. So you must be twenty-six now, I said, and I felt old and bitter just because I said it. Yes, I said, I'm an old maid. And I said: How can you call yourself old? You still have plenty of time to find someone. As if I was telling her: Leave my dead husband alone.

Yes, I said, I'm not in a rush. So you think I should go in? I think you should, I said. If you like I'll wait outside, and I thought that I was actually glad that she was here, because I'd been so alone lately. And I didn't know if I wanted her with me in the room or not. Which was more intimate? And I saw her hesitating, so I said, whatever you prefer, Alona, and suddenly my hand touched hers, and her hand was very cold, but still a hand, so I grabbed it and squeezed it hard and she said: You're right, Mira, I really should go in. Or else I'll never forgive myself. But what I really wanted to say was: And you, do you forgive me?

Because there was really something touching about her. Sexy and sad and touching, and it was obvious that she'd been through a lot since she was fifteen, but I had the feeling that something in her hadn't changed, the same something that he saw in her then, maybe the look in her eyes, which is something that never changes. I thought about the way she dressed, so neat and clean-cut, and how thin she was, and what beautiful hands she had. Not like mine. And that reminded me of his hands and how they had once hypnotized me. So are you going in? I asked and glanced at the room which seemed deserted, as if there were nobody in there anymore. Yes, I said, I think so, and I was sorry that she suddenly pulled her hand out of mine. So do you want me to go in with you, or would you rather I wait out here? And I didn't know what to say, so I said, maybe I'll go in for a few minutes, and you'll come afterward. But she went on standing there as if she was waiting for me to push her inside. And what I really wanted was for her to hold my hand again and take me away from there.

I think I'll go downstairs for a few minutes first, I said. I need a cigarette. What do you smoke? I asked. "Marlboro," I said. He smoked Nelson. Yes, I said, I know. He always smoked Nelson. And you? I wanted to ask, were you already smoking when you met him? You were so young. It's a terrible habit, I said, I wish I could quit. Have you tried? I asked because he tried so many times, because of me. For the sake of the children. No, I said, I never tried. So are you going downstairs? I asked and I saw that her hands were trembling. I don't know. I'm confused. I'm afraid to leave. I'm afraid that when I come back they'll tell me, you'll tell me. Go downstairs, Alona, I said. There's still some time left. It could take another few days. Go and smoke your cigarette. I'm here.

She's here. And, as usual, I'm running away from him. And both of us are adults now. She more than me. Almost old, in many ways. With her silver hair and glasses and slender neck and pearl neck-lace. Don't worry, I said. I'll wait for you here. Go downstairs and smoke. No, Mira, I'll go in and see him, because if I go downstairs I won't come back. I'll lose my nerve. But in a minute. Give me a second. Maybe I'll sit down for a minute. Did you get those here, the shoes, or are they from the States? These? I asked. From the States. They're nice, I said though they weren't. They look com-fortable, too. Yes, I said, and I looked at my shoes, clumsy hiking boots, they're really comfortable. My feet are too narrow for shoes like that, I said, yes, I said, mine are really very wide, and suddenly I was ashamed of my feet.

And it's sort of difficult driving in them, because they're so heavy that you don't feel the pedal. Never mind the gas, I said and thought of my own driving, and how nervous and reckless I was these days, what's important is the brakes. Right, I laughed, at least it's an automatic so there's no clutch. Did you buy a car yet? I asked. No, I said. It belongs to my parents. I don't have money yet. Just do me a favor, don't buy one like ours whatever you do. No, I said, what car do you have? As if I didn't know.

Was it you who scratched my car in the parking lot? I asked, because the day before yesterday someone left a big scratch on the driver's side, and she always parked next to me. It wasn't me, but I felt like confessing something, so I said: Yes. I wanted to leave a note. So that was your car? Yes, I said, it was our car. I'm sorry, I said. I'm a criminal. Tell me how much it'll cost to fix it and I'll give you a check right now, but I said: Forget it. It isn't too bad, even though the damage was pretty serious, but I felt sorry for her. I think I'll go in now, I said. Look how your hands are shaking. Yes, I said and looked at my hands, they are shaking a little, maybe because I haven't eaten all day. I have some gum, I said, if that will help. No thanks, I said, I'm going in, but first tell me how he looks. So I shouldn't be shocked. Terrible, I said, you won't recognize him, and suddenly I felt good saying this to her. Is he thin? I asked. Very, I said, but he's swollen from the medications, it's going to be difficult for you, Alona. I'm warning you. I know, I said, I probably won't recognize him. No, I said, nobody would. As if she were nobody.

She was nicer than I'd expected her to be, though I never thought of her as the enemy, because it wasn't he who left, but me. And I hated her less than I thought I would, though it didn't seem fair to me that I was the one who'd been with him all these years, and she was the one who got all the love. And was he your first? The question burst out of me without any warning. Yes, I said, and they say that you never forget the first. No, I said, you never forget. I tried to remember my first time, and that winter night in the dorms, and all I could remember was a face hovering over me with closed eyes, and me staring at the space heater.

And I think I was lucky that he was the first, because someone else might have taken advantage of me, you know, broken my heart. No, I said, Matti's not like that. You really were lucky. And your parents, did they know? No, I said, to this day they don't. My mother suspected, but she never asked. Yes, I said, mothers are like that. They're afraid to know. True, I said. And his mother, does she know? No. She died a few months after we got married. Oh, I said, what a pity. Yes, but it's better this way, because imagine what she would have to go through now seeing him like this. Just imagine.

So she knows exactly what I know, the same body with minor changes due to age. Maybe she doesn't know the little paunch, which is new, but she surely remembers the pimples on his back. And I've been with so many men since then, that I don't remember what his body looks like, only that he had a little fuzz on his chest, a strange little patch of hair, as if someone tried to plant grass there and failed. And what else does she know about him? And does she know our secrets? What did he teach her in a year? And what secrets did we have anyway? So this is the girl he held in his sleep? Is he conscious? I asked. No, I said, he's been unconscious for two days now.

She cried. The tears of someone for whom crying is part of a daily routine, and I envied her, because I haven't cried even once since I found out. I'm sorry, I said, I'm just stressed out. And I quickly put my hand on her shoulder, and at first she recoiled, and then she just stood there crying with my hand on her shoulder, like a blanket. You have no idea what I've been through, I said to her, hating myself for the self-pitying tone. I can imagine, I said, and I looked at my hand, which was big and ugly with bitten fingernails, compared to her tiny shoulder. It must have been awful for you. Yes, I said, awful. Do you know what it's like to see your husband dying in front of your eyes? Your family coming apart in your hands? No, I said, but I can see how devoted you are to him, and I thought of this shoulder, if it had been the support he deserved, because he was good, good to me, a good man, and he deserved someone who'd be good to him too. Yes, I said, and she blew her nose, and when she bent down to throw the tissue away her shoulder slipped from under my hand, so I quickly put my arm around her waist, which was narrow, like her feet, and I could feel her bones under my fingers, just as he must have felt when he held her, if he held her, and I said: Come, Mira, let's sit down.

We stared at the TV that was standing on a shelf suspended from the ceiling and soundlessly broadcasting the news, and the ward was empty, and the big ashtray was full of Styrofoam cups and soda cans and candy wrappers and plastic bags and newspapers and a few lipstick-stained cigarette butts though smoking was forbidden, so I also lit a cigarette and offered her one, and she said: No thanks. I don't smoke. And I remembered that she said that she was always asking him to quit, and that he tried and couldn't.

So now he won't smoke anymore either, I said, and again I burst out crying, because I remembered when they came to take him in the ambulance and he was lying on the stretcher covered with a sheet he suddenly woke up and said: Don't forget my cigarettes, and without thinking I took two packs from the kitchen drawer and threw them into the bag I packed for him, but he hadn't smoked a single one since then.

And we sat for a while in silence, with her sniffing and deftly drying her eyes with the edge of the crumpled tissue, and me taking deep puffs on my cigarette and blowing the smoke out straight ahead, so as not to bother her, and seeing out of the corner of my eye the pearl-colored stockings she was wearing matched her necklace, she was now stroking with one hand while the other was clutching her purse.

And I wanted her to come home with me, so that at least she would see the children, what he's leaving behind, and so that the shadow he brought into our home wouldn't completely vanish, because suddenly I started missing the shadow too, but I didn't dare ask her, because what was I to her, other than the dull wife of her great childhood adventure.

And I wanted to ask her if we could stay in touch. Be friends or something. But I hesitated, because I knew it would sound unnatural, because what did we have in common aside from this strange temporary intimacy, and an unconscious man lying a few feet away, who was more hers than mine, because she had his children who were now tucked away in bed in their pajamas, and suddenly I felt so single and barren, and I wanted to cry too, but the tears wouldn't come.

Look at the time, I said. I've been here all day. You lose all sense of time in a place like this. Maybe I should call home to see how the children are. And I thought: Who can I call? Maybe I'll wait a few more minutes, I said, my mother must be putting them to bed now. Aren't they asleep by now? I asked. No, she smiled, they're naughty. Especially the little one. What's the little one's name? Shahar, I said, and it was soothing, to say my son's name. And the older one? Uri, I said. That's a nice mane. Yes. I laughed. I always liked that name. Matti too. He chose it, actually. He's very attached to him. And Shahar? I asked. To him too, to both of them, but he has a special bond with Uri, and I wanted to say to her, it's because of you, but I didn't know how she'd react, if she'd see it as an accusation, and suddenly I didn't know if it was true or just a theory I'd developed to protect myself from the depression I sank into after I gave birth to Uri. What kind of a bond? I asked, and what I really wanted to know was: What kind of a father is he? Something that would never even have occurred to me to think about when I knew him. They're a lot alike, I said, the spitting image of each other, and I remembered what I was thinking at his circumcision, after I recovered from all the festivities, that giving birth ruined my chances of ever remaining as young as she did for him. Does he have green eyes, too? I asked. Exactly the same eyes, and eyebrows, you wouldn't believe it, and the hair, even though Matti doesn't have too much left, and the smile, Alona, if you could just see his smile.

A guilty smile? I asked. Yes, she laughed, exactly. You have to see that child to believe it, and this was my opportunity to invite her over, but I didn't dare. And Shahar? I asked. Who does he look like? Only out of politeness, because talking about Matti's smile and his son's brought me back to our café, which I dropped into a few days ago and saw that nothing had changed, except that they'd enclosed the courtyard and put up a glass roof, and I sat alone in the roofed courtyard, and the waiter, who was really old now, came up to me and took my order and didn't recognize me.

You know, I said, how many times I tried to imagine what you looked like? Really? I said. And how did you imagine me? I don't know, suddenly I was embarrassed, because what could I say? I imagined you more or less as you are. Maybe a little younger. I was, I said, I was a lot younger. And for some reason I thought you had black hair. No, I said, it was never black, mousy brown is my natural color. So do you henna it? I asked and looked at her hair, searching for mouse-brown roots, or is it dyed? Both, I said, for years now. I have to do it again. I haven't done it since I came back, but I'm sick of this color. I want to go back to my natural color, but it's a problem, because while it grows out I can't hide the roots.

The head nurse who had finished her shift passed by and looked at us for a minute, because she was used to seeing us apart, and she didn't know if she should come up to us and she said from a distance: If you need anything, Mira, to make a phone call, or coffee, if you'd like us to make up a bed for you, just say so. And I said: No, I'm fine, come meet Alona, she's a friend of ours.

So I'll go and call and see how the kids are, I said, if you want you can go in now, and I'll wait outside. Yes, I said, I'll go in now, and I stood up and closed the zipper on my bag and I said: So you're going to call now? Yes, I said, I should. I'm such a worrier. So I'll go in now, I said. Yes, I said, go in, Alona, and suddenly, I don't know why, I hugged her.

And finally I began to cry, at first hesitantly and then really hard, I couldn't stop, and I whispered: It's okay to cry, Alona, and I felt guilty that because of me she was stuck here in the corridor in an embrace with a phone card in her hand, and the delicate scent of her perfume, unable to call and find out how her kids were. And she was warm and soft and round with the angry tears of a child, and the head nurse who came back to the ward to get something lowered her eyes, so as not to interrupt or spoil it for us. And I didn't want to stop crying, because I started enjoying it, and because she was a little taller than I my tears wet the thin material of her blouse, I think it was silk, and I was glad I had no makeup on, because I would have left a stain.

Are you okay? I asked. Yes, I said, but maybe I'll go have another cigarette first, and I laughed: You addicts, and I laughed too and wiped my eyes on my sleeve, and I offered her a tissue but I said: That's okay, go and make your phone call, Mira, I'll be here waiting for you. So I said: I'll be back in a minute, and in the few minutes I was alone I thought about the difference in the way she cried and I did, and what it said about us.

My mother said everything was all right and asked how he was, if there was any change, and I said no, and I wanted to tell her that I'd met her, but I said: If Shahar wakes up, tell him I'll be home later. Uri threw up, she said. I bought them cookies at the bakery. Why, Mother? I wanted to scold her, because she knew they weren't allowed, but I said: Never mind. Make him tea if he throws up again. There are lemons in the fridge. And I went to wash my face, and I thought about how beautiful she looked when she cried, and what he had done when she cried with him.

And I thought about the phone ringing in an apartment somewhere, I didn't even know where he lived now, and an elderly woman rushing to get it before it wakes up the children, and maybe on the way she straightens her skirt the way her daughter does, and holding the receiver close to her mouth, and reporting in a whisper how their day was, what they did, what they bought, what they had for dinner, and when they went to sleep.

And in the bathroom mirror I saw how puffy my eyes were, and I washed my face and drank some water from the faucet, because I remembered that I hadn't had anything to drink all day, because at eight in the morning they'd called and said: You'd better come. He's having difficulty breathing. So I left my coffee on the counter and ran to the car, it's a good thing I was already dressed, and I got stuck in the traffic and I thought: What does "difficulty breathing" mean, and maybe they're lying and he's already dead, and this is the routine thing to say over the phone? And suddenly I began honking for everybody to get out of the way, wishing they were all dead.

And I thought how selfish I was, that ever since I heard I was thinking only of myself and longing only for myself, and how I'd missed my last chance to ask him about myself, because maybe a month ago it would have still been possible: So how are you and how are you feeling, tell me what you remember. And now it was only good-bye, and I didn't have to come here and I could have just said: "Yes, I heard," when people asked me "Have you heard?" instead of sneaking around here for two weeks like a thief, but I came, and all I did was sit on the lawn and chain-smoked thinking only about myself.

And when I returned from the bathroom I saw the tips of her shoes from the corridor, and I stood still for a minute and thinking, how strange, this intimacy, after seeing her wandering around here for two weeks, and the head nurse once asked me: Who is she? Do you know her? After almost ten years in which I tried to exorcise her from my life, those shoes, this circumstantial intimacy.

I feel like such an idiot, I said when she came back and sat down beside me, smelling of hospital soap, not having the guts to go in. Chickening out like this. Don't feel bad, I said, I can understand. For me it was a gradual process, you'll be seeing him like this all at once. Yes, I said, but I must. Or else I'll never forgive myself.

And I stood up and walked down the corridor, and quickly passed his room as if I'd made a mistake, and got to the big window at the end and turned around, and saw her standing there holding the tissue in her hand and playing with her pearl necklace, and I wanted to call out to her: What do you need this for? Give it up, go home! Go home to your parents! And I wanted to run to her so that she would put her arms around me again and say: You don't have to. Don't go in. But she just stood there, frozen next to the window, looking at me. And I was choking on my tears, and I started walking back slowly, and I passed his room, and turned back again, and stood outside the door, and listened, and I thought that maybe I should go and sit down again, so that she could do what she had to do, because maybe my presence was what was stopping her, and I saw that she was turning to go and I waved to her and signaled: Wait for me!

We sat and stared at the TV. She lit a cigarette and stared at the screen, breathing heavily, as if she had just run a marathon and she was resting. I was so ashamed, for being such a coward, and I was glad that at least the TV was there, so I didn't have to look her in the eye. I glanced at my watch and saw that it was already after ten, and I didn't know whether I should go home and wait, or wait here. We were together for just a year, just a year and such a long time ago, so why is it so important to say good-bye now? And if I ever start a new life, what would it be like? Because maybe I never said good-bye the proper way. And how much time has to pass before I'm allowed to think of a new beginning without him? Because I want a family. Definitely. Like hers. Two kids. And a home. And I'll be a widow now. Like my mother. And I really have to decide what kind of a life I should have. And maybe settle down. Find someone. And buy a car. I don't have the strength to sit in mourning for seven days, and what will I wear to the funeral, and should I bring the children. Because I never really had a real life, just plans, and maybe if I stayed with him, let him mature me at his own pace, I could have been a widow now instead of her. And the neighbors will come over, and offer to help, and get on my nerves, especially the one who said Happy New Year, she's a real pain. Because who am I now? What status do I have? I don't even qualify as an ex. And I don't have anyone to talk to either. About the sorrow. Because how can I go and confess to my mother now? She knows anyway. She always knew.

And I don't have any friends. I never had. And I can already imagine them all coming: Eli and Hagit and Dan and Liora, bringing food, playing with the kids, whispering in the kitchen and talking about him in the past tense. Because I want to be normal. Not someone who runs from one man to the other, from one continent to another, and dyes her hair a different color every day, and wonders now if she lost out on the one true love of her life. I wonder if she'll come visit while I'm in mourning. If what started between us here will last, our little romance. Because it's much more normal to lose a husband than to be someone who's never had a real home and maybe never will. And I envy her a little for being able to walk out of here and not having to explain anything to anyone or console two little children, or be consoled. If only I'd let myself spend that second summer with him. What harm could it have done? Relatively speaking I'm still young. Maybe I would have fallen in love with him. And maybe I should really try and do what I've always been so terrified of: being alone. Because the truth is that I'm sick of wandering, and I'm tired of feeling so old. I don't want to be her big sister. I don't want to be a myth, but something real. If she only knew how much I hated her.

I'll walk out of here and get into the car and turn the radio on and light another cigarette and start the engine, but where will I go? My apartment is still empty, there's only a mattress on the floor and books in boxes and the big ugly closet the previous tenants left. And my mother will hug me and say: "Yes, Mira, it's over. Now you can cry. Cry, Mira," and I'll ask her: "Did you keep my poems, by any chance?" And she'll say: "What poems, Alona?" As if she didn't know, as if the real sin was not writing them, but keeping them, and I'll say: "You know, Mom," and she'll go to their bedroom and climb on a chair and open the closet and pretend to be searching and take down from the top shelf an old shoe box with a shoelace tied around it, and give it to me. And I'll cry, oh how I'll cry, but this time not tears for him, or for the children, or obligatory tears for the world to see, but tears for myself, which might even have a little joy in them.

I ran into his room and took the duffel bag out of the night table. It was quiet in there. Not a breath. Not a rustle of sheets. Nothing. I was on my knees with my back to him, and I quickly went through the contents and for a second my fingers touched the folded underwear, and I pulled my hand out as if I'd been burned. It was cold in the room, even though it was warm outside, and the white light from the corridor came in through the open door and cast the shadow on the wall of the legs of his bed. And then I remembered it was in the side compartment, where the zipper always got stuck, where I put his cigarettes, and I didn't want to start battling with the zipper now but I knew that she was waiting there, in front of the TV, and that I had to hurry, because maybe she wouldn't be there anymore when I returned, that she'd leave without saying good-bye, just like she couldn't say good-bye to him either, and the zipper opened without effort, without a sound, and my fingers delved deep into bits of paper and lint and crumbs of tobacco, and a sticky sucking candy, until they suddenly touched it, cold and metallic, and I closed the bag and pushed it under the bed and left the room and ran back, and she was sitting there staring at her shoes and smoking and when she raised her head and looked at me and smiled I saw that there were no tears in her eyes anymore, and the look of guilt was gone too, that childish glance expecting punishment, and I walked up and handed it to her.

About the Author

Yael Hedaya was born in Jerusalem in 1964. A former humor columnist for the Hebrew daily *Yediot Aharonot*, she teaches journalism and creative writing. *House-broken* has been translated into Dutch, German, French, and Italian; it is Hedaya's first book to appear in English.